ROMANCE!

"A wonderful story of true love and a hero who can fight as well as any man but only when he is forced to!"

—*Roberta Gellis,*
THE ROSELYNDE CHRONICLES

WAR!

"An amazingly interesting story that captures the reader with its battle scenes between the early pioneers, the English soldiers and the Indians!"

—*Donald Clayton Porter,*
WHITE INDIAN SERIES

HONOR!

"A fast-moving account that shows the honor on the Indians' side as well as on the pioneers' and His Majesty's forces!"

—*William Stuart Long,*
THE AUSTRALIANS

ADVENTURE!

"The reader's attention is riveted to the adventures surrounding this important part in the making of America!"

—*Dana Fuller Ross,*
WAGONS WEST

Northwest Territory, Book 1

WARPATH

BOLD WOMEN
AND
BRAVE MEN
LIVING AMERICA'S
GREATEST ADVENTURE!

OWEN SUTHERLAND. Rugged frontiersman, he'd come to the New World with old wounds—and old hatreds—that must still be healed...

MAYLA. Owen's Ottawa wife, who carries his child—she would take grave risks to protect her passionate love...

MAJOR GLADWIN. He would fight against overwhelming odds to prevent his Fort Detroit command from falling to hostile tribes...

ELLA BENTLY. Gladwin's spirited sister—bred as an English lady, she would learn to love her wilderness home and the sun-bronzed trapper with the brooding eyes...

CHIEF PONTIAC. An aging warrior with an ageless dream, he would lead his people in a desperate fight for freedom...

MAJOR DUVALL. The pompous British officer who carried the secret of Sutherland's past to America and rivaled him for Ella Bently's heart...

MARY HAMILTON. The golden-haired captive of the Delaware Indians—she promised to live on for her lover...

DUNCAN McEWAN. The youthful ensign whose feats of bravery saved the life of TAMANO, Sutherland's Indian bloodbrother...

ANDRE BRETON. Owen's arch-enemy, the vicious French *voyageur* who left a trail of tears everywhere he went...

NORTHWEST TERRITORY·BOOK I

WARPATH

OLIVER PAYNE

 Created by the producers of
The Kent Family Chronicles,
Wagons West, **The Australians**,
and **White Indian** Series.

EXECUTIVE PRODUCER, LYLE KENYON ENGEL

ℬ

BERKLEY BOOKS, NEW YORK

WARPATH

A Berkley Book / published by arrangement with
Book Creations, Inc.

PRINTING HISTORY
Berkley edition / March 1982

Produced by Book Creations, Inc.
Executive Producer: Lyle Kenyon Engel
For information address: Berkley Publishing Corporation,
200 Madison Avenue, New York, New York 10016.

ISBN: 0-425-05452-7

A BERKLEY BOOK® TM 757,375

Voor onze ouders
For our parents

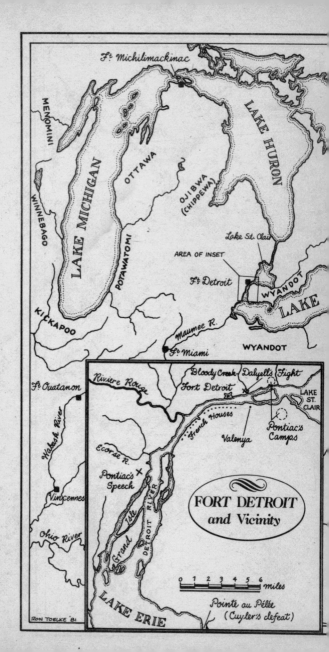

Ft Michilimackinac

MENOMINI

WINNEBAGO

LAKE MICHIGAN

OTTAWA

OJIBWA (CHIPPEWA)

POTAWATOMI

KICKAPOO

Lake St Clair

AREA OF INSET

Ft Detroit

WYANDOT

LAKE

Maumee R.

Ft Miami

WYANDOT

LAKE HURON

Ft Ouatanon

Wabash River

Vincennes

Ohio River

Riviere Rouge

Ecorse R.

Pontiac's Speech

Grand Isle

DETROIT RIVER

French Houses

Bloody Creek

Fort Detroit

Valenya

Dalyell's Fight

LAKE ST. CLAIR

Pontiac's Camps

FORT DETROIT and Vicinity

0 1 2 3 4 5 6 miles

Pointe au Pélle (Cuyler's defeat)

LAKE ERIE

RON TOELKE '81

Forts and Settlements in America 1763

Quebec

St. Lawrence River

Montreal

HURON

LAKE ONTARIO

Crown Point

Ticonderoga

Oswego

Mohawk River

Ft. Niagara

Genesee R.

IROQUOIS

Albany

New York

Hudson River

Ft. Presque Isle

Ft. Le Boeuf

Allegheny R.

Venango

DELAWARE

Pennsylvania

Susquehanna R.

New York

Delaware R.

New Jersey

Ft. Pitt

Bushy Run

Ft. Ligonier

Ft. Bedford

Carlisle

Philadelphia

Monongahela River

SHAWNEE

Baltimore

Maryland

Delaware

Potomac River

ATLANTIC OCEAN

Virginia

Norfolk

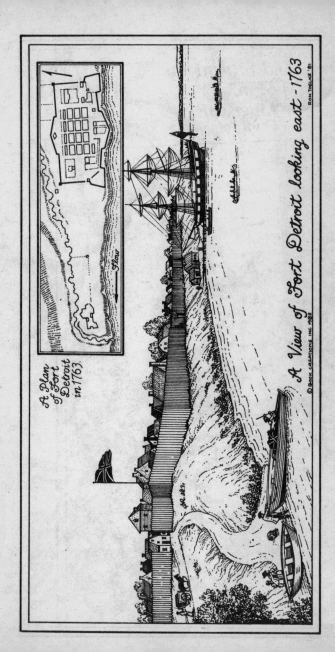

A Plan of Fort Detroit in 1763.

A View of Fort Detroit looking east - 1763

Ron Toelke '81

© Book Creations Inc 1982

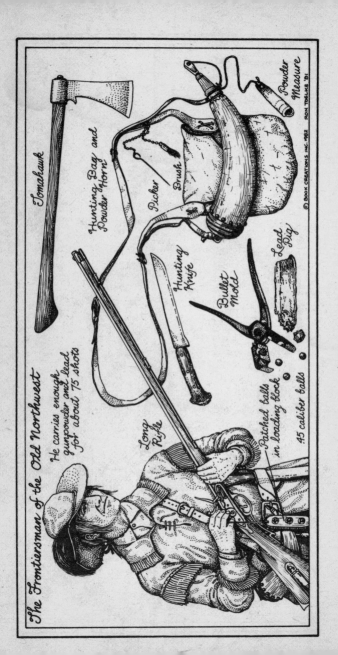

The Frontiersman of the Old Northwest

He carries enough gunpowder and lead for about 75 shots

Tomahawk

Hunting Bag and Powder Horn

Picker

Brush

Hunting Knife

Long Rifle

Bullet Mold

Lead Pig

Powder Measure

Patched balls in loading block

.45 caliber balls

© BOOK CREATIONS, INC. 1982

RON TOELKE '81

You must give up the practice of purchasing the good behaviour of the Indians by presents.... Tell them if they commit hostilities, they must not only expect the severest retaliation, but an entire destruction of all their nations, for I am firmly resolved wherever they give me occasion to extirpate them root and branch....

—*Letter from General Jeffrey Amherst, Commander-in-Chief of the British Army in North America, to Sir William Johnson, Superintendent of Indian Affairs, 1761*

In October, 1762, thick clouds of inky blackness gathered above the fort and settlement of Detroit. The river darkened beneath the awful shadows, and the forest was wrapped in double gloom. Drops of rain began to fall of strong sulphurous odor. Throughout the winter, the shower of black rain was the foremost topic of fireside talks, and dreary forebodings of evil disturbed the breast of many a timorous matron.

—**The Conspiracy of Pontiac**
by Francis Parkman

Cast my life abroad and plunder
all my past of memory;
purge my heart with marveling wonder,
blest by Nature's harmony.

—*Owen Sutherland*
Fort Detroit, 1763

PROLOGUE

In 1761 a prophet rose among the Delaware Indians, a people whose gift for prophecy was well known and respected by every tribe. He wandered through the wilderness, from the Appalachian Mountains in the East to the sacred islands of the inland seas in the Northwest, calling on all Indian nations to rise up before it was too late and drive out the English invaders.

Thousands flocked to hear his warning that the Indian must purify himself, must return to the old ways of the forefathers, and reject the ways of the white man. The prophet was the voice of the Indian soul, the desperate voice of a people face-to-face with doom. He called on them to unite as one people and fight a holy war against the arrogant English, who had defeated the French and now reigned supreme and unchallenged, and did not love the Indian. Now there was no French army to fight alongside the warriors and stop land-hungry English settlers from pushing over the eastern mountains and taking the sacred hunting lands for their own. Until the French returned with soldiers and thunder guns, only the Indian remained to stem the English flood.

In a dream, the Great Spirit told the prophet:

You have forgotten the traditions of your ancestors, and to forget them is to forsake your nature as an Indian. Clothe yourselves in skins; use only the stone lance and arrows of old, and do not let your war dead go unavenged. Why do you suffer these English dogs to dwell among you? Cast them out! Rise up against them and return the hunting grounds to your children. Stand before the Master of Life with a proud heart, as an Indian, with all the strength of your mighty race at your command!

Tribe after tribe obeyed the teachings of the prophet. They threw away flint and steel, cloth and white man's tools; and they sought the revelation of their spirits.

But the white man's musket remained. For hunting, it was far superior to the bow, and for driving out the English, it would serve well.

PART ONE

The Omen

chapter 1

THE STRAITS

For two days, rain fell steadily. Streams rose, and the straits became a torrent, sweeping muddy and swift down from Lake Saint Clair into Lake Erie. On the morning of the third day the rain stopped, and sun broke through. It was bright, warm, and windless, but the waters still raged, so the Indians stayed home to smoke and gamble and talk of the past; they knew better than to risk the angry straits after a storm. In Huron and Ottawa villages, squaws packed furs into bales for the coming trip to Fort Detroit, the trading post halfway up the straits, where the narrows bent suddenly from north to east. But that journey must wait until tomorrow—or perhaps the next day, if the gambling was good.

The French settlers living in cabins scattered along the shoreline also avoided the straits until the flood subsided, and they had taught the English soldiers and traders at Detroit to do the same. No one who knew the straits would risk a canoe or bateau on this April afternoon in 1763, but there were always newcomers whose inexperience and ignorance were dangerous.

Newcomers to this wild country had much to learn—newcomers such as the weary travelers in two whaleboats who entered the straits from Lake Erie and took the eastern channel, hoping to reach the fort by nightfall.

The whaleboats were thirty feet long, sleek, and worthy of the challenge offered by these waters. Durable and graceful, pointed at both ends, they passed between green islands, making slow but steady progress as soldiers in both boats rowed against the current. Scarlet uniforms were dark with sweat, and tunics flapped open to the air. Occasionally a soldier cast a wistful glance at the sail brailed to the lateen yard overhead.

3

A wind would have hurried the whaleboats through the channel, but there was no breeze today. To reach Detroit they had to row.

In the stern of each boat a soldier stood, steering with a long tiller that fought him, wrenching and jerking as the current rushed first on one side, then the other. The tillerman kept the bow headed into the flow, lest a sudden surge turn the boat broadside against the full force of the flood. In this rough water, to capsize meant death.

The second craft, manned by eight soldiers, followed twenty yards behind the first whaleboat, which carried a group of civilians huddled in the center seats. Four soldiers, paired before and behind the passengers, rowed this boat, in which there was at least one person who knew these waters: Garth Morely, a grizzled, bearded fur trader from Detroit. He knelt in the bow, peering upstream, and shook his head slowly. He had told the major several times not to try this passage under such turbulent conditions. Now, with the water turning even more quarrelsome, Morely decided to warn the officer once again. In a creaking voice he called over his shoulder.

"Water's gettin' too high here, Major. Worse than I ever seen it. I told thee I don't like this. Best be ready for trouble!" He spat over the side and squinted at the rapids foaming around the shores of the small islands close by the boat.

A tall officer rose from his seat near the civilians and stepped over three worn-out, sleeping children lying with their heads in the laps of two women, their mothers. The soldiers paused at their oars as Major Alex Duvall of the 80th Regiment worked his way with difficulty past them. Though he was no boatsman, he was responsible for this expedition, which had come all the way from Fort Little Niagara, three weeks and two hundred miles away at the east end of Lake Erie. Duvall did not know the straits, but he had still insisted, against Garth Morely's advice, that they try to make Detroit today. He was exasperated with Morely's persistent warnings. Now he reluctantly came to the trader, who said:

"Land, Major." Morely took the flat black hat from his head and wiped away spittle straggling from his beard. "This time of year, thee never knows what can happen on these waters. I never seen the straits so high. I tell thee, thee must land, Major. It be high time to make for dry land. Fast!"

Major Duvall sighed. He was a sharp contrast to the squat trader, who wore a long, ragged coat. Duvall's uniform was sparkling clean, for he had changed into a fresh tunic that morning in anticipation of reaching Detroit. Smooth-shaven and trim, he looked the perfect image of a British officer, but all his experience on the battlefield had not prepared him for this hard journey through an endless wilderness—a journey of discomfort, cruel blackflies, and surly provincials such as grubby trader Morely. Duvall sighed again, for he saw Morely was right—as he had been so often on this damnable trip. The water was getting rougher. The boats bobbed and thumped clumsily at best. Without a stiff breeze at their backs, they could never get through the channel against this current.

"What do you suggest, Mister Morely?" Duvall asked quietly, annoyed at the delay as much as at this man's maddening insolence.

Morely spat over the side again. Then he pointed off to the right at the near shore two hundred yards away, where a cove promised shelter.

"Best put in there for the day and tonight," he said. "If it don't rain again, then the water be fallin', and we can go on tomorrow. We have to beat across current now, but the water's calmer over there, and we can make camp."

Duvall removed his tricorn, waving it to the soldiers in the boat following. Then he shouted to the burly young sergeant at his whaleboat's tiller, ordering him to turn to shore. The water was powerful, and the tillerman needed all his strength to move the stiffening rudder and turn the boat. But he brought it round too fast, and the craft fell away suddenly, nearly spinning, throwing Morely and Duvall off their feet.

"Easy there, Sergeant McEwan!" Morely bellowed as he hung on to the bow. "Do that again and we'll turn turtle, lad! Easy does it!"

In the center of the boat, the children woke with a jolt. One was a sandy-haired boy of eight, and the others were sturdy lads of seven and six. The oldest boy rubbed his head where it had bumped against wood.

"What's happened, Ma?" he asked a pretty woman of about thirty, who pushed back his hair and saw a welt growing.

"Just rough water, that's all, Jeremy." She eased her tired son's head back onto her lap. "It seems we'll be traveling one more day before you see your Uncle Henry again. But we've waited this long . . ."

Ella Bently gazed across the troubled water to the shoreline, thick with tamarack pine and scrub oak. It was a beautiful country, even if it was so flat. There were no gentle hills or sudden peaks as in her last home in western Massachusetts, but she liked the endless horizon and the overwhelming sky. At times she missed Massachusetts, though she had been gone only three months. But what was there really to miss? There was nothing to go back for now. Only the past, only memories, nothing else. She must look ahead.

Ahead. To England again—to the country she had left forever ten years ago. Was England really ahead? After so much change and so many years, could she be happy in England at her brother's estate in Derbyshire? Questions! Such a waste of time! She had firmly decided to go back to England. She and Jeremy would soon return with her brother, Major Henry Gladwin, when he turned over the command of Fort Detroit to Alex Duvall. It would be a new life once more, and she would make it a good one. She always had done that, even when she first came to America. That had not been easy, either.

Ella looked down at Jeremy, who was asleep again. He would be a lord's nephew, no longer a New England provincial boy; and she would be expected to live as she had been born to live—as an English country lady. A strand of blond hair fell across her face, and she pushed it back. Her hair needed brushing. In Derbyshire, there was no place for unbrushed hair nor for rough muslin dresses such as the one she wore. In Derbyshire was the life she had left behind, the life before John, before her son.

It would be old ways and tradition again, formality and propriety—a life she had seldom thought about during the five years of marriage to John Bently. With John she was too happy to wonder what might have been if she had stayed in England. Like her he would have loved the land out here. He would have loved the adventure, the immensity, and the unbounded nature. For, indeed, it was this sense of adventure, this love of the wilderness country, that had prompted Ella to meet her brother out here in Detroit, rather than in a nearby, more established community like Quebec. She was eager to see the northwest country, eager to have her son see Henry and the fort he commanded. Her brother would now be a very important man in Jeremy's life for some time to come; he would be the father that the boy had lost.

Ella's thoughts were interrupted as Major Duvall sat down next to her and smiled.

"Well, Mistress Bently, it seems you'll have to wait until

tomorrow for your reunion with your brother. I'm afraid we must camp until the river falls. But there is some compensation, for we've got a lovely day ahead of us, and we'll be well rested for the last few miles, eh?"

He smiled again, charming and handsome. Ella returned his smile and was about to speak when a portly woman sitting across from her said, "Yes, 'tis best to wait 'til the water's down. 'Tis bad today. Even Injuns won't go out on water rough as this!" She wheezed and opened her linsey blouse a bit more—as far as her large bosom allowed. She was Lettie Morely, the fur trader's wife. She, her husband, and their sons were returning from a trading journey to Niagara.

Next to Lettie sat the Reverend Angus Lee, a young Scotch-Irish Presbyterian minister who, half-asleep, swayed and weaved in his seat like a charmed cobra, defying gravity and the rude pitching of the whaleboat. He opened one eyelid, thought better of it, and let it drop again.

Ella removed her straw hat and fanned herself. The sun was hot, the air thick. She was about to speak to Duvall when, with a whiplike force, the whaleboat suddenly swerved, tugging Lettie Morely's feet off the planking, heaving her backwards, arms flailing, whacking the drowsy reverend off his seat with a crash.

Duvall gripped Ella's shoulder, but the violent rocking knocked them from their seats. They bumped against the screaming children, helplessly trying to hold on to anything they could catch. Soldiers growled when their grips broke, and oars jerked loose from locks. At the tiller, Sergeant McEwan swore and fought to right the boat, which had swung sideways to the current and was reeling downstream out of control.

On the floor of the boat Ella clutched Jeremy against her. Duvall struggled to get to his feet, but the pitching threw him down again. Only McEwan held fast, battling with all his strength at the tiller. Ella held onto the seat with one arm and to Jeremy with the other. The world whirled faster and faster. Kegs and baskets slid free and smashed together. The boat rolled and nearly heeled over.

Someone shouted in terror, and Ella's whaleboat jarred to a stop with a shuddering crunch. They had collided with the second boat. Wood splintered, oars locked, and the boats hurled into a savage spin. Jeremy was ripped from Ella's grasp. She reached for him, but the boat tipped wildly, and the boy toppled over the edge. Ella screamed and threw herself to the gunwale, just catching his legs, holding on with all her might as the sky spun madly and water splashed over her.

Another crashing concussion banged Ella's head against the side of the boat, and when she recovered, Jeremy was gone. She floundered in panic, stunned. Men were screaming. Dazed, she shook her head and cried out for Jeremy. The boat had stopped moving. From what seemed like a great distance she heard Garth Morely shouting, "Soldier! Soldier! Hold it! Here! No! Godrotting no! No!" But where was Jeremy? She shouted his name again and again. People lay in a tumbled confusion of arms and legs.

"Ma! Ma!"

"Jeremy!" She saw him at last.

He was pressed shaken and frightened against the side of the boat, his head bleeding slightly. But he was there! He was safe! Ella crawled to him and held him close. Her bleary mind cleared. She looked up to see Morely and Duvall leaning over the side of the boat, which was tilted up at the bow.

Morely's head dropped, and his eyes closed. Duvall stood up and smashed his fist into a palm.

"Gone!" Duvall groaned. "Damn my eyes! Gone! Every last one of them!" Hatless, drenched with water, Duvall looked over the side and slowly shook his head. "Gone," he murmured. "And we're grounded!"

Ella sat up and saw why Duvall was dismayed. The second craft had capsized. Its soldiers were overboard, all lost! Ella began to tremble. Eight men were dead—dragged away by the water.

No one spoke. The only sound was the river rushing past. Ella trembled harder. Horror took her, and she sat down, hands covering her face. Jeremy put his arms over her shoulders. She tried to breathe, but air came only in gasps.

"Grounded!" Morely said and stood up.

Ella opened her eyes and touched her son's worried face. She looked up at Morely and Duvall, who were searching over the side, fore and aft, pushing past groggy soldiers, nearly stepping on the groaning Reverend Lee lying on the bottom of the whaleboat. Lee stirred and tried to sit up. It seemed they all were still in the boat, shaken and bruised but alive. The other whaleboat had been driven against shoals and turned over; the stricken craft lay keel-up on the rocks. All around, water surged unmercifully, and there was no sign of anyone swimming. Duvall shouted to Morely:

"If we can push clear of this and get the boat adrift, we can—"

"No, Major!" Morely interrupted. "We can't just drift off into this current! We try that without gettin' a line to shore first and we'll join them lads!" He cast a glance at the overturned whaleboat. "No, if we drift we be capsizin' for sure. For sure. Current's too strong to push off so sudden. We got to get a line to shore and tie it round a tree. Then we can haul her off and pull into those quiet waters."

Morely waved toward the little cove that the boats had almost reached before they went out of control in the current. The boat was stranded less than forty yards from an arc of large boulders. If they could get inside its shelter, they would be safe.

Reverend Lee moaned, and Lettie Morely pulled him onto his seat. All the while, she apologized for bumping into the stunned minister, who heard nothing in his frantic search for arms and legs. Finding them all unbroken, Lee drew spectacles from a pocket of his frock coat and pushed them onto his thin nose. Like a bird searching for a hidden cat, he looked about him.

Ella asked, "Are you all right, Reverend Lee?"

Lee fluttered and cleared his throat. "Oh! Oh, yes, thank you, Mistress Bently. Thank the Lord! Thank the Lord! What happened? Where are we? Is everyone all right?"

Lee turned and peered toward Morely. When he saw the prow of the whaleboat pointing up at the sky, the reverend started and gasped, "Mercy! Mercy!" He looked quickly over the side and saw the capsized boat. "Wha—Dear God! Where are those men? What happened to them?"

Morely scratched his beard and looked into the distance. Without emotion the trader said, "There ain't no more men, Reverend. Thee came out here to save souls. Well, thy ministry can begin right now; and if we don't get this boat away from these rocks, thy prayers will be for thine own soul and for the rest of this company's, as well."

"Good God, Morely, why talk like that?" Duvall asked the trader, who was staring hard at the tree line beyond a beach. "If the river's going down as you say, we can stay here and be safely away by morning. We can sleep . . ."

Morely turned abruptly from the officer and reached down into his kit bag. He drew out a pistol and checked the priming. Then he looked again at the shore and nodded toward it.

"It's not the river I'm thinkin' about, Major," he said softly. "It's that."

Everyone looked at the land.

"Injuns!" Lettie Morely spoke for all.

Standing on a rocky promontory about a hundred and fifty yards away were two buckskin-clad figures, tall and unmoving, both carrying muskets.

"But we're at peace now, Morely!" Duvall sputtered. "The war's been over these three years. Why should we fear a few savages?"

Morely spat again into the water, never taking his eyes from the Indians.

"Major," Morely said. "There won't be peace out here until the redskins understand the French lost the last war and the English are now their fathers. Right now, there ain't many Injuns that admit that. No, these Injuns fought alongside the French, and they lost with the French, and Injuns don't like to lose. No. They be Chippeways up there, I'd say, and every chance they get to molest the English, if they know they can get away safely, they'll take it."

Then Morely spoke softly to Duvall to keep from further frightening the women and children. But Ella heard him say, "They'll wait until just before dawn, when the river's down, then they'll put out with canoes and slip up on us in the dark. On land we could stand 'em off with these soldiers, but here . . ."

He looked up at the Indians again, but they were gone.

Morely spoke loudly: "We got to get this hunk of timber off these rocks and into a quiet place. If anyone has any ideas, let's hear 'em now. We need to get a line to shore and then pull the boat free."

The well-built Sergeant McEwan stood up at the stern and said: "I can swim." He began removing his red tunic. "Tie a line about my waist. Once I'm ashore I'll wrap the line around a tree and pull the boat free, then we'll get her to the bank."

The major put a hand on the youth's shoulder.

"I won't order you to do this, Sergeant," Duvall said.

McEwan made no reply but bent down to remove his boots.

"If thee ain't lucky," Morely said standing over him, "that water be a-drowndin' thee, lad."

"I know, fur trader," McEwan said, without bravado. He stood up, and his powerful muscles rippled underneath a white cotton shirt. He looked at the tortured current and said, "I like my chances out there better than waiting here to be taken at some redskin's leisure."

"If I could swim a stroke, I'd do the same, Sergeant," Major Duvall said as he brought McEwan the coiled rope and helped tie it around his waist. "Can you make it, Sergeant?"

"We'll see, sir," McEwan said and tightened the rope about his girth. "Keep the line slack unless I start to lose control and get pulled away. But don't pull on it until I wave for you to."

Morely took the rope in both hands; the end was lashed to a cleat. McEwan clambered onto the side of the whaleboat, his legs dangling over. He took a long look at the terrible raging water and then leaped.

"God go with thee," Lettie Morely murmured, pressing her hands to her lips.

McEwan sank, and his head rose suddenly, dark and glistening. Ella gave a little scream of fright when he was quickly swept away. Morely rapidly played out rope until McEwan's head showed for a moment in a calmer pool. Then he seemed to gather himself again and struck out toward shore. But when he swam out of the quieter spot, McEwan was dragged away and went under.

"Pull him up! Pull him up!" Ella pleaded.

Morely and Duvall hauled on the rope, but McEwan stayed under. Everyone was shouting, but it was no use. Then Morely blared:

"Let it go!" They released their grip on the line, giving out several yards very fast. McEwan's head bobbed up again, for the taut rope had held him down against the force of the current. Then they pulled the rope tight once more, controlling him, and McEwan got hold of some low, flat rocks just above the surface. He paused there, gasping for breath.

"Blast!" growled Duvall. "The lad's beached just like us. He can't go forward, and we can't haul him in."

McEwan climbed slowly onto the rocks and lay on his back, chest heaving. Ella saw blood gleam on his forehead. He was halfway from the boat to the shore, with the furious river between.

"Well, Major, it looks like we be takin' our chances with the redskins," Morely said and turned away from the defeated Sergeant McEwan. "We ain't movin' until the river falls. Be sure our friends'll come visitin' 'afore then."

Ella watched the despondent McEwan, who was sitting now, knees up, forehead resting on his arms.

"We can't just do *nothing*." Duvall struck his palm again.

Morely looked at the shoreline and stiffened. "Looks like we won't have to wait, Major."

On the shore, near a white beach two hundred yards upstream, the same two figures appeared. Ella felt fright grip her. Everyone was standing and staring at the two Indians. Soldiers reached for muskets, and Duvall put a hand on his sword. Even Sergeant McEwan, from his perch on the flat rock downstream, had seen the men on the beach, and his eyes were on them. The only sounds were the monotonous rush of the river and the occasional rattle of a ramrod pressing a bullet home in a musket barrel.

The men on land moved farther upstream, and one of them seemed to be removing his shirt and leggins.

"Get the children below the gunwales!" Major Duvall said to Ella and Lettie. "And stay there yourselves."

Lettie scurried her two boys to shelter in the stern of the boat and beckoned for Jeremy to follow them. The boy looked up into his mother's face.

"What's happening, Ma?"

"It's nothing, son," Ella said and pushed him gently toward Lettie Morely. "Just go sit with the other boys, and keep busy for a while. Stay below the side of the boat. Go on, now."

She looked back at the two men on shore and wondered whether there were others lurking in the trees. What were they trying to do? The one who had removed his shirt and leggins was making his way into the water, already at his waist.

The men in the whaleboat were tense, their muskets ready.

"Maybe this one wants to parley," Duvall said, not taking his eyes from the figure, who was swimming now.

"I don't trust these varmints," Morely said through his teeth. "If they try to sweet-talk us, watch out. They may even offer to help us ashore if it serves their thievin' purpose."

"But how can you be sure they're not friendly?" Duvall asked, his eyes on the swimmer, who was working out of calm water and into the swifter stream, moving steadily toward the stranded whaleboat. "Maybe they expect a reward—"

"Major, I been in this country too many years to trust the Injun," Morley replied. "When they're kind, be on thy guard. If they be generous, be even more careful. They steal and murder just for the sport. And this Injun comin' out now is riskin' his neck far too much for my likin'. He ain't swimmin' out here just to save us. No. He be after what we got."

Morely's voice fell as he told the officer: "And women are choice prizes for a buck. Be ready, Major. If he wants to talk, be careful. There's no tellin' how many others are waitin' in the woods for us to be brought to shore nice as you please, and then . . ."

The swimmer moved slowly at first, using the shelter of a small peninsula to make headway in the easier water. Then he pushed farther into the flood. He did not aim directly for the whaleboat, but he swam out into the driving current, and then he was caught and dashed forward in a torrent of sucking foam. If he went past too quickly or missed his calculation, he would be rushed out into the broad river like the soldiers who had drowned.

The man swam powerfully, now heading right at the boat. The company watching were amazed at his courage and determination to reach them.

"That redskin's goin' to great pains to get himself deaded," Morely said, a hatchet loose in his hand. "If the river don't do it, and if he don't have a good reason for why he came out here, I'll oblige the heathen's wish for death."

As the man hurtled at the longboat, soldiers stared alternately from him to the trees, searching for signs of more warriors. The children were huddled in silence. Lettie had a grip on one of her husband's pistols. Reverend Lee held his Bible, his lips moving silently, rapidly, eyes on the swimmer, who swept against the boat and banged hard against its hull, then disappeared between the overturned craft and the stranded whaleboat. Morely and Duvall bent low, peering over the side. Then at the opposite gunwale a dark hand reached up, and Ella gasped. Morely and Duvall leaped around, and the fur trader raised the hatchet.

"Hold on, you! What do you want?" he shouted, then snarled fiercely in an Indian tongue.

From below in the water a deep voice said, "Mind your manners, Morely, if you want out of this mess you've got yourself into!"

Morely's hatchet clattered to the planking and his eyes went wide with delight. He reached over the gunwale and laughed. "Sutherland! Sutherland, you rascal! Hah! Why didn't you tell us it was you? Pull him up, lads; he's one of us! Hah! Pull him up!"

Two soldiers rushed to help Morely haul in a dripping man, who collapsed on the deck and coughed up river water. He was naked to the waist, strongly muscled, and had black hair tied back in a short queue. A small Indian bow and several arrows were slung to his waist, and on his chest was a dark green tattoo that looked like a turtle. He caught his breath and got to his feet near the fur trader, who beamed at him.

"I thought thee a redskin comin' to trick us into the hands of his cronies." Morely chuckled, and Sutherland grinned down at him, for he stood a head above every other man in the boat. In his late thirties, he was clean-shaven, his face dark and ruddy. Only young McEwan, trapped on the rocks, could match this man's raw strength.

Ella's breath caught when the man looked at her, his gaze lasting longer than was comfortable. Then his eyes darted from one member of the company to the other as he removed the Indian bow from his belt thong. Major Duvall's cold voice cut through the lull, and Sutherland looked up quickly when the officer said, "So you are out here after all, Sutherland. I'd heard it said you'd come out here, and now I've seen it for myself."

Duvall's voice was almost a sneer. Sutherland, tense, straightened to his full height. His face was drawn, flushed, and he glared at Duvall. It seemed that every ounce of his strength flowed, controlled, toward Major Duvall, who raised his chin with forced disdain.

Sutherland looked the stiff officer up and down, then said, "Somehow I always knew I'd be meeting you again." Then the frontiersman continued untying the bow and arrows. "I see you're a major. I'm surprised; I thought you'd be someone's adjutant general by now."

The others in the boat stood listening, uncomprehending, while something strong and distant passed between these two men. Reverend Lee broke the spell.

"I say, sir," he said to Sutherland and waved his hands nervously. "As you can see, we've run afoul of these rocks, and it's a very tragic, nasty mess. Can you get us out of this frightful predicament? You see you're our only hope, for there are Indians out there. You're our only hope, sir—that is, after the Good Lord, of course!"

Sutherland strung the bow and looked at Lee, who fumbled with his Bible.

"Aye, Reverend." Sutherland's voice had a deep Scots ripple. "There are indeed Indians out there—a party of them just came up with me from Oswego. But you won't have to worry about them. However, I don't think you want to remain out here tonight, not if you might wake up to find yourself adrift in the flood. So let's see what we and the Good Lord can do to get you out of this predicament. We and the Good Lord, as well as my Indian friend on shore and this heathen bow and arrow."

A smile broke across his face. It was a face lined with experience that was obviously hard-earned, and it was handsome in a rugged way. From about his waist Sutherland unraveled a long length of string and tied it to an arrow. The Indian was standing, waiting on the beach. As Sutherland worked, Morely guessed the plan and tied the other end of the string to the spare line coiled on the floor of the whaleboat.

Duvall stepped between them and straightened his black officer's tricorn, which was losing some of its gold braid. The braid slumped over the major's shoulder, but he seemed not to notice it. He stared into Sutherland's impassive eyes.

"Now, see here, Sutherland, if you can help us get to safety, then I am willing to be most generous and shall be more than happy to pay you whatever you consider fair for your troubles. I'll even throw in a jug of high wine for that redskin retainer of yours, if—"

"Tell me, Alex," Sutherland said slowly and folded his arms. "What's your skin worth to you?"

Duvall stepped back. "Now just a minute—"

"As for your high wine," Sutherland said and glanced at the Indian on shore, "don't let Tamano know you're insulting him with an offer of high wine, or the first chance he gets he might dump you in the river."

Duvall darkened, and his neck bulged red.

"Now, now, Owen," said Morely, wiping his nose with the back of his hand. "The major here didn't mean to insult thee, and it be no time to get on thy high horse, lad. Now, thee knows well enough that when thee gets us safe and sound ashore we be in thy debt in a manner that can't be paid with material things, eh? Now, lad, let's be gettin' down to business."

Morely turned a false grin toward Sutherland, who lost his anger and faced the shore again.

"All right, Morely, but if Lettie wasn't with you I might not have come out here at all." Then he looked at Ella and the children. "Lettie and the other civilians as well, of course."

Sutherland fired the arrow, and it plunked into the ground

at the Indian's feet. Tamano pulled in the slender cord until
the thicker line was in his hands, then he hauled the line around
a tree, reaching it up over a stout branch. The rope was already
lashed to the bow of the whaleboat. Tamano pulled the rope
tight, and Sutherland tested it. The line ran from the boat across
the water three feet above the surface to the bough of a pine
tree at the edge of the woods.

"Now," Sutherland said and straddled the side of the boat,
"if we can get the men across, hand over hand on this rope,
then we'll have enough muscle to hold the boat against the
current and guide it into shore. There you can wait until the
river falls and head out for the fort in the morning."

Sutherland brought his other leg over the side of the boat
and yanked the rope several times to feel its tension. Then he
said, "Look sharp, lads, for this river still wants you. She'll
pull you down if you don't hold tight to this line. Come one
at a time, and once you start to go, don't stop!"

Sutherland dropped his legs into the water and dangled a
moment on the bouncing rope, and Ella thought his eyes sought
hers for an instant. She looked quickly away, then turned back
immediately, but he was already thrusting himself hand over
hand across the river toward the land.

chapter 2

OLD ENEMIES

Sutherland was soon wading ashore. The soldiers followed him, one at a time, rapidly heaving themselves along the length of rope, their legs splashing in the water that surged angrily against them, seeking to drag them away.

When the soldiers were all on land and stood in a group near Sutherland and Tamano, Morely followed, swearing and grunting and growling oaths as he pulled himself the forty yards to shore. When the trader staggered out of the water, huffing and puffing, his face running with sweat, he collapsed.

"That be young man's work, Owen," Morely panted, drawing out a red handkerchief. "For a moment there I thought I was to be drug off by the damned river. Hey! Here comes the good reverend. We best watch for him; he might..."

A wavering Reverend Lee carefully climbed over the side of the longboat and swung heavily into the water. Sutherland was about to tell the man to remain in the boat, but the minister was moving now, jouncing and swaying as he fought to keep hold of the line. Everyone, both in the boat and on land, was silent, watching the slender minister struggle as the river clutched at him. With one weakening grip after another, Lee jerked along the rope, his face agonized with effort.

Sergeant McEwan, still beached on the rocks downstream, cheered Lee onward.

"Hold tight, Reverend!" McEwan's voice was shrill above the sound of the river. "You're nearly there! Hold tight and go on! Go on!"

But Lee was too exhausted to hear McEwan. He slowed his pace and looked longingly at the soldiers on shore. He stopped and writhed in the rushing water, his arms spent. He hung

17

limply, dangling, with his body at an angle and the rushing water pulling at him relentlessly.

He tried to hold on and gave a long moan. His hands had no feeling left. He tried to hold, but he could not. He slipped, just managing to keep his grip.

Before anyone could move, Tamano sprang to the rope, yanking himself along it with marvelous strength.

Lee's faint voice rose above the waters: "Help me. Help me, please."

Tamano was on him, and the Indian's arm reached for his waist, but Lee collapsed. Tamano lunged at him, one hand holding the lifeline and the other grasping at Lee's coat. The line bounced. Lee's head rose, and he uttered a lost scream. The line bowed to the water, and the two men were dragged down.

Ella and Lettie shrieked as the men struggled. Sutherland shouted, "Hold him! Hold him, Tamano!"

But there was nothing anyone on shore could do, for another man's weight bounding along that line would snatch it from Tamano's tenuous grip, and they would both be gone. Sutherland and the others shouted encouragement and stamped about in the water near the beach.

Tamano went under, then came up again. He had Lee's face out of the water for a moment, but it went under once again. Tamano fought against the river with all his might, but the river was overwhelming.

The Indian's hand slid grudgingly from the rope, then broke free, and the two men plunged away in the torrent, swirling together, Tamano still holding the minister. They were battered into boulders, went under brown foam, came up again, and spun away. Tamano held fast.

Another yell rose above the river's roar.

Downstream from the drowning men, Sergeant McEwan, with the rope still tied about his waist, leaped into their path and wrested them to a stop. He wrapped arms and legs about them, and the water pulled them under. He and Tamano fought to the surface and sucked great gulps of air before they went under again. When they came up, Lee was held fiercely between them. The line kept them from being carried away. Tamano forced Lee's head above water, and McEwan, his legs locked around them both, pulled on the rope to equalize the river's assault. Thus they floated, suspended.

Then, when they were under control, Tamano and McEwan,

encumbered by Lee, struck out for the shelter of large rocks closer in to shore. They found still, deep water behind a massive tangle of roots, drifted logs, and boulders. There they pushed Lee, who was barely breathing, up onto driftwood.

McEwan and Tamano floated for a moment before they found the breath to nod at each other and grin.

"I owe you my life, soldier," Tamano said, and they looked on each other with respect. "Make you brother."

A voice called down from atop the driftwood. It was Sutherland. The blockage of the water reached all the way to shore, and Sutherland had hopped and climbed over the rocks to get to them. Behind came the soldiers.

"Well done, lad!" Sutherland said to McEwan and reached down to give the sergeant and Tamano a hand up. Lee was coughing water now, regaining consciousness. "Where do you come from, Sergeant?"

"Aberdeenshire, sir," McEwan replied and took the other's hand. "Bucksburn."

"Away!" Sutherland laughed, and his eyes warmed as they shook hands. "I'm an Aberdonian myself, though I've been gone these past ten year!"

Duvall harshly interrupted.

"All right, all right, we're not finished yet. We've got to get the boat ashore before any heathens come up and cause some mischief."

Tamano looked at Sutherland, who ignored Duvall and turned away to help carry Lee back to the beach.

Soon the men were hauling the longboat free. At last the craft was dragged into the shallows, where the whaleboat drew so much water that it was not possible to bring it up onto dry ground without unloading it. So Morely and Duvall carried the two women through the knee-deep water. Duvall bore Ella to dry land just as Sutherland came to speak to him. The major listened while still holding Ella in his arms.

"Since I'm on my way to Detroit myself," Sutherland said, "I'd enjoy traveling with you in the whaleboat for the last part of the trip. I've three canoes beached downstream with Indian paddlers, but Tamano can go back and arrange—"

"I'm sorry." Duvall shook his head. "We can't take you in our boat, Sutherland, for we're already much too crowded, and I'm afraid I can't risk—"

"Major!" Ella kicked her legs a little. "Would you kindly put me down?"

Startled, Duvall placed the woman on her feet and turned to Sutherland, but Ella spoke first.

"Major Duvall, these men saved our lives! Surely you won't deny Mr. Sutherland the courtesy of passage to Detroit!"

Flustered, Duvall tightened his lips. "Mistress Bently, the safety of this party is my responsibility, and I'm concerned about doing what is best for all of you. An overloaded boat—"

"Thank you for your kind words, ma'am." Sutherland bowed slightly and touched his forehead. "We'll be on our way, and when you arrive at the fort, we'll see you there."

"But, Mr. Sutherland," Ella insisted, "won't you at least give us the opportunity to thank you for all you've done? Join us for supper tonight."

Sutherland smiled and bowed again. "Ma'am, that would be a pleasure."

With that, Sutherland turned and strode away, beckoning to Tamano, who was talking with McEwan. For the first time, Ella realized that all Sutherland was wearing since he had removed his leggins was a deerskin breechcloth. His naked buttocks startled her, and she snatched her eyes back to the longboat, where soldiers were unloading supplies. When she was sure Sutherland was out of sight, Ella walked along the beach, leaving Morely and Duvall standing near the whaleboat.

"And what have thee against Owen Sutherland, Major?" asked the provincial.

Duvall turned indignantly to Morely, and his face was hard. Morely's eyes were penetrating under their bushy brows.

"What makes you think I've got something against him?"

Morely nodded slowly. "Don't thee? Thee seem to know each other, though this be thy own first time in this country."

Duvall let out a long sigh and cast his glance over the tumultuous river that swarmed through the channel between low islands and the mainland.

"Yes, I've met the man before," he said. "Years ago. And you're right, I hold something against him. But what it is I won't discuss here, Mr. Morely. It's too damning."

"To Owen?"

"Why, of course to him!" Duvall snapped at the nonchalant Morely, who rubbed the stubble on his chin. "That man . . . that man cost me dearly, and cost a lot of men their . . ." Duvall seemed to shudder back anger, and he contained himself with difficulty.

"I've heard enough," Morely muttered and hiked up the belt under his coat. "Major, thee should know now that Owen Sutherland be one of the best-regarded traders on this frontier. Injuns and whites, even the Frenchy frog-eaters, have never had a bad word to say about him. Myself, I've been through a tight squeeze with him more times than I like to recall. Sutherland is one of the bravest men I know—"

"I don't doubt his courage, Mr. Morely!" Duvall's teeth were clenched, and the words barely escaped his lips. "But I knew him as a soldier. He was an officer in my old regiment, the Black Watch Highlanders, and he never knew the meaning of obeying an order—"

"Major," Morely interrupted and removed his hat to wipe it free of sweat. "This be a different land than the old country, and even different than back East. One man don't go tellin' such things about another man that he ain't prepared to back up. And back up with a weapon. Now I ain't sayin' thy words be slanderous..."

Duvall bristled.

"...but I be tellin' thee that Owen Sutherland be no man to cross. He's a friend of Major Henry Gladwin's, too."

Duvall listened and brooded. He stared across the river.

"Now, Major," Morely continued as he put the hat back on his head, "I'll thank thee to tell me no more about Owen Sutherland. Out here a man's past is left behind, and what he does today is all that matters. The British Army ain't the law here yet. A man makes his own laws if he's strong enough. Or he obeys another's laws if he ain't—"

Duvall had taken all he could.

"Now see here, Morely! This is English territory now, under English law! Neither heathens nor vagabond traders can disobey that law without feeling the wrath of the crown. And where English law prevails, English authority shall watch those whom it has marked as lawbreakers—civil or military—to be sure they never disobey again."

Duvall's voice trembled as he went on:

"Believe me, Mr. Morely, when I assume command of Fort Detroit, things on this frontier will no longer be lax. This frontier shall become safe for law-abiding Englishmen, even if it must become safe over the bones of outlaws and renegades. Owen Sutherland, for one, will be under the closest scrutiny and must never be found wanting if he desires to keep his trading license."

With a look of disgust Morely spat a dark tobacco-stained glob that plopped into the water near their feet. Then he wiped his mouth and looked at the collection of barrels, blankets, and firewood fast becoming a camp. "I best organize to search for them poor lads we lost," he mumbled and turned away.

Duvall stood, feeling empty, staring at the muddy water flowing past, thinking of another time long ago when he was younger.

The soldiers built a pair of lean-tos from bent saplings and pine boughs. The shelters were on opposite sides of the cooking fire, and each could hold six or seven sleepers. Lettie and Ella prepared a meal of boiled wild onions and whitefish netted by the soldiers. Just before food was served, Sutherland arrived and cheered the travelers by handing over a brace of Canada geese, plucked and cleaned and ready for the spit. In a hogshide bag slung over his shoulder he carried two bottles of Spanish sherry wine.

"It seems like the right occasion for this." He handed the sherry to Sergeant McEwan, seated near the fire. "The living should be grateful, and Henry Gladwin's sherry might lift our spirits. I'm sure he'd agree that his sister's safety is cause enough to splice the main brace with the sherry he asked me to fetch him up from Oswego."

Ella smiled and sat on a blanket next to Jeremy, who was hungrily watching the geese begin to cook.

"You seem to know Henry very well, Mr. Sutherland." She brushed a lock of hair away from her face. Her hair was fixed neatly at the back of her neck, and she had changed into a clean, dark blue skirt and blouse overlaid by a white apron that crossed her shoulders and gathered above her waist. "Spanish sherry was always his favorite. But even celebrating his sister's rescue might not be excuse enough to drink up two bottles."

Sutherland sat next to her and poked at the fire with a long stick.

"Well," he said and blew out the flame on the stick, "he'll be going back to England in a few months, and there he can get all the sherry he desires. By the way, if you'll forgive my asking, are you coming all this way just to visit with him for a few months?"

Ella shook her head. "No, Mr. Sutherland, I and my son Jeremy intend to depart from Detroit with Henry. We're returning to England with him on a ship from Quebec this autumn."

Sutherland was surprised. "Most people make the journey from east to west, and not from the colonies back to England."

"I know. I made that trip to the colonies ten years ago with my late husband," she said. "Frankly, I never thought I would ever go back to England again." She was still a moment, and Sutherland did not press for more.

After some time of quiet among the gloomy survivors, Lettie Morely and a soldier ladled out whitefish and onions, and the broiled geese were divided and served out on wooden plates. The night was settling about them, and the firelight grew stronger in the darkness, warming them all.

Hungry men eating and the clatter of knives and pewter mugs were the only sounds other than the occasional distant laughter of a loon somewhere at the edge of the river.

Soon the geese were accounted for, and the sherry was splashed into mugs. In the silence the memory of the day's tragedy gathered itself, and Duvall offered a toast to Providence, which had brought them to safety. Duncan McEwan surprised the officer, and not pleasantly, by adding the names of Sutherland and Tamano to the toast of thanks.

Light came into the sky. Reverend Lee said softly, "The moon is rising."

Above the shadowed islands across the water, a glimmer of bright light peeked at them.

Lee spoke again, his melodious voice buoying up the weary spirits of everyone around the fire on that cool April evening.

"With how sad steps, O Moon, thou climb'st the skies!
How silently and with how wan a face!
What! may it be that even in heavenly place
That busy archer his sharp arrows tries?
Sure, if that . . . if that . . ."

Lee's voice slipped away as he thought for the next words. But it was Sutherland who remembered them.

". . . if that long-with-love-acquainted eyes
Can judge of love, thou feel'st a lover's case;
I read it in thy looks. Thy languished grace,
To me, that feel the like, thy state descries."

Then Sutherland gave a little laugh and said, "I'm afraid I can't remember much more either, Reverend Lee."

"I'm amazed," Ella said and surprised herself, "that you should even know that much."

He looked at her, and the fire lit his amused eyes. He tossed a stick into the blaze and gave that same short laugh again. He said absently, "We all come from somewhere else, and usually from where there are no Indians or bears."

Morely's hoarse cackle came from across the fire.

"Thee ought to hear him on the trail or in a canoe, Mistress Bently. That lad can go for miles and miles recitin' that feller Shakespeare and them other po-ates that any good God-fearin' trader would think downright frivvylus. Aye, it's a wonder to me how Owen ever manages to get any huntin' done with all his recitin' and spoutin'. I think he enchants them critters and charms 'em right into his sack, yes."

The laugh was shared by everyone, it seemed, but the sleepy children and a somber Major Duvall, who from the beginning had suggested that two fires be built: one for the soldiers and another for himself and the civilians. He sat, arms about his knees, his tricorn still on his head, with its sliver of broken gold-edging limp on his shoulder.

"I find it remarkable and strange," Ella said, "that a frontiersman would recite poetry."

"There are many strange men out here, Mistress Bently," Sutherland replied and looked closely at her.

Reverend Lee asked the question that she had thought but believed too forward to ask: "And where, Mr. Sutherland, did you learn the works of Sir Philip Sidney?"

"Edinburgh University, Reverend," Sutherland replied. "Back then, poetry was more important to me than Indian trading. Those were younger days."

"Admit it, Owen," Morely teased. "Thee still writes a verse or two when paper and ink get in thy hands."

Sutherland smiled and said nothing.

"And if you'll forgive my impertinent questions, sir," Lee went on and wriggled his legs under his bottom, trying to sit cross-legged like an Indian, the way Sutherland sat, "what brought you so far from Edinburgh University?"

Sutherland's eyes reflected the firelight, but Ella thought they seemed somehow darker now. Before speaking, he glanced at Major Duvall, who stared into the fire.

"Who knows, Reverend?" Sutherland said, looking at the sincere minister. "I could tell everything I've done, and perhaps why it was done, but as to how I came to be here, I'll never be able to explain that. But I love it here. I love the wilderness and the tranquillity. At last I've found where I belong."

"But isn't it lonely out here in the wilderness, Mr. Sutherland?" Ella couldn't help asking, and again she brushed back the straggling wisp of hair on her forehead.

He smiled. "I'm not alone . . ." He went silent.

Ella wanted to ask him who he was with, but before she could speak Sutherland turned and said to Duvall, "And, Major, how long will you be in this country?"

Duvall looked up. His face was drawn and not cordial when he said, "As long as it takes to put this place under the firm rule of King George. I'm assuming command at Detroit, although sometimes I wonder why I ever came to this godforsaken place."

He slapped the back of his neck.

"Mosquitoes and flies. Flies and mosquitoes! Drat them!" Duvall leaned back into the darkness, as though he had no desire to keep up conversation with Sutherland. "Let's break out another ration of rum, Sergeant McEwan; it would do us good."

Half-slumbering soldiers stirred at the thought of rum. McEwan brought out the keg and gathered in the mugs sent his way.

No one spoke for a time as the soldiers guzzled. Finishing his rum and smacking his lips, McEwan finally said, "There's a song popular in Philadelphia, called 'Drink to Me Only with Thine Eyes.' Has anyone heard it? No? Well, it's a good song, and I'll teach it to you."

One of the soldiers trying to sleep in the dark lean-to called, "I hope there's no wolves about, Dunkie. They'll take to your singing and come in."

Determined now, McEwan waited until the laughter died and began the song in an uncertain but brave voice that soon became a steady tenor. By the time he had finished the first verse, Lettie and Ella were humming the melody, and before long the song carried across the river as they all joined in. When it was done, they laughed and clapped.

"I'll bet the lasses died when you sang that way to them, Duncan," Lettie Morely coyly smiled.

But the soldier lying in the lean-to piped up before McEwan could answer. "For sure a lot of Dunkie's lasses in Philadelphia died, but it was usually of old age."

They laughed again, and McEwan tossed the empty keg into the lean-to at the soldier. Another tune came up, and they were off again. The evening passed in singing and talking, with Sutherland and Jeremy Bently becoming fast friends before the boy fell asleep. The moon was high and bright by the time they allowed the fire to burn low. Then Sutherland bid the party good night and returned to his own camp downstream.

When he had gone, Ella murmured to no one in particular: "A very unusual man."

"Aye, Mistress Bently," said the gruff Morely, who leaned back in his pine-branch bedding and pulled a blanket over his shoulders. "Owen Sutherland be indeed an unusual man. Educated like a schoolmaster, he be, but as good a trader as any in this country.

"He don't talk much about it, but Sutherland is a blood brother of the Ottawa, and they're the strongest tribe out here. A few years back, he come up with some Spaniards and was caught by the Ottawa. They killed his partners and took him to be tortured. But he laughed in their faces when they tried to make him beg. Thee'll see he ain't got fingernails on the last three fingers of his right hand."

Ella shuddered, and Lettie mumbled that Morely should go to sleep and not give folks bad dreams, but he went on:

"They respected Sutherland so much that they adopted him on the spot. Pulled every hair but a scalp lock out of his head, though it growed back now. And they scrubbed him in the river till his white blood was all gone away and only Indian remained. They gave him that green tattoo thee seed upon his breast. Aye, that Owen Sutherland just may be as much Indian as he be white, even if he knows a poem or two."

Morely yawned and curled up against his wife, who lay with her back to him. The air grew chilly as the night deepened.

Ella sat on the edge of darkness. The dying firelight played about her face. Nearby, Jeremy slept. Morely was snoring, one arm thrown over Lettie, who lay next to her two boys. Duvall and the soldiers were blanketed in the opposite lean-to and around the campfire. Only young Sergeant McEwan was still awake. He stood watch down by the water's edge, where the ~oon flashed off the surface and silhouetted him walking ~vly toward her.

In a moment McEwan was standing across the campfire from Ella.

"Will you be needin' more firewood, ma'am?" he asked.

She looked up at him and thought he was about twenty; he seemed very young. At thirty, and a widow for nearly six years, Ella felt as though she were growing old.

"No, thank you, Duncan," she said. "I should be asleep by now, but it's not so easy after all that's happened today."

"Aye," McEwan said and crouched, staring at the fire, his eyes glinting sadly. "I lost good friends today."

Lettie Morely grunted. Her husband snorted once and purred. McEwan looked at Ella, and she found it easy to look back. He was like her brother in some ways, open and genuine. He was not like so many men who had sought her attention after the death of her husband—so many who had flirted with her even before John died.

"That's what being a soldier is all about, though, isn't it?" she asked him.

He stirred the coals and tossed on another dry stick.

"It is, ma'am. And that's why I aim to get out before I end up like those fellows did this afternoon. I won't die before my time." He looked up, and his grin was a little forced, she thought. "Be sure of that, ma'am, I intend to live a full and hearty life, as I always have done. I'll get out of this army soon, and then I'll die when I'm good and ready to."

"Will you get that kind of life out here, Duncan?"

He thought a minute.

"Here you make life what you want it to be," he said and stood up, looking down at her. "I volunteered to come out with Major Duvall's party because there's a future out here. I'm resigning from the army in a few months, and I intend to stay here, get a farm or do a bit of tradin'.

"There's excitement out here. Life and excitement and opportunity that I can't find at home in Scotland. There the English have taken everything from us. But here, a man can be what he wants, and not what some English lord wills." He nodded and grinned again, but this time it was not forced. "Yes, ma'am, I'll find what I'm after out here."

They were quiet again, and Ella listened to the river.

McEwan said good night and walked back out to where the moonlight lifted off the swirling water, and Ella was alone.

She lay back on her blanket next to Jeremy. She pulled his blanket over his shoulders and slipped under her own. He was a good boy . . . remarkable how he looked more like his father every day. Ella hoped he would be happy in England. It would be a great change for him—for both of them—so far from all they had come to love. As Sergeant McEwan said, life is what you make it. She would make it good, for Jeremy's sake.

chapter 3

FORT DETROIT

It was late morning of the next day, with a breeze filling the sail, when the whaleboat heeled around a bend in the river and came in sight of Fort Detroit, which sat on a little rise on the left bank.

The soldiers gave a cheer when Morely pointed at the fort, set like a wooden crown on a long, spruce-scattered meadow that rose up from the river and drifted away toward the horizon. Along the waterfront were rude cabins of French *habitants*. The fort had been turned over to the English by French soldiers three years before. Those soldiers had gone, but hundreds of French civilians—trappers and subsistence farmers, many of them half-breeds called *métis*—had nowhere else to go.

As the whaleboat moved steadily against the current, Ella watched small groups of Frenchmen and their women appear near houses and in fields. They paused to stare, and Ella waved to them, but they did not reply. Morely said they had no love for the English, and they didn't accept the defeat of the last war any more than did the Indians.

Clumps of fruit trees—peach and apple—were a pale green contrast against the darker evergreens. On both sides of the river, which was about nine hundred yards wide at this point, narrow fields were planted in the meadows and showed a hint of green from sprouting peas and lettuce. In other places the earth was dark where it had just been turned. Along much of the shore, cattails stuck out of the water, and here and there was a strip of sand where canoes were beached.

From the right-hand bank an Indian canoe set out to intercept the whaleboat. It darted sleek and swift as the six young braves paddled it across the waves. Painted brightly with symbols of fish and birds, the birchbark canoe came alongside, and Morely broke into a grunting banter with the Indians. They looked glum-faced and surly when he shouted rudely and waved them away.

"They wanted rum!" the trader said roughly. "They should know Garth Morely well enough by now," and he looked innocently at Major Duvall, "to know that I obey the law, of course. Gen'l Amherst says no rum tradin', and by Jove, Garth Morely is one fur trader what sticks by the dictates of his conscience, yes."

He looked at his wife for support, but she blushed and looked away as he went on about how he refused rum and gunpowder to the Indians.

Duvall, obviously skeptical, said nothing. Ella watched the canoe drop back. The warriors seemed to linger, as though they somehow hoped Morely would change his mind and call them on for a keg of rum. In a few minutes the canoe was far behind, and the whaleboat was drawing toward the fort, now five hundred yards ahead.

White smoke burst from one of the blockhouses that topped each corner of the fort, and a dull clap echoed on the river as cannon fired a salute. When Duvall remarked that it was strange they should give a salute to any occasional whaleboat coming upstream, Morely, whose headquarters and home were in the fort, said:

"There ain't no such thing as an occasional whaleboat, Major. They come only every month or so with provisions. But I expect the fort knows who's in the boat and is givin' its future commander a proper welcome."

If Duvall wondered how Major Gladwin knew that he was in this solitary whaleboat, he did not voice his question aloud. Everyone in the boat watched intently as the fort drew nearer. A dozen scarlet-coated soldiers came down to the waterfront, and there were two or three times as many other figures garbed in greens and dark browns and bright blue blankets, and some with copper skins were naked to the waist.

Duvall mumbled something about a strange welcoming party, and then fell silent. It was apparent that the rough-timbered bastion of Fort Detroit, with its pointed poles for walls, did not appeal to him any more than did the disorderly crowd assembling to greet them. New York and headquarters were all too fresh in his mind.

McEwan dropped the sail as they ran in closer to shore, and the soldiers took up oars to bring the craft in slowly to a crude dock where a dozen men were waiting. At any minute, E᷑ thought, the rickety wharf seemed likely to collapse from the weight and fall into the river.

She searched for her brother, Major Henry Gladwin. She had not seen him since nearly two years ago, when he had stopped in Massachusetts on his way back to England. He had married there, and stayed several months. But his wife had remained at home in Derbyshire when he returned to America to accept command of this lonely outpost and simultaneously be promoted to major. Now that Henry had earned his promotion, he was eager to get back to England.

Ella had wondered why a man so apparently well connected as Major Alexander Duvall would want to come to Detroit, so far from Amherst's New York headquarters. She had asked him that early in the trip. His confident reply was that General Amherst had suggested that the most important trading post in British North America was the right place for an ambitious officer in these times.

The soldiers on the dock were shouting and cheering as the whaleboat clumped against the timbers jutting out of the water. There were a few squaws, but most of the Indians were dark-eyed braves standing back and watching with impassive faces.

Then a quick movement in the crowd caught Ella's eye. Others on the dock seemed to draw back, and Major Henry Gladwin, tall and trim at thirty-five, stepped through them, smiling delightedly down at his sister. She was the first up the ladder, and she eagerly took her brother's hand, swung up, and hugged him as he laughed.

"You look wonderful," she said and stood back, holding his hands wide and looking him up and down. He was as robust as ever, and that pleased her, for he had come down with malaria when he first served as commandant at Fort Detroit.

All around, the wharf was bustling: Burly, short French and half-breed *voyageurs* hired by the army to carry baggage hustled down into the boat to heave up hundred-pound bales and crates with seemingly little effort to companions on the dock. While friends clapped the Morelys on the back and welcomed them home, Ella called Jeremy to shake hands with his uncle. The boy stood proudly next to Major Gladwin and tried to emulate the officer's bearing; his uncle Henry now seemed much more impressive than he had two years ago.

"I've heard a lot about you, sir," said Jeremy eagerly. "About the wars and about you being a hero, sir!"

"Well, well," Gladwin chuckled, his pale eyes bright and

clear. "I'll have to hear all about that from you one day. But, you know, I recently have heard much about you, my boy, from a fellow who says he's a friend of yours."

Jeremy was confused.

"From a fellow named Owen Sutherland," Gladwin said. Ella was surprised to hear he had already reached the fort, even though her whaleboat had been moving fast under sail most of the morning.

There was a commotion nearby, and Gladwin turned to see what it was about. His face suddenly transformed from annoyed interest to surprise.

"Major Duvall, sir!" he gasped and held out his hand to greet his counterpart. Distracted, Duvall was arguing with a French half-breed who was roughly dragging his trunk up from the boat and onto his massive shoulders. Duvall turned momentarily, and without ceremony shook hands with the embarrassed Gladwin.

"Forgive me, Major," Gladwin gathered himself. "But I was engaged in welcoming my sister, whom I haven't—"

Duvall snarled at the *métis,* who stood stoically with the chest on his shoulders, gazing into the middle distance beyond the infuriated major.

"Allez! Allez!" Duvall shouted and waved his arms at the man, who pretended he did not understand. Duvall raged at the black-bearded young frontiersman, and then Major Gladwin, serious and now over his initial embarrassment of forgetting to welcome Duvall properly, interrupted.

"My dear Major," Gladwin said and stepped between the furious Duvall and the *voyageur.* "What seems to be the trouble? This man is employed by us, and if you have a complaint, you should put it to his leader, not directly to him. And if I might say, sir," Gladwin lowered his voice so the other English at hand would not hear him so well, "you might conduct yourself in a manner that will not alienate these people any more than they already are."

Duvall jerked his head around to face Gladwin, and the dangling gold embroidery on his tricorn slapped about his shoulders foolishly.

"Major, this man has battered my valuable trunk nearly to bits! Have you no discipline here? Frenchmen or Indian half-breed, I don't care what he is, he has no right to be such a varlet in handling my baggage!"

He turned back to the Frenchman and hurled another wave

of epithets in a kind of French that this young ruffian no doubt thought belonged to a fop instead of a man on the frontier. When Gladwin again spoke to Duvall, this time more sternly, the *voyageur* let the sea chest fall from his shoulders, and it slid with a tinkling crash and a crunch onto the wooden dock. Duvall yelped and leaped for the chest as it tilted toward the water. The *voyageur* was gone by the time the red-faced officer got control of the heavy chest.

"Is this considered normal?" Duvall stormed and began to draw his sword from his scabbard, his eyes on the back of the withdrawing *voyageur*. "I'll teach them some manners!"

But Gladwin stood firmly before Major Duvall and took hold of his sword arm.

"That, Major," Gladwin said, and his eyes were hard as they bore down on Duvall, "that is quite enough. This, sir, is not Philadelphia, nor is it New York. It is not even Fort Niagara. Out here we are dependent on good relations with the *voyageurs*, and unless there is a reason for it, we shall show them every respect due them."

Duvall spluttered with rage and slammed the sword into its scabbard. Gladwin withdrew his hand from Duvall's wrist and stepped back, but he still stood squarely in front of the angry officer.

"We depend for our survival on the goodwill of the French community, Major," Gladwin said softly, but Ella, who was discreetly moving off the dock, heard every word. "We need their food and their trade goods as well as the strength of their backs. If you intend to assume command here, that is the first thing you must recognize. Without them you are helpless here. With them, you have the most important trading post in North America."

Duvall's flaming eyes were still on the back of the *voyageur*, who was sauntering up the dirt track toward the fort's open gates.

"French scum," Duvall hissed through his teeth. "The sooner we get English out here, the better off we'll be."

Gladwin motioned for an English soldier nearby to carry the chest up to the fort. Then he sighed heavily and grinned at Duvall.

"Now, Major, let's start again, shall we? Welcome to Fort Detroit, sir. As you shall see, we have been awaiting you." Gladwin's face then became serious. "I'm sorry to hear about your terrible loss yesterday. Terrible, indeed. Thank God you and the others," he said looking at Ella as they all began to walk up to the fort, "escaped without harm. Thank God."

"Yes," muttered Duvall, who was beginning to calm down, though as he walked he cast hostile glances at loitering Indians and Frenchmen who stood, unimpressed, smoking pipes. "We were unfortunate. I lost a good many of my valuables in that accident. Some essential belongings and several important paintings and papers . . ."

As they stepped up the slope to the gate, Duvall muttered about his goods now at the bottom of the Detroit River.

"How many men were lost?" Gladwin asked. His tone was very pointed, thought Ella, who had Jeremy hopping along at her side.

"What? Men?" Duvall puzzled. "Why, eight, I believe. Yes, eight. I have the returns of casualties written for your records, sir. Yes, eight men lost. Pity. And all those documents! And those paintings! Ah! They were priceless works."

Duvall cast his eyes about as they came to the fort's gate. Lounging near the gate were Indians in dirty red blankets, Frenchmen and their women in cheap cotton or buckskins, and a collection of nondescript English and provincial civilians.

"Rather loose here with security, I'd say, Major Gladwin," said Duvall. But Gladwin made no reply. Ella was sure the new officer was already planning how he would keep the gates shut, check all visitors to the stockade, and make sure these grimy Indians and French kept clear of the English fort unless they had business here.

But for the next three months, Major Henry Gladwin was still in command of Detroit—thirty-seven acres enclosed by a stockade that was six hundred feet long facing the river. There were sixty mostly log buildings inside the fort, which was taken along with six dependency forts from the French at the end of the fighting of the French and Indian War in 1760. Until relieved, Gladwin was the ranking officer here.

As they walked through the gate, Major Duvall clearly noticed the smart salute as the sentry brought his Brown Bess musket to present arms, eyes straight ahead, brass shining. Duvall nodded and went into the gate. There he stopped short.

"Welcome to Fort Detroit, Major Duvall," Gladwin said with a glimmer of a smile as he saw Duvall's face light with pleasure and surprise.

The entire garrison of Royal Americans, as the occupying regiment was named, stood rank upon rank. One hundred and twenty soldiers in red jackets faced with blue, blue knee breeches, and white linen stockings came smartly to attention, slapping muskets with their butts on the ground rigidly against the sides of their legs.

A drum rolled. A portly captain shouted a command, and the garrison expertly presented arms. Every man was steady and looked as fine as any line regiment should.

"Would the major do the honors of inspecting the troops?" Major Gladwin asked politely.

Duvall, his face composed, but his eyes intent on everything, nodded and stepped toward the soldiers, who were in file along a broad dirt street. The men had their backs to a row of log houses lining both sides of the avenue. While the drum beat steadily, Duvall strode along the ranks, stopping here and there to speak quietly to a junior officer. Ella and Jeremy, standing at the gate, watched the ceremony with pride; Major Gladwin had disarmed the haughty Duvall and clearly proven that he, too, knew soldiering.

While her brother and Duvall walked down the street, Ella glanced among the crowd of English and French traders standing about the porches of buildings, which seemed to be the trading warehouses. But she did not see the person she sought.

On reaching the end of the parade, Duvall turned and marched back, with Gladwin and the fat captain one step behind him. They reached the gate once more, and Ella heard Duvall say: "Nicely done, sir. Nicely done. This is more to my liking."

They walked away down another long street, and Ella followed. She heard the clatter as the soldiers simultaneously brought their rifles to parade rest once more. The drum stopped, and the only sound was the snapping of the Union Jack flying over the blockhouse near the water gate through which they had entered.

Gladwin motioned for Ella to come, and they walked along the street between the crude but cozy formerly French garrison buildings and storehouses. A few married Englishwomen nodded to her from windows here and there, then a voice called from behind, and she turned to see Lettie Morely huffing toward her.

"As soon as thee be settled, Mistress Bently," Lettie wheezed, "come an' visit us. We live down Saint Jacques Street, where the soldiers was standing, on the left a bit. Thee be staying at the commandant's house, and that's a lovely place, as good as any thee'll find on the frontier. Hurry off,

now, an we'll be a-gettin' together as soon as thee be settled.
Go on, now."

Ella walked faster to overtake the officers, who, with Jeremy
tagging behind them, were nearly at the end of the street. There
an open ground spread around a building with a single spire
that reminded Ella of a church; indeed it was the Catholic
Church of Sainte Anne.

As she caught up to the officers, who had slowed their pace
to accommodate her, Ella heard Duvall asking Gladwin how
he had known it was they when he ordered the gun to salute
while they were still so far down the river. And how, asked
Duvall, did Gladwin so efficiently turn out the entire garrison
in full dress, polished and clean, on such short notice?

"Well, Major," replied Gladwin, who smiled broadly, "we
had a few hours' advance warning. We have our reliable and
quick methods of communication out here, and one of them
happens to be a trader, a Scotsman named Owen Sutherland.
I believe you met him yesterday?"

Duvall's face soured, then he collected himself and nodded
assent.

"Is he here?" Ella said quickly as they began to walk on to
Gladwin's whitewashed clapboard house at the corner of the
parade ground opposite the church.

"He's down at the riverfront loading his canoes," said Gladwin. "He'll be joining us for dinner tonight. I thought you
would like that. He's a leader of the British traders here. For
that matter he's a leader of the Indians who trade with us, too.
A natural leader, that is. I say, Major Duvall, you'll have to
make a point of getting on this fellow Sutherland's good side—
though I daresay that won't be hard, for he's my best friend
here, and there's no finer man in the country. I suggest you
establish good relations with him right from the start, Major."

Duvall said nothing. He seemed, to Ella, to become more
bowed over then, for his hands went behind his back, and he
leaned forward, as if some burden were bearing him down.
Whatever troubled the major, she thought, it boded no good
for Owen Sutherland.

Several hours later, down at the river, Sutherland's canoes were
loaded with trade goods. He sent an Indian in one of them to
his cabin a few miles away, across the river and up the flat
shoreline. Tamano, who was talking and laughing with Sergeant McEwan, would take the other craft across later. After

dining with Gladwin and the others, Sutherland would take the
third canoe across himself the next morning. Though he was
eager to get home, Sutherland had accepted Gladwin's invitation because he guessed that Gladwin wanted him to help in
making the uneasy Indian situation very clear to Alex Duvall.
That, to Sutherland, was a good reason to resist crossing the
river as soon as the canoes were ready.

"Mr. Sutherland! Mr. Sutherland!"

He turned to see Jeremy Bently, legs flying, running down
the slope from the stockade. The boy was a strong, sandy-haired
youth with a face both handsome and cheerful.

"Mr. Sutherland," Jeremy breathlessly halted and asked,
"are you leaving, sir?"

"No, young fellow." Sutherland grinned and rubbed the
boy's head. "I'll be joining your uncle and mother tonight at
your new home."

"Well," Jeremy said and caught his breath; he was becoming
self-conscious. "I just realized I never thanked you for saving
us yesterday. You left so soon, but now I wanted to make sure
I told you, and I hope—I hope I see you again, sir."

Sutherland smiled down at the boy, whose eyes were bright
with admiration.

"Well, laddie, perhaps one day you'll return the favor if
you find me in need of a rescue, eh?"

"I don't think I'll be rescuing anyone for a few more years
yet. Not till I grow up, sir."

Sutherland laughed. "Now, tell me your name again, lad."

"Jeremy, sir. That was my pa's middle name. John Jeremy
Bently, he was." His face darkened. "But he's dead. Though
I remember him all right. Even if I was only little. I remember
him, 'cause my ma tells me so I don't forget. He was a hero,
too."

"A hero? You mean like your uncle?"

"Why, no. I mean, yes, of course. But I mean like you..."
Sutherland was about to tell the boy not to be so quick to judge,
but Jeremy went on, his eyes looking at nothing. "He died
when I was little, because he had been wounded with General
Braddock. After that, he never got well. Killed by those dirty
redskins. I hate 'em. Every redskin, I hate 'em."

"Hey," Sutherland said, chucking the boy's chin. "Your ma
didn't teach you to hate now, did she? It's not right to hate all
Indians, although I can understand why you feel the way you
do." The boy was glum, but he listened. "Now that you're out

in this country you'll have to learn about Indians, the way I did. Just like whites, there are good ones and bad ones, and they have their own rules to live by—rules that aren't like yours. But it does no good to hate them all. I know, for I've lived among them. And don't forget that Tamano, as much as anyone else, saved your life yesterday."

"Well, yes," Jeremy said uncertainly. "But he's different."

"Don't be so sure. What would you think if I told you that I was an Indian? Yes, I am, you know." Sutherland unbuttoned his coarse linen hunting shirt and opened it to show the boy the green tattoo of a turtle on his chest. "I'm an Indian now all right, and I don't like hearing a fine lad like yourself speak badly of me."

"Oh, but—but—I didn't mean to insult *you*, sir. I thought . . ."

"I know, lad," Sutherland said and buttoned the shirt, although Jeremy's eyes sought another look at the turtle tattoo. "Now, if you like, I've got some time on my hands this afternoon. What do you say to learning something about Indians? I'll teach you."

Jeremy's confusion vanished, replaced with excitement. "That, sir, would be—would be wonderful. I'll tell my ma!"

They walked up to the fort, and Sutherland said one day he would take Jeremy across the river if he liked, and there he could meet some Indian youngsters. The boy was even more excited.

"Yes," Sutherland said wryly. "Never know but you might like to be an Indian yourself."

"I'd have to ask my ma first."

"Of course. And I'll teach you to shoot a bow and arrow, how to make them—"

"And hunt and fish like them?"

"And I'll tell you about the mysterious and mischievous giant called Menabozho, the manitou."

They entered the fort's gate and walked to the Rue Sainte Anne, as the French had called the long street down the center of the fort leading from the west stockade to the parade grounds. The English had already changed the name to Saint Anne Street.

"What's a manitou?" Jeremy asked as he skipped along.

"A manitou is a spirit, a power that's usually invisible except when it wants to be seen or sometimes to do mischief."

"Like a ghost?"

"No." Sutherland and Jeremy strode into the broad, dusty parade ground and approached the commandant's house, where

Ella stood on the porch, watching them. "No, not like a ghost. But it's a sacred spirit of nature that has special powers, magic powers, to help people and animals. They guide good hunters to game if the hunters are pure in heart and brave. Manitou is an Algonquin word. The Iroquois say *orenda,* and the Sioux say *wakan,* but they're all the same thing. The manitou helps the Indian—"

Jeremy interrupted in mid-hop. "And hurts the whites?"

"Well, now, that's a good question," Sutherland muttered and rubbed his chin, which needed shaving. "A good question. Does Menabozho hurt whites . . . ?"

It was remarkable, thought Ella as they approached, how naturally good these two looked together; and she felt herself a little silly for thinking that. But it was nice to watch. Neither had noticed her yet. Jeremy's open admiration of Sutherland was understandable, she thought. A man like that was good for a boy to know.

Sutherland thoroughly enjoyed the boy's company. As they paddled quietly downriver, he hoped that one day he would have a son like this. Many, in fact. Jeremy was paddling at the prow of the birch canoe, and Sutherland, wearing a doeskin shirt and a wide-brimmed black beaverskin hat, paddled in the stern.

They had begun with plans to fish, and they had netted a good deal. Now they were silently drifting close to shore, exploring the reed-grown thickets at the water's edge. Here and there were the sturdy French cabins, and Sutherland seemed to know them all, for the *habitants* came to call to him and welcome him back with words that Jeremy did not understand. Sutherland replied easily, and he seemed to have something different and important to say to each of them. They were rough, simple people, grown into the river land they had inherited. Their clothes were comfortable dark greens and dingy tan. They wore bright red caps and sashes, and it seemed every man had a beard and every woman was pregnant or laden with a baby.

In the unsettled stretches of riverbank, groves of shadblow trees flushed greenish white, ambitious against the pale greens of budding maples and scrub oak. Flurries of ducks squawked above the canoe to land again a short distance away, chattering and annoyed at the intrusion of Sutherland's craft. They turned and headed the canoe upstream once more toward the fort.

"I see you have many friends among the French, Mr. Sutherland," Jeremy said and turned, his paddle across his knees.

"I know them like I know the Indians, lad." Sutherland
paddled strongly against the current coming down at them.
Before Jeremy could say what was on his mind, Sutherland
spoke. "You're going to tell me that the French were at the
battle when—when Braddock was defeated in the last war."

Jeremy nodded and turned away to look at the water flowing
by, clear now that the muddy flooding had stopped.

"Well, lad, I didn't fight in the last war. I was up here, but
I was on no side. I've done my soldiering. I've nothing against
the French."

"You *were* a soldier, then?" Jeremy turned once more, his
face expectant.

Sutherland nodded. "But those days are long gone, and I
fought in Europe, not America."

"In what regiment?"

"The Black Watch."

"The Highlanders?" Jeremy nearly turned right around. His
eyes poured out admiration. "My pa fought alongside Highlanders. They're the best and the most famous—"

Sutherland's chuckling stopped the boy from going further.

"Turn around and paddle, lad. The Indians think men should
never talk in a canoe. They don't talk of the past when they're
traveling. They just travel. And as for me—that's not a memory
I like to recall."

"But we won the war!" Jeremy twisted back, then immediately returned to paddling and listened for Sutherland's reply.
It was slow in coming.

"Who won, lad? Maybe the king and his court won something. I never knew a soldier who won a thing, though many
of them lost all they had and nary a thanks for it. This is the
life, lad, and if you like it here, perhaps you'll come back when
you're grown and make it your home. For now that the war
is over, there soon won't be a need for regiments or battles or
glory."

Jeremy thought about that. They were approaching the fort
again. For the first time he noticed a schooner, its sails furled,
anchored a few yards offshore. It was the *Huron*, one of the
two British ships that traveled Lake Erie and supplied Detroit
from Fort Niagara. Duvall's party had come in whaleboats
because both ships had been at Fort Detroit when the major
was eager to depart from Niagara.

"Mr. Sutherland, that seems strange to me," Jeremy said after thinking about the trader's last words. "I've never ever heard a soldier say he didn't want to remember the battles he has won."

"Maybe not, lad. But now you have met one. But perhaps you haven't listened close enough when men talk of war, or you'd have heard enough to agree with me. If you do have to go to war, perhaps you'll learn why it's not something to remember happily. Perhaps you'll learn never to go to war again."

That evening, just after dark, the table in Henry Gladwin's small dining room was laid in a manner of elegance not seen since 1760, when the French left for Fort Vincennes in the West. Candles glinted golden on an elaborate candelabrum; their flames cast warmth on good English china and flatware set for six on the polished table in the center of the room. Gladwin's favorite sherry stood sentry in the middle of the table, and Ella had found a cluster of daffodils to set in a white vase near the wine. Precious crystal carefully crated from New York gleamed at each plate. Ella was exhilarated when she stepped into the room with Gladwin at her side.

"It's like a dream, Henry." She glided around the table, her pale blue brocade gown swishing against the chairs. The candles flickered as she swept past. "It's really a dream to be here after all we've come through."

She looked at her brother, who admired her simple beauty. The only other woman he knew who could dress in a rich gown and not wear an ornament at her neck, yet still look complete, was Frances, his new wife, who awaited his return to England. As Ella arranged the knives more precisely, Gladwin wondered how his sister could ever again adjust to life in England.

In the next room the orderly opened the door, and they heard the clump of heavy boots. Ella patted her hair, which was tied back with a bit of blue silk ribbon. It seemed to Gladwin that his sister's anticipation dimmed somewhat when she saw it was Duvall who had come into the house. The tall major stood in the doorway and bowed to them both, his powdered wig shining in the candlelight.

They greeted him, and Ella cordially remarked that she thought her brother's orderly had masterfully prepared the table. "It seems like a dream," she said once more.

"And you, Mistress Bently," said the handsome officer,

whose eyes sought hers, "are even more lovely than a dream tonight."

She was not ready for his compliment, but it was a charming one, she thought, and she inclined her head in acknowledgement.

Duvall stepped into the room and moved to her. His voice was soft. "You seem," and his chest heaved upwards as he spoke, "to have actually blossomed after our arduous journey, mistress. I do believe it has made you even more enchanting to my unworthy eyes."

Deftly, with his eyes on hers, he accepted her hand and kissed it. Then with a flourish Duvall flicked a fine silk handkerchief from his sleeve, and at the same moment a silver snuff box appeared in his left hand. With all the proficiency of an experienced gentleman, Duvall sniffed once and twice from the pinch his thumb brought skillfully to his nostrils. He did not offer Gladwin a pinch, for he already knew the other major did not indulge in snuff.

Ella, in that moment, knew she was indeed in the presence of an officer who was of the sort currently populating the general staff in New York as well as in England. Duvall's scarlet coat positively blushed with color. His ample gold braid and brass buttons were asparkle with a light that seemed to come from within and not from the candles, which were feeble by comparison. The officer's clean-shaven face and proud blue eyes glowed in the aura of his uniform.

They were alone now, for her brother had gone to the darkened outer room to welcome another arrival, and Ella realized with surprise that Duvall sensed she was staring at him.

She smiled and nodded, and Duvall allowed a self-assured smirk to creep across his face. His eyes held hers then, as though she had given a silent promise.

"Well, well! Here we are at the finest table I've had the good fortune to admire in these three long years at Fort Detroit!"

The cheerful voice burst from Captain Donald Campbell, the portly second-in-command at Detroit who, it seemed, had done ample justice to many a good table in his day. The ruddy-faced, grinning officer politely kissed Ella's hand and heartily shook hands with Duvall, who bowed but said little.

"Magnificent!" Campbell rubbed his hands and chortled to Major Gladwin, who clapped him on the shoulder in agreement. "You've been positively inspired by the arrival of your sister and Major Duvall, sir! Positively inspired! And I daresay this fine table positively inspires me as well!"

Campbell took another look at Ella and composed himself, his chubby, strong hands clasped contentedly at his chest. He was heavy, but he carried himself like an officer. He was distinguished and blessed with a kind face, Ella thought.

"And you, Mistress Bently, you look positively inspiring. You look lovely this evening, mistress."

Ella let her eyes drop momentarily, then smiled at Campbell. "You're too kind, Captain—"

"Not at all." But that was not Campbell who spoke.

The deep voice from the shadows of the doorway caught Ella unawares, and her smile left her as she looked at Owen Sutherland, who entered the room. Dressed in a loose linen smock, almost white and tied at the waist with a bright red *voyageur*'s sash, Sutherland was a dashing figure; wearing knee breeches, silk stockings, and with his hair tied back, he looked like a country squire.

"I've always thought Captain Campbell knew beauty when he saw it," Sutherland said and bowed to Ella, who floated her hand toward him, even though he had hardly moved from the doorway. In two strides he was there and kissed her hand. Unlike Duvall's, his eyes did not play with hers, and he stepped back with a cordial half-bow to greet Campbell and Gladwin. Duvall's face simmered with unguarded dislike.

"You must be relieved," Sutherland said to Gladwin, who was not as broad nor as tall as himself, "that your sister is at last in safe hands."

If that was meant as a barb to prod Duvall, it worked. The officer moved suddenly and Ella turned to him. But instead of anger, as she expected, a placid smile was on Duvall's face. "Mistress Bently, would you do me the honor of being seated next to me this evening?"

She had no choice. Duvall held her chair with a flourish. Gladwin spoke as someone else came in the front door:

"Reverend Lee! Ah, yes. Welcome! Now we can begin!" He shook hands cordially with the slender minister, who seemed to be perking up somewhat now that he was preparing to tend to a new flock, even if many of them were Roman Catholic and more interested in the Jesuit priests across the river who lived among Wyandot Hurons.

"Am I the last to arrive? I had thought I would meet the

renowned Sir Robert Davers, who has come out here from England."

"No, I'm afraid that's not possible," said Gladwin as they moved toward the table and the orderly entered to pour the wine. "Sir Robert is somewhere downriver for another day or so. That fellow is the most energetic gentleman I've ever encountered. So eager to learn, so profoundly fascinated with the ordinary lives of Indians. By Jove, he's a whirlwind around here, constantly going out and then returning for a brief stay. Ever since he came a few months ago, he's been wonderful company, though he can't play chess like you, Owen. More's the pity, for I don't see enough of you these days, either."

Gladwin explained that Sir Robert Davers was an English gentleman who had for many months been traveling about North America—an adventurer and a man who so genially mingled with the wealthiest and the most humble, that he was welcome everywhere, including Fort Detroit where he had lived in Gladwin's own house since his arrival before last winter.

Lee looked through his candle-splashed spectacles at Sutherland, who sat on his left next to Donald Campbell. Ella was on his right, and Duvall next to her. The minister and Gladwin were at opposite ends of the table.

"I say, Mr. Sutherland." Lee squinted. "What was the name of that remarkable Indian who saved me yesterday?"

"Tamano," Sutherland replied and touched the base of his glass, which the orderly had now filled with sherry. "He's a Chippewa from up near Michilimackinac, a few hundred miles north of here."

"Tamano," Lee mused. "Yes. Remarkable fellow indeed. Tell me, is he a Christian?"

Sutherland cleared his throat to restrain laughter. Good-naturedly, he said, "No, Reverend, Tamano is not a Christian. I presume you have no regrets at being rescued by a heathen? So far, I understand, he has no regrets at saving a Christian."

Lee was a bit blank, but with an effort at comprehension, he said, "Yes, of course. Of course." Then he thought for a moment. "I say, Mr. Sutherland, would you kindly tell Tamano that he is always welcome to visit me. At any time. Anytime he desires a talk, or perhaps some advice, or maybe he'll have a question or two about us Christians, you know. Lord knows he's seen enough of the Papist French to turn him against anyone with a cross, but perhaps—just perhaps—he might find a talk with me—well, fascinating."

A smiling Major Gladwin said, "I daresay, Reverend, that the only advice our good friend Tamano would ever seek from a Christian minister would be how to keep the already Christianized Indians from getting drunk and staying drunk on a trader's high wine."

Lee's mouth dropped open. Duvall looked annoyed, and Sutherland half smiled as he glanced at the minister. It was Duvall who spoke first, and his voice was indignant.

"Do you mean that even the Christian Indians are debauched, Major?"

"Yes, Major Duvall," Gladwin replied. "I really did not intend my comment to sound as flippant as it did, sir, but Owen or Captain Campbell here can attest to the debauchery of a great many of the Indians here. It's against General Amherst's directives, but I do not have the force to prevent it. Traders ply the Indians with rum and high wine, get them drunk, keep them drunk, and cheat them at every turn while they trade with them.

"The Indians are furious when they recover, and they hate many of our English traders as a result. But they are ensnared, just as many of our own people in England and in the provinces are snared by demon rum. They come back for more of the same after they've worked for months to replenish their furs and trade goods. They are poor as church mice all the time, because they drink away what the corrupt trader gives them in his despicable bargain. They fight terribly among themselves and, when intoxicated, kill each other and their wives. It's a sad affair, indeed."

They thought about it, and then Sutherland said, "But that's changing in some villages these days. Last year there was a Delaware, a prophet they called him, who wandered among the villages and told them to do away with rum and high wine. He convinced them, too. He was a true mystic. I saw him sway hundreds of Indians, and they threw away white man's cloth and tools as well as drink. He called on them to return to the ways of their forefathers. The eager young ones were especially moved. They're the most restless, and they were impressed with his visions. They even went off into the forest to have their own visions. They are deeply sincere."

"Why, that seems very noble, Mr. Sutherland," said Ella.

"If the white man has done so much evil to destroy the Indian's simpler life, then perhaps a return to the ways of those earlier times will bring the Indians contentment."

Sutherland sat back in his chair and looked troubled. He pursed his lips before he spoke. "Would that it were as simple as all that, Mistress Bently." He glanced at Major Gladwin, whose eyes, darkened now, were downcast. "But this prophet has also been calling on the Indians to drive out the English by brute force, and they believe they can. There has been talk on the frontier of a general uprising against all the English forts by the massed strength of the tribes."

The ensuing silence was broken by Major Duvall, who looked mildly vexed by the notion that savages could trouble the British Army, let alone this evening's pleasure.

"Isn't it time after all these years of war that the heathens realize there's no hope in making a nuisance of themselves? Haven't they been beaten badly enough? Have they forgotten so quickly, or do they need another lesson? General Amherst firmly believes they do."

He looked at Gladwin, but it was Sutherland who answered.

"Major Duvall, when you've spent some time in the wilderness, you'll learn that the Indians bear a deep hatred for the English. They resent giving up land to the English, who have snatched it from the French. They consider the land you are sitting on to be theirs and believe it was merely loaned to the French in order to carry out the war against the English. But it was loaned after bargaining—and that the English have never done.

"They know nothing of the peace treaty being drawn up in Europe at this moment. They expect that the French King— their Great French Father, they call him—will at any moment send soldiers to drive out the English once more. In these past three years they have tolerated your soldiers here, but they look for—"

"Tolerated *our* soldiers?" Duvall was incredulous. "*Our* soldiers? You speak as though you were an Indian yourself, or a Frenchman! Since when did you become one of them that you could refer to His Majesty's forces as other than your own people, Sutherland?"

"Steady, Major," Gladwin said, his voice tinged with annoyance.

Lee was looking at his knuckles. Campbell was eager to get on with drinking the sherry near his fingers on the table. Ella was looking from Sutherland to Duvall and back again, and she sensed once more the deep hostility that she had felt when they had first encountered each other on the whaleboat.

Sutherland lifted his head and folded his arms. "You, of all people, Duvall, need not ask me that question."

Duvall sniffed. No one spoke. Captain Campbell stirred in his chair.

Duvall went on, this time more calmly, and he addressed Major Gladwin. "My dear sir, surely if there had been the slightest thought in General Amherst's mind that there might be Indian trouble out here, he would have told me about it long ago. As it is, he said nothing of the kind. I for one am not inclined to gossip about dangers that do not exist. Surely, sir, General Amherst is thoroughly acquainted with the situation here."

Gladwin ran a forefinger around the rim of his sherry glass as he answered in slow, carefully chosen words. He looked directly at Duvall.

"No matter how good or how successful General Amherst was in pitched battle against the French, he knows very little about the ways of the Indian," Gladwin said. "We know, in fact, that he hates them with every bone in his body."

Duvall conceded that point with a shrug. Gladwin went on.

"It's largely because of the general's policies forbidding the trading of ammunition and gunpowder to the Indians that they are hostile to us now."

Duvall was startled by this blasphemy, which bordered on downright insubordination to General Amherst, an unbending and harsh commander of all the British Army in North America—the man who determined Indian policy. But before Duvall could respond, Gladwin went on:

"Indians are dependent on ball and powder for their hunting. The bow and arrow is a weapon largely of the past. They hunt for food and for furs to trade with. If they can't hunt for trade goods to get from us what they have always been given by the French and have come to depend on—tools, blankets, trinkets, knives, food, and such—then they face starvation and ultimate extermination.

"Furthermore, our English traders have undersold the hundreds of French traders and *voyageurs* who used to supply the Indians. Many of the *voyageurs* are *métis*—half-breeds themselves—and they hate us worse than the Indians do. We've destroyed their business and driven them into poverty.

There are many friendly Frenchmen here who are with us, but there are as many if not more who would be delighted to see the English forced out or annihilated by the Indians. They often try to incite the Indians against us, and they have very nearly been successful in the past two years. Uprisings have more than once been nipped by strong shows of force in the nick of time, but if the Indians are determined to attack our posts, they have the numbers to do it."

Duvall looked troubled. "Lord Amherst never mentioned any of this to me—"

"I wonder, Major," Campbell said as he leaned toward Duvall, "did the good general tell you about the black rain?"

Duvall scoffed and looked in appeal to Major Gladwin. "Black rain? Black rain, indeed, sir! What is all this about?"

Major Gladwin reached behind him to the cupboard against the wall and brought out a small bottle filled with a black, glistening liquid. He handed the bottle to Duvall, who turned it over and then set it with a sharp click on the table.

"This is a bottle of ink, I presume," Duvall muttered, once more annoyed at distracting frivolity.

"True, Major," said a twinkling-eyed Campbell, who again leaned over the table toward him. "It works just as well as ink, and we've used it as such. But it's not ink, sir. It's rain. Black rain."

Duvall sucked at his cheeks, but said nothing.

"What you see in that bottle, Major Duvall," said Gladwin matter-of-factly, "is rainwater that fell for two days last autumn. It came down from a daytime sky that was dark as the darkest night. It was horribly haunting, as Captain Campbell or Owen here could relate. But black rain indeed fell, and it looked just as you see it in that little bottle."

"All right, all right, gentlemen." Duvall clapped his hands once and clenched them. "Before we savor this delicious sherry before us, please be so kind as to tell me just what this mysterious black rain has to do with Indians or Frenchmen or General Amherst or me."

"Major Duvall," said Gladwin, again speaking slowly with measured words, "to the general staff in New York Town, black rain may seem nothing more than a trifling subject for friendly conversation. But to the superstitious Indians out here that black rain is a portent of evil. It gives credence to the prattling of their mystical prophet; it warns that doom is at hand. This black rain, sir, contributes another element to the unsettled conditions that are threatening war."

Again no one spoke. Duvall was restless now. Gladwin went on: "The Indians are nervous about what the English intend to do with them, and now there is a great war chief named Pontiac, who is calling on them to take the warpath—"

"Pontiac?" Duvall was surprised, nearly dismayed. "Why, he was the war chief who led the attack against General Braddock in fifty-five."

Ella gasped. Gladwin looked pained. Ella's husband had fallen in that disaster, and he had been an invalid for three long years before he died. Duvall sensed the tension and was confused.

"Ah, gentlemen," said the meek and pleasant voice of a smiling Reverend Lee, who seemed not to have noticed Ella's distress. "I see that Major Gladwin's orderly has been peeking at us through the door there to determine if we are ready to dine. Yet our sherry has not been touched, for no one has done the honors of a toast. But first allow me to suggest that I bless our repast, if we all are ready."

Captain Campbell, his glass prematurely raised for a toast, mumbled and nodded to Lee, then put his glass down again. They bowed their heads as Lee solemnly chanted a well-practiced grace and threw in a few references to peace and harmony and all God's children, red, white, and mixed. Ella glanced at Sutherland and saw he was not praying. He was looking thoughtfully at her. When she met his gaze and did not look down, he was surprised and let his eyes drop just as Reverend Lee said "Amen."

"And now a toast!" said Captain Campbell, his rosy face beaming, for he could already taste the wine. He raised his glass. "If I may do the honors, Major Gladwin? Thank you. That our work prosper in peace and harmony—between soldier and civilian, among Indian, French, and white—and may we all cooperate unselfishly so that His Majesty will always be adorned with beaver hats, and Major Gladwin's pantry always be adorned with Spanish sherry."

They clinked glasses all about, and Campbell drained his glass while the others were hardly done with the formalities. The orderly came in to pour another round of wine, then left to fetch the roast beef.

Conversation turned to Duvall's news of the latest English fashions to reach New York. Then they discussed his plans to build a Protestant chapel; until it was built, Reverend Lee would have to hold services in an unused barracks. And in the fall there would also be a school and a teacher for the children . . .

The meal was delicious, and the sherry they drank allowed the conversation to flow agreeably. After dinner they adjourned to the living room, where more comfortable chairs were set in a semicircle about a glowing fire in the hearth. The orderly brought in the candelabrum, and there they sat until Captain Campbell and Reverend Lee took their leave an hour later.

Sutherland also rose to go, and Gladwin stood with him. "Are you staying in the fort tonight, Owen?" Gladwin asked.

"Yes, at the Morely trading house. Then I'll be off in the morning. It will be good to get back to Valenya."

"Valenya?" Ella brightened. "What a lovely name. Is that an Indian name?"

"Yes," Sutherland said. "It refers to singing stones. For behind our cabin are great stones, and the north wind whirls through them, seeming to sing at times."

"Did you name it so?" she asked, fascinated and looking very pretty in the firelight.

"No, Mistress Bently," Sutherland said with a distant look in his eyes. "Mayla did."

"Mayla? Who is Mayla?"

Gladwin grinned as though congratulating his friend Sutherland. "Why, Mayla is the most beautiful Indian woman I've ever seen, sister. She's an Ottawa, and she's Owen's wife, the lucky fellow!"

Ella's glass nearly slipped to the floor, but she caught it without spilling the port. Sutherland kissed her hand, bowed a polite farewell, and was gone.

Beside her sat the contented Alex Duvall. Her brother sat down and poked up the fire, but somehow Ella did not feel its warmth.

chapter 4

MAYLA

Before the first soft light of morning lit the pines across the Detroit River, Sutherland was on his way, paddling the twenty-foot canoe laden with trade goods and supplies out into the current.

The sun was new in the sky and the day hinted at warmth when he slid the canoe into a cove just below a rough cabin set back from the water. Behind the cabin were dark outlines of massive rocks that huddled as though clustered for companionship on that low shoreline. This was Valenya.

Sutherland leaped over the side and splashed into the water to haul the canoe onto land. He heard a shout from the garden near the cabin, and he grinned, turned, and swept the broad hat from his head. A figure, dark and slim, raced toward him. At first, the girl running to him might look like a child. But as she hurled herself into his arms and he swung her around, her supple figure in the fringed, rough flaxen dress and the fire in her eyes revealed she was a mature, beautiful woman— Sutherland's woman.

He shouted "Mayla!" and laughed and hugged her close.

"Donoway! My Donoway!" She panted his Indian name and spoke the language of the Ottawa. "You are home at last!"

Her legs were long and well shaped down to her pretty bare feet. Her eyes shone, dark and excited, and her hair hung unbraided and glossy down her back. He buried his face in it and kissed her neck roughly, squeezing her until she yelped.

"You have been away too long, husband!" she scolded. "Why did Tamano come back to my sister, Lela, yesterday and you still remained at the fort when you knew your Mayla was waiting for you? You stay away too long! You spend too much time in the backcountry with the black bears! You like the bears too much and your woman not enough!"

Sutherland grinned and kissed her again, harder and then gentler and then deeply until she yielded against him. They stood knee-deep in water, her feet off the ground, her legs curled up behind her as she kissed her man.

"You're right, woman," he said and moved back to look at her. "I am too much with the bears. But look, the black bear has taught me well how to love my wife. Like this, see!"

He wrapped his arms about her and squeezed the breath from her. She gasped a shriek and pulled his head toward her face and bit his ear. He shouted and squeezed harder. She made no sound but bit him again hard, and he jumped back and dropped her.

"Hey, woman! Hey, you'll bite my ear off! Hey!" She splashed into the water, but he caught her up before she was completely soaked. She laughed with joy as he picked her up and carried her to the sandy bank, where he fell next to her, a contented smile on his face.

"Hey, husband!" She looked suddenly like a child then. "Husband," and she put her hands on his face, "we are blessed." She took his hand and placed the palm against her stomach. "Feel your child growing, Donoway."

Sutherland's eyes went wide, and he got to his knees. He looked deeply into Mayla's dark and beautiful face.

"How long has it been?" he said with words that could almost not be heard. He looked at her tummy and at his hand there as she answered.

"I have been carrying nearly four moons. When you were away with the black bears I felt it come to be. So, my husband, do not squeeze your Mayla as the bears squeeze. Your son needs room to grow."

Sutherland pulled her to kneeling and took her face in his hands as she touched fingers to his lips. He drew her close and kissed her gently on both eyes.

"I am glad to be home, Mayla," he said.

After the canoe was unloaded and the wares stored in the cabin—which resembled an Indian lodge in its round, bark-covered front section but was framed square with logs in its rear portions—the lovers spent the rest of the morning in the fur-covered bed, happy in each other's arms.

It was noon when Sutherland awoke. Thinking Mayla still asleep, he covered her with the fur blanket and went to his pack, which was beside the stone hearth. He sought out the silver pendant he had exchanged at Oswego for the finest river-otter pelts. He held the pendant before him: It was an inch long, a molded silver tube of simplest design and perfect crafts-manship, gleaming in the warm afternoon sun that fell through the cabin's windows.

He thought he heard a sound like breath catching, but when he glanced at Mayla, she was unmoving. He knew better, though. He stifled a grin as he went to the bed, all the while humming a *voyageur* paddling song.

He pinched her leg.

"Oh!" Mayla sat up quickly. "Why did you do that?"

Her eyes glanced at his hand below the edge of the bed, where the pendant was concealed in his fist.

"Because you were pretending to be asleep," he said.

"What if I was?" Then she knew he was amused by her curiosity, and her eyes flashed. She fell back, pretending in-difference, and looked up at him from her lovely soft naked-ness.

He continued to sing the *voyageur*'s song and Mayla grunted, "Ridiculous song!" She turned to face the wall, re-fusing to give Sutherland the satisfaction of teasing her.

Something cool touched her shoulder. The song stopped. She spun and looked in wonder at the magnificent silver pendant that sparkled as it lay on her breast. She sat up, not daring to touch it. He reached around and fastened it about her neck and kissed her.

Mayla drew quickly away, put one hand on his cheek, and with the other touched the treasure around her neck.

"Donoway," she whispered. "This is far too beautiful for me—"

"Too beautiful?" He kissed her again. "My woman, it is not beautiful enough for you."

She flushed and smiled and lay back once more, taking her man into her arms.

"I'm hungry." Sutherland yawned as he awoke and sat up.

Mayla was already awake. She had been lying awake for some time, watching the fading afternoon light give way to evening. The cabin was dim.

"Let's eat, wife," Sutherland said and, with another deep and satisfied yawn, dropped his legs off the bed. "Let's eat before it's time to sleep again."

He turned with a smile to Mayla lying against the wall, but her worried eyes caught him.

"Hey!" he said and slapped her leg. "What's got you gone so far away?"

She pulled him back beside her and put his face on the bed next to hers. "I worry, Donoway. Hold me, and then listen to what I have to tell you."

Sutherland slid his arm under her head. He waited. Then she leaned up on one elbow.

"Trouble is coming, my husband. It is coming very soon, before the corn is planted."

Sutherland said nothing. Mayla, whose family lived in the Ottawa village a few miles upstream, had spoken to him before about unrest and the evil it promised.

"Much has happened here since you have been away. Even now a great gathering of the tribes goes on downriver at the mouth of the Ecorse. Chief Pontiac has been calling on the Indians to combine their strength to show the English that they will no longer accept the insults and humiliation heaped on them by the redcoats since the Great French Father took away his sons."

He sighed and lay on his back looking up at the dark ceiling of the cabin.

"Well, maybe," he said, "a large party of chiefs from all the tribes meeting with the English will be just the medicine needed to show that fool Amherst how powerful the Indians can be. Maybe that's the only way he'll treat right with the Indians."

She was silent, but Sutherland was thinking and did not go on.

"It is deeper than that, my husband," she said. "Much deeper than just a gathering to talk about showing strength. There are many warriors and chiefs who want war. The *voyageurs* are telling them French soldiers are coming back soon, and they are believed. Pontiac said two great French armies are already marching here to drive out the English after the Indians rise up first. Is that true, Donoway?"

Sutherland sat up then. "Pontiac believes the *voyageurs?*"

"Yes," Mayla said pensively. She sat up, bringing her knees against her cheek, her long hair falling over her shoulders.

"He is sure the French are coming soon, and many chiefs believe him—want to believe him. Is it true? Will the French come if the Indians rise?"

"No, my love, no. In fact the treaty between England and France is being signed right now. France will never again hold this country."

He was restless, impatient now, and he pulled on his buckskin breechclout and Indian leggins, tying them to a rawhide belt about his waist.

"Pontiac is weighing the matter now," Mayla said as she watched him dress. "It may be that he will attack the English. And if he does, none will be spared."

"Gladwin must know this!" Sutherland said as he drew the flaxen smock over his head and slipped his arms into the sleeves. "He must be warned. If he's ready and shows them he is ready, Pontiac may not attack. Perhaps Pontiac will be willing to talk. If there's still time."

"There are many warriors, Donoway," Mayla said sadly. "Too many for the English soldiers here to stand against. If the attack comes, whether the soldiers at Fort Detroit are ready or not, they will be lost. And if the attack succeeds, every English trader here will be killed or driven out." She paused and breathed uneasily. "My husband, I fear for you."

He looked at her.

"Our people love you, Donoway," she said and seemed truly afraid. "But there are many Indians who hate all traders who are English, and they may come for you if there is trouble. Even though you are now of Ottawa blood, you are thought by many Indians to be English."

His face surprised her with a grin, and he shook his head slowly and chuckled. "Me, being called an Englishman by anybody! What would my auld faither say to that? I don't think it would make him laugh." Then he was serious again. "I have to warn Gladwin at the fort," he said. "If Pontiac knows I've done that, he'll want to kill me, that's sure. But it will have to be done, and done in secret. But first, I'm going to try to get to Pontiac and stop this madness before it's too late. Pontiac may win at first, but in the end England will be too strong for him, and his entire nation will be destroyed. Amherst's just the man to enjoy doing that. The English king wants this land. If he has to, Amherst will kill every Indian man, woman, or child who stands in his way."

Sutherland was dressed now. Mayla covered her shoulders

with the pelt blanket and went to the hearth. She stirred a pot of sweet corn soup that was still warm, though the cooking fire had gone out. Sutherland readied a pack for the short trip back across the river and downstream ten miles to the council camp at the Ecorse. Mayla poured soup into a wooden bowl, and he ate hungrily. Bread and strips of venison were also laid before him, but it was not the leisurely evening meal they had both hoped for on his return. Mayla had known he would go when he heard of the gathering at the Ecorse River. That was why she had not told him at first, had waited until they had been together for a few peaceful hours.

"How long do you think they'll wait before they decide to attack, if indeed they do?" he asked her as he opened the door and they went outside.

"After the council has decided, it will be but a day or two before they strike." She held his knapsack while he slung it over his shoulders.

"Where is Tamano?" he asked. "Will he join me in this?"

"He is gone with my sister, Lela," she replied. They walked past a second cabin, dark and empty, where Tamano lived with his wife—Mayla's younger sister. "They have gone north for some days and will not be back to help you."

He threw his long rifle, powder horn, and bullet bag into the canoe and followed with the knapsack. He turned and Mayla moved against him.

"Be careful, Donoway," she said. "There are many who will not love you for what you say to Pontiac. And there are *voyageurs* who will be looked upon as liars if you are believed and not they."

Sutherland smiled, then kissed her long and slowly. He held her face before him a moment, and neither wished for him to go. Soon Mayla stood alone on the gravel beach. The sun was low in the sky and the colors of twilight were filtering deep blue from the east behind her. The red sunset was touched with a chill. She drew the fur blanket closer about her. She felt the silver pendant at her throat and touched it as she watched Sutherland's canoe disappearing across the river. Her baby was uneasy.

It was the fourteenth day of the Green Month—by English reckoning, April 26—of the last peaceful spring the northwest country would know for many years to come.

·   ·   ·

Reverend Lee lost no time in taking charge of Fort Detroit's spiritual welfare. In a country that had for centuries been the private domain of Jesuit priests, Lee was the first Protestant minister ever to attempt breaking ground for his faith. On the morning of his first full day in Fort Detroit, Lee enviously watched the Indians who had been Christianized attend the Catholic morning services with the *habitants* in the Church of Sainte Anne. In the converted barracks allotted to him by Gladwin, he prepared to assemble his own flock, hoping against hope that he would soon make inroads with the Indians. The natives were his challenge, his ambition as a missionary of the word. But he knew it would take time to win their trust, to attract them to what Lee knew was the one true belief.

In the meantime Lee was happy with the kind and generous response the British were making to his arrival. Several, including Lettie Morely, had eagerly agreed to join him in forming a small choir, planning to have a first rehearsal this evening. Lee was buoyed by the enthusiasm of the singers, if not by their voices. But tone and harmony would come with time, he was certain.

When evening came, Lee assembled his choir in the council house. His group included two French women from the settlement along the river, both of whom delighted in singing and asked if they might participate in the rehearsals at least. Lee was glad for their presence. As it turned out, they were excellent singers—like all the French thereabouts, it seemed.

The session was wonderful; the council house fairly resounded with vigor and good tone, and the joyous Lee directed his charges with enthusiasm and cheer. Three hymns were taken up with commendable harmony and spirit by the twelve singers standing in two rows, Lee directing them by waving his wooden flute. The two French women had added the skill that the choir needed, and Lee was thrilled at this first accomplishment—which also marked a small step toward improving relations with the *habitants*, he realized. He swayed to the music, his flute describing elaborate arcs and spirals like a wand, lifting the music to its heights and softening it perfectly at the subtle tones. He delicately, gently guided his charges through a difficult phrase, exulting in the magnificent rendition, when without warning a blaring, honking voice broke out, crushing the others like a sick bull bellowing among nightingales. Lee froze, his flute stuck in midair, his mouth hanging open. The singing stopped, but the sick bull kept bellowing, and Lee gaped over his shoulder to see a ragged, dingy figure standing in the shadows near the doorway.

After a few moments the blaring voice stopped, and the ragged figure stepped into the light of the candles. Someone in the choir tittered, and another chuckled out loud. Lee was staring into the dull eyes of the dirtiest, homeliest Indian he had ever seen.

Lee exclaimed, "Just what do you...? Just who do you...?" Anger welled in him, but he remembered Christian charity, and he also remembered that he must make a good impression on the first Indians he met so he would not turn them away from him.

Lee peered closely at this woebegone man, who was decked out in dirty feathers, wearing dull and torn leggins, and covered with at least four old English trade shirts. He grinned broadly at Lee, who saw there wasn't a tooth in the fellow's head. Nor was there much light in the man's eye, just the dullness that comes from too much drink.

"That there be the Prince of Wales, Reverend," Lettie Morely said, and tried not to laugh at the serious minister. "I mean that be what we calls him, like... I mean he baint really the prince... Oh, Reverend," she said bashfully as the choir members laughed, "thee knows what I mean. Them Injuns all gets such names from us."

Lee nodded but still stared uncertainly at the grinning old Indian.

Lettie said, "The prince wants ter be a Christian, Reverend, don't thee, Prince?"

At that the Indian grinned even more broadly, thumped himself hard on the chest, and reeled a little. He smelled of liquor.

"Prince be Christian, thee know it, aye, aye!" the burly old man said, grunting. He reeled as he proudly said, "Sing good, Prince do! Aye, aye! Sing for the rev'nd. Aye, aye!" He nodded once.

Lee looked closer at the man, as though searching for some beauty, some natural truth, some goodness, but he sighed, for he could see nothing. Perhaps he would after a few years on the frontier, he thought. Yes, and he had to start his missionary work somewhere. Who was he to question the hand of God?

"Prince sing, Rev'nd, aye, aye!" The old warrior reeled and thumped his chest again.

In a moment the confused young minister had the stinking,

reeling Prince of Wales standing at the end of the back row, and the choir started once again.

But as everyone but the reverend and the prince had known, it was hopeless. Nothing could cure the sick bull. The voices of nightingales were not up to that task. Lee's faint hopes were quickly dashed. Finally everyone stopped singing—all but the prince, who droned on, his voice now melancholy—and Lettie spoke up.

"Ah, Reverend, there's one thing that might help matters . . . Well, thee might make the prince here happy and not hurt his feelin's if he was to have a copper or two for his pocket so's he could—ah—well—get himself somethin' to drink. No rum, of course—no, that be agin' the rules, but he'd be happy with a pint of beer or two."

The men in the group fumbled about for coins, but none had money with them. It was up to Reverend Lee to find some change, attract the prince's attention, and stop his singing, then to offer him the coppers to go off and have a beer.

This was done politely, and for the first time, light appeared in the Indian's eyes. He nodded slowly, grinned again, and stuck the money in a shirt pocket. He bowed deeply to the choir, then to Lee, then to the choir again, and Lee just caught the Indian's shoulders to keep him from knocking his forehead on the floor. The prince stood straight up and thumped his chest.

"Amen, Rev'nd. Aye, aye! Amen!"

With great dignity the Indian made his way to the door, opened it, and gave the whites another profound "amen."

When the old man was gone, Lee began again, slightly distracted by the reek of bear grease and aging dirt that clung to the air. But soon he had nightingales once more. Then as an afterthought, with one hand waving the flute in time to the music, Lee hurried to the door, closed it, and dropped the wooden bar into place to keep it that way.

The moon gave light to the river, and Sutherland paddled through the darkness tinged with silver; but by the time his canoe was within a mile of the mouth of the River Ecorse, he needed no moonlight to guide him. Downriver the fires of the mightiest encampment of Indians ever seen in North America glowed like a thousand fireflies.

Sutherland brought his paddle into the canoe and let the craft drift with the current as he gazed in awe at the field of campfires covering the riverbank on his right. He had not been aware of this gathering on his first return up the river because a six-mile-long island lay between the encampment and the far channel near the opposite bank, where his canoes had passed two days ago.

He smelled smoke, and when he was closer to the riverbank, he heard a humming babble, like a hive of bees. The sounds of drums and rattles mingled with the steady drone of humanity. In that moment Owen Sutherland knew his world was about to change forever.

Troubled but purposeful, Sutherland hauled the canoe ashore. In the moonlight and the flickering luster of firelight he saw canoes drawn up on the bank like an endless herd of beached water creatures. He took up his long rifle and knapsack and started toward the camp.

As he walked through them, the strangers—and there were thousands of strangers—drew back uncertainly, glowering in the light of the flames. Dark and glinting eyes turned to him wherever he went. There were no familiar faces in the first cluster of wigwams, which he recognized as Chippewa. There were great numbers of Chippewa at this gathering, and they must have come many, many miles for days and perhaps weeks of travel to reach the Ecorse.

Dogs barked and snapped, and he kicked them away. Women in dirty buckskins retreated as he passed. Young braves stood up suddenly and glared at him. Children stopped running and watched, as though they had come from distant places where white men were seldom seen.

Sutherland walked rapidly past the Chippewa lodges and saw many more hastily erected wigwams that, like the Chippewa structures, were covered with green bark recently stripped from the paper birches along the river. They had not been here long.

These were Wyandot Huron from across the Detroit River. They knew him, and some children ran up calling his name. He nodded and rubbed their heads. But few warriors or women he knew called out greetings. Even here among friends, he noted that eyes were guiltily averted, as though he had caught them at a secret. And he had.

When he passed among the Detroit Ottawa, some women called to him and asked if he had brought goods to trade. A friendly face here and there smiled, and then, as though suddenly realizing Sutherland was close to the English, smiles evaporated to uncertainty and apprehension. Sutherland strode on.

Through the dark and chattering camp he went, and he saw Delaware and Shawnee from the Ohio Valley in the distant south; Eel River Miami from the west, and Mississagua, Potawatomi, Kickapoo, and Piankashaw turned out in strength. There were many Ottawa, and there were others he did not know, but he recognized Sac, Menomini, Sioux, Osage, Algonquin; and he knew there were many more tribes among the laughing, singing, and dancing Indians swarming over every foot of that dark plain on the south bank of the Ecorse.

In the two months Sutherland had been away, Pontiac had sent out scores of wampum belts—black-and-red war belts, apparently—and had called these thousands of Indians together. Now he understood why Tamano had left with Lela. His friend wanted no part in what was to come. Yet Sutherland knew that he had to try to slow the tide of war now fast rising to a flood. Here on the River Ecorse was its first inundation.

Somewhere in the center of the massed wigwams, longhouses, and round lodges was the council ground where he would find Pontiac. The night was filled with sounds of war, and Owen Sutherland felt fear.

He needed no direction to the largest fire, the council fire, that flamed in the heart of the camp where the drums beat loudest. There sat many warriors, talking and smoking in a massive circle around the great fire. In a reddish haze Sutherland saw they were adorned with the finest feathers, their clay-stiffened hair standing straight out like the crests of proud birds of prey. Warriors strutted and preened, and bear-greased chests shone in the firelight with an eerie glow. Faces were streaked with paints of purple, green, vermillion, and white. Some were blackened with ashes that made scars prominent stripes of courage; others were marked with harsh tattoos that retold stories of manitous and portrayed symbols of worship. In the darkness their wild raiment seemed a flutter of shadows and darting light. The fire's circle was tinged red, as with the promise of blood.

Sutherland stopped when he came to the edge of the council circle. He saw a lounging crowd of drunken *voyageurs* sitting in a little knot at the other side of the council ground. More like Indians than whites, they sported feathers and bangles about their buckskins and fringed leggins. The red sashes strapped about their waists and the scarlet stocking caps were woɪn as though they were uniforms, and they gleamed more vainly than any Indian colors.

Sutherland knew many *voyageurs,* and he was friends with the best of them. But these were not the best, and when they saw him appear in the circle of light, they stopped smoking, sat up, and prodded one another with elbows until the eyes of every *métis* were on him. Many Indians went quiet as well, turned and glared.

Sutherland strode across the circle and around the fire until he stood before an old man covered with a blanket and seated with his legs crossed. He waited for the white-haired Ottawa to motion that he sit, and then did so. Rumbling passed among the Indians and *voyageurs,* but when the old Indian handed Sutherland a pipe to smoke in friendship, the Indian talk returned to normal, although the Frenchmen were silent. Sutherland smoked three puffs and passed the red-stone pipe back to the old man, who smoked and passed it to another. Sutherland glanced at the *voyageurs* and saw among them the stumpy, powerful hulk of André Breton. This was the most dangerous of these dangerous *métis.* He was known to Sutherland as a violent and ruthless man, a leader among the less worthy *métis* and *voyageurs,* and he held some sway at Fort Detroit. There he was employed as an interpreter from time to time, and his clever command of English and of most Indian tongues made him a valuable interpreter who was often used by Henry Gladwin.

Sutherland knew well that the Frenchman was serving his own interests at the moment and not Gladwin's in being here. Breton stared at Sutherland, but this *voyageur*'s eyes were not angry or threatening like those of his companions. Rather they were placid, confident, and touched with scorn. Breton bowed to Sutherland and chewed on his pipe stem. As usual he wore three long black feathers in his red stocking cap. They were raven feathers, and that was his nickname in the Ottawa tongue—the Raven.

Sutherland looked away from Breton without returning his greeting. Ogala, the old man seated next to Sutherland, was speaking in a throaty, cracking voice:

"My daughter's husband has returned from the ends of the lake. He has returned at a time when his people are faced with a great decision. Has he come to join them in their united purpose?"

Sutherland waited the appropriate ten minutes before replying to Mayla's father.

"I have come to see the great chief Pontiac, and to ask him why his sons are dressed for war. I have come to join my people in their purpose if it is their purpose to keep peace in our land."

After Ogala had waited a few moments, the old man said, "There is little talk of peace in this gathering, my son. Talk of peace shall be lost amid the songs of war."

Sutherland's presence was not forgotten by the Indians around the council fire—many of them war chiefs—but they went on with their storytelling and bragging as though he were not a white man. The great orations had not yet begun, and if the mighty Pontiac permitted this adopted Ottawa to remain among them when they began the next morning—as Ogala later told Sutherland they would—then there were none here who would oppose Pontiac's will.

"Ogala shall be blessed with a grandchild," Sutherland said at last, and the old man looked at him, but his eyes were not glad, as the Scotsman had expected they would be. His eyes were expressionless.

The old man said, "It is good, my son. But this is not a time to be happy. Maybe the Indian will never be happy again after these days upon the Ecorse. Maybe the Indian children of our day will be the last. Ogala has spoken."

Sutherland understood by this that Ogala wished not to discuss the future or the circumstances that had brought these masses of Indians to the edge of war.

"Ogala, I wish to parley with Pontiac before the decision is made."

Ogala did not look up. After some time he said, "Pontiac is meeting with the manitous and with the spirits. He is in the medicine lodge alone. He seeks his vision; he has promised it would be revealed to us tomorrow. It is a time for wisdom, my son, and the spirits will tell the Indian through Pontiac what we must do."

Just then Sutherland noticed Mayla's younger brother, named Molo, seated across the fire. The young warrior nodded to Sutherland, rose, and walked away. Molo looked back furtively, and Sutherland knew he should follow. He politely took leave of Ogala and walked through the crowd, ignoring the dark stares of the *voyageurs*.

A little distance from the crowd at the council fire, Molo waited for Sutherland. The young man was slender and strong; Molo had learned much about fighting with the knife and tomahawk from Sutherland. They had often hunted deer and trapped together. Sutherland taught him about the long rifle, and Molo taught his sister's husband how to track game and how to live in the wild. If there was anyone in this encampment Sutherland could trust, it was Molo. When he joined the young man in the shadows of an Ottawa lodge, Sutherland saw Molo was troubled.

"Why have you come here, Donoway?" Molo asked.

"To stop this war," Sutherland answered without a second thought.

"It cannot be stopped, my brother," Molo said. "The English have brought it on. We do not wish this war, but we must fight or be destroyed. Donoway, if you stay in this place too long, there are men who will kill you."

They were alternately in darkness and reflected firelight as warriors moved past, throwing shadows against them. In the poor light Sutherland saw the determination of an Ottawa brave rising in Molo's young face.

"And you, my younger brother," Sutherland said intently, "will you be destroyed with these other young men in a hopeless war against the English Great Father and his many sons?"

"I am Ottawa!" Molo replied. This question was not one to ask a warrior, and Sutherland knew it was almost an insult to Molo's manhood to have been asked such a question.

"Yes, Molo," Sutherland said. "You will make a fine warrior, my brother. But I hope for all of us that this war is not to be."

Molo glanced about him at the prying, curious looks that fell upon them from strolling braves. Then he beckoned for Sutherland to follow him, and they walked toward the lodge of the family of Molo's wife, where the young brave was staying during the council gathering.

"Here," said Molo, and he walked into the low doorway, holding back the buckskin flap. "You must stay here tonight and be gone in the morning, Donoway. You are not safe, for there are warriors who believe you'll warn the English of our plans."

Sutherland stood in the dull glow of a small cooking fire in the center of the little lodge.

"There are thousands of Indians here, just a few miles from

the fort, Molo," Sutherland said. I hardly think Gladwin does not know of this and what is to be decided here. I even saw Breton, his *métis* interpreter, at the council fire. He'll tell Gladwin, I presume." Sutherland knew that was unlikely, but he wanted Molo to bear out his suspicions that Breton was inciting the tribes.

Molo looked long and doubtfully at Sutherland. "That *métis*," the young brave said, "is calling for war. He has promised French armies. He has warned of English plans to destroy us all. He'll not be the eyes of the English at Detroit. He is the eyes of the Indian, Donoway. And he has spoken against you."

Sutherland flushed, and he turned to leave the lodge, but Molo held his arm. Sutherland felt then the growing strength in the youth. He looked at Molo.

"Do not return to the council fire tonight, Donoway. And do not challenge Breton—not yet. The warriors are waiting for Pontiac's vision, and nothing shall be permitted to come between now and then. Stay here tonight. If you wish to listen to our council and orations tomorrow, then I cannot stop you. But tonight, my brother, do not intrude on the visions of Pontiac, for none will forgive you. If you now challenge Breton, the warriors will kill you for committing sacrilege on this holy night."

Sutherland knew Molo was speaking the truth. He lay down where Molo showed him he could sleep, wrapped himself in a cheap English trade blanket full of holes, and watched as the small fire burned out. He listened to the drums, to the rattles, and to the voices of strong men ready to die.

The clatter of Molo's wife carrying bowls and ladles out the door of the lodge woke Sutherland. He shook his head clear and tugged on his leggins. Molo was deep asleep against the other side of the round wigwam. Sutherland stepped out into the somber light of a cloudy dawn, and what he saw was a marvel even more shocking than the sight of the encampment in the dark.

As far as Sutherland could see were thousands of birch and animal-hide dwellings. Smoke from morning fires cast a gray cloud that hung low in the gloomy sky. Squaws walked here and there with buckets of water and armloads of firewood. The entire meadow that rose from the Detroit River and from the mouth of the Ecorse was alive with Indians preparing meals.

Counting the wickiups, wigwams, and longhouses crowded over the plain, Sutherland estimated that nearly twenty thousand Indians were there. There were probably eight or nine thousand warriors of all ages.

Sutherland spent the morning near Molo's lodge. He learned that Pontiac had seen his vision, and the war chief would speak to the gathered tribes before the day was very old. In the east, clouds began to disperse, and a strong sun burst through with shafts of light that soon became a blue sky. When the men began to move out of camp, Sutherland joined Molo and Ogala in the walk toward open ground farther up the Ecorse. The women and the children also prepared to go, but they waited until the plumed and painted warriors were well ahead of them before they followed. The men, quiet now compared to the night before, took their places in a mass, grouped together by tribe and clan on a long slope. They faced the crest of the rise where, at the proper time, Pontiac would appear.

The flower of Indian manhood from the lands between the Mississippi in the west, the Ohio to the east and south, and the Ottawa River to the north were gathered in all their savage, warlike splendor. Half-naked Chippewa, the most numerous of the warriors, came with quivers hanging at their backs, and light, deadly war clubs at their sides. Wrapped in gaudy blankets were the Ottawa, the tribe of Pontiac himself. There were Wyandot Huron in bright painted shirts that fluttered in the breeze, and there were Sioux, joined by Delaware and Shawnee. They all sprouted with feathers, and their leggins hung with tinkling bells. Rattles clicked, and skin drums thumped on every side. The rhythms of each drum's driving beat were charmed together by the magic of the Indian soul. Until this day, that soul had never before been arrayed in such awesome strength.

Pipes began to pass; soon there were thousands of them sending smoke in vanishing wreaths above the heads of the seated warriors. Then the roar of conversation was hushed. It was silent. Pontiac had come.

Sutherland was seated in the center of the mass, about twenty yards from the top of the slope where Pontiac appeared. A stocky, aging warrior, he wore a broad belt of red and black beads over his shoulders, hanging to the ground. This was the wampum belt of the warpath. A white, shining crescent pendant dangled from Pontiac's nose, and he was painted black and red—the colors of war. His chest, back, and legs were tattooed, and he wore only a loincloth suspended on a thong around his waist. Beaten silver bands adorned his arms and glittered as he raised his hands solemnly, majestically. The warriors were attentive. It had begun.

A breeze lifted and swept the eagle feathers back on Pontiac's head as the sun broke through the last scattered clouds, and the Indians felt the grandeur of that moment. Every dark eye was on Pontiac.

"Friends and brothers!" His voice was deep and consumed the stillness. "It is the holy will of the Great Spirit that we should come together today. The Great Spirit orders all things. He has withdrawn his garment from the sun so that our eyes may see in its light. He has opened our ears, that we may hear his commandments, and our hearts are one, that we may comprehend in our deepest being the meaning of our destiny."

His hands were still raised in supplication to the Master of Life, and the warriors were awed by Pontiac's swelling, growing power, which seemed to pervade every one of them with the mystic fire of unity. Sutherland felt the war chief's magnetism course through the crowd and even thrill him with its primitive strength.

"My brothers and friends, it has been many moons since last our people went with honor to the longhouses of the white man. Since the day our brothers the French left the forts to the English redcoats, our chiefs and warriors have been treated as dogs and slaves."

Grumbles of assent and guttural ejaculations of anger rose from the host seated on the slope before Pontiac. The French *voyageurs,* gathered not far from Sutherland in the middle of the warriors, nodded and cast winking glances at one another. Then they heeded as Pontiac spoke again.

"The commanders of the English forts treat us with contempt. It is time they learned to respect the people who permit them to remain on this, our sacred land."

Another grumble, this time louder, as bows clattered and tomahawks were raised and shaken.

"The soldiers of the English drive away the Indian, even when we come to the forts in peace, to trade or to smoke the pipe of friendship. They bring us no gifts as befits our rank and our station as the first people of this country. They do us no honor. They are no respecters of our spirits or of our ancestors or of our holy places. The English are arrogant, and they are rude. Hear me, O brothers and friends. The English are dangerous to us."

At that the Indians made no sound. Pontiac waited until the gravity of his words penetrated. Sutherland was uneasy but sat unmoving, lest he attract the attention of some indignant brave who might take a sudden dislike to him and his white blood.

"Yes, brothers and friends, the English are a danger to our peoples! They have driven away the French, our brothers who are the sons of the Great French Father across the sea, and now they wait until they have the strength to drive us away, to destroy us!"

A cruel and savage shout went up from the warriors, and many of them jumped to their feet, brandishing knives and hurling threats at the skies. Muskets appeared and were held up. Pontiac was silent as the braves released their anger, yelping and whooping, chanting for revenge.

Then after some time, Pontiac raised an arm stiffly, and they became silent once more.

"The English come to our lands in ever-greater numbers. Like the locusts, they descend on our forests, and they burn them down. Like butchers, they dig their steel blades into the heart of the earth to grow their corn and oats. They come among us as traders, but they are really thieves. They come among us as friends, but they deceive us with tricks and cheating.

"Everywhere English cabins appear. Their pale children multiply and grow and spread like a poison in our lands. They do not love the Indian. Our world has changed since our French brothers left, and it is not good.

"But even as I speak to you, brothers and friends, the world is changing again. The manitous have told me that the day of the Indian has come once more. The manitous look upon our people with favor, and they have promised me in great visions that the long night of humiliation is passing. That long night will continue to pass if the Indian learns purity of heart and soul. The manitous have told me, brothers and friends, that the Indian must abandon the ways of the English. The Indian must cast away English tools and poison fire drink! The Indian must return to the ways of our mighty ancestors, when life was good, game was plenty, and the forests were ours.

"Yes, brothers and friends, the world is changing, even as I speak, for now the Great French Father has awakened from his long sleep. The Great French Father has heard the cries of his red children; he knows he has been asleep, and now he will avenge his red children who are so close to his heart. Yes, my brothers, even as I speak, he has sent his great bateaux up the Saint Lawrence River, and there are mighty thunder guns and vast numbers of young men who have come to win back Canada. They have come to wreak vengeance on the English, who have troubled us for so long with their arrogance, and who seek with their hearts to destroy us and take our land! Together we shall destroy the English!"

Sutherland watched the smug faces of the *métis* as the Indians burst again into hopping and shouting in angry delight. He felt insignificant, useless there.

Pontiac held up the great belt of war, and the sun exploded upon its redness and blazed the fiery lust of vengeance into every Indian heart. They whooped and screeched and promised death to their enemies.

"Brothers and friends!" Pontiac's voice rose against the waves of anger, and the braves became silent once more. "The Indian warrior shall once again fight side by side with the French as we did on that great day on the Monongahela, when we destroyed the English Army, shot them by the hundreds from ambush, like a massacre of roosting pigeons!"

Another great roar of approval went up. The *métis* were laughing now. Breton was there, and he sat with haughty disdain and looked at Sutherland, who ignored him only with difficulty. Pontiac told of that great defeat of General Braddock in the French and Indian War near what was now Fort Pitt, when more than nine hundred British and provincials were slaughtered by Indians and French. Pontiac was a leader that day, and the ease of the victory, the war chief said, proved that the English were nothing to destroy. If the Great French Father had been awake, Pontiac said, he would never have allowed the English to take this country. Now he is awake once more, and he is angry.

"My brothers and friends, I shall tell you the story which the Delaware prophet who came amongst us some seasons ago told me. It is the tale of my own vision. Open your hearts, that my words may enter and be understood:

"There was an Indian who had the desire to learn wisdom from the Master of Life. But being ignorant of where to find Him, the Indian turned to fasting, dreaming, and magical incantations. By these means, it was revealed to him that he must move forward in a straight and undeviating course to reach the abode of the Great Spirit.

"He equipped himself and set out on the journey with high hopes and confidence. But his journey was not an easy one. He took many wrong turns and false trails, and every time, he turned back without success.

"At length, emerging from the forest, lost and without hope, the Indian saw before him a mountain, dazzling white. But its ascent was so steep that he could go no farther.

"Then the figure of a beautiful woman dressed in white came to him. She asked how could he hope, burdened as he was with an English kettle, trade goods, ammunition, tools, and musket, to climb the shining mountain? She told him to throw away those things and wash himself in the stream. In that way the Indian would be prepared to stand before the Master of Life.

"My brothers and friends, this Indian did as he was told and climbed the mountain; he found himself on a rich and beautiful plain upon which was the abode of the Master of Life, and standing before the unspeakable splendor of the Master of Life, the Indian heard these words . . ."

Pontiac paused here. Not a sound came from the enthralled audience. Even the wind seemed to have stilled its fluttering of feathers, and Pontiac spoke in a deeper voice:

". . . 'I am the Maker of heaven and earth, of the trees and lakes and rivers. I am the Maker of mankind, and because I love you, you must do My will. The land on which you dwell I have made for you and not for others. Why do you suffer the white men to dwell among you?

"'My children,' you have forgotten the customs and sacred traditions of your forefathers. You can no longer do without the guns, knives, kettles, and blankets of the English. And what is worse, you crave the firewater which turns you into fools.'"

Even the *métis*, the French half-breeds, were hushed by the majesty of Pontiac's oration.

"'Fling all these things away!'" Pontiac's voice boomed and echoed across the plain of humanity. "'Live as your wise forefathers before you! And as for these English—these dogs dressed in red, who have come to rob your hunting grounds— wipe them from the face of the earth!'"

The Indians surged into a frenzy. The *métis* whooped madly with them, caught up by the anger and the frustration of three

years under English domination. André Breton, alone among
the half-breeds, was impassive, his thick arms folded, a long
pipe clinging to his mouth. Next to him was a Delaware war
chief, Sin-gat, who shouted as he reveled in accord with the
field of Indians and clapped the unmoving Breton on the back.
Breton sat quietly brooding. Sutherland presumed Breton was
pondering the next lie he would tell Pontiac—the next lie about
French armies and sleeping French kings. But if the lie were
discovered before the uprising began, Breton would be a dead
man.

Pontiac spoke for another half hour. When he was done,
every Indian in the encampment was eager for English blood.
There were enough Indians gathered here to destroy every settlement on the frontier. If this force moved upstream against
Detroit, the fort would fall in moments.

Pontiac railed against the practice of magic to do evil,
against drinking rum and high wine, and against the evils of
English traders. He promised that the strength of all Indian
nations, from the Mississippi to the Ottawa rivers, would unite
in a planned attack before another moon rose.

Then Pontiac lowered the belt of war from his shoulders
and raised a tomahawk that was painted red and cast it into the
dust. That was the signal calling on those who would stand
with him to take up the tomahawk. The first to do so was Sin-
gat, the friend of Breton. The naked warrior, powerful of shoulder and with long hair flying from his feathered warbonnet,
bounded to Pontiac. He raised the tomahawk and chanted a
wild and fierce promise to drink the blood of the English, to
cut out their hearts and eat them. Sin-gat, to the cheers and
whoops of the six hundred Delaware seated together, dashed
the tomahawk into the earth. Another warrior chief rose to
swear the allegiance of his people, and Sin-gat strutted to his
place at the side of Breton.

Before he sat down, Sin-gat glared with open hatred at
Sutherland, who smoked his pipe slowly and listened without
apparent emotion as the speeches went on. But he felt Sin-gat's
hate.

This was no moment for Sutherland to talk to Pontiac. Perhaps when the passions of the Ecorse encampment were calmed
by the passage of time, Sutherland could meet with Pontiac
and try to reason with him. The war chief respected Sutherland.
It was Pontiac who, admiring Sutherland's courage during ritual
torture, had called for his release when he was first captured.

And it was Pontiac who had given Sutherland his Ottawa name, Donoway—which meant "fearless in the flames." For Sutherland's test had been by fire, and he had not flinched, although he still bore the scars of that long night.

Sutherland must immediately canoe from the Ecorse and warn Gladwin to be prepared. Then after the Indians had departed for their distant villages, he would meet with Pontiac and tell him of the lies Breton had spread. There would be no French army. There could be no ultimate victory against the English, only great bloodshed. Sutherland must make that clear to Pontiac, even if it meant crossing the path of André Breton. And no doubt it meant just that.

Far away in the East, at the southern tip of New York City, the headquarters of the British Army in North America was crowded with curious onlookers. Officers, private secretaries, and provincial officials all ogled at the bizarre assemblage of Indians sitting on benches in the waiting room of the office of the commander, General Sir Jeffrey Amherst. The whites giggled and joked to each other as they pretended to be coming on official business. In fact they were there to get a good look at the stolid, silent, but wildly garbed Iroquois chiefs who sat sullenly in the elegant waiting room.

Behind the closed door of the commander's office, voices rose and fell, obviously in anger, sometimes with threats. Neither the Indians nor the spectators knew exactly what was being said in the privacy of that office, but it was obvious that the Superintendent of Indian Affairs, Sir William Johnson, was in the thick of a bitter argument with the headstrong General Amherst.

Inside his office General Amherst rose from his chair and slammed his fist on the desk. He stared straight into the flaming eyes of Sir William, and neither spoke for a long moment. Both men were used to getting their own way. One was a lifelong commander of men, the victor who had led the British Army over the French in the seven-years'-long French and Indian War: Amherst was a lanky man, whose bright scarlet coat and glittering adornments did little to improve his remarkable homeliness. His face seemed chiseled from an old tree root, his red eyebrows bristled with anger.

The other, Sir William, was an Irishman of low birth but good connections who had made a vast fortune and acquired immense influence with the Iroquois in western New York Province. He was a tall, dark, powerfully built man, whose short temper was then under temporary control in this confrontation with Amherst. Known as Warraghiyagey to the Mohawks, who had adopted him, Johnson had thus far lived up to the meaning of this name: "the man who undertakes great things." As a revered leader of the Mohawks, Johnson was listened to when he sat at the councils of the great League of the Iroquois, in which the Mohawks were one of six tribes. Johnson singlehandedly had brought the Iroquois League into an alliance with the British in the last war—an alliance that turned the tide against the French and their Indian allies, an alliance that ultimately guaranteed the defeat of the French and their Indians.

Dressed now in a fine coat of green, with rich lace and shining buttons, Johnson did not look at all like a man who cast off such clothes and took on the dress of a Mohawk chief. At this moment of bitter dispute Sir Jeffrey must have found it difficult to imagine the dignified Sir William dancing the calumet with sweating, bear-greased, and painted warriors. But this was that very man who faced Amherst now. Johnson was dressed like a white man, but he had come to speak for the Iroquois. And Amherst did not like what he had to say.

"For the last time, sir," Amherst said in a hissing voice, "you will not tell me how to administer the military affairs of this country! You will not presume to tell me that I must give skulking, stinking savages gifts in order to preserve their friendship. You will not tell me to grovel at the feet of some drunken buck and beg him not to join his litter-mates in attacking British forts! You will not, sir, presume anything at all with regard to military affairs in these colonies! Not at all! Do you understand me?"

Johnson did not flinch. He had faced the wrath of enemy Indians and had spoken up for the English when the Indians had been betrayed by them more than once. He knew what sort of man Jeffrey Amherst was. He knew now it was no use trying to convince him to change his policies with respect to treatment of the Indians. But Sir William Johnson had a commission from the king, a commission independent of Amherst's control. And his own welfare, along with the welfare of thousands of other whites with holdings near Indian country, was in grave peril if the Indians rose.

So when Amherst turned his back and stared, fuming, out the window of his headquarters at the mouth of the Hudson River, Johnson rose and said softly: "Whatever is done by the military will not alter my intentions, Sir Jeffrey. No matter what reckless behavior is carried out by the military, I shall go on with my attempts to prevent the Iroquois from joining an uprising."

Amherst was barely restraining his fury as he glared over his shoulder at Johnson, who said, "You see, Sir Jeffrey, there will be an uprising for the very reasons I have told you. And if the Iroquois join it, there will not be a soldier alive from the Mississippi to Albany, and no amount of stubborn disbelief will prevent your house of cards from tumbling down over your head!"

"Get out!" Amherst shouted. "Get out and take that rabble out there with you! Damned provincial upstart! Get out before I call the guard, and—"

Amherst was quivering with rage, but Johnson did not move. Then Johnson said, "Will you have your guards arrest the king's Superintendent of Indian Affairs, General?" There was a long pause as the two men stared at each other with open hatred. "Mark my words," Johnson went on, "your policies will deluge this country with blood; and all the laurels you have won as a commander in the field will melt away overnight."

Johnson turned and stalked from the room, leaving the maddened Amherst with a torrent of confusion in his agonized mind. He was due to return to England in a few months, there to be honored for his leadership against the French. He wanted no more of the responsibility for protecting this country. He wanted out, and he wanted never again to meet the likes of that upstart Irish provincial who called himself an Indian!

Several times before, alarms of uprising had turned out to be false. Why would William Johnson be now so doggedly asserting that the frontier faced grave danger? Power! That had to be it! Johnson wanted power and influence! He wanted to stir up fear among the English and then take the credit for pacifying the Indians. That had to be it, Amherst thought as he sat down heavily at his desk. Johnson's warnings that the regular British Army might suffer defeats at the hands of primitive Indians were, to him, utterly unthinkable.

chapter 5

"I OWE THEM NOTHING!"

"Come meet Sir Robert!" Henry Gladwin said to coax Ella away from the daffodils she was arranging in a Delft blue vase. "Come on!" Her brother caught her enthusiastically by the arm and hurried her out of the sitting room and onto the parade grounds.

"He's just coming upriver now," Gladwin went on. "As fine an English gentleman as you'd ever want to meet. He'll be going back soon after we leave, and perhaps you'll both be glad to get acquainted."

He grinned as they walked quickly to the water gate, which was open and busy with traders bringing pelts up from their canoes. Ella was almost annoyed at her brother's matchmaking attempts. He meant well enough, but she felt a sight: Her white cotton dress needed ironing, and her hair was out of control and over her shoulders.

Gladwin chuckled and led her by the elbow down to the gate through the bottleneck of traders, Indians, and trappers moving lethargically in and out the gate.

"Henry, don't expect me to jump at every unmarried gentleman you send my way! And please don't hurry so. He'll think I'm as eager as you are to meet him. Is Sir Robert so very special, then?"

"Special? Why, yes, I'd say so. Never met a finer, happier man. Nobody plays chess like he can—except Owen Sutherland and myself, of course—and his conversation is delightful. Been everywhere, seen everything, and knows everyone of any importance from New York to Montreal! Ah! There he comes now!"

Gladwin was waving gaily at the snub-nosed bateau being rowed up the Detroit River. A tall man, simply dressed, stood in the bow. He shouted, then lifted his hat and waved back at Gladwin. Sir Robert Davers, a young English nobleman who had been traveling all over North America, had settled at Detroit last winter largely because he liked the company of her brother. He was a striking man, tanned and rugged-looking from years of wilderness living, but he wore a powdered wig, as was proper for a gentleman. His face was youthful, intelligent, and lively. He nodded to Ella and raised his tricorn again as the bateau glided up onto the beach. Gladwin hurried to his friend, shaking hands, joking, and being very unsoldierly. It was apparent Gladwin hungered for the company of gentry like this Sir Robert. Henry would be grateful to get back to England.

When she was introduced, Ella curtsied slightly and saw Sir Robert had blue eyes and an easy, refined manner.

"Mistress Bently." Sir Robert bowed and kissed her hand. "I see your brother was telling me less than the truth when he talked so proudly of you. Indeed, mistress, I am honored to make your acquaintance."

"And I yours, Sir Robert. My brother has spoken very highly of you. It seems you are a good match, two gentlemen here in the wilderness."

They turned to stroll up to the stockade, Ella taking her brother's arm and Sir Robert walking at the other side.

"I rather love this wilderness." Sir Robert swept his arm grandly at the fort and river. "I find it infinitely less tedious than London or Paris. Here the people are close to nature at its purest. True, I'm blessed to have had Major Gladwin for companionship, and he has been most accommodating, but I think I would have been enchanted by this place even if I had never met him. And now that you are here, Mistress Bently, I daresay that life in the wilderness will be as marvelous as anyone might hope for."

She blushed at that, for it was a bit more forward than she liked. Yet Davers was charming, open, obviously a kind fellow. Davers was talking to Gladwin as they entered the fort's gate, discussing the Indians.

"Yes, Henry, it was a glorious sight. Thousands upon thousands of Indians of every single shape, size, and color, writhing and hurrooing about the riverbank not more than half a dozen miles downstream. I thought you were down there giving away buckets of bullets and rum the way they were carrying on. Didn't you know about it?"

Gladwin looked as though he had forgotten something, then he slowly nodded and said, "Yes, Sir Robert, I had heard they would be gathering there. I don't know why they're meeting, but they've been restless of late. But I didn't know they'd gather in such numbers. Thousands, you say?"

"Tens of thousands, Henry!" Sir Robert described with a flow of his hands the scene he had witnessed. "Everywhere at the mouth of the Ecorse. I wanted to stop, but these *voyageurs* in my bateau refused. Blankly refused! Strange, eh? They rowed even harder then, as though they hadn't been at it since morning. I say, we did have a lovely journey to the islands at the west end of Lake Erie. Hard rowing it was coming back, but it's fine country. Fine country. Mistress Bently, have you seen much of the country in this wilderness? No? Well, we'll do something about that, eh? Perhaps a picnic upriver. Marvelous place. Alive and sweet with fruit blossoms."

Sir Robert bantered with Ella, and she found him unabashed and very engaging in a lively sort of way. Why, she wondered, was Henry suddenly so glum? Was it the news of the Indian gathering? Well, a picnic, now, that would be a nice change. The country certainly was lovely. It would be more lovely if it were seen with a picnic basket rather than from the whaleboat that had been her constant purgatory for two weeks from Niagara. The gracious Sir Robert Davers would be pleasant company, as long as he had no objections to Jeremy coming along.

Alex Duvall met them at the gate, bowing to Ella and being introduced by Gladwin to Sir Robert. He and the English adventurer liked each other immediately, and Duvall commented that the gentleman's presence in this intellectual desert was heartily welcome. Then he bowed again to Ella and reminded her that they had planned to stroll along the river's edge that day.

"Here," he said, taking a volume of Shakespeare's sonnets from his tunic, "we have some nourishment for our famished souls, Mistress Bently."

Ella smiled. She loved the sonnets, and Duvall had touched her warmly with this thoughtfulness. They took leave of Sir Robert and her unusually somber brother, who seemed deep in thought, and together they walked down to the river's edge, where they observed the rules of decorum and sat on a bench in full view of the water gate. Duvall read to her, and she, in turn chose her favorites to read. It was a thoroughly pleasant diversion, and Ella felt the strain of the journey from the East gradually lifting.

"Won't it be wonderful for you to be home again?" Duvall asked her during an interlude between sonnets. He was sitting on the bench with her, erect and proper, a twinkle in his eye as he spoke.

Ella thought of home then, but it was New England that first came to mind, not England, and she hadn't expected that. She knew Duvall meant England, and she thought a moment, but before she could reply, he spoke again.

"Yes, back home," he said. He was rueful, almost dreamy as he went on with a sigh, "This command out here was an opportunity for me, an opportunity for advancement, and that's why I accepted it. I could have stayed in New York—not a bad little town it is—but out here there's much happening of importance, as you well know. Once this country is firmly in British control, it promises to deliver great wealth to the crown, and the man who is responsible for stabilizing this lawless land will be in the thoughts of the king himself." He sighed again. "But this responsibility won't be easy. Especially because I long to be at home in England, not isolated in this barren frontier."

Duvall looked at her now and said, "I envy you, mistress. If I could, I'd return with you to England. But—but I have my duty." As he spoke, Ella felt Duvall's distress at being in so remote a country, so far from the culture and sophistication of England. It made her a trifle uncomfortable to think that he believed she also was so restless out here. Certainly there was much truth in what Duvall told her about the delights of the Old World across the sea, and Ella was sure that once she was back there again, her link with America would fade, and she would find happiness in the social circles of her brother and their relatives. But she was not restless. She thought this wilderness was, as Sir Robert had said, quite marvelous.

England seemed all so very far away just then. The river was especially enchanting to her at that moment, and it seemed that Shakespeare's sonnets had never sounded quite so beautiful as they did when read aloud in this tranquil wilderness setting. Jeremy, too, seemed to thrive out here. Indeed, she had never seen the boy look as happy as he had the day he and Owen Sutherland went out fishing together. Ella well understood her son's great pleasure in being with Owen Sutherland. He was a man such as Jeremy's father had been.

It was very late in the afternoon when the last boasting war chief picked up and threw down the red-painted tomahawk of war. The Indians began to drift away, and Sutherland quickly headed for his canoe.

This was no time to argue with Pontiac, but there would be another opportunity. Right now he must alert Henry Gladwin to be ready for trouble. Warriors were beginning to chant and dance in their tribal encampments. Fires were being stoked. The ceremonies would be calm during the rest of that day, when the spirit of light ruled the world—the right-handed manitou twin. But when the left-handed twin came to reign over the night, dancing would become frenzied, and singing would be a celebration of angry mysticism under the rule of darkness.

Sutherland tossed his gear into the canoe and laid his rifle carefully against a thwart. He pushed the canoe lightly into the water and stepped in; soon he was stroking away from the noisy camp.

Then came a volley of gunfire. He stopped and turned to see a second canoe being shoved into the water by three braves, one of them Molo. The musket smoke rose above them, and their muskets were still aimed up at the sky. Some Indians in the encampment seemed to like the idea of firing off muskets, and gunfire suddenly rattled and clattered throughout the camp, accompanied by yelps and whoops.

Molo's canoe drew alongside Sutherland, who was waiting. The Scotsman listened as Molo spoke.

"My brother Donoway," Molo said, "our great war chief Pontiac asked me to convey to you that he is honored to have seen you among the listeners today."

Molo waited for Sutherland to speak, but nothing came. Sutherland suspected something. Would Pontiac give him an audience now?

"But our chief Pontiac," Molo went on, and he was forcing his eyes to meet Sutherland's, "is troubled in his heart. He worries that Donoway might go to Fort Detroit to tell his friends what has taken place here. And that is not good, for to do so would mean Donoway's death."

Sutherland tensed, but he showed none of the surprise that came over him.

"And so, Donoway, to protect you from death, I and my two cousins you see with me shall accompany you back to Valenya, where I'll visit with my sister, and we'll remain with you until what must be done is done."

Sutherland saw more than embarrassment in Molo's dark eyes. The young brave was not merely abashed that he must stand guard over Sutherland, he was obviously disappointed to have been given a task that would keep him from the early fighting.

Without a word Sutherland put his paddle blade into the clear water and pushed off. Molo followed, making sure Sutherland would not turn off when he came to Fort Detroit.

When the two canoes reached Valenya, Mayla was standing, watching on the shore. She took the arms of her brother, welcomed him, and at the same moment saw the gloom about her husband, who walked without speaking up to the cabin.

"Is the council finished, my brother?" she asked Molo and then noticed the unhappiness in his face, too. "Why are you here with our cousins?"

"We have come because Pontiac sent us to watch over Donoway, my sister," Molo said, and the sense of responsibility hardened him from within. "He'll not be permitted to warn the English. We'll stay until it is too late for him to go to them. Then your husband may leave if he chooses."

Mayla went weak for a moment, but recovered. Sutherland was already throwing open the door to the cabin, and he vanished inside. Mayla muttered that she would bring the young men food, then she ran up the hill after Sutherland. The Ottawa braves went to the shelter of a stand of pine trees and settled down.

Mayla came into the cabin and closed the door behind her. She leaned against it, her breath quick and short. Sutherland was standing near the fireplace, his arm on the stone mantel, his forehead pressed against his fist. He turned to her and said, "They are ready. Pontiac sent Molo here. I don't know when they'll strike, but it will be soon. Soon. And if I am to go, it will have to be over your brother."

She gasped and hurried to his side.

"And if I do not go, Mayla, it will be the end. The end of everything as we know it. I must go. I *must* go."

He moved away from her and sat down at the table.

"Either I warn Gladwin or I speak to Pontiac before the

trouble begins and make him see the truth. I had no chance yesterday or today, but as soon as he returns to his village, I'll go to him and tell him what I know. Perhaps it will not be too late then. Surely it can't be too late then!"

Mayla sat next to him, and she ran her trembling fingers down his arm and took his hand. He looked at her with eyes that were angry and sad, hopeless yet determined to try something, no matter how dangerous, no matter how impossible.

"I must go to Pontiac," Sutherland said. "I must keep him from this. No one can win. If the Indians destroy the whites they see before them, more will come, and yet many, many more. They'll come until the Indians are wiped out. There must be peace—"

"Peace!" Mayla's voice quivered. She restrained her own fear and fury with great effort. "Peace, my husband? Can there be peace with the English here? Have they given my people a choice in this? It seems the English seek this bloodshed. They have forced us to go to war! I am not sure the English *truly* want peace!"

Sutherland's eyes were distant. Into his mind Mayla's words whirled, but they rang true. She went on, impassioned, indignant.

"The English refuse to give the Indian powder and lead. Yet they offer to trade for our furs, which we cannot get without ammunition. We cannot even bring home food without loaded muskets! The English scorn us! They take our land. The English have brought my people to the edge of disaster, Donoway! Do they truly want peace? Is that peace a peace without the Indian? Is that the English peace? Have my people any choice but to fight? To die? Hear me, my husband, whom I respect and love with all my being, even before my own people. Hear me! You understand what the English have done. Surely you know they have driven us to this—suicide! No matter who strikes first, this war shall come. The English have . . . They . . ."

She shuddered and wept and laid her head against his forearm resting on the table. Sutherland kissed her cheek.

"And what, my wife, would you have me do?"

She raised her head. Tears swept down her face. "My husband, this war is coming, but it is not our war. It is the war of the English and my people. But when I became your woman, I knew I was no longer wholly of my people. Yes, I knew I had chosen a new life, and I did not know where that life would lead me. I have sworn to live forever with you, and that I long to do. I wish to bear your sons and to teach your daughters the way of the new life."

She quickly wiped her tears away and leaned toward Sutherland, who was listening closely.

"My husband, I shall always be loyal to you, but I beg you, do not become involved in this war!"

She trembled again and brought his hands awkwardly against her swollen middle.

"Our child is not Indian and not white. It is our child, and others like our child who will shape the future of the new world. Our children will be stronger than all the generals and all the war chiefs. They born of white and red will create new blood, and that blood must be allowed to live!

"Hear me, my husband. Let us leave this land and go, if we must, to the far mountains. Let us depart before this evil time is upon us. Let us travel to the north. I no longer wish to remain here. My husband, I do not wish to see my people destroyed. I do not wish to see the English destroyed. Donoway—"

Sutherland stood, bringing her to her feet. His misery smoldered in his eyes. He drew her close.

"Mayla, my wife, understand me. If Gladwin knows the Indians are about to attack, he'll be ready for it. If he is ready, then Pontiac, who is a wise leader, must see the hopelessness of an attack, and he'll call it off. He must. And if the English understand how much power the Indian can bring to bear against them, then they must consider the grievances of your people and the grievances of all Indians!"

He hoped, he wished that were true. Mayla looked at him, her lip trembling, her eyes confessing that she knew her husband was not convinced by what he said.

"My Mayla," he whispered, "have we any other hope but that?" She pushed her face against his chest and sobbed. "My Mayla, Pontiac must be told the truth. Gladwin must be told. If Pontiac knows Detroit won't fall quickly because the soldiers are prepared, then war might never begin. And then this fool Lord Amherst shall see how wrong his policies have been!"

Mayla pulled back, a vision of hope mingled with doubt. "Do you really think so?"

"I must."

"And do you think—" She forced back a sob and took a

deep breath. "Do you think that if Henry Gladwin knew of Pontiac's plan he would be able to defend the fort? Would he be able to prevent Pontiac from starting the war?"

Sutherland sighed and mustered determination. "He could. He could, I'm certain!" Sutherland cast his gaze out the window that looked upon the river, and he imagined Detroit, so vulnerable now. "He must! If I cannot bring Pontiac to believe the uselessness of what he is planning to do, then it is our only hope that Gladwin can stop this!"

Mayla turned his head to face her.

"Then tell me, Donoway, what shall we do if we cannot help stop this war? Do we remain here?"

His answer was quick, for he had long ago made the decision never to take part in another English war.

"My wife, you know that I have already chosen not to live with the English again. That is how I came to you. Yet I cannot fight against them with your people, and even Pontiac knows that. If there is to be a war, my love, we shall do as you say. We'll depart for the north country. To the mountains, if we must. We'll not stay here. We'll go where our children can grow strong. That I promise you, Mayla!"

For the next several days, Sutherland was caged. He paced the cabin. He roamed about the beach and outbuildings. He worked with a frenzy. Always the eyes of Molo or one of his cousins watched him. To leave in secret would bring shame on Molo's head and incur eternal hatred. But with Molo watching, the only other way to get to the fort was to fight the young men. That he wished not to do, for not only would it ally him with the English against his adopted people, but he also loved Molo.

It was more than the prospect of war that gnawed at Sutherland's mind: It was also the realization that again he had come to a crossroads, and it was a crossroads of decision he thought he had passed forever. But again he was faced with choosing his way of life, choosing his very substance as a man. That same decision he had made when he left Scotland as a soldier of fortune. Here in the wilderness, adopted by the Ottawa, married to Mayla, he believed his past had been permanently purged. The ritual washing in the river during the Ottawa adoption ceremonies had, he once believed, symbolically severed all ties with the old life. But they had not. The same choice had come round once more: Stand with the British no matter how bitter life might be for Mayla and for children to come, or take leave of British ties forever and depart with Mayla for the far country.

Yet he knew the relentless movement of the British would one day bring them to wherever he wandered. Had they not even found him in this wilderness after nearly twenty years? And irony of ironies, Alex Duvall himself was the future commander of Fort Detroit, the focal point for Sutherland's thriving livelihood as a fur trader.

If Donoway alone were to decide, it would be to choose Mayla's way and depart the country. But the specter of war proved to Donoway that Owen Sutherland was still very much a part of his life, and Owen Sutherland could not abandon the English settlements in the face of doom.

One night, as he lay in the dark cabin, worry kept sleep from him. Staring at darkness, he let his mind tumble and turn, reaching to anger, subsiding to misery, and overwhelmed by frustration. Beside him lay Mayla under the warm furs. Her back was to him, and she lay very still, but Sutherland sensed she was also unsleeping.

He rolled on his side and looked across the dim room to where the embers of the fire glowed. Despair found him again. It was so useless, so impossible to resolve! Mayla was right— English and Indians alike were set on fighting, if not now, then later. What could he do to prevent the inevitable?

He sighed and gazed at the points of light in the hearth's ashes. His thoughts went to the baby in Mayla's growing womb. He flopped onto his back and stared upward, then turned and put an arm over Mayla. Through all the confusion and anguish of these days, she was a haven to him, the focus of his life, the reason for his very existence. Mayla's happiness was most important of all.

Mayla and the child were the answer to every question. Their well-being was the ultimate guide for any decision. First, Mayla and the child. First . . . Then his mind fought him. How could he run? How could he leave without at least trying to prevent the storm that was gathering? Sutherland grumbled and rolled over to face the weak firelight.

"Husband?"

He turned his head to Mayla and listened. She had not moved and still lay facing the wall.

"Husband, you should sleep."

"I'm sorry, my love. I didn't mean to keep you awake.

Don't worry about me now. You sleep." He kissed her shoulder. "I'm going for a walk, and—"

As he began to get out of bed, Mayla grasped his shoulder. In the faint light he looked down and saw her eyes, dark and hinting tears.

"Stay," she whispered. "Stay with me now, Donoway. I need you by me. Stay."

She drew him down, and he propped on his elbow. He caressed her soft, warm body, soothing her. His hand met the bulging tummy and felt it tight and promising. They lay in silence, then suddenly a little jolt from within Mayla startled him so that he sat up and drew his hand away.

"Did that—did that hurt you?" he asked, amazed.

Mayla giggled. "No, husband. You?"

He smiled and felt her fullness again. He came close against her, his hand over her womb. The baby kicked, and Sutherland made a sound of delight. He moved his hand to another spot, and it kicked him again. He chuckled and lay down as Mayla nestled into him, pressing her face against his cheek and kissing him.

"Strong baby," he said and let the kicking come to him again and again.

After some time he said, "Are you sure that doesn't hurt you?" But Mayla did not answer, for she was asleep. He was glad for that; he felt sleepy himself and yawned. Now there was nothing in the world but that silent cabin, with Mayla and the strong baby in her womb. Sutherland drifted off at last and slept. For tonight, at least, if only for tonight, he was satisfied, close to the woman he loved.

In the restless days that followed, Sutherland repaired canoes with a hungry vigor. He patched and tarred the forty-foot *canot du nord* until every seam and stitch was tight and sealed. Then he patched again, working with the anger of a frustrated man. His hands moved quickly, savagely, whipping the palette knife laden with hot pine tar over the seams where the birch was stitched together. The smaller half-canoe was also repaired— repaired as it never had been before. Between spurts of angry work Sutherland paused, and his eyes often drifted toward the horizon and downstream where Detroit sat, awaiting its fate. Ignorant, proud, the fort was like so much that was English: victorious in the world and smug in the certainty that the spirit of Britannia would always triumph.

Sutherland tried to keep his mind blank, but the troubles kept plaguing him, nipping like blackflies, complaining like an empty stomach. He ignored the friendly conversation of Molo, knowing he could never again make friendly talk as they had in past days. Molo did not know it, but his young life was in the hands of his sister's husband, who was seriously considering how to keep from humiliating the warrior by escaping from under his nose. And the darker thought of what he would do if Molo interfered also flitted at Sutherland from time to time.

For now, though, the first question in Sutherland's mind was how he could prevent Pontiac from striking. How could he stop it? And what did he owe the British after all the humiliation they had heaped on him years ago?

"Nothing!" he muttered angrily to himself and jammed the hot pitch into a seam where the birch had again split apart because of his overworking and softening it. "I owe them nothing! Nothing!"

He laughed a little helpless laugh of irony and threw the sticky palette knife into the canoe. He knelt at the edge of the water and looked across to the opposite shore. Late-morning sunshine splashed green along the distant line of trees and flashed on the whitewashed walls of French *habitant* homes.

Long ago he had resolved that he owed the British nothing. So why bring this question up now? He had successfully kept from taking sides in the great conflict recently lost by the French. Even though he had become fast friends with Henry Gladwin, he owed the British nothing. What good would a warning really do? The English might be ready for an attack and temporarily prevent the Indians from launching one, but British policies, as Pontiac had said, and as even Mayla had said, left the Indians no other choice but to go to war. Sadly enough, war was inevitable unless the English changed their Indian policies.

He sat down on the shingle beach and watched wavelets lap against the shore. Coming and going, coming and going. The river was like the lifeblood of humanity, the unquenchable human urge for survival. Peace and war, war and peace. Life would go on like that out here no matter who defeated whom.

The words of a poem drifted into his consciousness—a poem about choosing, about living—but he cast them away. This was no time for poems. It was a time, raw and bitter, for decision.

This country would remain after the Amhersts, the Pontiacs, and the Sutherlands had passed on. What difference did it make in the course of human history if Owen Sutherland chose a side in an insignificant bit of bloodshed on a vast wilderness? What difference if he chose to depart for more peaceful country?

Mayla was right. It was better to depart forever and, as he once long ago had promised himself, never to look back.

"Donoway!"

Mayla came to him, and he wondered at how serenely lovely she was. She walked down the beach, and her wide red leggins flapped in the breeze. Her motherhood was hidden beneath the loose and graceful light blue overdress of English calico tied at the waist by a white muslin belt.

He stood, and she touched him with one hand.

"My husband, I go to my mother's lodge today. Tomorrow I shall return and bring what news I can for you. I shall try to find out when Pontiac is planning to attack."

They held one another, and then she climbed into the half-canoe as he pushed it farther into the water. With a final smile for him, she paddled away.

Sutherland threw himself again into his work. Steel traps were oiled and mended; fishing nets were repaired; furs were unbaled and sorted, counted and counted again, stacked and put away until the time—who knew when?—that they could be traded at Detroit. His Pennsylvania rifle, the only one of its kind in the northwest, was cleaned and polished until its maple stock gleamed. He held it up and aimed across the river.

The muzzle-loader, made in 1761 by a Pennsylvania genius, had a quality that the standard musket of the day did not: It was rifled with spiral grooves inside the barrel that aimed the ball in a deadly accurate path. The time spent making cartridges of greased paper enclosing musket balls and the hours polishing the rifle were the only distraction from Sutherland's inner turmoil.

Strange, he thought, for a former soldier to have such a fine and deadly long rifle and never to have used it to kill a man. That was another irony that swept through Sutherland during those maddening days of confinement at peaceful Valenya.

That evening, in the solitude of the cabin, Sutherland went to a wooden chest and took out a slender, canvas-covered package. He laid it on the table and flipped back the canvas. In the light of the fire and a whale-oil lamp, Sutherland held up a Highland officer's sword. It was the claymore, slender and straight, that he had worn throughout the campaign in Europe. It shone as it had on the day eighteen years ago when last he wore it. Of every memento of that time, the claymore was the only one he had not cast away.

Sutherland strapped the scabbard around his waist and lifted the sword. Its hilt was shielded by an intricately worked basket that protected the fist of the one who wielded it. He flayed the darkness once, twice, and the blade glittered. It felt easy in his hand, as though meant for it. Indeed, as a young officer, Sutherland had commissioned the sword to be made to his specifications.

He decided to wear it on his embassy to chief Pontiac. The old warrior had never before seen him with the claymore, and in these days an imposing manner had much influence on the Indian. Sutherland lightly slid the sword into its scabbard. It certainly was imposing.

He removed the sword and belt and hung them on the wall near the fireplace. Strange to see the claymore in readiness again. Well, these were strange times.

The claymore had given Sutherland a lift. It reunited him with something intangible—something he had once been very proud of. The sword was more than a memento. It was a proof of a man's character, and even though nearly twenty years had lapsed, much of it in a wilderness, the excitement called up by wearing that sword again told Owen Sutherland that the Ottawa baptism had not washed away all his Highland blood. What Highland blood remained was kindling warm on the eve of the war.

When Mayla came back the next morning, she found Sutherland looking bleak and weary. He had not slept much, nor had he eaten. She greeted him eagerly, anxiously, and tried not to fret over his pallor. Tamano and Lela, her sister, had gone up to Lake Saint Clair, she said, and when they would come back no one knew. Sutherland wished he had the counsel of his friend just then, but he did not blame Tamano for leaving rather than being compelled to join the attack on Detroit.

They walked arm in arm up to the cabin, and she said only what could be heard by her brother and the other braves. Once inside and with the door closed, they sat at the table and Mayla told all she had learned:

"Tomorrow," she began, "Pontiac and forty of his warriors will go to the fort, and there they will smoke the pipe of friendship with Gladwin, as is the custom each spring. But when they are in the fort, Pontiac's braves and leading war chiefs will search out the defenses of the fort. They will spy out weak places and count the defenders so that a plan for the final attack can be carefully made.

"Then, having made a favorable impression on Gladwin, who no doubt will believe they are sincere in their expression of love for the English, Pontiac will promise to come back another day to dance the calumet in greater numbers in honor of the English. When they return, a belt of wampum will be offered to Gladwin as a gift. But when Pontiac turns the belt over, that will be a sign for the attack to begin. Then the English will be killed to the very last."

Mayla's eyes, though lit by the golden morning light that slanted through the rear window and across her face, were empty.

The day was lovely, the sun bright and warm. The long grass on the slope above the river rippled happily in the breeze as Jeremy Bently ran and laughed with Sergeant Duncan McEwan. Both carried fishing poles and soon were wading barefoot at the river's edge. On the crest of the rise above the river, Ella Bently sat between Alex Duvall and Sir Robert Davers. They were finishing their picnic, and the blankets they sat on were littered with empty plates and glasses.

Sir Robert took from the wicker picnic basket the last bottle of German wine and poured three glasses while Duvall finished his strident point about the frivolity and lack of restraint exhibited by modern music. Sir Robert poured the wine and waited to disagree again.

"I tell you, Sir Robert," Duvall said, wagging a finger, "this distortion of true music, this false exuberance is typical of so much that is wrong with our age! Too much freedom, not enough discipline! Too much urgent striving after gratification of the senses! I tell you, Sir Robert, this new music is very insubstantial! It's unchristian!"

"Now, now, Alex," Sir Robert kindly chided, handing the glasses round. Ella took hers and watched Jeremy laughing and splashing with McEwan down at the water. "If one is caught up by the excitement of the new music—and it certainly is exciting and beautiful—then there is no *false* exuberance. Its elegance is captivating. And I, for one, find the form inspired! We're not so controlled by the idealism that spurred on the artists and musicians of our grandfathers. Now we are fulfilled by the glorification of the moment. Fulfilled by this moment of being rather than by dreaming of the past! Yes, my dear Alex, this age is marvelous in originality and enthusiasm for life at its most beautiful! And our music is a manifestation of the genius of our age. I find it wonderful. What do you think, Mistress Bently?"

Ella was startled by the question, for she had been following only at a distance. She was glad to be out of the confinement of the fort, and the Detroit River looked exquisitely lovely at that moment. She apologized, and Sir Robert repeated his question.

"I'm afraid I've been away from England for so long that I hardly ever consider culture or its vocabulary these days." She smiled and drank her wine. "But as a young woman I became enamored of the spinet, and I have loved playing it ever since. The music I enjoyed most—before I was compelled to sell my spinet—were the compositions of Rameau and Daquin."

"Hah!" Sir Robert slapped his knee and grinned. "There you are, Alex! The lady is musically inclined, has obviously fine taste, and *she* loves the new mode! So how can you dispute both of us?"

"Rameau? Daquin?" Duvall asked before draining his glass. "They're Frenchmen, aren't they? Well, it's a pity that an Englishwoman should find the music of Frenchmen so appealing." The wine was already filtering into Duvall's words. "Pity, yes. I say, Mistress Bently," and he said this half in jest, "couldn't you have been moved by an Englishman rather than a Frenchman? Even a German would be more appropriate. Our beloved Handel was German by birth! And what about the fine music of Henry Purcell or John Dowland? At least they were British!"

"Dowland was Irish," corrected a mock-serious Sir Robert, who splashed more wine into Duvall's glass.

"There's hardly enough evidence to support the theory that he was Irish," Duvall murmured. "But even if he were Irish, that's better than being a Frenchman."

"Which reminds me!" Sir Robert clapped his hands and fought back laughter. "Our Reverend Lee has already labored very hard to assemble a little choral group, and I heard them singing yesterday as sweet as mating nightingales. Well, that's fine. The difficulty is that Reverend Lee gathered his little flock of nightingales expressly to sing during his services, but—" He giggled here and started Ella and Duvall giggling, too, although they had no idea what was funny. "—but the best of them are French and Catholics, and they refuse to sing in his little church after all his work. But the poor fellow loves music so much he can't resist bringing them into the choir!"

They laughed again in sympathy with the minister, who was trying so hard to bring culture to Fort Detroit. Lee had even gathered a number of musicians together to form a chamber group. Some were English and some French, and the music they played was quite good and appreciated by those who had heard it.

"By the way, Mistress Bently," Sir Robert said, "do you know one of the French *habitants* in the fort has a nice old spinet that isn't used? Yes, indeed! As soon as we return, I'll inquire about it, and perhaps we can get hold of it for a reasonable sum. One of my avocations is toying with instruments. Perhaps all it needs is a voicing and a tuning, and then you'll really have to play for us on Sundays."

Ella was aglow at the prospect. "Dear Sir Robert! What a joy it would be to play again! Do you really think it possible?"

"Yes," said Duvall, and he filled his glass once more, "but won't you please learn some pieces from your native land, Mistress Bently? After all, those Frenchmen are—are Frenchmen!"

"If I'm not being too inquisitive, Mistress Bently," asked Sir Robert, "why on earth did you sell a spinet if you love the instrument so much? Such an instrument is nearly impossible to come by in the colonies."

Ella looked down at her white dress and smoothed away the folds.

"It was not long after my husband died," she said. "We were in distress—financially—during his long illness. Ultimately, when he died, I had to sell the spinet . . . many valuables, eventually the farm. That became my reason for joining Major Gladwin, to return to England where—where life would, he believes, be easier for my son and me."

An embarrassed silence passed over them. Duvall cleared his throat. Sir Robert spoke: "Forgive my question, for it was not—"

"No, no, Sir Robert." Ella smiled. "Please do not apologize, for it was a fair question indeed. Now this is wonderful news about the spinet at the fort. It will be like old times."

"I say," said Duvall and cleared his throat sleepily. "Can you play 'The World Turned Upside Down'?"

"Now that," laughed Sir Robert, "is indeed modern music!"

Thanks to the presence of the Frenchwomen, the sound at the choir rehearsal that May afternoon was exhilarating, and Reverend Lee forgot his disappointment over the unwillingness of the French to sing in his church. But the group had barely completed the first hymn when the sick bull joined in once more from the shadows over near the door.

The singers stopped as Lee, mumbling with annoyance because he had failed to bolt the door, wasted no time in stepping over to the newcomer, whom he expected to be the Prince of Wales. But as he approached the shabby figure in the half-light, he was surprised to see it was not the prince at all, though this would be an appropriate protégé, for the man was equally shabby and dirty. The old Indian moved forward to greet Lee, grasping his hand, shaking it vigorously, and grunting "amen," over and over again.

Lee eyed the Indian quickly, then drew out some coins he had brought for just such an occasion. Muttering "yes, yes," and patting the Indian on the shoulder, Lee showed the man out, ignoring the bowing and moaned "amens." But before the door was closed, in stepped none other than the Prince of Wales himself, a vacant grin on his face, and his eyes alight, no doubt with the thought of drinking beer. Lee gritted his teeth, found another copper, and guided the two sick bulls outside. This time he barred the door.

But it was not long before there was a knocking. Lee ignored it, determined not to be disturbed by anything—particularly by the Prince of Wales!

But the knocking went on doggedly, monotonously, almost rhythmically, nonstop. Lee tried drawing out more volume from his singers, but that was no use, for the knocking grew louder at the same time. And in the places where the choir took breaths or paused, the ponderous banging jarred them without cease. At last, lowering his flute in the middle of a shaky pianissimo transition, Lee stamped to the door, ripped up the bar, and yanked it away.

"Amen, amen," grumbled at least ten gravelly voices, and Lee staggered back as into the council house trooped a crowd of aged Indian men, all bowing, hands praying, and muttering sincere "amens."

The choir members hooted and roared with laughter, and Lettie Morely collapsed into a chair, wiping away tears. Reverend Lee was simply speechless.

chapter 6

SUTHERLAND'S DISHONOR

The afternoon of the following day was also sunny and bright. Sitting with her son on the porch of Gladwin's white house, Ella stared thoughtfully across the parade ground at the French Church of Sainte Anne, where *habitants* had already come, worshipped, and gone. In the distance Ella could hear the awful sound of Indians singing over in the council house. Apparently Reverend Lee had undertaken to teach English hymns to some of the more pious ones. Ella thought that was quite charming of the good reverend, but she wondered at his endurance, being shut up in the echoing room with those dismal sounds. It reminded her of a slaughterhouse.

She looked over at Jeremy and said, "You know, son, you really must learn your French while you have the opportunity to use it with so many Frenchmen about." She picked up some knitting which she had neglected for several days.

Jeremy nodded but did not let up burnishing his fishing pole with tallow as Sergeant McEwan had told him to do.

"But, Ma, why can't Reverend Lee teach me to speak the kind of French that's spoken by the *Canadiens* out here? Why do we have to learn the old classics, the—"

"Because, my boy, the French that's spoken out on the frontier is not pure French. A Frenchman from France would never understand it, and he would laugh you out of France if you spoke that way to him."

"Perhaps," Jeremy said and laid the pole down. "But we're in Canada now, and when I try to speak proper to the French boys here, they laugh at me! They tease me for being a little gentleman and all!"

"Then be a gentleman . . ."

Her voice trailed off as a clamor arose near the opposite end of the fort. Soldiers came from the barracks and ran to their posts. Traders stepped into the street and looked up the Rue Sainte Anne toward the west gate.

"Indians approaching!" a sentry shouted to Henry Gladwin as the officer came out of his front door. "Lots of them, Major. And they're all painted!"

Fascinated, Ella and Jeremy stood up to look down the Rue Sainte Anne. Major Gladwin was in the company of his interpreter, André Breton. Ella did not like the look of this man, although her brother insisted Breton was an excellent interpreter. Breton, Henry had told her, had even been to the great meeting of the Indians at the Ecorse River, and the French half-breed had assured Gladwin that the Indians were making the normal complaints, but it was nothing more serious.

As the two men walked past Ella and Jeremy, she heard Gladwin say, "Tell them they can't come in. First I want to hear from Pontiac all that happened at the Ecorse council. Ask why he's been keeping that from us. If he'll report why he called them together, then I'll talk with him. Not before."

"But, Major," Breton appealed. "I have already told you this meeting was nothing remarkable. You must not turn them away, or there might be trouble, Major. They come every spring to the fort to dance and smoke the calumet in honor of the commandant of the fort. To turn them away after they have come to honor you would be a great insult, I assure you. They are not carrying arms—"

Captain Campbell appeared alongside them and said, "Breton's right, sir. We have no choice but to let them in and show them the respect they expect from us, sir. They'll come to the parade ground, dance, make long speeches, and smoke with you. They'll expect some gift in return for their honoring you— some bread, tobacco, and beer will do well enough. If you don't let them come in, as Breton said, there may be unpleasant repercussions, some hard feelings that we don't want."

Sir Robert Davers now appeared at Ella's side, and he smiled cordially to her and Jeremy, who showed little interest in him, even though the gentleman rubbed the boy's head in a friendly way. Gladwin sighed and waved his arms in exasperation.

"All right, all right, Breton, you and Captain Campbell lead them in and get this over with. At least Sir Robert and Jeremy here might find it all interesting. I, for one, counted on an afternoon without duties of state and tiresome Indian speeches. Bring them in."

With that, Gladwin turned on his heel and strode back to the porch, where he settled on a chair with Sir Robert beside him. Ella and Jeremy went into the house to watch through an open window behind Gladwin. From this vantage point she would be able to look directly at Pontiac when he made his speech to her brother.

A moment later, down the Rue Sainte Anne came a wild and proud array of Indians, most bare-chested, and some in only loincloths. Others had brightly beaded leggins of buckskin, and none carried any weapon other than a hunting knife. Most bore calumet pipes of clay or red sandstone.

As the crowd gathered near Gladwin's porch, Ella watched in fascination, noting the savage tattoos that often covered every visible inch of a warrior, including the legs and buttocks. Their faces, however, were unpainted. The Indians sat in a large crescent behind Pontiac, who looked grimly imposing even without ceremonial paint. At a respectful distance, the residents and off-duty soldiers gathered to watch the proceedings.

Gladwin did not rise but nodded gravely to Pontiac, who stepped forward. Then the major stood and shook hands with the war chief, and Breton interpreted their polite but cool greetings.

Pontiac presented Gladwin with an ornate, ebony-colored pipe and then raised his hand to signal his warriors to prepare for the dancing. Some braves drove a long stake into the ground at the center of the parade, and other Indians, including Pontiac, sat placidly smoking. Gladwin politely puffed three times on the pipe Pontiac had given him and passed it to Sir Robert and then to Campbell and Duvall.

When the pipes were out, a small group of warriors began a frantic, chanting dance about the pole. The singing grew more frenzied, and the capering matched the voices in intensity and excitement. Ella and Jeremy watched, enthralled, as the braves leaped and pranced, howled, and yelped in a circle for more than an hour.

From time to time Ella's attention was caught by the occasional arrival of a warrior who appeared from somewhere in the fort, as though he had been wandering alone. One by one they came, unobtrusively sitting down and nonchalantly acting as though they had been there all the time. She saw at least six of these newcomers slipping without a word into the edge of the massed Indians, but she thought nothing of it.

Then Pontiac stood, and the dancing abruptly ceased. The powerfully built, dark-faced chieftain advanced to within a few feet of Gladwin, and with a loud voice, spoke quickly for several minutes.

"He looks frightening," Jeremy whispered to his mother, who shushed him as Breton began to interpret for Gladwin:

"Major Gladwin, Pontiac and all his Ottawa have come to tell you how much they love their English brothers. They are your friends now and shall continue to be for as long as the grass grows and the rivers run. He thanks you for whatever favors you have granted him and his people, and he apologizes that this calumet party is so small. But, he says, many of his people are still at the winter hunting grounds in the south. When they return in a few days, Pontiac and all his young men shall pay you a formal visit in such numbers and with such enthusiasm and eagerness that the feelings of the Indians will be clearly shown to the English. The love the Indian bears for his English Father will be quite apparent. Pontiac now asks, as a token of the English commander's friendship, that his party here be provided with a little tobacco, bread, and rum."

Gladwin smiled slightly and said to Breton, "Tell him that we are greatly honored by his visit and heartily appreciate the friendship of the Ottawa for the English. Tell him he can be sure that whatever friendship he and his people hold for us and whatever deeds of friendship they do for us shall be returned in like measure to him and his people. We look forward to the next visit he intends for us. Tell him that bread and tobacco shall be given as tokens of our esteem for the Ottawa, but tell him that my chief does not permit me to give Indians rum, so they shall have beer, instead, to drink as our guests."

With extreme gravity and without a hint of disappointment over the withholding of rum, the Indians accepted bread, beer, and tobacco. They chewed the bread and drank the beer with solemnity. When all were finished, Pontiac rose and shook hands with Gladwin once more. Then the party crowded past the group of spectators, which opened to give them room. In silence they went out through the west gate, which was closed behind them.

Alex Duvall spoke to the pensive Sir Robert Davers seated next to Gladwin. "That was a closer look at these northwestern Indians than we Englishmen will ever have."

Gladwin was up and walking away with Captain Campbell, who was joking and chuckling at his commander's side.

"Closer than all but Owen Sutherland, you mean," Sir Robert said and rose to stretch his legs. Ella and Jeremy were still seated at the window, but neither Sir Robert nor Duvall noticed them. "It seems," Sir Robert went on with a stifled yawn, "that Owen Sutherland has seen more than any of us have of the Indians. From what he says, he certainly knows a lot about them."

Ella did not intend to listen to the conversation.

Duvall snorted. "Sutherland, yes. Well, he's not an Englishman. He's a Scotchman, and by now, maybe he's not even a Scotchman anymore. I daresay he's more savage than the savage, or at least he's as uncivilized as they. Have you seen the way he sports his arse about in those leggins and breechclout? No self-respecting Scotchman would do that, even if the worst of them still yearn to wear the kilt! Though we put a stop to that after we whipped them in the rebellion of forty-five."

Duvall glanced up to the window to see Ella staring at him. He flushed and apologized and bowed, his tricorn in hand.

"Forgive my language, Mistress Bently, I did not realize you were at hand," he said and then became charmingly gracious once more. "I say, mistress, how did you enjoy your first calumet dance, eh? Was it worth making that long journey out here to view such unsurpassed primitive entertainment? I daresay it was!"

"You shouldn't speak like that about Owen Sutherland!"

It was Jeremy's angry voice that expressed Ella's own thoughts, but she shushed him and apologized to Duvall for her son's outburst. Jeremy roughly pulled his head back from the window.

Ella looked at Duvall and Sir Robert. "Fascinating," she said, and left the window without excusing herself.

Duvall spoke with surprise. "Well, she's in a snippety mood at the moment, eh, Sir Robert? Why was she so short, do you suppose?"

Sir Robert stepped down from the porch and put a friendly arm over the major's shoulders, directing him away from Gladwin's house.

"Perhaps, Major," Sir Robert said with a smile, "she doesn't like to hear you make insulting remarks about Owen Sutherland. After all, he did save her life and the boy's, I understand."

Duvall stopped in his tracks and stepped back from Sir Robert, whose eyes were mischievous.

Duvall was annoyed. "Come now, Sir Robert, surely you haven't been out here in the wilds so long that you would think a churl like Sutherland could ever be the fancy of an English-woman of breeding like Ella Bently! No, no, my good fellow. No, no, indeed."

They walked toward the officers' mess, which was a low, rough-hewn building set against the river wall. Duvall laughed again but without conviction.

"Strange things happen in the colonies, especially in the wilderness." Sir Robert was teasing, but his words cut deeply. "This is the age of reason, the day of enlightenment, and the day of equality of human beings, as I've been reading so often lately, even in English books, not just from Frenchmen like Rousseau. So perhaps our lady—"

"Let's not have any more such talk," Duvall said with a wave of a hand. "I can see by your own big eyes that you're smitten by Ella Bently as much as anyone."

"As much as you?" Sir Robert winked.

"Well, Sir Robert, are you sure you want to risk taking this journey up to Lake Saint Clair tomorrow? Eh? You'll be leaving her to me, you know. That might be a fatal mistake on your part. Out of sight, out of mind."

Sir Robert laughed, although his companion was correct. Ella attracted him strongly. Duvall spoke again. "You spend so much time puttering about in this wilderness that you might forget you're English! You might even end up like Owen Sutherland, married to a heathen doxy!"

At that, Sir Robert was taken aback. He stopped, and Duvall paused, too. Normally Sir Robert genuinely liked Duvall's company, but this constant berating of Sutherland, whom Davers respected, was curious and even irritating.

"I say, Alex, aren't you being a bit unfair to Sutherland? After all, I've known the man for some months, and he seems quite a remarkable fellow, well-respected by the Indians, the French, by the British, and by Major Gladwin, whose judgment I trust implicitly. You tell me you knew him years ago. Why do you hold such a grudge against—"

"Grudge?" Duvall was inflamed, but he quickly looked away and gathered himself. His chest heaved suddenly and he struggled to compose his breathing. Then he turned back to Davers, who was looking closely at him.

"A grudge? I hold no grudge, although you are correct, Sir Robert, in recognizing that I hold the man in no esteem. Perhaps it is because I know him better than anyone on this frontier. I know him for what he is. The opinions of heathens and of French traders I hold to no account. They see no deeper than a man's strength of arm or his ability to hold his rum—both of which I credit Sutherland possesses in abundance. As for Major Gladwin's high opinion of Sutherland, he would not be the first good officer whose head has been turned by Sutherland's deception and self-seeking devices!"

Sir Robert was uneasy as soldiers walking past overheard the conversation and looked at them. Duvall's face was now nearly as red as his scarlet coat. His neck puffed and swelled in the restraining black collar.

"Major—" But Davers was cut off.

"Sir Robert, I have seen more of Owen Sutherland than Major Gladwin or Captain Campbell or you have seen of him all together. I have seen him in circumstances when a man's mettle is tested, and I assure you, he failed the test! Failed miserably! And his failure cost the lives of many—"

"My dear sir!" Sir Robert exclaimed. "My dear sir! This is not talk for a pleasant spring afternoon!" Exhibiting the innate charm that had won love and friendship from New York to Boston, Philadelphia to Montreal, Davers smiled and once more cast an arm over Duvall's shoulders. "Come, come, Alex, let's think of other things. Let's consider pleasanter subjects over a mug or two of Jamaican rum, eh? The officers' mess won't be busy at this time of day. Come, I won't have the pleasure of a table and chair for days to come on this journey to Saint Clair. Nor will I have any news about New York and our mutual friends there, whom you've so recently seen. Come, come, good fellow!"

Duvall sighed and cooled somewhat as they began to walk to the officers' mess. Cheered, Davers went on: "Let's forget this scandal between you and Suth—"

"Scandal! Scandal, you say?" Duvall was furious again. Soldiers cast furtive glances at him, and he returned their curiosity with a scathing look. Then to Davers he said, "There is no scandal that involves me, Sir Robert! You probably imagine that Sutherland and I vied for the same woman and I lost, eh?"

"Well, Alex, I must admit—"

"Yes, that's it! You believe I hold a grudge against Sutherland, and that's why I intend to be so hard on him when I become commander!"

"You what?"

"Yes! I intend keeping him in close surveillance! I'll issue trading licenses here, and Sutherland had damned well better meet all the requirements, or he'll lose his privileges like that!" He snapped his fingers in Sir Robert's startled face. "Now, Sir Robert, let's have that rum, and I'll tell you what I know about your noble Owen Sutherland, so you, at least—unlike Henry Gladwin—won't be duped by false appearances." His voice dropped to a whisper before they entered the door of the officers' mess. "Gladwin cannot see through Sutherland—he cannot recognize the truth about that man's sordid past. But at least a gentleman like yourself, a man with friends in high places, can understand my motives when I become commander of this post! If any questions are asked publicly about who receives and who does not receive a trading license, then you, at least, will know the truth and be able to defend me should I not be present if controversy arises."

Davers was too fascinated and too curious about this whole affair to do what he knew he as a gentleman ought to do at that moment—which was take leave of the angry Duvall and hear no more.

"Why would you rescind his license, Alex?"

"That, my friend, is precisely what I wish to explain, if you'll grant me the courtesy of listening to a story you undoubtedly will find difficult to believe. But it's true. Hear me out and I'll let you be the judge of my feelings toward Owen Sutherland."

Duvall began to push open the dark door, but Davers held back, reluctant now that he had seen a strange anxiety in Duvall's eyes.

"Alex," he protested. "I really would rather not—"

"Sir Robert, I shall in months to come depend upon your support in this matter, for no one else on this frontier knows the truth about a man who is said to be a leader of the trading group here. Listen, Sir Robert, did you know that Colonel Brockhurst will be coming here in a few months to inspect these posts?"

"Brockhurst? You mean the former commander of the Highlanders?"

"The same. He was once my superior officer, and Sutherland's, too. Just like Gladwin, Brockhurst is a good man who's been taken in by Sutherland; been blinded by the Scotchman's charm. If Sutherland gets Brockhurst's ear, I know he'll do everything in his power to embarrass me! I swear he will, for he has tried it in the past! That man will do everything he can to blacken my character before Brockhurst, and I tell you, Sir Robert, Brockhurst actually admires that scoundrel! He'll believe him, no matter what I do. That is why I desire you to hear my side of the story. I ask you to hear me out, sir, and as a gentleman, you must do me that courtesy."

Davers hesitated again.

"It's not for my sake!" Duvall insisted. "It's for the sake of this post and all the people who depend on it! Will you hear me, sir?"

Davers nodded, but with obvious distaste. Yet he had come this far, and Duvall was hinting at an interesting story: a man of Sutherland's stature guilty of unsavory deeds. Duvall pushed the door again, and Sir Robert went first into the dim room crowded with tables and chairs, the only light coming from three small windows. For the first time in his life Sir Robert Davers was reluctant to share an old story with a soldier over a mug of Jamaican rum.

Afternoon was drawing to an end as Owen Sutherland stood on the beach at Valenya and stared into the setting sun. In the middle of the river two dozen Ottawa canoes were passing upstream, as though the strong current were no hindrance at all. Molo and the two other braves joined Sutherland to watch the canoes.

"It is Pontiac returning from Detroit," Molo said.

Sutherland now resolved to act. He said to Molo, "My brother, I shall go to the lodge of Pontiac tonight, before the darkness comes and the left-handed twin rules us. You may come with me, if you choose. But I give you my word, I shall go to no other place."

"We shall come," Molo said. "I trust your word, Donoway, but we are eager to hear the news of what happened today, and we wish to hear how our chief will carry out his plans."

"Tonight," said Sutherland as he began to walk up to the cabin, "I hope Chief Pontiac will listen to the words of a white man who speaks the truth."

"Hey," Molo called cheerfully. "You are Donoway, an Ottawa."

"Tonight," Sutherland called back, "you and your brothers shall see the spirit of Owen Sutherland descend into my body, for Owen Sutherland loves the Ottawa, and he will speak to them of the English army."

In a few moments Sutherland had strapped to his waist the claymore, light and worthy. In the cabin he kissed Mayla, and then they walked down to where Molo waited in Sutherland's canoe. The other youths followed in the second canoe.

"May the manitous protect you, my husband," Mayla said softly from the shore. "Speak the truth, Donoway, and come back to me."

When they were some distance from the shore—Sutherland in the bow of the canoe—he suddenly stopped paddling and turned to look at Mayla on shore, but she was gone. That was unusual, for she always watched until he was out of sight. At that moment, he wished he did not have to leave. A powerful urge to return fought within him.

"Donoway." Molo brought him back. "If you desire to reach Pontiac while the right-handed twin rules the world, then you must paddle."

On the shore Mayla saw Sutherland turn and look for her, and she waved eagerly, but he did not wave back. Perhaps he could not see her in the play of light and shadows. She waved harder, but still he did not respond. To her disappointment he turned away and went on paddling.

She wished so that he would not leave. Her hand drifted to the silver pendant, and she held it a moment. It was hard to feel it because her hands were cold, almost numb, although the afternoon was quite warm. She clutched the pendant and whispered a farewell to Donoway. She whispered, but the words sounded an echo through her mind, an echo that did not fade, even though she went as quickly as she could back up the slope to their lonely cabin.

Inside the officers' mess it was dark. Sir Robert and Alex Duvall sat at a table near the window. The mess was empty, for it was two hours before the meal would be served, and most officers were off enjoying the end of a fine spring day instead of drinking at the officers' tavern, which was no more than a small wooden countertop at the opposite end of the room.

Duvall bawled at the kitchen door, and someone inside dropped a mug clanging to the floor. An orderly, young and sleepy-eyed, with hair frozen askew, burst out the door and apologized for not hearing them come in. Sir Robert looked out the thick provincial glass used to glaze the windows, and Duvall ordered rum. When it came and the orderly disappeared once more, both men drank thirstily, Duvall particularly so, as he drained his mug in a few moments. The rum was a strong batch, and Sir Robert wondered whether he should caution Duvall about drinking so quickly on an empty stomach. But before he could speak, the officer took off his tricorn and said:

"It is not my wish to scandalize anyone, Sir Robert." He belched and poured a second mug of rum. "Nor to spread false rumor, but soon I shall have responsibility for this post. At least someone I respect will have heard my story in case there are repercussions . . . Now, hear my story, and believe it or ignore it, as you see fit.

"Mind you," Duvall added and took another swig of burning rum, "the facts of the matter are all on record with the War Ministry. With the department of courts-martial, as a matter of fact. And anyone may look into them to judge the truth of what I am about to tell you."

Sir Robert was genuinely interested now. He finished his mug and took up the pitcher to pour another. He refilled both mugs as Duvall began:

"Eighteen years ago I was a captain in the Black Watch Regiment fighting in the Flemish Lowlands against the French. Owen Sutherland was an ensign in my company, employed as a dispatch rider carrying messages between general headquarters and our regiment. Colonel Brockhurst was a major then, and he was in charge of the regiment because the officer who would normally have been in command had fallen.

"We were in bitterly close combat, the worst I have ever seen. It was almost winter, and the campaign weather had very nearly ended. Rain and snow were expected at any time to prevent an army's movement over that country. Well, we were struggling with the French for control of several strategic towns which would offer whoever held them through winter a good place to attack from in the spring. But whoever was driven away from these towns would be forced to give up possession of the entire countryside, for the army couldn't winter in open encampments without suffering great hardship.

"It fell on our regiment, the Highlanders, to keep an important French supply line closed. This supply line ran through country that was cut by a deep river, and the river could be crossed only by a bridge that we held. If the French could not cross it, they could never bring up reinforcements in time to break the siege. But if they got across the bridge, they could fall upon our main army from the rear and put it in a perilous position. It was up to our regiment to defend this crossing at all costs, and we did it time and again, against impossible odds. We paid heavily, though, and all our commanding officers were killed or wounded. Major Brockhurst was also carried from the field, and I, a lowly captain, was given command of the regiment in its most desperate hour."

More rum was brought, and Sir Robert remembered those battles of the War of the Austrian Succession, which had been known in America as King George's War. The treaty that was signed in 1748 had been, in actuality, only a truce, for in 1755 hostilities between the French and the English broke out again. The Seven Years' War, as it had been called, had also spilled over into America—where it was known as the French and Indian War. At this very moment, terms of the peace were being worked out in Paris—a peace that was expected to cede all French territory east of the Mississippi to Great Britain, including Fort Detroit. Duvall went on:

"While our army was about to take the key towns, my regiment did its duty. The French tried to bring reinforcements across the bridge, but we held them off, and we had very few cannon, mind you. We did it with musketry and bayonet counterattacks. Glorious! It was a glorious defense, sir!

"But they kept coming at us. We destroyed them, and more came. More and again more. But we held them off. They desperately wanted that bridge. They had to get across to strike our army from behind, and they did everything, sacrificed everything to try it. But we held them! By God, we held them!"

The strain of those days crept back into Duvall's face. Sir Robert saw a young captain who gave his last ounce of strength to rally his men against a superior enemy. Duvall talked about that fighting, about its horrors, its anguish, and about its merciless drain on his innermost strength. His eyes grew dark, his face showed deeply lined in the fading sunlight tunneling into the room through the window near them. Duvall drank and continued; he spoke as though conversing with himself, answering his own questions, replying with scorn to random thoughts of possible defeat.

"At last, the French had had enough. We had not slept for

days. Here I was, a man of twenty, a temporary commander in the most critical aspect of the entire campaign. And they never sent one man for reinforcement!"

"Did you ask for reinforcement?"

"Did I *have* to ask? By God, man, surely you can see that a commander cannot show signs of fear or of doubt that he can carry out his duties. Did I *have* to ask? Were my superiors not soldiers who could understand the hell I was going through hour after hour, day after day? Did I have to ask? *Of course I did not ask!* I refused to crawl to those pompous fools! If they were not men enough to know what I was steadily enduring to protect them, how could I beg for reinforcements?"

"And someone else of superior rank might have been sent to take over command?" Sir Robert tried but failed to say this gently.

Duvall's rum-washed eyes seemed to wince, but he recovered quickly. "Well, no matter. The fact is that I held those frog-eaters, and without any reinforcements. I beat everything they could send against me. Damned frog-eaters! Hah! Stopped them dead!"

"It was a difficult time, Alex," Sir Robert said softly, but Duvall seemed not to hear, guzzled rum, and came back to his tale.

"I turned them back. Days and nights of constant fighting, but I withstood them. They had failed. I won! By good God in heaven, I won!"

Duvall clumsily smashed his fist against the tabletop and the orderly dashed from the kitchen, but Duvall eyed him cruelly. "What do you want? Go on, get! I'll call you when I want more! Out!" He wiped his mouth. "Where was I?"

His voice was thickening, but his excitement was growing as he spoke. Words came out with sprays of spittle, and his face hardened.

"I had those frog-eaters beaten, I tell you!"

He calmed then and chuckled to himself, a low, quiet chuckle. Slowly he shook his head. Sunlight glinted in the spittle on his cheek.

"Your men must have behaved admirably under these conditions," Sir Robert said, urging on the story.

"What? Men? Oh, yes, of course! Did their duty, behaved well, as they were expected to. As soldiers should, by God! Better, or I'd have chopped them to pieces myself, and they

knew it well. I put fear into them, I did. That's the only way
to deal with their kind!"

"As I have heard," said Sir Robert, growing uneasy at the
tale, which was deteriorating into a tipsy ranting, "Scottish
soldiers are the best infantry in the world today. Brave
and—"

"Bah!" Duvall waved heavily at those words. "They're just
soldiers like any others. Good if they have English officers.
Mind you, it's the officers make an army fight, and English
officers are the finest, no matter what the troops under their
command! Yes, even the Scotch are all right with English
officers and if they can use a good Brown Bess musket instead
of those barbarian claymores!"

"Sutherland was an ensign with you?" Davers asked carefully, hoping not to set Duvall into another rage. To Sir Robert's
surprise, Duvall seemed to gather himself for his next words
and became quiet, his voice a low hiss.

"Now we come to the crucial part of my story, Sir Robert.
Listen closely, and then tell me what kind of man this Owen
Sutherland is."

Duvall pushed his empty mug aside and leaned on the table.

"All our spies told me the French were beaten, would never
attack again. These were good spies, Sir Robert. They told me
the French had lost heavily attacking me. Everywhere the enemy were withdrawing, and soon those towns would be taken
by our main army. I could rest! At long glorious last, I could
rest! Three days and nights I had not slept, understand! But
now, I could rest. My troops were on alert in their defenses,
and I gave orders to be informed of any suspicious enemy
movement. I would have come to the battlefront at a moment's
notice. But surely you can understand, Sir Robert, I was bone
tired. Tired! Exhausted in my very soul. I craved rest, but I
was careful enough to prepare my subordinates—particularly
Owen Sutherland, who was my main courier—to wake me in
case of attack."

Sir Robert watched as Duvall's thoughts drifted away once
more, and he seemed again to be talking to himself.

"My spies assured me the French were beaten. So I went
to a captured inn and—and slept."

Duvall paused, looking vaguely at Sir Robert, who was sure
he was not being seen.

"I slept, sweet merciful—I slept. And, my God, I deserved

that sleep! I deserved it! But—but when I awoke and came downstairs . . ." His hands went against his face and clawed his white wig, loosening it. "I went downstairs and found that— that bastard! Owen Sutherland! My main courier! And how do you think I found him?" He began to chuckle softly again and slowly shake his head. "I found my courier asleep—asleep on a divan. Asleep like an innocent babe. Asleep! And in his innocent arms were dispatches from my forces to the south on our side of the river. Dispatches that called me to the front immediately, for the French had crossed on barges in the south and were attacking with heavy cavalry! Heavy cavalry, by God! In that flat country! Heavy French cavalry against me, and all I had were a few infantry. But even then I could have held them, if only—if only that bastard Sutherland had brought me the dispatches instead of falling asleep!" He pounded the table. "Yes, Sir Robert, your noble Owen Sutherland thought a good night's sleep was more important to him than delivering the most critical message of the war to his superior.

"Yes, most important of the war! For if those messages had come, I could have organized the defense. I would have held back the French as I had before, and—and they could not have surprised our army from the rear. Yes, they surprised our army after they drove past my leaderless regiment!

"They swept past us as though we were chaff in the wind. Swept past because I was not informed. I could have held them back! But Sutherland fell asleep! Surely you understand! I would have stayed at the front, but my spies were so certain, so sure that the French were finished!"

"Were they Frenchmen, these spies?" Sir Robert asked.

"No, no, of course not. They were French-speaking Walloons, and you know they have no sympathies with the French, or at least they don't if they're paid well enough—and I paid them well, and paid them out of my own damned pocket! But it did no good, not one whit of good. By the time I came downstairs in that inn, the battle was lost. The French had swept past us and were already rolling up our main army's flank. It was all we could do to escape back to our own lines without being captured."

"You and Sutherland?"

"Yes! I took that duty-shirking bastard with me, though I should have left him to fend for himself! The rest of the regiment was nearly destroyed."

Duvall, crestfallen, seemed as though he were nearly destroyed as well. His face drawn, he looked up angrily at Sir
Robert and spoke again:

"Our main army was driven back to the Channel ports for
the winter. The French won the field, and all we had gained
in the year before had been lost. Instead of being in a strategic
position to strike the following spring, we found ourselves
nearly driven off the Continent. And, as a result of that battle,
as a result of Owen Sutherland not delivering that message
directly to me, as a result of Owen Sutherland falling asleep
instead of obeying orders like any soldier would, as a result
of all those little things, the war dragged on, and thousands
died. Peace would have been signed the next spring, with
France bowing and scraping for good terms, but that did not
happen, Sir Robert, and the blame lies on the shoulders of
Owen Sutherland!"

Davers thought in silence. He saw Duvall was too distressed
by bad memories and strong rum to be reasoned with at that
moment. He knew that Duvall might have exaggerated the
importance of his own engagement, and perhaps the French
heavy cavalry would have broken through anyway, but there
was no point in pressing the issue. He was ready to get up to
leave when Duvall went on again, with a voice both spiteful
and frustrated.

"They court-martialed him. Court-martialed him, and they
could have sentenced him to a firing squad."

"Why didn't they?"

Duvall sneered. "Because he was the protégé of James
Brockhurst. He deserved to be shot, but Brockhurst sat on that
court-martial, and they listened to Sutherland's lying story."

Duvall looked more like a sickly old gossip than a king's
officer just then.

"Sutherland told them some false tale about coming to my
lodgings and being met by two Walloons who said I was asleep
and not to be disturbed. Well, one thing led to another, Sutherland said—" Duvall scoffed and looked into his mug, which
was empty, so he clanged it on the table. "He said they drugged
him!" Duvall looked at Sir Robert and forced a smile across
his face, as though he were waiting for Sir Robert to break into
laughter. When Davers did not even grin, Duvall shook his
head hopelessly and looked down at the table.

"Drugged him, indeed!" Duvall growled. "He had the insolence to claim the men who met him were spies for the French! Spies! In my very own quarters! Insolent, impudent lying swine! Trying to cast those kinds of accusations—"

"Who were they, then?"

"Who?" Duvall sputtered and his mouth worked furiously. "Why, nobody! Nobody! There was nobody there at all when he came! It was all a lie! Sutherland was making up a lie to protect himself and cast doubt upon me! Upon *me!* After all I had suffered!"

Duvall's head was in his hands. Sir Robert tried to coax him to his feet, fearing the major would break into tears suddenly, and that officers might come in for dinner and see him. But Duvall went on, his voice cold and hateful again:

"The truth is that Sutherland wanted a sleep, and he took it, no matter what the consequences might be. French heavy cavalry or no. He took his sleep!"

"But why did the court-martial not execute him?" Davers asked.

"Because—because—because Owen Sutherland always has been the favorite of the commanding officer, just as he is the favorite of Henry Gladwin. He was the favorite of Colonel Brockhurst, who stood up for him. But Sutherland resigned his commission because he couldn't stand the cloud of suspicion hanging over him. For my own part, I stuck it out with that damnable Scotch regiment until seven years ago, when I sold my commission and bought another in the 80th Foot."

Duvall's eyes were glassy, filling with the tears Sir Robert had expected.

"Believe it or not, Sir Robert," Duvall trembled, "there was even some opinion on that court-martial that I—that I—after all I had done alone, all I had borne for their sakes—that I . . . that those Walloon spies were really French—I mean—"

"Now, now, Alex," Sir Robert muttered kindly and raised Duvall by one limp arm. Duvall lurched against him, and Davers led him outside. "Let's get you to your quarters before the others come in."

Davers slapped Duvall's tricorn on at a decent angle. Duvall struggled for sobriety, and they stepped into the sun, which had weakened but felt bright after the dim officers' mess. As quickly and discreetly as he could, Davers led the stumbling Duvall along back alleys to the officer's cabin. Inside, Davers eased his companion onto the narrow bed, removed his tunic and boots, tossed a fine Dutch blanket—no doubt a souvenir of those sad days—over his chest, and left the room.

Himself feeling the dizzying strength of that Jamaican, Sir Robert decided to alert the orderly in the officers' mess to reserve this particular keg for only the most important occasions, and then only when Sir Robert himself was present.

It was a shame to waste fine rum like that. It should be saved for a ball or a celebration when the young women of the fort were on hand. Rum like that could go a long way to breaking down formalities or defenses. Look what it had done to Alex Duvall.

chapter 7

THE FIGHT

Sutherland lifted a sack filled with twists of tobacco from his canoe and slung it over his shoulder. He picked up his long rifle and walked into Pontiac's camp. There were a few greetings, for this was the village of Mayla's people, and he knew everyone here. These people had been at the Ecorse meeting, also, and now they were home. Sutherland hoped they had tempered their eagerness for war.

He found Pontiac seated before a low, round lodge in the company of a dozen Ottawa village chiefs and war chiefs. Sutherland approached the Indian leader, stopped a few feet away, raised his hand in greeting, and waited until Pontiac acknowledged his presence. In the fading light, Sutherland sensed hostility in many of the chiefs and warriors in Pontiac's court. Out of the corner of his eye he saw the *voyageurs,* perhaps a score of them, wander idly toward the circle, Breton among them.

Pontiac nodded a reserved welcome. Sutherland stepped forward, placed his rifle on the ground at his feet, and took out a long twist of tobacco.

"May this gift of tobacco, my chief Pontiac, open your heart and the hearts of your warriors gathered here for my counsel."

Sutherland held out the tobacco, and Pontiac, still seated, accepted it politely. The tobacco was passed around, and the *voyageurs* sat down among the Indians. Pipes were lit in silence. Pontiac motioned Sutherland to sit at his right hand. After some time, when the pipes were finished, Pontiac asked Sutherland to present his counsel. Sutherland stood and raised his arms in greeting to the group, which had grown considerably since he had come. The sun was very low now, but it had not yet vanished beyond the horizon. As long as there was light, his appeal for peace could be heard. In the darkness the Indians were ruled by the left-handed Malsum, the creator of evil things

and the brother of Gluskap, creator of good and vanquisher of
Malsum. In the morning Gluskap drives Malsum from the face
of the earth to take refuge in the underworld, where he becomes
a wolf. But Malsum returns to the earth's surface at night,
when his spirit rules, and the realm of death and witchcraft
replaces the light world of goodness. Thus the words of peace
would have no power if spoken after dark, and Sutherland's
plea for reason would fall on the ears of men who would
consider them impotent.

But as Sutherland stood before these Ottawa leaders, he
grasped in sudden despair the ironic meaning of the setting sun.
He had little time to speak, and no matter what he said, the
day was soon bound to give way to night.

"My brothers and friends," he began in a voice that carried
across the council grounds. "It has been too long since Donoway has been among you, for I have been many moons in the
East at the trading post called Oswego. Now that I am returned,
my heart is heavy, for I see my brothers and the sons of my
brothers painted for war. Now I come to you as one who knows
the English, as one who is a brother of the Ottawa, and as one
who loves both peoples.

"May my unworthy gift of tobacco open your hearts, that
my words might be understood, and may this setting sun be
but a passing phase to be revived by the spirits of light, just
as your thoughts of war may pass and give way once more to
reason and patience."

The warriors were restless. They had expected such words
from Donoway, and they were not glad to hear them. His words
were not, as he had hoped, falling on open hearts. But he went
on.

"I return to my home and learn that wampum belts of war
are being sent far and wide. I sit at the great council at the
Ecorse, and I hear the cry for English blood. My heart is heavy,
brothers and friends. For I am afraid for you.

"The warriors of all the Indian nations are strong in battle,
and they are justified to be angry with the English. They are
justified to be eager to pit their strength in battle against the
strength of the English. But they will die if they do so."

A great stirring now, and the sun began to sink. The *voyageurs* grumbled, and one spat scornfully on the ground. That
was Breton.

Sutherland said: "I know the anger of the Indians, and I
understand it. Also I know that all Englishmen are not evil,

nor are they weak in battle. I ask my brothers and friends to have patience with the English, for they are new in this land, and they are learning the ways of the Indian. The English have been here but three years, my brothers, and that is not a long time for two peoples to make peace between them. They, like the Indian, had many sons slain in the last war, and they, like the Indian, still suffer from their wounds. There is bitterness on both sides, and that is why we must be patient."

Sutherland spoke on about the injustice of English trading policies. He agreed that the Indians were not being supplied with powder and ball, and he urged that the Indians show their massed force peacefully to General Amherst, that he might understand the gravity of their anger. The last rays of sunlight glinted on the silver hilt of the claymore at his side, as he told them not to bring on a war that could only have a tragic end.

"Do not, my brothers, believe that the English will be easily defeated. If you kill all English who are now in your lands, more will come, for they are like the leaves on the trees. You cannot stop up the way forever, and when they come with thunder guns, and when the forest is filled with English soldiers, their revenge will be total, and the day of the Indian will be at an end."

The warriors sat sullenly. *Voyageurs* seethed.

"There is hope for peace and prosperity only if you do not carry out this war. Show your force and let the English see its majesty. But do not use it yet. You are all valorous in battle; none are more courageous. But the English are as the grains of sand, and they, too, are brave. You know these words to be true, my brothers.

"I have heard that a bad bird has told you that the Great French Father has sent a mighty army of his sons to fight with you, that he has wakened from a long sleep and will soon drive out the English. I tell you, now, my brothers, that bad bird lies!"

He paused here, and the crowd sat surly but silent. Sutherland turned to confront the *voyageurs*, stared hard at them, and said, "Without a French army at your side, there is no hope for victory. Hear me, you brave warriors, who are wise and will choose your moment to die, that bad bird is a wicked bird, for it seeks to drink your blood, to pillage your lost land, and to ravish your women."

The *voyageurs* were astonished, and anger rose in their faces. Sutherland spoke again:

"There will be no French army. The Great French Father has forgotten his red children! I say the bad bird—"

"Lies! Lies! All Lies!" André Breton was on his feet, his massive, stubby body quivering from head to foot. "This English cur lies!"

The sun was behind the distant horizon, and the last light had gone from the sky. Sutherland folded his arms and looked at Pontiac, whose face was unmoving despite this unforgivable breach of formality by the maddened Breton, who leaped into the clearing.

"This English cur wants only his own English curs to dwell in this country!" Breton spat out. "He is a spy for them. You have seen him at the fort many times, brothers, and you should know that all this English cur cares for is his own profit and nothing for the Indian! And when the Great French Father sends his sons to fight alongside the Indian, English curs like this one will be done away with forever! He is a traitor to the Indian; he is a wolf in the clothing of a lamb!"

Pontiac raised his hand, and Breton, trembling, stood with clenched fists, the black feathers stuck in his stocking cap rattling silently.

"My brother," Pontiac said to Breton. "It is not right to speak out before Donoway has presented his counsel. Donoway shall finish his words."

"I have finished, Pontiac," Sutherland said solemnly. "Truth ended with the setting of the sun. Now it is the time of darkness, the time of lies; and since the evil twin now rules, I shall say no more, lest my words be misjudged."

"Do not believe him!" Breton shouted in a deep and bellowing voice. The *métis* put his hand to his tomahawk and took one short step toward Sutherland, who raised a hand and spoke to Pontiac.

"I have come in peace, but I have not come to be insulted by this *métis* who is filled with blind hate. I shall have revenge, Pontiac, and I shall have it now!"

The Indians yelped and whooped in anticipation of a fight. But Pontiac stood and said, "Will you soil the sanctity of this council with bloodshed, Donoway?"

Sutherland looked at Breton, who had his tomahawk in hand now, and was glaring, ready to attack.

"The sanctity of this council has already been soiled by the lies of André Breton."

Breton went for Sutherland, but three braves leaped between

them and held the wild Frenchman back. Pontiac also stepped forward and said, "So be it." The Indians set up a noisy clamor, shaking rattles, waving tomahawks, thirsting for the fight. "It shall be," said Pontiac, "the duel of knives."

Sutherland stepped back, and Molo, his face aglow with admiration, accepted Sutherland's shirt. Sutherland put the sheathed claymore into Molo's hands, then drew out his dirk from its place against his shin. He turned to face the Frenchman. Breton flicked his wicked hunting knife, and its blade flashed in the firelight. Sin-gat, the Delaware chief, was standing at Breton's side; he took the knife and stepped into the crowd a moment, then he returned, grinning, and handed the knife back to his companion. The hunting knife in Breton's hand no longer shone. It seemed smeared with something brown and foul.

Molo whispered, "Have care, Donoway, for that Delaware has poisoned Breton's knife."

Sutherland walked back into the circle of gleeful warriors, who clapped and slapped their thighs in anticipation, cheering and laughing. Pontiac waved a hand to begin.

The two men circled slowly. Breton, several inches shorter than Sutherland, was the stronger. His naked chest puffed and rippled as he crouched, feinting, ready to strike. Years of carrying hundreds of pounds over long portages had strengthened and toned his body until it was as strong as steel, tempered so that it did not know fatigue. He flaunted the knife before Sutherland's face, taunting, mocking with his dirty blade.

Sutherland was the finer physical specimen, tall, agile, and long-muscled. He leaned forward, intent, waiting for Breton's first move. They circled. The Indians roared. The green turtle tattoo on Sutherland's chest, slick with sweat, gleamed in the reddish light of the council fire. The sun was down. Stars glittered in the deepening sky.

Breton came in, but Sutherland jabbed, surprising him, forcing him back as the Scottish dirk darted and drew blood across the Frenchman's cheek. The Indians shouted and leaped in approval of the clever blade.

Breton's shock instantly vanished, and the *métis* grinned and stood up straight. He swept the stocking cap from his head, flourished it, and bowed low to Sutherland, who stayed in his crouch. Then Breton cast the cap away and wiped the blood from his chin. He moved to Sutherland again.

They circled. Their eyes fixed hot and white upon each other's knives. Sutherland feinted and struck for Breton's face, but Breton was ready, and he leaped back and slid to Sutherland's right, where the knife arm of the Scotsman was outstretched. Breton shrieked and stabbed at Sutherland's neck, but Sutherland dropped, and the blade whisked a hair's breadth over his shoulder. Breton brought it down and flicked back with it, and Sutherland's neck gave out a thin line of blood from ear to shoulder. Breton jumped back as Sutherland's knife came up savagely, then he kicked, caught Sutherland on the chin, and the Scotsman tumbled backwards but sprang to his feet to meet Breton's charge.

Breton was upon Sutherland too fast to stop his momentum, but as Sutherland brought up his dirk, Breton jumped feet-first at Sutherland's chest. Sutherland sidestepped and dug the dirk into the Frenchman's thigh, but the dirk was wrenched away by the force, whipped out of Sutherland's grip.

Before Sutherland could move, Breton was on his feet. The bloody dirk lay where it landed—at the side of Sin-gat, who, laughing, picked it up and held it like a toy in his grimy hands.

Breton began to laugh even though blood ran from his face and spurted from his thick upper leg. He laughed, threw back his head, and roared. The *voyageurs* and Delawares clapped and cheered, but the Ottawa were quiet.

Sutherland rose to his full height and stood with his hands at his sides. Breton, still cackling in his throat, moved in for the kill. Sutherland let his shoulders drop helplessly, and he looked as though in appeal to Pontiac. Those who hated him chanted: "Kill! Kill the Englishman! Kill!"

Sutherland glanced at Breton, then back to Pontiac. Breton was moving in slowly, carefully. As if to retreat, Sutherland took a quick step to Pontiac. Breton saw his chance and leaped, knife aimed at Sutherland's abdomen. But Sutherland's step had been calculated, and he was ready for Breton's charge. He slid down on his back under the airborne Breton, kicked up at the same time, and caught the Frenchman a hard whack in the groin.

Breton grunted, rolled, and got to his feet. Sutherland, whose back was to Sin-gat, spun and kicked the Delaware in the face. Sin-gat staggered, and Sutherland snatched his dirk away. The Ottawa cheered, no one louder than young Molo. Breton attacked, but Sutherland sprang aside, and the clumsy, lurching Breton missed and sprawled against the furious Sin-gat, who angrily pushed him off.

Again the powerful *voyageur*, his face and leg bleeding,

advanced toward Sutherland, who feinted a forward rush and knife thrust. Breton kicked for the dirk, but Sutherland pulled it back and threw himself under the kick, hurling against Breton's standing leg, driving his knife into the same thigh he had already wounded.

Breton roared in pain and twisted away, bringing his own knife down at Sutherland's back, but the Scotsman was already behind him, slipping clear.

The swarthy Frenchman paused, surprised. He looked at the crouching, tense Sutherland, and a glint of humor came into his eyes. The Indians were muttering, and they began to clamor. Breton suddenly laughed as savagely as he had laughed when Sutherland's knife was torn from his hands.

Molo shouted, "Donoway! Your knife, Donoway!"

Sutherland looked down at the knife in his hand and saw why Breton was laughing. The dirk's narrow blade had snapped at the hilt when Breton had so powerfully wrenched away his wounded leg. Sutherland was again disarmed.

He looked up to see the Frenchman kick something out of the dust: the bloody blade of the dirk. Breton's thigh bled heavily, but it was of no consequence now, for the matter would be decided momentarily. Breton looked down at the blood running from his wounds; he clucked his tongue and slowly shook his shaggy head.

"You should know better than to trust an English blade. English blades always break against good French flesh. Now," and he moved confidently at Sutherland, "let me show you how French steel cuts. It was made for English throats."

Breton closed in. Sutherland readied for the last effort. The Frenchman did a shifty little dance. He was toying with his victim. Breton increased the tempo of his dance, closing the distance between them. Sutherland was being worked into a corner, with the mass of Indians, shouting and yelping, at his back.

Then Sutherland stood straight up, folded his arms, and grinned. He stared at Breton and began to laugh softly. Breton stopped in his tracks. Then he spat, concentrated on Sutherland's heart, where his knife would sink, and stepped forward.

But Breton stopped short, five paces away. He would take no chances with this tricky Sutherland. He estimated the situation.

"Come on, coward!" Sutherland shouted. "Use that filthy blade if you know how! Or are you too afraid I might snatch it and sink it into your guts? Coward."

Breton's face went the color of the fire, and his jaw clenched so tight that teeth seemed about to pop clear. He stepped forward. Sutherland shouted at him; startled, Breton hesitated. He hesitated for only one brief instant, but it was enough. With Molo leading the laughter, the Ottawa chiefs and warriors burst out in hooting and howling at this taunting they had never expected to see. Donaway, "fearless in the flames," was as recklessly brave as ever, and the Ottawa loved him.

Sutherland made more of the moment by dropping to his knees, his arms still folded, no more than four steps from Breton. The Ottawa cheered louder. Sutherland put his arms out as though appealing for Breton to come kill him.

But Breton only came on slowly. His eyes glittered as he brought the knife to point at Sutherland. He was three paces, then two from Sutherland. Breton's face became a cold grin, and he said, "Do you think that I am such a fool. I will not let anger make me lose my head—"

But before Breton's words were out of his mouth, Sutherland was driving him backwards, the Scotsman's shoulder into his midsection, crashing him to the ground with a jarring thud. Breton flailed with arms and legs, and Sutherland was cut high on his left ribs and forced to break away. Sutherland stood back, heaving for air, blood covering his side. Breton, who still had his knife, got slowly, painfully, to his feet. Sutherland had taken him down with every ounce of force he could muster, and Breton could not get his breath. His mouth hung open, his eyes were glassy as he swayed, stepping toward Sutherland. He weakly waved the knife. He wheezed, and blood came up into his mouth. He coughed and retched a bloody flood onto the ground, lurched, and nearly went down. Still he could not breathe, and his face was turning blue. Sutherland, also feeling himself sway, stepped forward, but Breton summoned his strength and whipped up the knife, holding it before him. Sutherland moved to his left, then to his right, and he saw Breton did not respond well. This was the moment.

Sutherland threw both feet simultaneously at Breton's broad chest and staggered him backwards. The burning slash of Breton's knife bit Sutherland's leg. Breton reeled but did not fall; again he lurched toward Sutherland, who lay on the ground, and struck down with his knife, but Sutherland was gone. The tottering, crouching Frenchman turned, and Sutherland's fist, weighted by the hilt of the broken dirk, crunched down on his head, just behind the ear. With a grunt, the *voyageur* slumped and dropped his knife at his side.

In agony Sutherland fell to his knees and picked up the Frenchman's knife. The deliriously happy Ottawa cried for Breton's blood. Sutherland had no strength left. He nearly collapsed over his enemy's unconscious body. Then he saw the throat was exposed. One thrust, and . . .

But he could not kill that way. Not without passion—and his passion was drained with his strength. He could not slit Breton's throat.

The din of the Ottawa hurled thunderously down upon him. "Kill, kill, kill him! Kill, kill, kill him! Kill, kill, kill him! Kill, kill . . ." Their hoarse voices rose louder and louder, washing like a stormy sea inside Sutherland's head. He could barely see. Blood was in his eyes; the flames of wounds ripped at him. He was cut everywhere.

He raised his head. Breton was unmoving.

Sutherland slowly stood up.

"Kill, kill, kill him!"

He stepped back.

"Kill, kill, kill him!" Molo was the loudest of all.

"Kill, kill, kill him!"

Sutherland tossed the knife toward Pontiac, and it fell at the war chief's feet.

"Kill, kill . . ." The chant weakened.

Sutherland walked to Pontiac. The chant died. Annoyed muttering swept the Ottawa. Sutherland slowly raised his eyes to the chief. The warriors became silent to hear his words.

"I do not kill a helpless man!" Sutherland said and was surprised at the force of his voice. "If it must be, Breton and I shall meet again. But I shall not kill him while he is helpless."

The muttering amongst the Ottawa and Delaware and the *voyageurs* went from dismay to anger. Breton had been humiliated even more severely by not being slain as a proud, vanquished warrior who deserved to be slain. Sutherland knew that, but he still could not do it. The voices grew to a roar. Then, strangely, they went quiet. A weak Sutherland noticed Pontiac was staring past him, and he turned. There, at the opposite end of the circle, stood the giant Sin-gat, fierce and hateful.

Sutherland brought himself around square to Sin-gat, who said ponderously, "A man who cannot kill shows weakness." Sin-gat's chest heaved.

Sutherland drew himself up and was about to speak when suddenly Molo was at his side, the youth's hand on his scalping knife. But before Molo could defend the battered Sutherland, Pontiac spoke:

"Stop! Enough has been said and done this night. We have councils to hold tomorrow, and I wish nothing to come between the Ottawa and the Delaware. We have enemies in plenty to face without fighting each other." Pontiac looked at Molo, who clearly would have stood for Sutherland against a mature warrior who was more than his match. Molo's eyes burned, but he stepped back in deference to his chief, who spoke to the entire company. "Tonight, we shall have peace amongst ourselves, and we shall have an answer to Donoway's counsel when the sun returns."

The gathering was over. Sutherland leaned against Molo, who, carrying the claymore and rifle, led him away from the fire, past the admiring Ottawa who clapped Sutherland's bloody back and shouted encouragement. They walked through the darkness to Molo's lodge, and behind, *voyageurs* picked up the pulped Breton and bore him off.

"You have made a dangerous enemy of Sin-gat," Molo said to the staggering Sutherland. "He wants your blood, my brother."

"Yes," Sutherland said painfully. "He may have his chance, but first we'd better get this body of mine cleaned, for already I feel the sting of whatever Breton fouled his knife with. It burns. It burns, Molo."

Molo laid Donoway in the lodge, where the young man's wife hurried in to swab and bathe the wounds. Sutherland wished for the forgetfulness of sleep, but the awful burning in so many wounded places nagged him awake. Even cold water, herbal swabbing, powders, and cleansing by Molo's squaw did not stop the awful burning. Fire seared through his throbbing heart, into his loins, and burst into his numbed brain.

Several hours later, Sutherland passed out. He was unconscious, but his body was not in restful sleep. It was ablaze in a hellish netherworld, where the left-handed twin, Malsum, ruler of evil, scourged his victims. The face of the wolf laughed as Sutherland burned, and the face became the face of André Breton, hateful, cruel, laughing as Sutherland burned.

Then light came, and the wolf's face became the slim, worried face of Tamano, dark and grave. Lela was also there, beautiful like her sister. The burning went on and on, but the daylight was cool. Where was Mayla? He wanted her—he wanted her so. Why had she not watched from the beach? Where was she? In the dimness of the late-afternoon sun, she was nowhere to be seen. Mayla. Mayla!

Cool water on his face. Tamano again. Lela. Where was Mayla? Then he passed out again.

That night, when Sutherland awoke, a small fire burned in the lodge. His lips were dry. His shriveled voice asked for water. Lela again was there, and so was Tamano.

Lela gave him water from a wooden bowl; Tamano was looking down over her shoulder. Sutherland's head fell back. His body was stiff; every muscle ached. He could hardly move.

"It seems," said Tamano in his familiar deep voice, "that the victor has very nearly been vanquished."

Sutherland looked up in search of a touch of humor in Tamano's stolid face. But there was none.

"Indeed," he weakly replied. "Poison."

"You have passed the fever of the poison, and soon you must eat," said Lela as she leaned over him and wiped his face with a wet cloth. "You must rid yourself of the filth that has entered your blood, and to do that, you must eat."

"Those wounds will take time to heal," Tamano said, glancing up and down Sutherland's bandaged body.

Sutherland lifted his head and looked down. There were bindings of muslin around both legs, his chest, and over his right shoulder.

"And you know, Tamano, I won." Sutherland managed a faint smile.

"Yes," Tamano said, "but Breton is doing better than you. Today he has already departed for Fort Detroit. His poison was stronger than your blows. You should have killed him, my brother. One day, he will try to kill you."

"He—" Sutherland tried unsuccessfully to lean on an elbow. He lay back again. "I thought you were gone north," he said weakly.

Tamano nodded. "We went north because we wished no part in this fight. But when I was gone, I feared you would try something dangerous, and I wanted to be here either to stop you or to take you north with us. It seems I was too late."

Sutherland said nothing. Then he thought about Pontiac and tried to sit up.

"The reply to my counsel! Pontiac promised to give it to me today."

Tamano shook his head, and Lela pushed Sutherland back down. Tamano spoke. "The answer was given to me, for you have been in the lands of darkness all day, and much has happened in that time."

Tamano glanced behind him, got up, and closed the skin covering to the lodge door. Then he came back and knelt beside Lela.

"There will be war, Donoway. It has been decided this morning, and what you told them has not been heard."

Sutherland lay silent. Lela poured some broth steaming into a bowl hollowed from a gourd.

"When does it begin?" Sutherland asked, gazing up at the ceiling of the lodge, where faint gray smoke disappeared through a hole in which stars glimmered.

Tamano looked grim. "It will begin the day after tomorrow." He told Sutherland about Pontiac's plan to enter the fort on false pretenses of peace and ritual dancing. Then, when a signal was given, the attack would begin. Sutherland lay ashen-faced, hardly feeling the pain of his wounds.

"This must be stopped, Tamano," he said.

"I cannot help you, my brother, for I am to be guarded as you are guarded. I cannot go to Gladwin, although I would do it if I could."

Sutherland looked at Lela. "Will you tell your sister what has happened? Will you go to her and tell her I am well and shall come back to her soon? She'll worry if you do not."

Lela nodded. "I'll depart in the morning for Valenya. You must wait until the next day. Your wounds must heal before you move."

Sutherland pursed his dry lips. He was helpless. The attack would come in two days, and he could not stop it. He turned his face away, and the burning pain crept back into his limbs. It had been years since Owen Sutherland had felt tears. But he felt them now.

The next morning was gusty, as it often was in that low-lying country. Sir Robert Davers was ready at the break of dawn to be off from his overnight encampment on an island near the western shore of Lake Saint Clair. His bateau was shoved into the rippling water by two of the eleven men assigned to his party by Henry Gladwin. He climbed from a rock into the bow of the flat-nosed boat. Lieutenant Charles Robertson, one of the more cordial and clever of the junior officers at Detroit,

was the welcome commander of the expedition, and Davers
was the mind that directed it. They were on their way to sound
the mouth of the Saint Clair River, which entered the north end
of Lake Saint Clair. The river came down from Lake Huron,
where Michilimackinac, a key fort and trading post, stood. If
the river was deep enough, the sloop *Michigan* could make its
way north to supply this distant post located where the western
lakes joined Huron. The sloop could more efficiently supply
the strategic post at Michilimackinac than could the usual slow
and expensive convoy of bateaux rowed by large numbers of
men. If soundings proved the river deep enough for the sloop,
this trip would be a valuable one for English trading interests.

On his lap Davers held a fine new rifle he had recently been
given as a gift by an English trader. He was a handsome sight,
sitting nobly, staring ahead as the rowers beat their way along
the low, forested shores of Lake Saint Clair. He breathed deeply
and wondered if he could ever return to England and be content
where there was no majestic wilderness like this. A flock of
Canada geese in arrow formation gabbled overhead. The wind
blew, and the lake frothed and pitched the bateau. Sir Robert
Davers was a very happy man.

It was May 6, and Owen Sutherland was regaining his strength
in the lodge of Molo. He told Molo and Tamano he would
depart the next day for Valenya. Meanwhile, at his home, Lela
had already told Mayla about the fight and had assured her that
Sutherland had recovered and would come soon. The sisters
sat sadly outside the small cabin. The younger, Lela, spoke:

"There is nothing that can be done. It is best to leave this
country forever, and Donoway agrees. We shall go to the country of the Assiniboines, where my husband is known, and we
shall begin again. It is good country, rich and wide, and there
is peace."

Mayla sat quietly. Now and again, she would let the moccasin onto which she was sewing bright beads drop to her lap,
and she looked bleakly across the river toward Fort Detroit.
Then resolutely she returned to her beadwork. Lela had told
her the plans for the coming attack: It would take place tomorrow, and it seemed there was no way to stop it it.

chapter **8**

MAYLA'S WARNING

The spinet was magnificent. It needed only a slight tuning, for the French trader who had owned it had played it every day until he died two months ago and left it to his unmusical wife. When Sir Robert approached the widow about buying, she was at first hesitant to part with an object of such sentimental attachment, especially to an Englishman. But when she met Ella and heard her play, the Frenchwoman was soon won over, pleased that the spinet would be played by one who loved its music as much as her late husband had. After several days of coaxing and delicate negotiations, a price was agreed upon—Sir Robert and Gladwin vied to buy it, and finally agreed to share the cost—but it was Friday before the woman could bear to part with it, and Davers had already left on his journey north. That afternoon, a few soldiers carried the delicate triangular instrument carefully to the high-ceilinged council house near the river gate, where balls and special ceremonies were held. There Ella could play to her heart's content.

Henry watched as Ella fiddled with the tuning hammer, playing scales and intervals and tuning a string at a time until she was satisfied with the pitch. Then she played a sparkling Rameau *sonatine* for her brother.

"Reverend Lee will be utterly delighted to have your spinet as part of his growing musical company," Gladwin said as Ella sat at the glossy, dark spinet.

"He will, Henry," Ella replied, and her hands rippled over the keys, evoking a bright harmony of sound. "And someone else will be just as excited about this—Sir Robert!"

But at that moment Sir Robert Davers was thinking aimlessly about yesterday evening's strange encounter with several

French lumberjacks. The Englishman and his expedition had shared the woodsmen's campfire. It was not especially unusual that the Frenchmen were not cordial, but what had struck Davers as strange was the nervous manner of one Frenchman, who had gripped Sir Robert by the arm just as the English were departing.

The man was afraid, it seemed, to let his French comrades hear his words, and what he said was very curious. The words returned clearly to Sir Robert's mind: "Listen!" the Frenchman had whispered. "Danger! Listen to me! Danger! Indians! Go back to fort! Quickly! Warn them! Attack! Danger!"

Curious—and even more so because as soon as a second Frenchman walked up as if to overhear what was said, the nervous man startled and confused Davers by bursting into laughter and slapping Sir Robert on the shoulder before turning away to rejoin his comrades. Very curious, indeed.

Lieutenant Robertson's voice broke into Sir Robert's thoughts: "Do you really believe there is a Northwest Passage to the Orient somewhere in this country, Sir Robert?" The handsome, cheerful young officer grinned doubtfully.

"What's that? Northwest Passage? Why certainly, certainly, Lieutenant. If we're fortunate, we may even discover that doorway to the Orient on one of these little sounding expeditions, what? Why, certainly. It wouldn't surprise me at all if one of these days our fellow marking the depths should toss his weight overboard and have it sink down a hundred fathoms, and there we have the threshold of the western ocean!" He clapped his hands and rubbed them warmly. "Ah! Wonderful day! Wonderful country, this!"

They were in the lower channels of the marshy mouth of the Saint Clair River. At one side of the boat a middle-aged sailor, one of two seamen on the expedition, was dropping the weighted sounding line into the water and calling out the marks, which Lieutenant Robertson entered in a leather-bound log. So far it looked as if the sloop *Michigan* could get upstream if it had a good wind behind it. The downstream current was indeed strong, but a good wind would do it, Davers thought.

Six soldiers pulled hard on the oars. Davers looked over the side into the deep green water, admiring a fish and talking with a young English trader who had volunteered to come along with his Pawnee slave, who was now holding the tiller at the stern.

Suddenly Sir Robert saw something move on the shore. He looked up at the thick trees crowding the bank and was startled to see a grappling hook tied to a long rope whiz through the air and land in the boat, latching onto the gunwale and yanking the craft to a stop. Sir Robert did not hear the shot that killed him. He fell back without a sound, a musket ball between the eyes.

Lieutenant Robertson and the two sailors were shot dead at the same instant. Wild shrieking burst from the trees at the shoreline; the boat was wrenched by the grappling hook into the shore; and before the stunned soldiers could resist, Indians and a Frenchman were upon them, tomahawking and stabbing every one. The white trader collapsed in shock, and his Pawnee slave was beaten unconscious by the laughing Frenchman.

Two excited Indians hurled Robertson's limp body onto a rock, where it was stripped naked. The Frenchman took the powder horn and rifle that had belonged to Davers. The attackers did not kill the Pawnee or the trader, who were taken prisoner. Then they snatched their trophies: With one foot holding down the body, the Indians sliced circles in the skulls of the dead and yanked the scalps free with terrible exultant yells of triumph.

Whooping Indians, chattering and laughing, watched as their chief yanked out his tomahawk and hacked away great chunks of flesh from the limbs of Lieutenant Robertson. They divided up the flesh and tore at it like dogs, slobbering and devouring with devilish gusto. Blood stained their greasy, painted chests as they consumed the magic power of the enemy and gave themselves his strength in battle.

The Indian leader drove his knife into the dead officer's breast and cut it open, exposing the heart, then slashing it free. He bit deeply and ripped away a bloody chunk. Laughing triumphantly, he threw the heart to his warriors, and one by one they bit into it.

First blood had been shed in Pontiac's uprising. The chief had avenged himself in part for a recent insult at the hands of the English. The chief was the Delaware, Sin-gat. But until this heart was that of Owen Sutherland, Sin-gat would never be satisfied.

It was still light when Mayla pushed the half-canoe into the river and splashed aboard. She lifted the paddle and waved once to Lela, who stood at the door of the cabin. Mayla stroked out into the river's current, paddled into midstream, and set off for Fort Detroit.

Ella Bently had not felt so content in years. The last hour spent at the spinet had freed her from care, and she strolled with a light step back to her brother's house. She felt like a young girl, even pretty. The three more months she and Jeremy would remain with Henry Gladwin on this frontier would pass quickly enough now that she had the spinet.

Jeremy ran up to her, panting for breath.

"Ma, I just met two boys who live in a cabin on an island with their mother, and they want me to come stay with them for a few days! Can I?"

"On an island? Oh, you must mean Mrs. Turnbull. Well, I'm sure it can be arranged, if Mrs. Turnbull doesn't mind. Maybe you can help them and show how we used to farm at home in Massachusetts."

In Massachusetts. She said that without a real twinge of melancholy. She sighed and smiled and took her boy's hand. For the first time since they had sold the farm, Ella felt she had a future. And even the present was rather nice as well.

"They want me to come tomorrow," Jeremy said.

"They do? Yes, perhaps I could take you over there myself. I've a mind to see something else of this country, and if your uncle can arrange for someone to row us out there, it would be a nice diversion."

Jeremy was excited, and he leaped with joy and ran ahead.

"Hold on!" Ella shouted. He turned back, fidgety with happiness. "This Mrs. Turnbull just became a widow, as I understand it, so don't go making any remarks or asking questions that would make it unpleasant for her, do you hear?"

Jeremy shouted that he did and raced off. Ella smiled to herself. The gusting wind, fresh and cool, bustled her muslin dress as she walked down Rue Saint Louis toward her home. Rue Saint Louis—that sounded better than Saint Louis Street. More charming than the English version.

A single snare drum rattled in the center of the parade ground while a guard detail lowered the Union Jack. Ella, like everyone else passing at that moment, paused out of respect to the flag. It was folded, the detail marched off, and she went on through shadows that were long in the early evening. She entered the house and greeted her brother, who was seated at the table in the dark sitting room, a quill working in his hand.

"Light a candle; you'll ruin your eyes, Henry," she said gaily and went up the narrow stairs to her room. There she changed into a warmer house dress of linsey, straightened her hair, and was about to go down and prepare the meal when she heard someone come in.

Downstairs Henry's voice sounded surprised. Ella heard the stranger speaking. It appeared to be a woman. Curious, Ella leaned out of the door of her room and listened. It was a woman, and she was French or Indian, for her words came out in halting, broken English. The name "Mayla" drifted up to her. Mayla! Yes! That was the name of Sutherland's Indian wife.

Ella could not resist a brief look at this girl, who was said to be so lovely. She tiptoed out of her door and along the short hallway. A board creaked, and she stopped until she knew the voices had not paused, then she went to the head of the stairs and looked around the wall and down.

Henry had lit a candle, and he now sat across the table from a dark, long-haired girl. No more than a girl at all, she seemed. In the dim light, Ella could make out eyes that glowed, and even in this circumstance, it was clear the girl was very beautiful. Ella felt just a touch of restlessness. Satisfied that she now knew what kind of woman this Mayla was, she began to draw back from her vantage point. But she paused when she heard Henry suddenly raise his voice.

"Tomorrow! Good God, Mayla! Are you absolutely certain? We've had rumors like this before, but—"

"Tomorrow," the girl said in a husky voice that sounded strained and nervous. "It is tomorrow. Pontiac come with warriors. Squaws have blankets; under blankets, tomahawks."

Ella's mind opened. She wondered what they were talking about. The Indian girl went on.

"Pontiac bring wampum to Gladwin. When he give wampum, he turn it over, and that signal to strike. Henry Gladwin die first. Then others. No one live but those who become slaves."

Henry muttered the name of the Lord and rubbed his eyes. Then he shook away dismay and asked about Sutherland.

"Donoway go try stop Pontiac, but he fail. Mayla sister say my man fight with *voyageur* who tell Indian big lie about

French army. My man win, but Pontiac want to believe lie. Pontiac lose great face if he cannot believe French. Great face, because many, many thousand Indian follow Pontiac now. They follow him to die if he say."

The strength had drained from Ella's body. She listened, paralyzed, as Mayla told the Indian plan to Gladwin. It was completely dark outside by the time Mayla finished. Gladwin promised to be prepared, and he thanked the girl, showing her out a back door. He sat down heavily at the table. The light from the single candle flickered and glittered on his officer's gold braid. Above, Ella released a trembling sigh and moved back to her room. The board creaked again, a groaning creak in the darkness.

"Ella?" Henry called. She stepped back to the head of the stairs and looked down into the pool of light where her brother sat, sad-eyed, with the lives of every English soul on his shoulders. She came down the steps and put her hands on his. He gave her a wan smile.

"Don't worry, sister," he said, and tried to be soothing. "These alarms occur every now and again at Indian country posts. Don't fret over this. They always blow over. This isn't the first, and it won't be the last out here. We'll be ready when Pontiac comes with his henchmen, and that'll be enough to take the wind from his sails. You'll see."

Gladwin inhaled deeply and stood up. He buckled on his scabbard and fetched his tricorn from the hook near the door. He said he had some things to attend to and not to wait supper for him. He would eat with his officers. As Henry opened the door to leave, Ella said, "That's Owen Sutherland's wife, isn't it?"

"Yes, a good girl," Gladwin said and began to close the door.

"Very beautiful," Ella heard herself saying, but Gladwin was gone, and the door closed. Sutherland and the Indian girl were, she thought, a very fine match.

Outside in the darkness Mayla was hurrying along Rue Saint Louis toward the water gate, when a stocky figure stepped into her path. She stopped short, but not before long arms went around her and dragged her toward white flashing teeth and the stench of rum. She wrenched herself away and flitted a dagger against the big man's ribs. He grunted and jumped back into the gloom.

"Easy with that blade, squaw," a hoarse voice snarled in Ottawa, but there was a French tinge to it. "I meant no harm."

The shadow came closer to her, and she could see the suggestion of a face, grinning, leering.

"Stay back!" she warned and played the knife before him.

"No harm, squaw," the man said. "I just wanted a look at what kind of woman these English have for mistresses. You're a choice piece, squaw. Who were you with tonight?" Mayla noticed the silhouette of a feathered stocking cap against the deep blue sky. The man stepped back again and said with a flourish of his hand, "And does Donoway's woman return to him this night? If she should need some protection on her journey across the river, I, André Breton, am at your service."

Mayla's heart nearly stopped. She had not informed Gladwin that it was Breton who had told Pontiac those lies. She should go back and warn Gladwin of the treachery of this *métis*. She faltered. Enough had been said already. Donoway would tell Gladwin about the disloyalty of André Breton. Now she must return to Valenya before anyone knew she had come to Gladwin. She shivered when she saw Breton's eyes gleaming in the darkness. They looked hungry.

"No harm done, squaw," he chuckled and bowed and drifted away. From the night came his soft, hoarse words, "No harm done," and she fled from his cold laugh.

She ran to the gate, where two guards opened it for her, and it groaned on its hinges. She dashed out into the night, down to the river toward her waiting canoe.

The guards were closing the gate when a dark shadow pushed past and disappeared.

"Who was that, George?" one guard asked another.

"Looked like that Frenchy half-breed, the one the Major uses as interpreter sometime. You know, Breton or some such frog-eatin' name."

"Shouldn't we stop 'im, then take 'im to the corporal?"

George barred the closed gate. "Ah, come on, Freddy, we're due off any minute. We go chasin' that froggie an' we'll be out all night. Let 'im go! Who gives a damn about frog-eaters?"

The wooden bar thumped dully into its brackets.

Out on the broad, starlit Detroit River, André Breton paddled in the direction of Valenya. His side still ached, and it was often difficult to breathe, for Sutherland had cracked some ribs. But Sutherland would pay. He would pay tonight. Breton laughed to think that Sutherland was still recovering back at the Ottawa village, as an Indian had told him this afternoon. That meant this Ottawa girl was alone in their cabin.

He laughed again and coughed painfully. It was hard to breathe, damn that Sutherland! It was even hard to sing because of his smashed ribs, and paddling was torture. But it was worth it to be out on the river tonight. It was worth it to take revenge.

He laughed, and it hurt. He tried to sing but only coughed. Who ever heard of a *voyageur* who could not sing? He forced himself to sing softly. His paddle swept down and up, digging in to the rhythm of a lively *voyageur* song.

No soldier slept at Fort Detroit that night. As he had expected, Henry Gladwin was too busy seeing to the fort's defenses to return to his house for dinner. The men stood watch-shifts throughout the night. The small six-pound cannon were both taken to the parade ground from their station on the north wall tower. The guns were emplaced so their fire could sweep the parade and rake right up the Rue Sainte Anne toward the west gate at the opposite end of the fort.

Gladwin had a plan which he believed would head off Pontiac. When he heard it, Captain Campbell was not happy. The second officer was against letting large numbers of Indians bent on mischief into the fort at all. He called for closing off the fort to Indians until the trouble passed. But Gladwin warned that there was no time to bring all the English settlers outside the fort in to safety if Pontiac was pushed to attack the next day. Also, there was Sir Robert's expedition up on Lake Saint Clair to be considered. But if Pontiac could be stopped in his tracks, before the uprising began, then there would be enough time to alert the dependency garrisons scattered around the countryside in a radius of several hundred miles. Then settlers and traders could be brought into the fort in the lull between tomorrow's anticipated confrontation and any real attack by the Indians.

"But I believe," said Gladwin, "that what we'll show Pontiac on the morrow will change his plans. We'll bare our teeth, Captain, and we'll do it while he and his warriors are in our own lair. We'll show them we have no fear of them, and we'll put them in awe of the English lion, eh?"

Gladwin grinned jovially, but Captain Campbell merely patted his hungry stomach and puffed out his cheeks.

"I hope you're right, Major," Campbell said. "I'll send off couriers to the dependency forts immediately. This new young

Sergeant McEwan will go up to Michilimackinac with a French guide before dawn."

As Campbell departed, Gladwin readied himself to continue overseeing the preparations for tomorrow's dangerous confrontation with Pontiac. He paused, standing on the parade ground and surveying the torch-lit fort, busy with soldiers coming and going. Men were nailing shut storehouse windows, and the ramparts were occupied by extra guards. The entire garrison was under arms tonight. Gladwin knew his force would be ready.

At that moment he wished he had time to write to Frances, his wife at home in England. He wondered whether she had received his last letter yet. He had meant to write earlier that day, but this emergency had prevented that. He cast his eyes once more around the fort. Yes, all was in order. But Henry Gladwin felt uneasy. One never knew what might happen tomorrow. Somehow, before the night was done, he must find the time to pen a note to Frances. He refused to think that it might be the last she would receive from him. That kind of thinking distracted a man at critical moments, and Gladwin was determined not to be distracted by anything until he made it plain to Pontiac that an uprising was suicidal for the Indians.

Indeed, Frances Beridge Gladwin had received her husband's last letter, and she had read and reread it every day in the week since it had arrived here in Stubbing, Derbyshire. It had been read most often late at night, after she should have been asleep; and it was then that the letter did Frances the most good. She missed her husband, and she longed for his return to England.

It was late as she lay in bed, listening to a spring rain patter on the leaves outside. Frances had never thought the sound of rain could be so lonely. Somehow she felt especially tense tonight, but did not know why. She sat up and listened for a sound from her father, who was sleeping in the next room. He had been ill for much too long, and she feared his end might be coming. However, there was no sound, and if there had been, the nurse who slept in the chamber beyond her father's would be with him immediately. It was not her father's illness that caused her restlessness tonight. It was something else. Something, she sensed, was wrong with Henry.

Frances got out of bed, drew on her robe, and struck a light. She was a pretty woman, petite and fair, in her mid-twenties. With two candles flickering nearby, and the sound of a cold rain in the background, she sat down at her writing desk and took out Henry's letter once more. She read it through, and found no hint of trouble, no expectation of danger. That was like Henry, though: He seldom spoke of war or of his military responsibilities. In the few brief months he had been home last year—when they had married at last after years of betrothal—there was hardly a word spoken about the fighting he had done in America. But Frances knew what her husband had often faced; she knew he was at the slaughter of Braddock's army, and she knew he had seen some of the most bitter fighting of the American war.

Just what was he doing now? In her mind she tried to picture Fort Detroit. He had drawn a sketch of it once, even roughly showing the commander's house. Ella must be with him by now. That was good. Ella would see that Henry took care of himself. And young Jeremy must be growing. Frances felt warm inside then, thinking how fine it would be for her sister-in-law to return to England once more. Life would be wonderful when Henry and Ella and the boy lived here. They would be a happy family.

Then Frances looked down at the letter again, and that same uneasiness returned. She did not know why she felt so nervous. Even Henry's casual comments in the letter about the Indians being angry with British rule were not enough to trouble her. That sort of thing was normal on a frontier, and a soldier's wife must never worry for her man just because his duty was dangerous.

She sighed and folded the letter. It would be marvelous when he came back! She blew out the candles and went to bed once more. The rain had stopped, and there was a hint of dawn at the windows. The morning breeze clattered through branches outside, and Frances Gladwin drew the covers to her chin. But she knew she would not sleep this night.

When Mayla forced her canoe up on the pebbled shingle before her cabin, she sensed she was being followed. The night was too dark to see clearly, for the moon had not yet risen, but for the past half hour she had heard a sound, as of someone singing.

She jumped from the canoe, took a swift look across the water, and ran up to the cabin, where firelight glowed at the window. She smelled smoke from the fire. Perhaps Lela was still awake. Perhaps Tamano had come down from the Ottawa camp a day early. She pushed open the door.

Before she entered the cabin, she glanced out at the beach and saw the mass of a canoe draw up on shore. Fright caught her throat, and she slammed the door closed, dropping the iron bar across it.

"What's that?" gasped Lela from the bed, where she had been torn from sleep. In the murky room Lela was sitting up bleary-eyed, staring across at Mayla, who leaned back against the door.

"Someone is following!" Mayla breathed and ran into her sister's arms. "I met Breton at the fort. I think it is he! He comes now!"

Lela dashed to her traveling pack and pulled out a pistol. At the same time Mayla emptied water onto the fire from a kettle that hung over the hearth, sending smoke gusting into the room and up the chimney. The fire went out, and the room was dark. It was silent as the two women sat on the bed, listening.

The fire sizzled and hissed. The wind picked up and shook the trees. It came from the north, whistling a low, howling song through the standing rocks behind the cabin. The wind blew, and the stones sang. The women dared not speak. Then they heard it: Someone was walking around the cabin, walking with a dragging gait, as if his leg was hurt.

Slowly the steps drifted through the grass. They paused at a back window, but it was too high to see through. Then the steps went around to the front of the cabin. Lela gripped the pistol. Mayla drew out her dagger. They held each other.

Their breathing almost stopped.

There was a scratching at the door. The latch was yanked up, and a great weight heaved against it. The iron bar shuddered and clanked, but it held. A hoarse voice grumbled at the door. The latch went up and the door trembled again. Lela's pistol aimed.

Again, again, and again the door was battered. A snarl and a roar and another crash. But the bar stayed on its brackets. Mayla's fright shook her, and her mouth was dry.

Then it was still.

Whoever was there seemed to have gone away. The sisters sat in silence. They looked at each other, but they did not move.

After a long time, the fire stopped hissing and went out into complete blackness. Mayla came off the bed. She crept slowly toward the front window, but before she had gone halfway, the stumbling, almost limping step returned, and a flame glowed red at the left window.

"Fire!" Lela whispered, and Mayla stood ready in the center of the room.

A cold voice laughed. The torchlight played on the windows and ran over the ceiling of the cabin. A rifle butt smashed through the panes, and in flew a flaming torch, sizzling and crackling as it landed on the floor. Mayla swept it up and moved to hurl it back. But a musket roared, and Mayla staggered backwards, crashing hard against the wall. Lela screamed and fired her pistol at a man's head now peering through the window. With a shriek of anger, the head vanished from sight. Lela snatched up the torch and threw it back outside, then scrambled to Mayla, who was slumped, unmoving, on the floor.

"Mayla! Mayla!" Owen Sutherland sat straight up in his bedding and screamed. Near him, Tamano jerked awake and grasped his shoulders. Sutherland's eyes were glassy; his mouth was open. He was feverish again, for the poison had not yet left him completely.

Tamano coaxed him back down, murmuring that he should sleep. Sutherland lay, eyes wide, staring blankly up at the hole where the smoke of the dying fire escaped from the lodge to join the stars. He lay sweating, his chest rising and falling convulsively. Blood seeped from the wound at his side. Tamano took off the stained muslin bandage, washed it, and bound Sutherland's body again. He spoke to his friend and told him to sleep. But Sutherland, as though in a trance, said nothing. Then he began calling "Mayla, my Mayla. Come back. Mayla, come back . . ."

Tamano tightened the bandage and wiped sweat from Sutherland's flushed face. He assured Sutherland they would see Mayla in the morning, but he should sleep until tomorrow.

Tamano himself lay back; he wished Sutherland would close his eyes. The Chippewa felt helpless as he watched his friend in the light of the old crescent moon that fell through the hole in the lodge roof. Slowly, soundlessly now, Sutherland's lips moved, muttering his woman's name, begging her, begging her to come back.

PART TWO

The Rising

chapter **9**

PONTIAC'S TREACHERY

It was well past first light when Sutherland awoke. He sat up suddenly, and the soreness of many cuts clawed at him. But the memory of last night's dream was worse. He could still see a hazy vision of Mayla drifting away, drifting hopelessly away from him, and he could not stop her. He could not bring her back.

Tamano poked his head in under the hide flap covering the door to the lodge. "Donoway is awake; that is good," he said. "We must go soon, my brother."

Sutherland thought the Ottawa village sounded unusually busy this morning. He heard many people talking excitedly, and there was much movement outside. He struggled to his feet, and Tamano helped him pull the hunting shirt over his head. He tied his buckskin leggins below the knee, strapped on his sword, and picked up his rifle. Then they stepped out through the door into the early sunlight, and Sutherland stopped and stared. The camp was alive with warriors, hundreds of them, mostly Ottawa, but many Chippewa also. They were everywhere, grooming their heads, holding small mirrors before them to paint their faces with the vermillion of battle.

Guns, tomahawks, and knives lay at their sides. Those who had no guns had bows on their shoulders, and quivers of arrows hung loose on their backs. Many were cavorting together, wrapping themselves in blankets, nodding politely to friends, then whooping as they cast aside the blanket and brandished a sawed-off musket or a newly sharpened tomahawk that had been concealed. They all laughed and yelped together.

Tamano and Sutherland, aching all over, walked through the camp toward the canoes at the riverside. Soon Molo and his two cousins were with them and a little behind. The young warrior, who was painted with red over black and also prepared for war, looked glum, disappointed, for he would not be joining his brothers today.

Sutherland was deeply troubled, and he ignored all greetings as he and Tamano and their guards walked to the canoes. Not only did the dream of last night haunt him, but the hoplessness of this mad moment twisted inside his mind. War was coming, and there was nothing he could do to stop it.

By the time Sutherland reached his canoe, the great mass of Indians had already swarmed down to the river and were crowding into birch and elm-bark craft. It was an awesome sight, as the reds and blues, bright flashes of color and feathers, flooded the beach and then floated out in small groups onto the river.

Sutherland was about to wade through the water and get into the canoe when a voice called from behind. He turned and saw Pontiac himself, wrapped in a red trade blanket, standing haughtily and staring. Sutherland went to him.

"Donoway," Pontiac began, and the crescent of white bone at his nose dangled as he spoke, "must remain at his cabin until Pontiac permits him to leave. If he interferes in this war, he shall die."

Sutherland looked directly at Pontiac but said nothing. Then the chief turned away, followed by a score of lesser chiefs, all wrapped closely in blankets and all adorned with eagle feathers slanting from their brows. Pontiac strode toward his own canoe, which would take him to Fort Detroit.

There were between sixteen and nineteen Indians in each canoe, and scores of them slid heavily out into the stream flowing down from Lake Saint Clair. Sutherland and Tamano set off toward Valenya in one canoe, with Molo and his two cousins following reluctantly. The young braves cast frequent glances at the mass of canoes crossing the river and receding in the distance.

When they were nearly at Valenya, Sutherland spoke to Tamano, who was kneeling in the stern of the craft.

"You know, my brother, Mayla was right when she said we cannot stay here in these evil times. I'll do what she has said. We'll go to the northwest wilderness and there have our child. We'll begin again among those people, for they do not yet hate the English, and they have not yet been fouled by white man's rum. We'll depart today, Tamano, if you are ready."

Tamano said nothing, though he knew he would go with

Donoway. But somehow he could not bring himself to speak about departing yet, even though he and Lela had already started once for the north country. He could not say: Yes, I'll go with you, Donoway. But he did not know why.

"You mean I can't go to visit the Turnbull boys today?" Jeremy was in anguish as he looked at his mother, who was pouring him milk at the breakfast table. "You promised I could. What's wrong?"

Ella could not tell him of the growing danger. Henry had not come back last night, and it seemed her fleeting happiness yesterday afternoon had been a cruel hoax of destiny. She prayed that her brother was right when he said these Indian alarms were to be expected on the frontier, and that this one would pass as quickly as others had.

"Maybe tomorrow, son," Ella said weakly and stirred sugar into her black tea. "But not today, because your uncle needs all his soldiers to greet the Indians coming this afternoon. And you have to stay in the barracks on Rue Saint Jacques with the other English children."

"Why do we have to stay there?" he said plaintively. "I want to see—"

"Don't ask questions!" Ella snapped. She caught herself: "Please don't ask me now, Jeremy, dear. There's too much on my mind, and you'll know better at the end of the day. Perhaps you can go over tomorrow, when—when—"

"When what, Ma?"

She got up to walk away from the table so Jeremy would not see the insistent tears that filled her eyes.

Tamano was helping the wounded Sutherland out of the canoe at Valenya when Lela's shrieking cries brought them around to see her running toward them, shouting frantically, her arms spread wide. She shouted. "Mayla! Mayla! Donoway! Mayla!"

Lela stumbled against Tamano, who grasped her by both arms. She muttered hurriedly through sobs. Tamano wrenched around to stare at Sutherland, who shuddered one fierce moment, then with a strangled cry of horror dashed up the beach, the bloody bandage trailing from beneath his shirt. Tamano and Lela ran behind him as he burst through the cabin door. Suddenly he stopped.

On the bed lay Mayla. He sprang to her. He whispered her name. He touched her eyes. They were closed. He drew back the blanket that covered her breast, and there he saw the dull stain of blood spread over her body. He felt her face, her hands. Nothing. He put his head to her breast. Nothing. He put his face close to her lips. Nothing.

She was dead.

Sutherland sank to his knees. Again he shuddered.

He held her cold hand against his cheek. He fought down what wished to explode and destroy everything cruel. He restrained his fury, gulped it down, but it welled up like a flood, an awful, vacant, furious sadness. Mayla. Dead. He leaned his head against her and sobbed. He spoke her name in drowning anguish, and he surrendered to misery that surpassed all misery he had ever known.

He brought her hand to his lips. Then he felt the silver pendant gripped tightly between her fingers. Gently he drew it away. He pressed his brow against her breast and stayed that way for a long time.

Finally, Lela touched his shoulder. Tamano brought the devastated Sutherland to his feet. Silently they moved outside into cloudy sunlight. Then Sutherland heard the death chant being sung by Molo and his young cousins near the pine trees.

Sutherland, Tamano, and Lela moved away from the house and sat down in grass, facing the vast expanse of a gray river.

Sutherland at last said emptily: "Tell me, sister."

Lela told what happened. When she said Mayla had encountered Breton at the fort, Sutherland began to quiver. Then he looked up, his jaw clenched, his eyes murderous. "I should have killed him then," he whispered.

"We are not sure it was Breton who—who—" Lela bit her lip.

"You say you shot at him?" Sutherland asked, and he was beginning to cool, to calculate. "You say you think you wounded him?"

Lela nodded and wiped away tears. Sutherland got up and walked to the front of the cabin. Tamano followed, and with his friend he kneeled and searched the ground. There was blood scattered in the dust. The man had been shot.

"Look here!" Tamano said and picked up something. He handed it to Sutherland, who went very cold as he turned over a black raven feather.

Ella hurried the complaining Jeremy into the barracks on the Rue Saint Jacques, where the English women and children were gathering under the eyes of several guards and some armed traders. In double rows along the street that would be used by the Indians when they came that afternoon, the greater part of the garrison was assembled in red and blue lines standing at parade rest.

The soldiers had fixed bayonets and were turned out with shining brass and leather. They numbered only one hundred and twenty, and it was expected that the Indians would easily double that or perhaps treble it. But the garrison looked formidable and well disciplined, each man standing with his musket butt on the ground and one hand held at the small of the back. Ella glanced up and down the street, then prodded Jeremy up onto the porch and through the door of the long building. There were a large number of Indians in the fort this morning; they loitered in little knots, most wrapped in worn trade blankets, although the midday sun was warm. The Indians who roamed about were turned away by every trading house, told the house would open soon, soon, later, not now. But the morning passed with no business being done, although Saturday morning was normally the busiest trading day of all. It was May 7, and the fort was unusually hushed.

Ella entered the barracks, where twenty or more English and provincial children were keeping each other busy with games and grumbling. Nearly as many women—all pale and fretting under a brave exterior—were in the long, low room. Many women stood aimlessly at windows, staring outside, asking each other when they thought Pontiac would come. But none knew or cared to guess.

Lettie Morely was there, exuberant and friendly as ever. Hearty Lettie seemed too preoccupied with good cheer ever to feel the same anxiety others wore in their eyes as the hours passed. Lettie cajoled Ella into reading fairy tales to the children, and later, the portly woman struck up songs that even the most worried women found themselves singing. Poetry, games, singing, games, and more poetry whittled away the lingering time. Ella was at the glazed window that let in misty cool light from the street when there came a clattering at the end of the building. That section of the room was beginning to darken. Someone was closing the shutters, a voice said, and the speaker seemed short of breath. Had it begun now? someone else asked. There was no answer.

A thumping came at the door, and it was opened by a Royal American private who nodded, smiled, and let in Reverend

Lee. Several women fluttered toward him as he blew into the room, smiled, shook hands, smiled again, and raised his palms to quiet their many anxious questions. The children looked up, dubious, for many feared they were about to get an early Sunday school lesson or, at best, a prolonged French session.

But Lee had come for no such disagreeable purpose. He had come to lift the spirits of the women, and he called them together in sympathetically nasal tones. Major Gladwin, he said, had asked that he tell the women what to expect when the Indians came, and he assured them that they were not to worry. More shutters slammed closed and were nailed with a few sharp bangs on each.

"Now, then, when the Indians are inside the stockade," he began and brought the tips of his fingers and thumbs neatly together as he surveyed the anxious women gathered near him, "the gate will be closed, and Major Gladwin will accept Pontiac over at the council house . . ."

Ella thought fleetingly about her spinet, polished and tuned, standing helplessly in that same building. Soon there would be a crowd of Indians and soldiers, and who knew what might happen to the spinet? Foolish thought!

The soldiers sealing the shutters now reached the center of the room, where Lee was explaining how a drum would be heard tap-tapping the entire time the Indians would be in the fort.

". . . and if you should hear that drum stop tapping, then you are all to get down on the floor and stay there until you are told everything is—is safe—is finished."

"What will that mean?" asked a rather slow-witted woman, who glanced at the shadow of a shutter being thrust in front of the window near her and winced at every blow of the hammer.

"That will mean," Lee said softly so the children who had been bustled off to the other end of the room would not hear, "that trouble has begun. Some shooting is likely."

Several women sat down limply on soldiers' cots provided for sleeping—or for fainting.

Ella tried to find something to do with her tingling hands. Another shutter was nailed up, and the room became darker. Now the only light fell from three windowed cupolas set along the roof of the barracks.

"Now, now, ladies," Lee said and smiled brightly. "Major Gladwin assures me nothing at all will happen. The Indians are angry, and he'll listen to their complaints of course. But then they'll go away, and that'll be that!"

Apparently, thought Ella, Lee had not heard of Mayla's visit to Gladwin last night. It was unlikely that there would be nothing more to this than just a few speeches.

Lee spoke a few moments longer, answered questions with supreme optimism, and then went to the door of the barracks.

"So, ladies," Lee chirped, "don't worry, for the Good Lord is watching over his people. And remember, now, listen for the drum to stop. Only when it stops!"

Lee swung the door open, and Ella was standing with him as he went out. Before he was gone, she caught his arm and looked into his eyes and saw, for a moment, they were furtive and afraid.

"Pray for us, Reverend," Ella whispered.

"I am, Mistress Bently, I am." He put his tricorn on his head, forced another smile, and went outside into the milling crowd of gloom-faced Indians.

A soldier on the western wall suddenly shouted down that Pontiac and his Indians were on the way to the fort. Whites in the streets began to move out of the way, up onto porches or into houses where they reappeared at windows with muskets in their hands. The soldier standing gurard at the barracks where the children were kept suggested that Ella get inside so he could close the door. She moved out and told him to go ahead and close the door, saying she would go in directly, but first she wanted to watch the Indians come. The soldier was not keen on her idea, but he closed the door anyway and stood by it with his bayoneted musket at his side.

Most windows in the fort were shuttered. Every man was armed with musket, pistol, and hatchet or Indian axe. The French *habitants* had not come in to trade this morning, as they usually did on Saturdays, and that indicated something was afoot. The French who lived in the fort were either indoors or had gone away. Crowding along the Rue Saint Jacques were more than one hundred and fifty armed soldiers and traders. At the east end of the fort soldiers stood near the cannon, and a company of men were in rank near the council house just off the parade ground by the water gate.

The guard spoke to Ella again, but she could not remain in the confinement of the children's barracks. She stared nervously down the street, her heart thudding. Then the gate swung open to let in the Indians. The guard again said she should go into the barracks. She nodded and watched, transfixed.

There was a long train of blanketed, feathered, painted warriors stamping behind one Indian who led them in—Pontiac. She was sure Pontiac hesitated just a moment when he realized that the entire garrison was under arms. But he recovered immediately, came on, and so did the entourage of warriors, more than two hundred of them, who followed. Added to the host of Indians already in the fort, that meant there were at least three hundred warriors inside the walls.

Marching alongside the stoic Pontiac was Captain Campbell on one side and on the other a limping Frenchman Ella recognized as André Breton, the interpreter. Breton had a fresh wound on his face, from his left temple back to his ear under his red stocking cap, which was pulled down tightly over his head. Somewhere on the parade ground a snare drum tapped, tapped, tapped in rhythm to the tread of the Indians as they tramped into the fort—in rhythm to the pounding of Ella's heart.

They were walking toward the council house. She wondered what had been done about her spinet. But it was intense curiosity about her brother and how he would handle this affair— not fear for the welfare of her spinet—that sent Ella running around behind the barracks, darting along the north wall toward the council house. She kept to the edges of the parade ground, hurrying forward, driven by the great need to know what would happen. She could not be trapped in that barracks, for she had heard Mayla's warning: The signal to strike would be when Pontiac turned the wampum belt over and then drove his tomahawk into Henry . . .

Tap, tap, tap, the drum went on. Knots of hard-eyed Indians, painted garishly and flourishing plumes of feathers about their greasy buckskins, watched as she ran past them. There were Indians with heads shaven except for scalp locks that spewed from their crowns. There were Indians in bright, filthy blankets with bones in their noses. As she ran past one, he caught her eye and grinned stupidly.

Soldiers and traders scolded, urging her to go indoors, but on she went around the church and the army bakery, past the storehouse at the southeast corner of the stockade and past the commander's garden in an enclave at the corner of the fort. There! She stopped short at the corner of a building and watched as Campbell and Breton stood aside at the door of the council house and let Pontiac, with sixty chiefs and warriors, file slowly in.

All the while, the drum tap-tapped steadily.

Ella hurried to the rear of the council house, which had its back portions near the stockade. A group of men, all armed, were crowded at a window in the alley, looking in. When Ella pushed through them, they muttered a warning but gave her room. She peered inside.

The room was jammed with Indians. Red-coated soldiers with fixed bayonets lined the walls. The room was so crowded that these soldiers had little space to move. Several officers with one or two pistols stuck in their belts stood stiffly near Gladwin, who was seated at the extreme right of the dim chamber. Ella shuddered as she recalled Mayla's warning: Henry would be the first to die.

The drum tapped, and although the drummer was out on the parade ground, it seemed as though the tapping drifted to her from within the silent room itself.

There was the spinet, pushed into one corner and covered by canvas. Strange, she thought, how that spinet could interest her at this moment.

The Indians sat down silently on the floor. Their eyes flitted to the soldiers about them. They looked nervous and worried, for they knew they had been betrayed. They easily outnumbered the soldiers, but Indians seldom liked to fight a pitched battle if it were not a foregone conclusion that they would win without suffering great loss. If a fight began this afternoon, the outcome was very definitely in doubt. And no Indian had failed to notice the cannon aimed at them. All knew the gates of the fort had been closed and barricaded.

However, the warriors would fight bravely if Pontiac gave the command. Would he give the command even though his clever plot had been uncovered?

Gladwin immediately ordered the distribution of tobacco. No one else spoke. An atmosphere, heavy and ominous, settled upon the room. Bread was passed to the Indians, and they smoked and gnawed, none uttering a sound, all waiting. The drum tapped, tapped, tapped.

Time passed in chewing and puffing. Soldiers and Indians were sweating. The day was warm. Ella was standing in the shade looking in the window, and she smelled the fetid, sickly-sweet odor of bear-greased Indian drift from the steaming room.

The warriors ate and smoked. The drum tapped.

The entire fort was silent. No one moved.

Ella had the urge to return to Jeremy, who must be wondering where she was by now. But she wanted to stay. Or should she go?

Her decision was made as Chief Pontiac, who had sat at the forefront of his men for more than an hour, rose to face Gladwin. The drum tapped. Breton was translator.

Pontiac's face was drawn with anger, his eyes narrow as he began in a throaty voice: "Our people have come to you this day as is our custom," he said, and it was a clear insult that he did not formally address Gladwin or the English with a friendly greeting before he spoke. "We have come, as I foretold we would, to profess our friendship for the English and to smoke the pipe of peace." He paused, and as Breton leaned over Gladwin to interpret, his voice was loud enough for Ella to hear. The drum tapped.

Pontiac went on: "But why do I see so many of your young men outside this house carrying guns? Why should this be? We are greatly surprised, brother, to see all your soldiers under arms. Could it be some bad bird has sung in your ear ill news of your children and brothers the Indian? If that is so, we advise you, brothers, not to believe it. For, as you know, there are some bad birds who would like to see you rise up against your Indian brothers who have come in peace, and who have always been in perfect friendship with their brothers the English."

Breton completed the translation, and his voice was strangely in rhythm with the beating of the drum. Then the *métis* stopped. Pontiac waited for Gladwin's reply. Gladwin stared coolly at the chief. The drum tapped.

At last, without a hint of irritation or anger or fear in his voice, Gladwin said: "Pontiac should not be troubled by what he has seen of my young men armed and ready outside. Often this takes place for the sake of discipline and drill. But today I have heard that some other Indian nations are on their way to counsel here, and since I do not know them well and perhaps I should not trust them, I wish to have my garrison under arms when they arrive."

Breton translated to the impassive Pontiac, who stood staring at the seated Gladwin. Neither leader's eyes wavered.

Gladwin said: "And since I do not wish these strange nations to be insulted when they are received by armed soldiers, I chose to begin this procedure with the visit of our greatest friends, the Ottawa and Chippewa, since I am sure they will in no way take offense at it. And if they do not take offense, then how could these strange Indians who are coming take offense?"

Ella strained on tiptoe to see into the room. She discovered Major Duvall standing, glaring at her, near the door. Before she looked away from him, Duvall, trying to maintain his composure, jerked his head several times to indicate she should leave. She looked away and at Pontiac, who was listening to Breton's guttural translation of her brother's words into Ottawa. Pontiac looked even more terrible than before.

Breton's voice fell, and except for the drum, there was silence again. Pontiac stood looking at Gladwin. Time passed. The drum tapped. No one spoke.

Then Pontiac reached down into a blanket at his feet and drew something out. Officers in the room tensed. Hands went to pistols and hilts of swords. Ella felt fear as Pontiac casually held up a long green-and-white wampum belt in both hands. He held it forth to Gladwin, the white side up. When he turned this belt over, the killing would begin.

A tall man next to Ella accidently stepped hard on her foot. She gasped, and the sound echoed into the room. Pontiac paused. The drum went on.

Then Pontiac moved to Gladwin with the long, broad belt outstretched. Ella's teeth chattered; she wished she were in the barracks now. But, she thought sickeningly, even that might not be safe, and she whispered to herself, "Jeremy."

Henry Gladwin gazed steadily at Pontiac's eyes. The moment had come. The drum tapped.

Pontiac began to speak. He went on in a dull drone about the unhappiness of his people over the loss of six Ottawa chiefs during the past winter. The drum tapped. Ella forced shaking hands behind her skirts. Holding forth the belt, Pontiac said he hoped the English would give the Ottawa presents to banish their grief. Every eye was fixed on that belt. Even Breton's voice seemed numb as he simultaneously muttered the translation. Gladwin's steady, icy stare held Pontiac's eyes.

Pontiac ended his speech. Breton went on with the last of the translation, but before he could finish, Pontiac moved as though to turn the belt over. Breton's words stopped, half-spoken. Gladwin made a little quick motion with one hand. At the door Duvall relayed the message to the drummer, and the deadly tap broke into a loud rolling sound. Outside, scores of

English muskets clattered as they were slapped to force powder into the priming pan. Pontiac held the belt aloft.

The drum raced and raced and every man in the room was ready. Pontiac stepped forward, raised the belt a little higher, and brought it down. The drum raced and raced. But Pontiac did not turn the belt over.

With the drum rolling madly in the background, Henry Gladwin spoke in a loud voice.

"Pontiac, it is with deep sorrow that we hear the news of your loss. In memory of those six chiefs, we English shall present your people with six new suits of clothes and more bread. It is good to know that we have such loyal friends as the Ottawa, and I can assure you, Pontiac, that English friendship shall be extended to you and your people for as long as it is deserved.

"The strange tribes which are coming to counsel with us shall be made to know that this is the English way. But they shall also be told that at the first act of aggression against us, we shall retaliate with all our mighty power, with all our young men and all our great thunder guns, and we shall have *vengeance!*"

Gladwin and Pontiac stared at one another, and the drum raced. Then Pontiac finally seemed about to give the signal. But the moment passed. He spoke.

"It is not fitting that so few of our people have come to honor the English. We shall go now and in a few days return with our entire nation and counsel with you. Then we shall properly express the friendship that exists between the Indian and the English." He put down the wampum.

Gladwin said nothing. The drum still rolled.

Pontiac turned hard on his heels and paced from the council house, followed by glaring warriors and chiefs. In a few moments the drum changed once more from a rapid roll to a steady tap-tapping. The gates opened; the Indians filed sullenly out of the fort until every one of them was gone. The gates closed once more, and the whites breathed gratefully in relief.

Ella's heart was still beating madly, even when the snare drum stopped its pulse and a sentinel went round the fort to say that all was safe. She ran toward the barracks where Jeremy was with the other children and the women. She burst through the door and sought her son to hug him, embarrassing him with her emotion. He pulled away and told her not to be so fussy. But he was not unkind, and soon he was back with the others, who had found wood to whittle and stories to tell each other while the women, almost all of them exhausted from the tension, reclined on cots.

Lying on a bed, with her hand up to her eyes, Lettie Morely clucked her tongue and said, "That were some chancy thing for yon Major Gladwin ter do, it were." She looked over at Ella and shook her head slowly. "All them savages in among us, and all of 'em with guns and tommyhawks under them dirty blankets. Even their women had axes and whatnot under them blankets, they did. Chancy, it were, I'll say," and she lay back again, fanning her face with a pudgy hand.

The shutters were taken down from the windows and light splashed in.

"Thy brother be a brave man, indeed," Lettie said, short of breath. "But I daresay he be needin' a bit more learnin' about them heathens. No disrespect meant, Mistress Bently, but I say this was beginner's luck. Yes. Next time, them heathens won't be shufflin' off like a clutter of sheep if they come here armed an' ready for business. No. Thee best tell thy brother—an' no disrespect meant, mind thee—that the folk who know them Injuns hope he don't ever open the gates like this in time of trouble again. No. Mark me, mistress, there's no disrespect meant. Thy brother be a brave man. Yes." She continued fanning her pale face with her hand.

chapter 10

FEVER

Sergeant Duncan McEwan was not eager to make this trip north to Fort Michilimackinac, nearly two weeks' journey around Lake Saint Clair, through the Saint Clair River, and on out into Lake Huron for mile after mile of paddling. And he was no more pleased with the company of Jean Dusten, the *voyageur* serving as his guide.

Dusten was an aloof Frenchman, tiny and slim, a man who always needed a shave but never grew a beard. His age was hard to tell, but he seemed to be about fifty. Dusten constantly had a clay pipe jammed in the side of his mouth, and his chin was ever jutting upwards and out as though he sought to smell something or smelled something he'd rather not. He spoke little to McEwan, except to nod or shake his head. Since McEwan had left Fort Detroit early that morning, Dusten had been singularly uncommunicative.

At Michilimackinac McEwan would pass on the papers given him by Major Gladwin. If somehow the papers were lost, McEwan was to warn the fort at Michilimackinac that an uprising was threatening. This was the most remote outpost in North America, and one of the most important. There the rich fur trade thrived as the western Indians bartered their harvest for English goods. There the wealth of the vast interior was started on its way to eastern America and Europe. Michilimackinac was the heart of the northwest trade enterprise, a conduit for valuable furs that were sent down to Fort Detroit.

McEwan had suggested to Dusten that they paddle only by night, but the Frenchman had scoffed at the sergeant's idea and made light of what the Frenchman hinted was a touch of timidity about the young Scotsman. Inexperienced in the ways of Indians, McEwan permitted his pride to overrule his own good common sense. He was correct to want to travel only at night

in these uncertain times, but he did not want Dusten to think
him a coward.

"C'est ne pas grand-chose," the Frenchman had said at the
mention of a possible uprising—nothing to worry about. Perhaps not, McEwan thought. Then, perhaps it was.

They pressed on up to sandy, shallow Lake Saint Clair, and
then they paused as night drew close and it was time to camp.
McEwan was relieved to be ashore and out of sight. There were
a good number of Indians traveling on the water, and none cast
him a friendly eye when they saw his bright scarlet coat. That
set McEwan to wondering whether he ought to borrow one of
Dusten's greasy hunting shirts as a disguise, just in case hostiles
approached them. But he discarded that idea, too, for again it
would have given the cold Dusten something to chuckle at.
And the man had a way of chuckling softly, a chuckle that was
scornfully derisive, although it was full of humor and made it
difficult for the object of derision to stir up a good, unfettered
anger.

They camped that night along the pine-scrub shore of western Lake Saint Clair, a few hours north of the mouth of the
Detroit River, and an eternity away from the safety of British
arms.

The bleeding at Owen Sutherland's side had stopped, and Lela
was binding clean muslin strips about his torso as Tamano and
Molo paddled the canoe toward the Ottawa camp north of
Valenya. Digging a grave for Mayla had burst open the fes-
tering cuts behind his ribs, but Sutherland had wielded the
spade with a fury that left no room for pain. Pain and sadness
had been pressed back behind anger and obsession. The loss
of Mayla was buried for the moment, buried with every shov-
elful of earth he cast into her grave.

Now he sought André Breton, and he expected to find him
at Pontiac's camp. Young braves had come to Valenya late in
the afternoon to tell Molo the attack had not been carried off
against Detroit. Sutherland thought Breton would come back
to Pontiac that night.

Sutherland's canoe slid against the shore. He knew that his
burial of Mayla was not in the traditional manner of the Ottawa,
who put their dead on standing racks high above the ground
on poles. But Mayla had become a Christian in her years with
him, and he could not bring himself to give her an Ottawa
funeral. He was not that much an Indian.

The sun was almost down behind him as he walked up the beach with Tamano, Lela, and Molo with his two cousins coming behind. They were all somber, but none of them matched the terrible anguish and fury that was on the faces of the hundreds of Indian braves who slouched and sat about their lodges in the Ottawa camp. The failure of the surprise had filled them with poisoned spite. Sutherland walked toward Pontiac's lodge, ignoring hateful looks.

Molo went to tell his family about Mayla. He would say that Sutherland suggested they go to the grave to mourn, since there would not be an Ottawa funeral. The body should be left where it was buried behind the house, in the western shadow of the singing stones, marked with rocks and a temporary cross Sutherland swore would be replaced by a proper granite marker that would endure forever. Granite was the Scottish in him, for his city of Aberdeen on the eastern coast of Scotland was built almost all of granite. His heart still lay in splinters—some of it in the old country, and most of it in the shadow of the singing stones at Valenya, with the woman who taught him what it meant to love.

Sutherland was walking toward Pontiac's lodge when Tamano came to his side.

"Are you certain, my brother," Tamano asked in a low voice, "that you wish to see Pontiac at this time, when he will be troubled by his failure and will be angry?"

"I must," Sutherland said without looking at the Chippewa. "I want Pontiac's permission to go after Breton, whether that swine is here or in Detroit. If he won't accept my word that I want nothing more than to get Breton and that I'll not warn the British about anything else I might learn, then I'll go anyway."

"He might not let you leave yet," Tamano said.

"He'll have to kill me, then."

They walked a little way farther, and the lodge of Pontiac came into sight.

Tamano said in a whisper, "He might do that, Donoway."

The thought came into Sutherland's chilled and darkened mind that he would then take his revenge on Pontiac instead of Breton. It was Pontiac who brought about the uprising that Mayla had given her life to prevent. Although Sutherland sympathized with the plight of the Indian, his heart held no mercy for any man just then. Pontiac must allow him to go after Breton. Or he would kill Pontiac.

He arrived at Pontiac's lodge with no interference from the dark-eyed braves who glowered at him as he walked past. At the dwelling Sutherland spoke to subchiefs who sat sullenly outside. He wished to talk to Pontiac briefly, he told them. But the chiefs quickly said Sutherland could not meet with Pontiac. Before Sutherland could insist, Pontiac's drawn and lined visage appeared from under the flap of the lodge entrance. He beckoned.

Sutherland went in, and they sat around a small fire, just the two of them. In icy terms Sutherland told Pontiac about Mayla's death. Then he said he suspected it was Breton. He would kill Breton, he said plainly, no matter if he were an ally of Pontiac.

As the somber-faced chief sat unmoving for an hour, Sutherland remained silent, although he was thinking of Breton. Not of Mayla, not of the uprising, but of Breton.

At last, Pontiac spoke: "Breton," he said, "is not here. He is at Detroit." Pontiac was silent again, and Sutherland waited for him to say more. Finally the chief went on.

"There has been much unhappiness among my people this day. And now the fairest woman of her clan has been slain. Revenge is your duty, Donoway, and I know that I should kill you to prevent you from carrying it out, but I will not stop you.

"Today there is no more need for secrecy. The English know we mean to destroy them, and they are ready for our attack. But ten Englishmen have paid with their lives already, and not one drop of our blood has been spilled. That is a good omen, Donoway. The war has begun in earnest."

Sutherland had not told Pontiac that Mayla was the one who warned the fort. If he knew, Pontiac would never allow him to leave. Her death would have been warranted, and revenge against Breton would have been an attack on the Indians. Perhaps Breton did not know Mayla had given the Indian plot away. If he had known, he need only have told Pontiac, and her life would have been forfeit immediately.

"But I tell you now, Donoway, and you are warned. If you are found with the English when we take the fort, you shall be killed with them. And this time, Pontiac shall not spare you from death, whether by the arrow of an Ottawa or by the ritual of torture by flames. You shall die, Donoway, if you join the English."

Sutherland waited an appropriate ten minutes before answering Pontiac. But before he spoke, a recurrence of the

nausea of the past days swept over him. With difficulty he
ignored it.

"I do not go to join the English, Pontiac. I go to kill Breton.
Then I shall be departing from this country. I shall go north
and begin again. And, my chief, this war in which you engage
will result in many of our people being driven from this land,
I tell you—"

"Enough!" Pontiac's glare was dangerous. "You talk like
an Englishman! We have already heard your words, and they
were not accepted. I wish to hear no more. Go now, and have
your revenge. And be warned that you shall die if we catch
you with the English. Go. Pontiac has spoken."

Sutherland got up to leave. Dizziness swayed him.

"Donoway," Pontiac said quietly. Sutherland turned and
looked down at the chief, who was gazing at the fire before
him. "See to it that your blood is not spilled by my young men,
Donoway. And I pray that we shall meet again in happier times.
You have been a good trader, my son. Perhaps you shall be
one again, and in times of peace."

Sutherland went out among the babbling crowds of restless
warriors, many of whom were drinking rum in bitterness, while
others were kicking stray dogs and reviling their women. That
night was far different from the eager, glory-hungry celebration
of the morning when the warriors had painted themselves
bravely for a war that had not yet come to be. Like bile within
them, the hatred and savagery among these Indians was in need
of venting, and until that happened, they would be a seething
mass of unfulfilled passion—the passion of bloodlust.

At the canoe on the shore, Tamano stood with Lela. She
begged to go with them, but it was not possible. The danger
was uncertain, but trouble with the *voyageurs* as well as with
Sin-gat's Delawares could erupt when they went after Breton.
That was no place for Lela. She did not agree, but Tamano
spoke roughly, then gently, and she accepted his will. He
touched her face, then he and Sutherland were shooting the
canoe into the river, where darkness had already overtaken the
day.

They paddled toward the fort, and Sutherland felt the sickness come on him again. He had kept it off all that day, but
now, kneeling in the canoe, it took hold once more. He felt
the fever rising, and he fought it back. It must wait until he
had met Breton for the last time. Complete darkness came
about them, and the stars twinkled sharp in the blue-black of

the sky. But as they paddled, Sutherland, who was in the bow of the small canoe, felt the weakness begin to flood his vision. His ears rang. He paddled on but without real power.

Indeed, this next encounter with André Breton would be the last—for one or the other. Dizziness swept him again, but he paddled steadily. There was no bright confidence within Owen Sutherland now, as there had been before their first fight. He knew he was weakened.

The nausea came and went and came on again, and in a sort of haze he saw Mayla staring at him. He looked at her, but she seemed not to see him. He whispered her name, and she laughed at him, merry and teasing. Her dark eyes sought his, and they went searching, probing his very soul, as only her eyes could. Then she laughed again, the laugh of happy love. He tried to shout, but she laughed again and turned and ran, legs gliding, hair floating. She looked round over her shoulder and called his name. Laughing and beckoning, she ran down the beach, where sunshine gleamed on the sand. She splashed through the water. Mayla! He followed. But he could not! He ran, but his legs were leaden. He called her, but she did not hear him. It was dusk, and he was drifting out into the lake. Mayla stood on the beach, drawing a blanket about her shoulders. It was chill. He was drifting. She was hard to see. The sunset glinted color in bright, cold splashes. He was drifting, drifting. Tamano was telling him to paddle. He must go! Must go. Mayla, there on the beach, lifted her head. Or did she? She pulled the blanket closer. The canoe was far from shore. She waved! She saw him now, and he her. Hard to see, so hard to see. Softly she called him. Again, more softly. The canoe was drifting, drifting, drifting . . . Mayla. She was drifting. She called him . . .

"Donoway."

He heard his name.

"Donoway." It was Tamano's voice. Sutherland looked up at blurred darkness. Tamano's shadow loomed over him. Stars glittering, swinging, floating, drifting. Heat and cold. Mayla's face once more. Tamano's voice.

"Donoway!"

Sutherland felt icy sweat about his face and neck. He dragged himself back, back from the strange weakness of a world that numbed his senses. He ached for Mayla. He longed to touch her, to hold her. Then he was awake. He was in the canoe, and Tamano was over him, calling his name. He struggled to sit up, and the canoe rocked. He shook his head clear.

His side throbbed. It burned as though a foul lump of devil's brew clung to his ribs, reaching, clawing for his heart. Tamano called him.

"Yes . . . yes," he answered helplessly, and the sickness filled his being with burning. Slowly he came back. His head felt disconnected from his shoulders. Slowly it regained sensation. He looked over the swimming river, and the lights of Fort Detroit's sentry towers gleamed a warm yellow three hundred yards ahead.

"I'm all right," Sutherland mumbled. "I'll be all right. Let's just get over to the fort. This sickness will pass. It'll pass."

Tamano knew his friend well enough to resign himself to bringing in the canoe past the two ships, the *Huron* and the *Michigan*, that lay anchored in the clear darkness of the river. Sutherland had made up his mind to die, if need be, in facing Breton.

Tamano paddled past the wave-lapped *Huron*, which creaked and fluttered reefed canvas in the night breeze. He put into shore, lurching the canoe up, leaping into the shallow water and shoving it onto the sand. In the bow Sutherland sat, his head down, and he snapped it up as the canoe was grounded.

"Donoway," Tamano said gravely as he helped Sutherland from the canoe. "You cannot fight Breton now."

"I'll be all right," Sutherland panted, and he nearly stumbled as he pulled his rifle and gear from the canoe.

They went up through knee-high buffalo grass toward the fort's water gate. Tamano let Sutherland lean against him as they went up the slope. When they stood beneath the fort's stockade, Sutherland slumped to the ground. The Chippewa called up to the surprised sentry above, who chattered nervously for the corporal of the guard. In a few minutes the unconscious Sutherland, carried by a stoic Tamano, was being brought into Fort Detroit, delirious and dreaming about Mayla, whose face looked right at him all the while. But why did she not speak? Why did she not reply when he called her name?

Ella leaned over the fever-wracked Sutherland and laid another cold compress on his forehead. She wiped the sweat from his lips and neck and swabbed his heaving chest with cold water. The door behind her opened, and into the small, candle-lit room at the top of Gladwin's house came Jeremy with a tin bowl of fresh water. He stood beside her and looked down at the helpless figure of a man he had never imagined could be helpless.

"Will he get better, Ma?" the boy asked, eyes wide.

"Soon, darling," Ella said and wiped her own weary face. "He'll be fine soon. Now, you go off to bed, and I'll be in to see you in a few minutes. It's very late. Good night."

"But, Ma—"

"To bed." She summoned her strength to scuttle the boy out of the room, and then she closed the door and leaned wearily against it. It was after midnight. She hadn't noticed time passing until a few minutes ago when the German clock downstairs tolled twelve. She had been bathing Sutherland for more than three hours, ever since Henry had him carried up to the spare room.

Someone pushed the door. She turned, expecting Jeremy, but it was her brother. Gladwin's face bore the shadows and lines of lack of sleep. Ella smiled weakly at him and then knelt at Sutherland's bedside again. The dimly flickering candlelight gave Sutherland's face an even more scarlet cast.

"Still not better?" Gladwin muttered and stood at his sister's shoulder. "That wound's poisoned at his side. Wonder if the Indians threw him out like they did the other traders. Pity Tamano didn't stay around after he brought him. I've got men searching the post for that Indian, but he hasn't been brought in yet."

Ella pulled the bandages gently back from the ten-inch wound that ran in a lateral bluish line from his side under the armpit up to his shoulder blade. She swabbed and washed the cut, then washed out the bandage in the bowl of water Jeremy had brought. As she wrapped the bandage around Sutherland's hot, writhing body, Gladwin removed his black tricorn and sighed.

"You should get some sleep, sister," he said. "I can send up an orderly, or perhaps Mrs. Morely—"

"No." Ella was sharper than she meant to be. "I mean, I can do it, Henry. I've gone this long. I owe him my life and Jeremy's life. This is one small way to repay him. I want to." Her voice trailed off as she looked at Sutherland. "I want to. I only hope I can help him. Lord, let me be of some help to him."

"All right, sister. Damn! I can't take any sleep myself because of these alarms, and after today I don't know if Pontiac will really try to hit us or not. I hope he does nothing more than he's done so far, and I hope he realizes that we're ready for him . . ."

A voice called from downstairs, and Gladwin opened the door. He went into the darkened hall, listened a moment as Captain Campbell said something from below, then came back to Ella.

"Campbell says they've found Tamano over at Morely's trading house. I'm going to talk with him and find out what's happened to Owen. Perhaps Tamano knows something about this dratted trouble. Send the orderly for me if Sutherland awakes; he's asleep downstairs on the divan."

Then he was gone, clumping down the stairs, and Ella knew Jeremy must still be wide awake with all the excitement. She went to her son, bade him good night, then hurried back to her patient.

She sat on the floor, her head on her arm, resting on the bed. She dozed from time to time, but when Sutherland began to rant, she was startled awake. He sat up, body rigid, eyes wide, calling something Ella could not understand. She tried to force him down, but he was too strong.

His movement ruptured the wound at his side, and green pus mixed with blood gushed through the bandages and over her apron and the bedclothes. She snatched a towel and soaked up the mess, then carefully removed the bandages and pressed Sutherland down, talking softly, answering "Yes, yes, it's all right, yes," as he called a name and asked someone to speak to him, to come back to him. She pressed the cloth against the wound to force the infection out, all the time talking softly to him.

"It's all right, yes. All right. Lie down. Sleep."

Sutherland's glazed eyes and dry mouth were frozen open. From time to time he mumbled, asking her a question, but she could not make out its meaning. She answered as gently as she could, "Yes, yes. It's all right. Yes. Yes. Lie down. You must rest now." And he seemed to hear her. He seemed to understand. His eyes were still glazed, but now that the pus and blood had burst from the wound, he seemed somehow better. He lay more restful, and then, soon, he slept. His breathing eased, and his face became less feverish.

Ella watched, waited. At last he slept soundly.

• • •

Ella jerked awake, tingling. She was lying on the floor, a blanket beneath her, another on top, and sunlight was warm through the windows, spilling over her as though last night had been only a dream, a nightmare. She sat up.

It was not a nightmare. Sutherland lay in fresh sheets. He was asleep; his face was calm, and his chest moved slowly up and down. She knelt at his side. She let her breath out in relief and sat limply back down on the floor.

Heavy steps came up the stairs, and a woman was humming. The door opened, and the round, bright face of Lettie Morely poked in. She looked at Sutherland and then at the bedraggled Ella, who, trying to smile but failing, said, "The fever's broken. I think he's out of danger."

"I know, love." Lettie chuckled, went on with her humming, and came into the room. Her billowing linsey skirt swam in the small chamber. She put a hand on Sutherland's face and listened to his breathing. "I know, love, for I come in to see thee just before dawn at the major's request."

Ella looked down at the blankets crumpled about her, looked back up at Lettie, and began to ask, "Did you . . . ?"

"Aye, love," Lettie said with a cheerful smile. "I come in an' found thee asleep over Owen's chest, yonder."

Ella's hand went to her open mouth.

Lettie chuckled. "An' a pretty pitcher it was, too. Yes. Right pretty, I'll say."

Lettie puttered with Sutherland's blanket, still chuckling, as Ella scolded Lettie good-naturedly for her teasing, and Lettie laughed as she made to leave the room.

Then Sutherland's voice, deep but weak, said, "Ladies, can't I get some sleep around here?"

They both turned to see Sutherland's grinning face looking up at them. The paleness was there, but the fire was once more in his eyes, the fire that Ella had always liked to see in them. Ella held back, but Lettie bundled toward the wounded man.

"Well, well, Owen, it's about time thee was openin' them brown Scotch eyes o' thine so this young lady can get her own closed." Lettie helped Sutherland struggle to a sitting position, and she puffed a pillow behind his neck. All the while, she chattered on, "This lass been up all the night with thee, she has. Yes. She brought thee through that nasty fever. How did thee come by that ugly wound, anyhow? Been fightin' Indians? It's better now, yes. Thanks to Mistress Bently here."

While Lettie busied herself with Sutherland's bed, Ella was

looking down at her feet. Sutherland's eyes were on her. She looked up, and he gave a smile that did something within her, and she smiled back.

"My deepest gratitude, Mistress Bently," he said, and already his voice seemed stronger.

Lettie was suspended between them, looking from one to the other and back again. She brought her hands together and said, "I'll just fetch a pot o' tea and some bread with cheese for all of us. I'll leave thee to tell each other how thee spent the night together in the same bedroom!" She giggled and was halfway out the door when she paused and asked Ella to join her in private for a moment. Ella came out, and Lettie closed the door.

Exhausted and a little disturbed by Sutherland's steady gaze, Ella was glad to find herself in the coolness of the hallway above the stairs. Lettie drew her close and whispered, "Had to tell thee, mistress. Don't mention Owen's Indian woman. She's dead."

Ella lost her breath, and her heart stopped.

"Aye, she be dead, pore darlin'. Pore darlin' that lass were. Now, don't be a-talkin' about that. He'll be thinkin' about it, so try an' cheer him up."

"But . . ." Ella could think of nothing to say. "How do you—"

"Owen's Injun friend what brought him here come to my man last night an' told him. Said someone deaded her in her own cabin! Dreadful! Dreadful, it be. Yes. Now, thee be cheerin' that lad up while I gets some tea and whatnot. Go on! Get in there now."

Lettie went thumping down the stairs. Ella stood numbly by the closed door of Sutherland's room. Now she knew whose name he had been calling in his delirium. She could not go in. She paused, then began to breathe again. Jeremy's feet padded on the floor of his room. Then the sleepy-faced boy was next to her, standing in a nightgown that trailed over the rough boards. He yawned, then asked about Sutherland.

"He's all right now."

Before she could say more, Jeremy was whooping and barged into the room. He ran to Sutherland's side as Ella hurried in behind and apologized to her patient, who smiled at the admiring boy standing at the side of his bed.

"I'm sure glad you're better and not going to die, Mr.

Sutherland," Jeremy eagerly tossed out.

"You're glad? Well, so am I, laddie." Sutherland's grin drifted from his face as his eyes clouded over. "I'm glad, too, because I have some business to take care of."

He tried to swing his legs from the bed, but he slumped back against the pillow and sweat came to his face. Ella was at his side immediately, and even before she knew what she was doing, her hands were on a damp cloth and wiping his flushed, dazed face. He turned to look at her. She pulled her hand away, and then she smiled.

"You can't get up yet, Mr. Sutherland," she said. "Business or no."

His face was hard and angry now. "Does anyone else know I'm here? I mean other than the Morelys and Henry?"

Ella was startled by the darkness that had rushed into Sutherland's eyes. He gripped her wrist and held it tightly.

"Anyone?" he growled, and he seemed terrible, dangerous. She pulled her arm away and stood up.

"Mr. Sutherland—" She was about to scold, but then she remembered what Lettie had told her about Mayla being dead, and she realized what was in his eyes. At that same moment Sutherland's face fell and he rubbed his forehead.

"I'm sorry, mistress, I'm sorry." He looked up at her, and the fire was replaced with unfathomable sadness. Ella fell to her knees beside him. Jeremy, at her shoulder, said nothing.

"Forgive me, mistress," Sutherland said in what was little more than a whisper. "I—I just don't want anyone to know I'm here." He looked up at her, his eyes appealing. "Would you send for Henry? I must talk to him immediately."

She nodded and rose to leave. Lettie was at the door with a tray and a set of cups and steaming teapot on it. Ella was past her before Lettie could protest. She turned her dismay on Sutherland, who was lying back, looking straight up at the dark hewn timbers of the roof supports.

"Well, I say!" Lettie sputtered, setting the tray down on a chair next to the bed. "Here comes a cozy cup of English tea that thee won't find nowheres else in this wilderness, and thee goes and says somethin' that sends off thy company in a rush. Owen, my man's right! Sometimes thee has an awful hard Scotch head on thy shoulders, thee does."

Sutherland almost smiled. He turned to Lettie.

"Lass, hold my head up and pour some of that strong brew

down me, eh? And if it runs right out again through this hole in my ribs, make another pot and keep on bringing it until that muddy English tea stops up the leak."

Standing in the corner of the room, young Jeremy watched as Sutherland finished two cups of tea and lay back with a deep release of breath and a low groan. Lettie was gone. Sutherland did not know the boy had stayed when his mother left.

"Mr. Sutherland . . ."

Sutherland jumped in surprise, winced, and slowly shook his head, giving a small smile, thinking he certainly was out of sorts to be frightened by a boy. He looked at Jeremy, who walked toward the bed.

"Mr. Sutherland, did an Indian try to kill you?"

Sutherland thought a moment, then he raised his eyes to Jeremy standing at hand. "No, laddie. Not an Indian. If it was an Indian, he'd not have left me alive."

"Then, who?"

"Not time to ask that, lad. I've got some talking to do with your uncle. Maybe later you'll find out about this little mess I've got around myself."

Jeremy looked at the thick bandages about Sutherland's body. It must ache terribly, he thought. Being a soldier must mean suffering a lot of pain. He would learn how to accept pain like Owen Sutherland. One day he would be just as brave.

"Thinking hard, laddie?"

"What? Oh, yes. I was just thinking that your wound must— must hurt a lot. Does it?"

"A bit. But when you've got it, there's no use thinking about it, is there? No, the idea is not to get one to begin with, eh? Better learn how not to get wounded than how to stand up to pain."

"How did you know . . . ? I mean, that's what I was thinking—how to stand up to pain when you're a soldier. How did you know that's what I was thinking?"

Sutherland shifted himself and forced back a grunt of soreness. "I didn't, laddie. But I was thinking to myself how I should have learned long ago how not to get wounded." He smiled again, and the boy did, too. "That's the hardest part of being a good soldier, though. Mostly you learn how to live with wounds, not how to keep them from happening."

Jeremy looked down at the bandage showing a slight stain of blood. Sutherland reached carefully for the pot of tea standing on the chair nearby. Quickly Jeremy moved for it and poured a cup for his friend. They both smiled again. Jeremy wondered if he ever would be as much a man as Owen Sutherland. He sure would try hard to be.

When Gladwin came in, dressed in his scarlet uniform, young Jeremy left them alone and closed the door behind him. Gladwin moved away the cold tea and dried bloodied cloth strips from the chair next to the bed and sat down with the back of the chair before him.

"You look a damned sight better than you did last night," Gladwin said. "How'd you get that scratch? Pontiac's bucks?"

Sutherland sat up a little. "Not Pontiac's bucks. André Breton."

Gladwin scratched the back of his head under his white wig and nodded. "Yes, I suspected Breton was with the Indians in this affair. Your friend Tamano told me Breton was not to be trusted. But he didn't stay long enough to say Breton had given you that."

"Didn't stay?"

"No. He went just after Breton did—"

"Breton's gone?" Sutherland felt the wound pull as he forced himself up.

Gladwin nodded. "Sorry, Owen. Breton left in the night, soon after you came into the fort. I suppose he guessed that you would tell me about him. Traitorous swine that."

"How much did Tamano tell you?"

Gladwin's eyes met Sutherland's and held them. Then he said, "Everything about Mayla. I'm sorry, Owen."

Sutherland leaned his head back, feeling the soreness of his wounds. Gladwin spoke again.

"Do you have any idea who did it?"

Sutherland turned his head a little to Gladwin. "Didn't Tamano tell you that?"

Gladwin shook his head. Sutherland said, "Breton did it. And I came here to find him. Now he's gone. Tamano has gone after him, I'm sure. He'll find the bastard, and then I'll go for him."

"Not in this condition, you won't," Gladwin said. "You'll need some time to heal before you face that bear."

Sutherland looked at Gladwin. "Have you got all your people in the fort yet? The attack will be any time now."

Gladwin nodded slowly and sighed as his words came out. "We've got in who'll come in. But there are a few stubborn ones like the Fishers, who are minding our cattle out on Hog

Island. And there's Mrs. Trumbull with her two little boys; they won't come in either. She doesn't believe there's danger. There are a few traders still to be accounted for, and of course, Sir Robert's party up on Saint Clair."

Sutherland's face was drawn and his mouth twisted. "Better get them in, Henry. They're finished if you don't. Pontiac is serious. He says he's already done some killing."

Gladwin rose to leave. "Tamano said he'll be back for you as soon as he knows where they went. But I don't know—or I didn't know—what he meant by 'they.' I presume he means Breton and his cronies." Sutherland nodded. "You get well, and as soon as Tamano comes in, I'll send him to you. If there's anything I can do to help you bring in Breton, I'll do it. Get some rest, man. You'll need it if you're going after him."

All that day, May 8, a dejected and miserable Owen Sutherland lay abed in the small garret in Gladwin's house. Lettie Morely came to him from time to time, and Gladwin came up to look in and say Captain Campbell had parlayed outside the fort with Pontiac and a few of his chiefs. The Indians, said Gladwin, were playing their wild game called *baggataway*, or *la crosse*, as the Frenchmen called it. They were in a broad field near the fort, hundreds of them, painted and whooping, and Sutherland could hear them gabbling like faraway flocks of game birds.

Pontiac had again asked for admittance to the fort, Gladwin said, but he had been refused. Then the major left, and Sutherland slept.

It was late in the afternoon when Gladwin returned to the darkening room. The door opened, and Sutherland saw before him a shocked man whose face betrayed awful pain.

"Sir Robert has been killed!"

Sutherland closed his eyes.

"His whole party was taken three days ago on Saint Clair," Gladwin weakly went on. "A trader reported."

The room was quiet. In the distance the whooping rose as though in climax, as though all the hundreds of Indians collected on the fields were cheering simultaneously. Gladwin went to the small window and looked out to the northwest where the Indians were gathering in a great crowd and moving off toward their camp upriver. Silence returned.

"It's over," Gladwin said softly, and the fading sunlight

melted bright and warm on the shoulders of his red tunic, sparkling golden from his epaulets.

"No," Sutherland said and opened his eyes. "Nothing's over. It's just begun."

That night extra soldiers stood guard on the fort's ramparts. Already worn from a day spent strengthening the fortifications and preparing buckets and barrels of water to douse fire arrows, the men still labored, throwing up earthworks against the inside of the stockade walls to prevent fires. Those not working saw to their weapons, made bullets, and cleaned muskets.

Most of the English living outside the fort came in except, as Gladwin had said, the Fisher family, who did not want to leave the livestock on Hog Island. And the stubborn widow Turnbull swore she would stay and not be driven away from her dead husband's hard-won farm by a pack of dirty heathen Indians.

As the dim dawn light filtered into the garret, Sutherland awoke when Ella Bently came softly into his room.

"How are you, Mr. Sutherland?" she asked, standing in shadows that were silver with the early light.

"I'm fine, thank you, Mistress Bently," he said and sat up, easing himself forward. Ella pushed extra pillows behind him. "I'm glad you've come in, though, for I fear I must trouble you to change this bandage, ma'am. It's dried and is sticking to the wound."

She tenderly unbound his ribs and revealed the gash. The mottled bluishness was gone. It was turning a healthy pink now.

"It looks better," Ella said as she bathed him gently. "In a few days you'll be on your feet."

He did not look at her, but he drew a deep breath and said, "Not in a few days, ma'am. Today, if I'm right in guessing. Tamano will be back at the post tonight and will bring me some news that I'm wanting."

"You mean about Breton?" The words escaped her without thought. But when they were said, even before his face turned to search hers, Ella knew she had touched Sutherland. She soaked the bandage in the tin bowl on the chair. "Yes, Mr. Sutherland, I have heard why you want Breton. I—I am deeply sorry about your loss." She looked at him.

He stared at the end of the bed.

Ella tightened the clean bandage and put her hand under his back as he lay down against the pillows. She saw his linsey hunting shirt, bloody and dirty with old sweat, at the foot of the bed; she snatched it up and smiled in forced cheerfulness.

"This is filthy, sir. I'll just take it and—"

Something metallic tinkled on the floor. In the grayish light Ella found a silver pendant at her feet. She quickly picked it up and it dangled, gleaming before her.

"Why, this is lovely, Mr.—"

"Give me that!" Sutherland snatched it from her, gasping with pain at the effort.

She stepped back in surprise. Sutherland tucked the pendant under his blankets. He brooded, and she turned to leave.

"Mistress." His voice was hard. "Mistress, I'm sorry." His voice went kinder. "Forgive my rudeness, mistress." She looked at him and wondered why she felt so much like tears. "It's just that this—this token means very much to me, and I never want to part with it. I'm sorry."

"Not at all," she said, her eyes wet. She was halfway out the door when she turned. "I also have something very dear to me—something that reminds me of a loved one. I understand."

Then she was gone, and the door was closed.

Sutherland lay back and brought out the pendant; it lingered in the palm of his hand. Then he thought of Jeremy Bently. Yes, Ella did, indeed, have a precious memory of her past. He slid down and turned to the wall, but he could not sleep.

Ella did not know just why she was struggling with her emotions or why tears were coming. After putting Sutherland's shirt in a tub to soak, she walked quickly across the parade ground, heading for the water gate and out to the river. She was trembling a little, perhaps from weariness, perhaps from the strain of the past hours. She wiped her nose and sniffed.

"Mistress! Mistress Bently!"

She turned to see Alex Duvall striding rapidly toward her. She felt embarrassed then, wishing no one would see her like this. She quickly pushed back her straggling hair and averted her face to rub away tears.

"Mistress, I say, mistress, you seem troubled," Duvall said and looked closely at her.

She tried to smile but sniffed without meaning to, and Duvall stepped back, amazed. "Mistress, what has happened to you? You're covered in blood!"

Indeed, her apron was smeared with Owen Sutherland's blood, and so were her hands soiled from Sutherland's shirt and bandages. For a helpless moment Ella suspected there might also be blood on her face, where she had wiped the tears.

She told Duvall about Sutherland being wounded and abed in her brother's house. Although she knew Sutherland wanted as few people as possible to know he was there, she could not avoid telling the major. But when she saw Duvall's face darken and his mouth grow tight when he heard about Sutherland, she wished she had said nothing.

"This is no time to let an Indian-lover in the fort," Duvall muttered under his breath. "Who knows what he'll tell his friends about our defenses—"

Duvall cut himself short when he saw the intensity in Ella's eyes. She was confused at this, now even more deeply troubled.

"I'm sorry, mistress," he said gently, trying to relieve her misery. "Forgive my indiscretion, please. I see you've been under great strain, and I wish not to increase it. Won't you permit me to accompany you home? You really ought to—to get some rest and, if you'll permit me to say it, change into some fresh clothes."

Duvall was genuinely concerned for her well-being, she knew. With one last shaking sob she managed to smile at him. She began to take his arm when he offered it, but then drew back.

"The—the blood," she said, a little flustered. "I don't want to—"

"Come come," he said with a warm smile. "A soldier's tunic is none the worse for a little blood. It's said that scarlet isn't truly scarlet if it's never been stained with blood!"

She took his arm but tried to look closely at him to determine just how lightly he meant that comment. Duvall looked back at her and sensed what she was thinking.

"Not too much blood, naturally." He smiled again and patted her hand. Then whispering he said, "And it's best if it isn't one's own blood, of course."

She knew he meant well, and she appreciated his attempts to cheer her up. Alex Duvall, for all his bluster and stiff formality, was not so very self-centered after one got to know him.

· · ·

Word from Gladwin later that afternoon said Tamano would come for Sutherland that night. A French trader had brought the message. Perhaps Tamano knew of Breton's whereabouts. The dizziness had left Sutherland, and he had eaten well that day. At noon Lettie had brought boiled partridge and fried onions. Sutherland smoked his pipe, thinking. He would be patient until he found Breton. He watched the wreaths of gray drift up to the ceiling and curl into corners.

Suddenly muskets crackled in the distance, and men were shouting in the fort below. Sutherland struggled to his feet and went to the window. Across the fields he saw crowds of Indian braves running toward the fort. Men were up on the ramparts. Indian gunfire scattered from the empty cabins and the long grass. Some Indians were shooting at the fort from the cover of houses belonging to the French; others were hiding in orchards and behind fencerows. The shots spattered against the ramparts and thudded into the wooden stockade. Lead thunked near Sutherland's window, and he stepped back.

Soldiers began to fire, but there were few targets. On the tower near the north wall someone snatched the canvas from the fort's cannon. Soon the rattle of musketry was punctuated by the dull thud and clap of cannon hurling shot at groups of scurrying Indians. It was not much of a battle yet, but thick smoke already hung heavily about the fort. A haunting thrill surged through Sutherland—a thrill he had not expected to remember. His eyes were alight with the sense of battle.

Someone came up the stairs while Sutherland was painfully drawing on his clean hunting shirt. It was Ella. She stopped when she saw him, and her eyes revealed excitement and fear. Neither spoke, but she helped him ease his stiff left arm into the sleeve of his shirt. She stood back just as Gladwin pushed into the room.

The major shook his head and said, "You can't leave now."

"I'm going tonight. I'll find Tamano if he doesn't come here first now the fight has begun."

"Owen," Gladwin stood straight. "Owen, I'd be proud to employ you as our scout and interpreter."

"No," Sutherland said curtly. Then he buttoned the last button, and his gaze came level with the major's. "I'm grateful for what you've done for me, Henry, Mistress Bently. And I'm honored by your offer, Henry." He stood as dignified as the major, and Ella saw the image of an officer, for he had not lost that bearing. "But I am no longer a soldier, and I've no intention of becoming one again. I've no quarrel with these Indians. My future depends on getting along with them, not fighting them. I'll do what I can to return peace to this country—that I promise you, Henry—but don't ask me to take up arms against them. I won't."

They stood a moment, not talking, while the musketry went on like a hundred fires of wet wood spitting and barking. Now and again the cannon went off, and the soldiers gave out with a loud hurrah.

"And you know, Henry," Sutherland said, his eyes turning cold as he went to the corner for his rifle, "I've got my own mission to complete before anything else."

Gladwin said nothing. Sutherland buckled on his sword and moved to the door. Ella opened it.

"Thank you both. I shall return this favor one day. In the meantime I'll be with trader Morely until Tamano comes tonight. If there's anything I can do to help make peace again, I'll do it. Good-bye."

Sutherland shook hands with Gladwin and briefly held Ella's, which were chilled. Then he was gone.

He went directly to the trader's warehouse, where Morely invited him in for a drink.

"So thee be a-leavin' us at a time like this, eh, Owen?" Garth Morely said, pouring each of them a pewter mug of Jamaican rum as they stood in the dark trading warehouse. The keg was on the counter where Morely collected furs and weighed the flour that he traded to the Indians. In the distance, gunfire continued as soldiers and Indians took potshots at one another.

"Why don't thee pick thy side now an' stick to it, lad?" Morely said, handing a mug to Sutherland on the other side of the long counter. Sutherland took the rum, and they clinked. Morely muttered a "cheers," and they drank deeply.

"Thee well knows Lord Jeffrey Amherst'll be delighted when he hears about this risin'." Morely belched and said, "Pontiac's played right into the gentleman's hands, he has. Now Amherst has a right excuse to send soldiers and butcher them Injuns. That's what he's wanted ter do all along. An' thee be best off a-stayin' with thy own kind. This be no time to be fraternizin' with the enemy. No."

Morely licked rum from his lips and wiped his bearded face

with a hairy hand. Sutherland drank thoughtfully. The light was nearly gone from the trading house, and Morely looked across at Sutherland's shadowed form.

"Them that supports the Injuns in this bain't goin' ter have the love of General Amherst. Nor of this new bug-tit Duvall neither. No. Thee be best standin' with us until this be a-blowin' over, lad. Maybe thee can help when the time comes for punishin' 'em. Lord knows somebody'll have to keep Amherst from killin' 'em all. An' it don' do us traders no good if he do; thee can't trade with dead Injuns. No."

Sutherland drained his cup and put it on the counter. He pulled the newly filled knapsack toward himself and slung it painfully over his shoulder.

"Garth, I'm only after one thing, and that's André Breton, and I'll have him no matter what. I'm on nobody's side in this rising. If I have to go through Pontiac to get Breton, I'll do it. I hope I don't have to go through Henry Gladwin, because I'll do that, too."

They said nothing, and Sutherland began to move to the door. It was dark now but for the intermittent flash of a musket from the ramparts nearby.

"Well, lad," Morely said, and Sutherland turned to listen to his old friend, "it be thy life." Morely thought for a moment and then said, "But it seems that thee be a-wastin' thyself by havin' no patience. If thee waits until this is over, no Injuns'll be able to stop thee from gettin' at Breton."

"Aye," Sutherland said and opened the door. "But I want to get him before Jeffrey Amherst does."

It was dark by the time Tamano and Sutherland met at the sally port near the water gate. The sentry let them out into the night, then closed the door. The bar thudded down behind them as they slipped through the shadows to the water line and pushed off the canoe. Gunfire sporadically flickered here and there on the other three sides of the fort, and soldiers fired back from time to time. Upstream a cabin burned against the darkness. Tamano said it was the home of a widow named Turnbull. She and her two little boys had been scalped.

Tamano told Sutherland that Indians were searching everywhere for English to kill or take prisoner; traders were being set upon, and many of them murdered. The family of the soldier named Fisher guarding the fort's stock on Hog Island were either killed or taken prisoner. The three little girls were taken by Ottawa, their mother tortured to death before their eyes, and their father and two soldiers helping tend stock were killed on the spot.

Sutherland had nothing to say as he listened to Tamano's narrative of pillage and death. The French remained unharmed, since they had assured Pontiac of their loyalty to him. They had no other choice. They, too, would become victims if they dared oppose the uprising.

And Breton? He had gone north with some Chippewa and Delaware to meet with Sin-gat, who had already gone up toward Fort Michilimackinac at the straits between the western lakes and Lake Huron. They would stir up the Indians there and urge them to destroy the fort, garrison, and traders, Tamano said.

Sutherland felt the dull ache at his side. But he was stronger now. He felt purged, as though all his remorse for Mayla's death had been, for the moment, drained from him as the poison had drained from his wound. He could not paddle yet, for his wound was raw. In the stern of the canoe, Tamano paddled steadily and strongly, and the canoe slid upstream in the center of the river's channel, past blazing English cabins and past the low fires of Indian encampments northeast of the fort.

The sound of muskets crackling melted behind them as they headed eastward through the darkened curve of the river north of Pontiac's camp on their right. In the canoe was food for a month—pemmican (dried buffalo meat), cornmeal, rum, and dried peas—as well as plenty of bullets, some pigs of lead, and a small keg of black powder for trade if they needed to win some Indian friends. There were also trinkets, beads, mirrors, and several trade blankets. Flints and vermillion paint, some bolts of cloth, and two English trade muskets were also in the canoe. In time of need, those goods might be valuable, for they represented items of wealth to an Indian. Certainly many a hostile warrior would enjoy including Owen Sutherland's scalp in the taking of such plunder. But Tamano was well known among the northern Chippewa, and Sutherland was counting on him to prevent trouble while they pursued Breton—and now the Delaware Sin-gat. No doubt this time Sin-gat would be part of the bargain, for Breton would likely be taken in the company of the Delaware.

The night was cool, and from Lake Saint Clair a few miles north a fresh breeze blew downriver, cool and soothing on Sutherland's wounds.

chapter **11**

BESIEGED

Duncan McEwan lay wrapped in his soldier's gray woolen blanket, looking at the campfire, which had burned low. The river lapped near the canoe he and his guide had pulled ashore and concealed with branches just before darkness. McEwan was decided now: He would insist they travel only at night—no matter how the Frenchman Jean Dusten chuckled. And if that twerp did chuckle, McEwan would wipe off the laugh with the back of his hand.

It was too quiet. It seemed there should be some sounds other than the steady breathing of Dusten lying on the opposite side of the fire and the monotonous lapping of Lake Huron's water against the shore.

It occurred to McEwan that they ought not to have a fire at night. If there were hostiles about—if the fears of Henry Gladwin were founded on truth—then they ought to be traveling more carefully. But Dusten was the woodsman, not McEwan. Why hadn't the Frenchman suggested no fire?

Dusten snored softly. The guide was not restless, so perhaps McEwan was unreasonable in his edginess. Just the same, he would put out the fire. He was about to throw back his blanket when a twig snapped behind him. He froze.

He listened, holding his breath. Dusten's snoring had stopped. Even the man's breathing seemed to have stopped. McEwan saw the faint gleam of the Frenchman's eye reflecting firelight. McEwan listened, then he breathed out and pretended he was sleeping. He stirred as though simply changing position, and he faced the trees behind him. His hand slipped onto the cold steel of the musket lying at his side. Then he saw another eye gleam in the firelight. This eye was in the shadows of the woods. Under the blanket, he drew out his hatchet. Then Dusten spoke quietly.

"I wouldn't do anything that would get you killed just yet, Sergeant. Just sit up nice and easy and maybe you live to see tomorrow." There was a pause, then came Dusten's oily snicker. "And then maybe not."

McEwan sat up and tossed the blanket from his shoulders. The trees and bushes around him came to life, and in a moment the campsite was filled with Indians. In the glow of the fire the warriors looked like hell's own devils. Their faces black with the soot of death, they were smeared, every inch of them, with streaks of red and yellow paint. In each hand was a tomahawk or a musket. McEwan stood and raised an open hand in the sign of peace. The braves looked at him with contempt.

"That not help now, Sergeant," Dusten said and chuckled again. Then the Frenchman tossed sticks into the fire, and it flared into a blaze. Still sitting, Dusten exchanged a few words with the oldest Indian, who seemed to be the leader, then the warriors sat down in a ring around the fire. McEwan sought a place to sit in the ring, but there was no room, and none of the Indians made an opening for him. Then the warrior in charge grabbed McEwan's canvas knapsack and jerked it open. McEwan moved as though to protest, but Dusten caught his eye, and the Scotsman hesitated.

"What do they want?" he asked Dusten.

"Want, Sergeant? They got what they want." The Frenchman pulled out the unlit pipe and stuck it in his mouth. Then he said, "They got you."

Several days after Sutherland left Fort Detroit, Ella and Lettie Morely sat in the living room of Gladwin's house carding lamb's wool into little cylinders for spinning. Ella's mind was being numbed by the state of siege that had descended like a fog over the spirits of everyone at Detroit. Her thoughts returned steadily to the memory of Jeremy asking permission to spend the night at Mrs. Turnbull's with the young boys there. There were moments when Ella saw Jeremy lying with the boys on the floor of their cabin before the savages set it ablaze. Those were the moments when she had to put aside the wool and step onto the porch to talk to her son who was sitting in a rocking chair drawing on a smooth board with charcoal.

She and Lettie were silently carding when they heard the stamp of Henry Gladwin's boots coming up the wooden steps

outside. They looked up when Gladwin threw open the door
and crashed past them, swearing, "Damn! Damn! Damn those
lying swine! Damn them! Damn them, I say!"

Gladwin pulled out a bottle of brandy kept tucked away
behind some old military officer's books. Angrily, he poured
himself a tumblerful. All the while he was grumbling, muttering, and hissing. Normally, Gladwin restrained anger at the
worst of times, and before women he was reserved even in his
most annoyed moments. Ella went to him and touched his
shoulder as he gulped down the drink and poured another.

"Lying swine! I knew he shouldn't have gone! I knew it!
Lying dirty swine!"

He looked at his sister as though she were in his way. His
lip quivered and dripped with brandy. He downed another full
tumbler and swallowed hard.

"Pontiac promised safe conduct!" he said and looked, unseeing, at the bookcase. "Swore safe conduct for Campbell and
Lieutenant McDougall. The swine! They asked to parley! Now
they're both taken!"

Ella felt a rush of fear; she began to tremble and stepped
back from her brother, who turned to face her.

"Promised safe conduct, and now I get word that the captain
and McDougall are prisoners! Prisoners, by God! Lying
swine!"

Gladwin seemed to be buckling under the strain of five days
of constant effort. He had been awake all night nearly every
night since the uprising began. He swung out of the room and
stamped upstairs to his chamber, snapping and growling all the
way. He had the brandy bottle in his fist, but there was no
glass. His door slammed shut.

It took a week of hard traveling to reach Lake Huron, and by
then Sutherland's wound had healed well enough for him to
paddle the canoe.

They kept to the shoreline as they went, and they avoided
when they could the many parties of Indians moving downstream on the Saint Clair River or coming down the lakeshore
toward Detroit. The Indians they encountered were passionate
in their wish for death to the English. They whooped and cursed
the English as they passed Sutherland's canoe, but there were
no incidents, for he or Tamano often had acquaintances among
them.

At villages, they stopped and asked what they could about

Breton. They learned he was on his way with a large party of Delaware and Chippewa up to Michilimackinac. Most Indians were silent when asked what was planned for the fort, but Tamano found out that Michilimackinac was soon to be attacked. Breton and the Indians he was with had boasted they would lead in the destruction of the post.

Then one morning, when departing from a little Chippewa town, they got news that made Tamano flush. An English courier had been taken prisoner by a band of Chippewa, and he was being brought to their village, which was south of Michilimackinac. There he would be tortured if he was man enough to deserve such a fate. Tamano had learned back at Detroit that McEwan—to whom he owed his life—had been sent as courier to Michilimackinac. The brave who told Tamano about the captured courier had seen him when the Chippewa band passed through a day ago. His description matched McEwan . . . eyes blue like the sky, added the Indian's wife, who apparently had taken a closer look at McEwan than her man had. And when they said he was traveling with the *voyageur* known as Dusten, Tamano knew the prisoner was indeed McEwan.

Now Tamano had his own quest. He must do what he could to free McEwan, his blood brother. He must try to save him even if it meant surrendering his own life to do it.

After more than two weeks of journeying with very little food, Duncan McEwan was near starvation when he was thrown forward on a sandy beach at a village in the north of Lake Huron. He lay wearily on his face, unable even to spit the sand from his dry mouth. Someone was slashing the leather thongs that bound his hands behind his back. The legs of many Indians were around him. He heard the noise of chattering and shouting women and children. He lifted his head and looked forward, up from the beach to see scores of low, rough huts and lodges of bark and skins. There was a flood of Indians—women and children and some old men—shrieking and laughing and gathering around McEwan into a long double column that swayed like the sluggish tail of a sleeping dog.

McEwan was hauled up sharply and pushed forward again. He stumbled but kept his feet. The leader of the Indians was jabbering at him and gesturing at the two long lines of Indians. McEwan looked down the corridor of Indians and saw they were carrying sticks and switches and clubs. They were laughing and shouting at him. They waved their weapons and leaned forward to look at him.

Dusten stood nearby. McEwan looked at the Frenchman, who bit a wad from a plug of tobacco and nonchalantly slipped the tobacco into a shirt pocket. Then he said, "You got to run through that line there to the other end, Sergeant."

McEwan looked again at the hundreds of women and children who capered and shouted at him. Then he turned back to Dusten.

"If you don't run, Sergeant, your throat'll be slit right here. If you get through, you be a slave or a son of somebody." Dusten chewed thoughtfully. "But don't think about that, Sergeant. Not many get through." He chuckled and turned away to spit.

McEwan took one great breath and then another. He rose to his full height and glanced around at the amused faces of the warriors who had captured him. He surged his last strength into his blood and felt it course hot and furious through his heart.

The gauntlet seemed endless. The faces were hungry. They taunted him. They cursed him. But he was ready.

He inhaled again and thrust out his chest. With a savage Highland war cry that for centuries had borne his clansmen to victory and to death, McEwan sprang into the seething corridor. Blows battered him, cut him, slashed and whacked him. He jumped over traps and swung his arms into the faces of women and children. They fell before him, and there were still more of them. He charged powerfully, and the agony rained down with every step. His mind became dull and groggy. He forced his legs to pump. Stinging sand struck his face, blinding him. He stumbled and lurched forward under cracks on his head. Blood ran into his eyes. But he did not fall. Clubs and switches and sticks stung and rocked him. He swung wildly with his fists. He screeched the war cry and stumbled again, desperate, with long, clumsy steps. Then he went down.

He fought himself to his knees, and the sounds of laughing and yelping were lost amidst the whack of sticks against his head and shoulders. Every part of him was being struck at the same time. But he blared the savage war cry and dragged himself to his feet again. He thudded forward and felt himself going down. This, he knew, would be the last time. He pitched ahead, and as everything went black, he found himself sunk in a mass of incredible softness.

When he came to, he heard Dusten softly chuckling. McEwan looked up through the haze of the inside of an Indian lodge and saw two dark, piglike eyes staring at him. He heard Dusten chuckling again.

McEwan fought for consciousness. He felt the war cry rising in his throat again. But he was too weak to fling it at the world. He was snared by those eyes, black and shining. As his sight cleared, he saw the eyes were not piglike at all. They were more like the eyes of a sleepy cow. They were the eyes of a woman. He forced light into his mind, and groaned. His whole body throbbed with pain. A voice, surely Dusten's, was saying something to the cow's eyes, and the cow's eyes seemed to be listening. At last McEwan saw the hulking body of a very fat Indian squaw. He pushed his aching body up on both elbows and saw in the twilight that the fat face with the cow eyes was smiling benevolently, almost lovingly at him. Dusten kept chuckling.

McEwan turned his stiff neck toward the chuckle and saw the Frenchman, his unlit pipe stuck in his face. Dusten was laughing softly.

McEwan looked back at the Indian woman and let his head drop down again. She wiped his face with a warm cloth. In the light he saw her broken teeth that he was sure must be yellow or green. She talked to him, and her voice was soothing and kind. She smiled.

"Bonne chance," said Dusten from the other side of the lodge. "You are lucky, *mon ami*. You have survived the gauntlet, and you have been blessed with this lovely Wesah-na. She is your wife."

McEwan was up on his elbows again, yanking away the rag from his face and gaping at Dusten, who let out a high, delighted squeal of hilarity. After a prolonged laugh, Dusten, almost breathless, said, "You are fortunate, Sergeant, for this woman will make a fine wife, and as you can see, she likes to eat. That must mean she likes to cook." He giggled again.

"But how did she—?"

Dusten stifled his giggle into a snicker. "This lovely Wesah-na rescued you when you reached her in the gauntlet. She caught you before they spanked you to dust." He spat an oily glob of tobacco into his hand and tossed it into the fire. "Wesah-na's husband was killed four years ago by the English, so that gives her the right to replace him from prisoners who run the gauntlet. All she has to do is catch the prisoner before he's killed, and he's hers by law. And she caught you, Sergeant. Be good to her, Sergeant, for she stands between you and death."

McEwan looked from the woman to Dusten and back again. Even in this dim light McEwan could see her dirty, greasy buckskin gown. Her fat fingers were grimy, the nails stubby and cracked. She smelled of bear grease and sweat, of stale food and a dirty mouth. McEwan lay back limply. Her hands caressed his face and chest. He felt himself fading again until all he could see were Wesah-na's beady eyes. Now they did indeed look like the eyes of a pig. She hung over him and her enormous breasts flooded his view. Then all McEwan remembered was how he had collapsed into a mass of incredible softness. The pain took him again, and, as he began to pass out, he heard Dusten laugh.

By May 30, the siege of Detroit was more than three weeks old. Already it strained the nerves of the fort's inhabitants, soldier and civilian alike. It was difficult to rest, for night after night intense shooting broke out on every side except for the river wall. Each night sleep came hard to those trapped within the fort. Sometimes the constant banging of muskets was interrupted by the scream of a soldier just wounded on the ramparts. At those moments tension rose higher, and sleep kept its distance.

Still, the several hundred soldiers and civilians in the fort were outwardly uncomplaining. Though restless and weary of the sustained imprisonment, they went about their daily tasks with good humor and courage. They were a hardy lot.

No attempt had been made to breach the walls, though small parties of warriors often slipped close to the fort and shot at sentries. Showing one's head over the parapet was a dangerous business. Foraging groups who volunteered to go after firewood were heavily guarded. Then they only went as far as the nearest available fencerow, pulled it down, and hurried back to the safety of the fort, usually under heavy fire from hidden Indians.

Henry Gladwin knew the Indians would not attempt a frontal attack in force, for it was not their method to risk heavy loss if an objective could be taken without casualties. Chief Pontiac had a different strategy—he planned to starve the British into surrender. Spies had told him that the fort was almost out of food and in danger of famine, and so the chief knew it was just a matter of time before Detroit and its inhabitants were in his hands. It would take much too long for the fort's supply ships, the *Huron* and the *Michigan,* to travel all the way to Fort Niagara and back again for food. And a convoy of whaleboats that had, according to Pontiac's spies, left Fort Niagara carrying soldiers, provisions, and ammunition, was already under surveillance by Indian scouts. Plans had been laid to attack the unsuspecting convoy at the first opportunity, and without these anticipated supplies Fort Detroit could not hold out against Pontiac's warriors.

But Pontiac's spies did not tell him everything. They did not know that many brave French *habitants* outside the fort were nightly making secret shipments of food to the fort's ships anchored near Detroit's water gate. Under cover of darkness the food was then brought inside to sustain the defenders. If Pontiac discovered who these Frenchmen were, they would die, and painfully. He had forced the French—seven hundred of them, who lived mostly outside the fort—to swear allegiance to him or be killed. Caught helpless in the middle of a bloody quarrel, they had done this. A few young Frenchmen even joined with Pontiac and were counseling him on the best way to take the fort. But, in the main, the French were noncombatants in a dangerous, precarious position.

By the end of May the fort's stores were gone, and it was the French pemmican, peas, and fish that sustained the beleaguered English. It was depressing, dull fare, but it was gratefully accepted and was all that stood between them and surrender. Who brought the food was a secret, and none in the fort spoke openly about it, for a slip of the tongue would mean death to the Frenchman and his entire family if Pontiac suspected treachery.

Without the aid of the *habitants*—who sought only peace and prosperity, no matter whose flag flew over Detroit—the fort would have fallen.

One gray dawn, Ella, Jeremy, and Gladwin sat at breakfast. The occasional report of a musket caused Ella to jump involuntarily. She was tired from night after night of harrowing gunfire; she could do little to keep from being startled. Nearby, Jeremy sat, sleepily pushing his fork at a plate of dried fish, hard army biscuit, and boiled peas. He looked exhausted, too, but it was not Jeremy's condition that worried Ella most just then. It was Henry's glumness. His face was sunken, and his eyes were dark. Since the siege began, her brother had not slept more than an hour each night. He was everywhere at once, seeing to a thousand details, keeping up spirits, and preparing for anything.

"You really must find some rest, Henry," Ella said and poured some twice-brewed black tea into his cup. He looked up with weary eyes and smiled to assure her. But it was a wan, unconvincing smile.

He said nothing. He continued to munch the food that was as lifeless as the sluggish routine that had descended on the fort in the past few weeks.

Ella spoke: "You really must get enough rest, Henry. You have to be strong in case—in case—" Her eyes darted to the sleepy boy, who looked listless in the pale light. Jeremy was too groggy to realize that his mother was hinting to Gladwin that he must be fresh and alert in case the Indians launched an all-out attack against the fort. Gladwin lifted his teacup and sipped in silence for a while.

"Don't fear, sister," he said as he set the cup down on its saucer. "The Indians will never do what you're thinking." Gladwin, too, was careful with his words so as not to alarm Jeremy, who picked weakly at his peas. "They won't risk the casualties of a full-scale attack—though I daresay they've got more than fifteen hundred braves by now. They hope to starve us out. But the regular supply convoy should be coming upriver any day now."

As far as Gladwin knew, Fort Niagara, the large base to the east on the tip of Lake Erie, still had heard nothing of the uprising. A convoy of whaleboats with nearly one hundred men to replace some of the garrison was scheduled to arrive soon. He had sent the armed sloop *Michigan* to anchor downriver to warn the approaching convoy to be alert for ambush. But the sloop had come under dangerous attack and was forced to return to the fort. Gladwin's thoughts were on the unsuspecting convoy. It was a strong force, but if it were unprepared for a surprise attack . . . He finished his tea.

"Henry," Ella said and cut some fish, "I'm not merely concerned about the Indians. I worry about some of the officers who, it seems, are not so eager to go on with the defense. They think Pontiac's offer of permitting us to leave safely—"

"Ella—"

"What I mean is that you have to be rested to deal with them as much as anything else. And I worry about you. You're trying to do everything yourself, Henry. You even were on the fort's tower, aiming the cannon yourself, and yesterday you risked your life when you went out to help tear down the fences where those Indians were hiding!"

"Someone has to." His voice was flat and tired.

"You must keep fit, Henry. Even if only to face your officers should they lose heart."

He looked at her and grinned. "Sister, sister. Let me worry about myself, eh? When this is over, there'll be lots of time to rest. And back home in England in a few more months, we'll all have a good rest together."

"Henry, can't Major Duvall take more of the responsibility from you?"

He did not look up from his breakfast, but slowly he shook his head. "Major Duvall would be glad to take over the entire command right now, Ella. But he doesn't have the experience. He's headstrong, though he's gallant enough. He's a good soldier, but he doesn't know much about fighting Indians—or making peace with them. I've already told him that if the siege is not broken by the time he would normally take over the command in two months, I'll remain in charge of the fort." He paused. "That means, Ella, that we shall not depart for England as scheduled."

He looked up, waiting. She dropped her eyes and said, "Of course that doesn't matter, Henry. We'll go when it's the right time." Suddenly the thought of leaving America chilled her, and that surprised her.

Gladwin was looking with mock scolding eyes at Jeremy, who was alert now, listening intently.

"Eat your breakfast, boy," Gladwin said and reached over the table to pinch the child's cheek.

"Uncle Henry," Jeremy said, stirring slightly. "Is it true the Indians will eat us if they—"

"Jeremy!" Ella gasped and pressed her napkin to her pale lips.

"Come now, Jeremy," Gladwin said. He looked down at his own fork and knife scratching at the peas and forced a smile. "Don't go listening to every rumor you hear. You want to be a soldier someday like your fa—like your Uncle Henry, correct?"

Jeremy nodded absently.

"Right! Then the first thing a good soldier must learn is to ignore rumor. Never let another's fears or worries bother you. Understand? Good. Now, what you're facing are those peas and soldier's biscuit. Eat now like a soldier, and perhaps this afternoon we'll tour the French trader warehouses and see if we can find you some maple sugar."

Gladwin winked at the boy and then continued, "Being a soldier means you'll have to learn how to ration your supplies, lad. You'll have to promise me—I mean, I'm giving you an order—to make your sugar last until the supply convoy comes in from Niagara."

Jeremy's face brightened, and he eagerly attacked his peas and fish. Ella smiled, but an excited shout from outside caught her. They listened. Was she hearing correctly? Yes! Henry was on his feet, staring out the windows. Yes! It was true! Someone indeed was shouting what she thought she heard!

"The supply convoy from Niagara! It's coming! It's coming!"

Gladwin went quickly to the door, opened it, and let in sunlight and a louder alarm that the convoy was indeed in sight. A young ensign jumped to the porch and told Gladwin, "Reinforcements! There must be sixteen boats coming upstream! They've come through at last, sir!"

The ensign ran with the rest of the growing crowd toward the river ramparts, where scores of soldiers and civilians were gathering to wave and halloo the boats. Gladwin turned in triumph and slapped his hands. Ella felt a profound relief.

Gladwin buckled on his sword belt. "Now we'll have all the tea we want, and Pontiac will have to think twice about sustaining this foolish adventure. He'll never starve us out!"

Gladwin was gone, and Ella and Jeremy followed outside. She pushed back her straggling hair and hurried with her son in hand across the parade ground, which was alive with shouting, laughing people climbing the stairs of the palisade ramparts overlooking the river.

Ella and Jeremy scampered up the narrow steps and looked over the pointed wall across the river. There, almost a mile away, the line of ponderous boats came upstream, oars lifting and slapping in the glint of sunshine on water.

"There they are!" Lettie Morely shouted and waved.

"Never thought soldiers could look so lovely," said a sleep-puffed Garth Morely, who nodded and grinned at her side. Morely slapped his wife eagerly on the back. She wheeled and kicked his shins. He grunted, wincing.

"Now we'll teach those heathens a lesson," said Major Duvall, who stood behind Ella and smiled warmly at her as she turned to acknowledge him. "There must be a hundred men in those boats."

Jeremy could not see over the palisade, so Duvall lifted him high onto his shoulders. The boy looked proud and excited to sit up there. Ella was surprised that the normally very formal Duvall would do such an unsoldierly thing in front of the entire garrison. Duvall grinned broadly when she looked at him.

She turned back to the blue river, and the breeze came off it into her face, wonderfully clean and refreshing, as though all the drabness and shadows of death that had mingled with the routine of fort life had gusted away. They did look lovely, those boats!

The soldiers in the whaleboats rowed steadily, gradually approaching, and the delighted people on the ramparts laughed and cheered and waved everything from handkerchiefs to undershirts. In the foremost whaleboat the Union Jack fluttered in the breeze, snapping proudly, and the scattering of red uniforms looked bright and gay against the river—it was, as Lettie Morely spouted, a marvelous sight!

There was a dull bang as soldiers fired the fort's cannon in salute. Three cheers went up in unified hip, hip, hurrah. But through it Ella heard Morely's voice mutter in an alien tone of worry.

"Strange," he said. "They be awful close ter shore. They be a mite close ter that Huron village down there. I don' like it, no. They ought ter put out further into the stream in case them Injuns start shootin'. The commander must think he's comin' ter a picnic."

Duvall came to Morely's side. "Perhaps the commander doesn't know about the uprising. Anyway, they're nearly clear of the Huron village now, and not a shot has been sent at them."

"Aye," Morely said slowly. "That worries me, too."

But Duvall was not worried. He bounced the happy Jeremy on his shoulders and said to Ella, "This is a cause to celebrate, eh, Mistress Bently? We must have a ball tonight in honor of these fine fellows coming up! Grand idea, that! Don't you agree? We all need a pleasant diversion from this affair. Grand idea!"

"They're too close for my likin'." Morely was talking, and Ella found herself listening. Her delight at the notion of a ball that evening was tarnished by the bearded trader's words.

"Somethin' baint right. No."

Duvall jabbered happily about the ball and how he would organize it personally. Ella listened, watching the approaching convoy at the same time. The oars dipped and pulled steadily in each craft. They were less than half a mile away now. She could clearly see the red backs of soldiers, with white straps crossed on them, heaving at the oars.

Morely was silent, unmoving. He was a statue amid the swarming, cheerful people jumping up and down on the rampart. Duvall spoke, his voice barely over the crowd noise.

"Well, Mr. Morely, the Indians haven't opened fire, you see. Apparently they've already turned tail and run. They must know we're about to teach them a lesson they won't forget. It seems as if they—"

A woman screamed a curdling shriek of terror. Men on the ramparts groaned. Ella jerked around to look at the convoy.

"Good sweet God, no!" Duvall whispered.

In every boat Indians stood up, and Ella's heart collapsed. Bronzed and naked, slashed with purple and vermillion, the savages waved their arms, taunting the fort.

"Taken!" Morely said softly. "All of 'em taken."

The woman screamed again. Then silence.

Every boat had several soldiers rowing, but they were prisoners. The Indians had hidden in the bottom of each whaleboat until the convoy was tantalizingly close to the fort yet still out of good musket range. Then they stood and jeered, rattling muskets above their heads, holding up scarlet clusters—what seemed to be human scalps.

From the deck of the schooner *Huron* soldiers and seamen cursed the Indians and shook their fists. Men on the ramparts began to shout for the prisoners to make a break for it. But the boats plodded past, and the warriors brazenly paraded their victory under the noses of the dismayed, helpless British.

Then a shock went through the spectators. Four soldiers in the first boat sprang at the two Indians guarding them. The boat rocked dangerously, and a soldier grappling with an Indian went overboard. The second Indian leaped into the water and was clubbed by a redcoat wielding an oar. The brave went under.

In the water the other Indian and the soldier rose and sank. When they came up, the Indian yanked his tomahawk free, struck down again and again, and the soldier vanished. Treading water, the Indian turned to see the whaleboat with three soldiers in it escaping toward the fort. He screamed angrily, and his comrades opened a sporadic fire from their whaleboats nearby. The three fleeing soldiers rowed with all their might, and the people on the ramparts urged and shouted for the desperate men to reach the safety of the *Huron* anchored a few hundred yards away. Musketry clattered from the deck of the *Huron*, and a small cannon blasted a spout in the water where a pursuing whaleboat began to edge after the fugitives.

Two of the men slumped in the boat, wounded by the Indian gunfire. But they struggled back to their oars and pulled again. A frantic few moments later they reached the *Huron*, and men came over the side with ropes to haul them up. In the distance the furious Indians yelled and hooted at the fort. Then they forced their captives to turn the boats in to the shore across the river where a camp had been set up.

Ella trembled, and her knees nearly buckled. Jeremy was at her side now. She felt faint. Duvall put his arm about her waist and held her as they turned sadly to the rampart's steps, where an unhappy crowd of British and provincials filtered back to their homes and barracks, hope completely gone. Women openly weeping hurried away for fear of creating a general panic or weakening of resolve.

"I'll be all right, Major, thank you," Ella said to Duvall, who supported her as they walked across the dusty parade ground. She looked up and tried unsuccessfully to smile at Duvall.

"I'd be honored to see you home, mistress," he said quietly and drew her waist against his side. "I must meet with Major Gladwin about this tragedy and how we shall cope with it. May I accompany you, mistress?"

Jeremy took his mother's hand and tugged.

"She'll be all right with me, sir," he said and looked up at his mother's ashen face. She glanced down at him and then looked again at Duvall, who drew back a bit.

"Really, I'm all right now, Major. Thank you. But as you see, I'm in good hands already."

She pulled away from his arm, which was reluctant to release her waist. Then Duvall bowed low and doffed his black tricorn. He strode smartly off toward Major Gladwin, who was storming down from the ramparts on the rickety stairs. In a moment the two of them were on their way to the water gate to send a man to the *Huron* for information about the lost supply column.

Ella sighed and walked with her son back to the commander's house. She went as quickly as her wobbly legs could bear her.

Inside the cool living room of the house Ella paused, leaning against the table to let her weakness pass. Jeremy stood at her side, silent, deep in thought. She sighed and straightened up, about to say something that would ease the boy's troubled mind. But her eyes caught the gleam of the little bottle—the bottle of black rain!

Uncertainly, Ella reached for the shiny vial and held it before her. Could this really mean what all the Indians believed it did? Black rain! Foolish superstition! She forced a scornful laugh and set the vial down on the shelf again. But she continued to stare at it. The bottle held her, hypnotizing.

Black rain promised doom, they said. And doom had come to those men of the relief convoy, and for others: Sir Robert, the Fishers, the Turnbulls. Sutherland's wife.

Black rain. Its promise of tragedy already had been amply fulfilled. Would there be even more? Ella knew very well there would be more woe before its promise was kept. How profound that woe would be for her and Jeremy, Ella preferred not to contemplate. She wrenched her gaze free of the bottle. Henry should throw it away!

She felt nauseated and thought of lying down for a while. Jeremy went off with friends, and Ella went upstairs to bed. The spring sun fell through the window, and its warmth soaked through her. Gradually her racing pulse slowed, and she was grateful when sleep came.

The scrape and thud of soldier's boots woke her. Below, the officers had come in. Ella had not slept long, for the sun still lingered on her bed. A voice downstairs began to tell the tale of the captured convoy.

"They was cut off two days ago, accordin' to them lads that escaped. On Pointe au Pélée, where they was camped, the Injuns caught 'em before they even got their fires lit for the night. Shot 'em down on the beach."

Ella, hypnotized by the gruff, nasal voice, listened as it told of the escape of only a few soldiers from that first ambush. Sixty-one men out of nearly one hundred were killed or captured.

"An' them that's taken won't make it through the night, by God! Them Injuns captivated kegs o' rum, by God! All that good rum! When they drinks it tonight, they'll celebrate by torturin' them captives, they will! By God!"

Ella faced the wall, covered her face with her hands, and wept until sleep took her again.

Sir William Johnson had never felt so exhausted. When he returned to Johnson Hall, his stately manor on the Mohawk River a few miles west of Schenectady, he collapsed into bed with his Mohawk mistress and fell asleep. When he awoke, he lay in darkness and recalled the events of the past few days—days of uncertainty and danger. He had been at the sacred Iroquois council fire at Onondaga for a week—a grueling week of dancing, of speeches, of debating, of threats, of warnings, and of more dancing. At last, in the face of bitter opposition from some western Seneca, and with every Indian there realizing that their fate hung on the whim of the English Great Father, Johnson won: He persuaded the leaders of the Six Nations to stay out of Pontiac's uprising, and he had won permission for British soldiers to pass through their lands on the way to fight the western Indians.

As Johnson lay with his sleeping mistress, he thought again of the terror on the frontier, and he knew well that his paradise here in western New York was in imminent danger until the uprising was defeated once and for all.

chapter **12**

MICHILIMACKINAC

It was June 2 when Sutherland and Tamano guided their canoe into the shallows near Fort Michilimackinac and beached the craft a few hundred yards below a large number of Indian canoes gathered on the shore. Sutherland preferred to approach the fort as inconspicuously as possible, for there was no way of knowing whether trouble had already begun there.

Concealing the canoe in the shelter of a clump of scrub oak and cedar, they clambered up a slope and, carrying their guns, walked along a riverside path leading to the fort.

The sound of shouting and wild cheering erupted from near the fort, which was out of sight beyond trees and bushes at the edge of the water. They quickened their pace but slowed suddenly when voices came to them as they reached the crowd of canoes belonging to Indians. From the bushes stepped two old Indians, brightly decked with blue and green trade blankets. They stopped short, staring as Tamano and Sutherland caught their eyes.

To Sutherland's surprise Tamano gave a shout and ran to them. He laughed and took the man in the blue blanket by the shoulders. The old warrior looked uncertainly at Sutherland, who came up and nodded to both men.

"This is my uncle, Donoway," Tamano said cheerfully, but the old man's eyes were clouded and dark when they left Sutherland and returned to Tamano, who quickly began to talk to him, asking about family and offering a gift of tobacco.

"I have heard of Donoway," the old man said, now looking hard at Sutherland. "He is always welcome in our towns. But—" He glanced at his comrade, who was beginning to walk toward the sound of shouting and yelling beyond the trees near the fort. "But today there will be many Indians at this fort who do not know Donoway, and they will not like him because his face is white. There will be warriors at this place who hate the English. Donoway is not safe here."

"Not safe?" Tamano asked, surprised. "Donoway is Ottawa adopted. We come in search of two men, and then we shall return to Detroit. We seek my brother, the English sergeant, McEwan, whom we have heard was taken by the Chippewa some days ago. And we seek the Frenchman, André Breton, for other reasons. Tell me, uncle, have you seen them? Do you know where we can find them?"

The old man thought a moment and looked up the trail where his friend had vanished among the bushes. Then he spoke slowly.

"The prisoner of whom you speak is known to me, nephew. He now lives down the coast two days by canoe. He has been taken as a squaw's husband. The Frenchman, Breton," he said, motioning with a hand at the shrieking through the trees, "is here." The noise carried louder now. It was no more than a hundred yards ahead.

Sutherland felt fury rising. Breton was here! He loosened the tomahawk in its belt and glanced at Tamano. Then he moved off toward the shouting. Tamano's uncle, who was staring at Sutherland's back with eyes that seemed able to penetrate the very depths of the earth, said quietly, "Donoway, you are in danger." Sutherland stopped and turned. "I shall show you," the old man said. "Come with me."

The warrior pulled his blanket tighter about his scraggly shoulders and stepped from the path and into the brush. Tamano and Sutherland followed, and in a moment the three of them stood at the edge of the bushes, looking out at a milling mass of sweating, running, fiercely feathered warriors charging headlong back and forth across a great clearing. Beyond loomed the wooden stockade of Michilimackinac.

"*Baggataway!*" Tamano's eyes gleamed with excitement. He watched the warriors—divided into two teams of more than a hundred on each side—throwing a ball by means of a stick with a small rawhide cradle woven into the crook at its end, catching the ball and running with it until men from the opposing team knocked it loose or downed the runner with a vicious whack.

"*Baggataway!*" Tamano exclaimed again. This game—called *la crosse* by the French because the stick looked like a bishop's crosier—was, after Lela, his greatest love. He was a champion among the Chippewa, and he had a goodly number of scars and broken bones to prove his courage in this contest, which was little short of war between opposing tribes. Sutherland watched silently as the braves kicked, pushed, and threw the ball as well as each other, with the object being, at last, to strike a post standing behind the other team's defense. The ball could be brought against the post in any manner except by carrying it with the hands, and the player with the ball could be brought down in any way possible. All was fair.

Clusters of English soldiers in crimson, and traders in greens, buckskins, and hunting shirts were gathered watching the game. Relief swept Sutherland to see there had been no attack yet. But something was in the air—a tension, a sense of danger that hung like a gathering storm, despite the apparently peaceful scene before him. He thought of Pontiac's warning that he would be killed if he took the side of the English. But that was no matter now, for he had to act: to tell the commander that this fort was in deadly peril. Then he would find Breton.

"Sac and Foxes against the Chippewa," Tamano said to Sutherland, not taking his eager eyes from the clubbing, running horde of braves painted for war. "Who is winning?" Tamano asked his uncle.

The old warrior replied to Tamano, "Today there will be no victors." He let a branch he was holding spring back into place, concealing much of the game from them.

Tamano politely waited for his uncle to elaborate on his cryptic statement. But first Sutherland said, "He's there!"

Tamano pushed away the bushes and saw Breton in the distance, strutting, sauntering up and down the field, black feathers fluttering on his red stocking cap. Chest puffed out, Breton laughed and joked with the Indian women who—strangely enough, for it was a warm day—were every one of them closely wrapped in blankets.

Sutherland moved forward, but the old Indian gripped his arm in a claw hand. Surprised, Sutherland looked back into beady eyes.

"Donoway," the Indian grunted, "you go to your death."

Sutherland felt anger boiling now. He barely contained himself enough to say, "I have beaten him before."

Tamano's uncle began to speak, but a blood-chilling shriek rose suddenly from the playing field, and all eyes turned toward a huge warrior whose cradle held the ball. It was as though a signal had been given. The player deliberately heaved the ball with a mighty throw at the gate of the fort, where a large group of squaws had gathered. The warriors gave a savage shout and rushed for the ball and the gate. To Sutherland's puzzlement, even Indians not in the game were running now.

Then there were little knots of quick, violent movement, flurries of men struggling. A soldier was on the ground and his legs kicked the air. An Indian was on top of him, striking with a tomahawk again and again. Soldiers and traders were running madly for the fort, and many were on the ground. The Indians rushing through the gate raised the shrieking yelp of the scalp cry. Breton was out of sight, apparently already in the fort. The squaws had cast aside their blankets, and some still were handing knives and tomahawks to their men.

There was little firing. The work was with the tomahawk and scalping knife. Scarlet lumps lay on the field here and there. The field was almost clear of human life, and the long grass waved lazily. Near the fort's gate an officer was surrounded by a dozen braves. He jabbed at them with his sword, fighting one off, but was struck from behind by another, and when he turned to defend himself, one came in and stabbed him again. He stood his hopeless ground against the laughing warriors who prolonged the sport until his flickering sword wounded too many of them. Then a warrior dealt a swift and cracking tomahawk blow that Sutherland heard across the clearing three hundred yards away.

Sutherland was still in the iron grip of the old Indian. He had come too late. Murderous yells and death cries rose from the fort. There was no real resistance, for the soldiers had no chance to organize. Soon the screaming from within the stockade faded.

Tamano spoke to his uncle. "I thank you, for you have indeed done us a service. We are in your debt, aged one."

The old man let his gaze drop. He released Sutherland's arm, pushed through the bushes, and walked slowly to the fort.

After Duncan McEwan had spent several days in the lodge of his new wife, his bruises from the gauntlet run were losing their ache. Wesah-na had tended his injuries very kindly; even her face seemed less ugly now, more gentle. McEwan had the freedom of the camp, although he was the center of attention wherever he went. His uniform had been stolen, and he now wore a greasy old buckskin shirt and tattered deerskin leggins—much like the poorest Indian alive.

He walked often near the edge of the river, and always he thought of escape. But flight must be carefully planned, for there were many young men eager to kill him. When he fled, he would steal a canoe, and he must have a head start of several hours.

McEwan knew well enough to stay out of the way of the bucks who eyed him with unmasked hatred. When they were drinking rum, he knew his life hung by the faintest thread, for Indians held no brave responsible for whatever was done under the influence of liquor. Though McEwan's murder would be an unfortunate loss for the blissfully happy Wesah-na, his hair would not be denied the man who took it, drunk or sober.

Now and again Dusten had come to visit, and McEwan learned from the Frenchman that the main body of braves from this village had gone north to attack Fort Michilimackinac. In his hours alone at the riverside McEwan was tormented by the thought that he had failed to reach the outpost to warn of the impending uprising. The fact that he was still alive, if only temporarily so, was little consolation to him when he thought of the danger to the fort's unwary garrison. Much of his time by the river, where he had found a secluded inlet girded by thick cattails and a stand of spruce, was spent thinking about Michilimackinac. He often prayed for its safety.

It was on one of these unhappy reveries that McEwan met Mary Hamilton. He was tossing pebbles uselessly into the still water, when he heard rustling in the cattails nearby. He was startled to see a white woman with blond hair moving into the water, dipping a bucket down to fill it. She was dressed in ankle-length doeskin, like a Chippewa squaw, and her hair was long and held back by a bright beaded headband. Even from twenty feet away McEwan saw her blue eyes.

She looked up, noticed him, and gasped. Hesitantly she began to retreat back through the spruce.

He rose and asked, "Who are you?"

She dropped the bucket, spilling the water over her feet and legs. She gaped at him, her breasts rising and falling as though frantic for air.

"Do you understand me?" he asked but dared not move toward her lest she bolt.

The girl glanced about quickly, picked up the wooden bucket, and moved into the spruce thicket at the tip of the crescent of bank forming the inlet. McEwan followed and ducked under the shaggy branches. Behind, the bank sloped up fifteen feet from the water, and under the spruce the ground was soft and shadowed from sight.

McEwan pushed in, and there in the dimness he saw the girl kneeling. He crawled beside her and said his name. She put a finger to her lips and beckoned him to come closer. He was at her shoulder, and she showed no fear.

"I have seen you," she whispered. "But I have not tried to meet you, for if we are discovered together, we'll die."

"Who are you?"

"Mary Hamilton. I was taken two weeks ago when traveling with my father and two brothers in a trading party heading for Sault Sainte Marie. They caught us on the shore of Lake Huron . . ." She bit her lower lip, and her eyes glinted with tears, then she shuddered a sigh and looked back at McEwan. "They killed—all of us—but—me—" She could hold back no longer, for she had contained her misery for two desolate weeks. Mary Hamilton collapsed into McEwan's arms, her face buried against his chest, and she struggled to keep her sobs from being heard by passing Indians. Her hands were cold as ice. She gripped fast to McEwan's hands and held them against her cheek, which was wet with tears.

"Forgive me, sir," she sniffed and looked away at the light beyond the sheltering pine branches. "But—for a moment to— to speak to one of my own . . ."

She let go then and wiped her face and nose with dirty hands that once had been soft and pretty; now they were bruised, scratched from toiling with the squaws.

She said, "I have been here for a week, but I'll be gone in a few days, they tell me."

"Gone? Where?" McEwan felt a surge of sympathy for this woman—beautiful and young and strong.

"I am to be given to a war chief by the Chippewa," she said and fought against sobbing once more. "He is a Delaware who is in the attack on Michilimackinac. He will come back soon and take me as—as—"

As his woman. McEwan's mind echoed what Mary did not say. She trembled again, and he reached for her. She fell into his arms and found a haven there, if only for a moment. Her body heaved silently.

"Listen," he said after some time, pushing her back and looking at her. "I intend to escape soon. I'd planned to go in a few weeks, but I can go sooner. I'll take a canoe, and you come with me. If you—"

"Yes!" she said breathlessly and nodded.

McEwan took her hands in his.

"You can't be afraid," he said.

She shook her head. "No." She seemed in a daze. "No, I shan't be afraid now. I was. But though it seems strange to me, I am afraid no longer. Your name?"

"McEwan. Duncan—"

A heavy rustling and tramping broke out back where they had first seen each other. Through the trees McEwan saw Wesah-na come stamping and crashing down the knee-length grass of the small slope. He looked at Mary, then pushed her back into the shadows and stepped out of the spruce toward the fat woman, who turned and glared at him. She broke into a flurry of scolding, hands on her broad hips, thundering at her new husband.

McEwan heard then a soft chuckling from the top of the slope. There stood Dusten, scoffing and chewing the end of his old pipe.

"Ah, *mon ami,*" Dusten laughed, "your sweetheart is not happy with you. You slipped away from her for too long. She says she was sick with worry, for she thought you had gone off and lost your hair to some buck."

McEwan looked from Dusten to the squaw and back again. She was fuming, and Dusten was still chortling in delight.

McEwan stepped up the slope and said to Dusten, "Tell her she needn't worry about me. But she must know that I, like any husband, need time alone—time to think! Tell her that, and say I find this place good for thinking, and I'll come here whenever I want to! Tell her that! Tell her if I am to be her husband, I expect to be honored as such." At the top of the slope McEwan turned and stared down at Wesah-na, who was open-faced, listening. "Tell her I'll come here each day, at dawn and at dusk! At dawn and at dusk!" He said it loud enough for Mary to hear from her hiding place beneath the pine branches. "Tell her, Frenchman, that I must come here to learn from the spirits how to be a good husband, but if she scolds me or is abusive, or if she follows me when I want to be alone, I'll lose face with my personal spirits, and then I'll be no use as her husband, and the warriors might as well kill me. Tell her that, Dusten. I'll be here every day at dawn and sunset, and I'll come alone! Let her be satisfied with her new husband, or she'll have no husband at all!"

Dusten laughed and said, "Very good, *mon ami,* very good. When I tell her, she'll be happy that she has claimed a husband who'll treat her as she should be treated, with severity. Hah, you are learning fast, *mon ami.* You may yet have a long and happy life among the Chippewa."

The Frenchman quickly translated, even throwing in some finger-wagging to accentuate McEwan's message. Wesah-na's face went from surprise to dismay and then to pride. At the end of the translation McEwan slapped his hands together sharply and shooed the squaw up the bank. She jumped in surprise, but she jiggled quickly enough toward him, past, and away to their lodge. McEwan thought he saw a faint smile on her face as she went by.

Late that afternoon Sutherland and Tamano made camp in a quiet bay a day's trip south of the lost Fort Michilimackinac. It was a fine spring day, alive with flocks of white-throated sparrows, thousands of them, traveling north. A cool breeze blew in off Lake Huron, which was rockier and steeper along the shore than was the low waterline south on the Detroit River and western Lake Erie.

With the canoe tucked away, the two men settled into a hollow in the ground that would conceal the glow of their campfire at night, and the dry wood fire would give off no smoke to reveal their presence to passing canoes. They cooked a quick meal of fried pemmican, greasy and filling, with corn-meal cakes known in the south as johnnycake, which were cooked on a flat, fire-heated rock. Now that they were north of the village where Tamano's uncle had told them McEwan was a prisoner, they would be more cautious about meeting Indians. Sutherland would remain in camp just above the town, and then Tamano would go alone to try to free his blood brother. But they must act soon, before the warriors crazed by the blood orgy that no doubt followed the fall of Michilimackinac returned to McEwan's village. Their lust for more white blood could mean McEwan's death by torture.

They lay on deerskin spread over pine needles; between them the embers of the fire glimmered. The sun was nearly down when Sutherland did what he had tried not to do every quiet moment for the past month—he thought of Mayla. He touched the silver pendant at his chest.

The wind rustled the bushes and stirred the fire's ashes,

flaring up the last coals, which flamed, dimmed, and then went nearly out. Sutherland rolled on his back, his fingers still touching the pendant inside his shirt.

"When you are at the Chippewa village," he said quietly to Tamano, "find out where Breton went after the attack."

Tamano looked up at the sky, which was a cold blue, with a hint of stars arriving.

"I hope," he said, "that Donoway does not lose his life when he takes his vengeance, for that will compel Tamano to avenge his death."

Sutherland pulled up his blanket and tried to sleep. The wind gusted again and scattered ashes, causing the hot coals to glow.

That same night McEwan left his lodge. Wesah-na lay asleep under a bearskin cover, snoring and muttering. The Indian camp was quiet now; cooking fires were dying, for there were few young men awake to keep them alive and tell tales about their prowess in hunting and war. McEwan quickly moved around the outer edge of the camp, keeping to the shadows, and slipped into the trees near the river and the inlet where he hoped Mary would be waiting.

As he went, he noticed three canoes that had just been repaired and were overturned and lying in the grass above the river less than a hundred yards from where he and Mary had met. That was close enough for him. He had watched some young men working on them all afternoon, had seen them tested and readied for the lake. One of these canoes would take him and Mary to freedom.

McEwan slipped down the grassy bank, already damp with the evening's dew, and moved through the darkness of the spruce stand where he had left Mary that morning. His heart thumped as he wondered whether she understood him when he said he would come. He hoped Wesah-na would not awaken and search for him. All was silent, and in the darkness a child cried out for its mother. Dogs yapped hungrily.

In the shadows someone caught a breath. McEwan sensed Mary's presence. She reached for his arm. He took her hand, and she pressed herself, trembling, against him, both of them kneeling on the soft carpet of pine needles. They listened for the sounds of Indians or Dusten approaching. After a few minutes they breathed easier.

"Tomorrow night, I am going," he said in a low voice. "If you still want to go, meet me here at this time. We'll take one of those canoes over there. Bring what food you can, and be sure to take warm clothes, for it's a long way to Detroit, and we'll be moving mostly at night. Take a blanket, and be sure, for heaven's sake, that no one suspects you. I'll hide a pouch of pemmican and some cornmeal here tomorrow morning. We'll be short of food, but there's no other choice."

She said nothing. She hardly breathed.

"Can you do it, lass?" he asked.

She moved then and sighed deeply. "I can do it, Duncan. Be sure of that."

"All right," he said and gripped her shoulders. "I'll leave first now. When I'm gone, slip back through the other side of the village. Much strength."

Mary, close and warm, moved against him. Her body was steady, firm against his. He put his arms about her, and she held him in silence. They drew back at arm's length, and he took her hands. They were not cold today.

Then he was gone, and Mary Hamilton knew she was not afraid to die.

At dawn McEwan awoke to find that the sweaty, earth-smelling woman who had lain with him was gone. In the half-light of morning he wrapped himself in a blanket, took up the pouch of pemmican and a small deerskin sack of cornmeal he had secreted in a corner of the lodge, and slipped outside.

The camp was stirring. His own woman's cooking fire was crackling and spitting, but she was apparently off gathering water or on some other errand. He moved quickly through the wakening camp, and soon he was at the river and down among the deeper shadows of the spruce.

Mary was there, and he was beside her, both pretending to be busy getting water. She looked about once, then slipped farther into the trees, in among the sweet scent of pine, where no one could find them easily. For several minutes they lay without talking.

"Mary," he said and reached to touch her cheek. "I ask you once more—are you certain you want to try this?"

"I'd rather try and fail than become the squaw of that Delaware, Duncan," she said. "I'll die, if that must be."

They said nothing for a time.

"Listen, Mary. There is no guarantee that we'll get away.

You must understand that. You may very well have to become his woman . . . no matter what hopes we have for escape tonight."

The light was coming. He could see her face now.

"I won't let him have me—I won't! I'll die first!"

"Mary! Don't! You must live, you must live—"

"Why? Why should I live like that?" She turned her head to the ground, her face in her hands.

"Because—" McEwan said gently and knelt next to her. "Because I want you to, Mary. And if the Lord permits, I'll come back for you one day. I promise that."

He brought her to sit next to him and caressed her hair. A bullfrog grumbled sleepily not far away. The chatter of children in the Chippewa camp drifted to them.

"I know we don't know each other . . ." he began. She looked up at him and pressed her palm against his lips.

"Duncan," she said, breathless. "I'm not sure how to say this, Duncan, but I—I fear that something will keep me from going with you."

"Don't say that!" He put her hand against his breast.

"I wish I could not say it, Duncan. But—but I—I think you'll not take me with you."

"Mary—"

She pressed her hand against his lips again and came to her knees, facing him. "Listen to me, Duncan. I may become the squaw of that savage if I agree to your request not to die instead—"

"Mary, lass—"

"Duncan, do not speak now, for I must ask you—"

He brought her against him, urgent, hard, and kissed her forehead, hair, and then her lips. She yielded and leaned against him. The wind lifted her hair against his face. She struggled against weeping and looked at him.

"Duncan, I fear and hate the dreadful thought of being taken by that savage. I fear it!" Her voice was controlled now. "I fear it all the more because—because I have never—" she dropped her eyes, "—never known a man."

It was as though all her strength left her at that moment. McEwan closed his eyes and held her against him. She pushed back and faced him squarely.

"I have never known a man, Duncan." She was determined now. "And I loathe with all my being the thought of this savage . . . that he would be the one who—who would be the one who—"

Her words were lost as McEwan kissed her lips. He brought her down on the bed of pine earth, and he kissed her deeply. Passion surged within him, and he was lost in absolute joy.

But he jerked his head up suddenly when the hoarse laughter of Chippewa men lifted on the breeze. He tensed, and his hair bristled. But the Indians were far off. He looked down at Mary's beautiful face. She seemed so innocent. A sudden pang of emptiness, of hopelessness twisted at McEwan's heart. The harsh reality of their captivity came to him like an awful weight. But Mary's eyes were closed; she seemed content, as though she heard nothing; she knew nothing—nothing but happiness just then.

"Mary," he said softly, and she opened her eyes. She sensed his uneasiness and reached for his face, touching it lightly. "Mary, promise me now—whatever happens—promise you'll live for me. Live until I can make you my wife."

She smiled faintly. For a moment it seemed she, too, heard the savage sounds of the Indian village. Her eyes went distant, then returned and filled with love again. Her hand wandered over his lips and eyes and behind his head, where she clutched his hair. She nodded quickly.

"I'll live, Duncan. I'll live because you've given me a reason to. No matter what. Ah, Duncan, let's not talk—"

He kissed her roughly, and she giggled like a country girl without a care in the world—like a love-struck lass pursued and caught by her first youthful lover. "I love you," she whispered.

Then McEwan came to her, and he was gentle, for he loved Mary Hamilton.

The sun was bright and carefree when they left their concealment. He scooped water from the river with her bucket, and their hands touched with a flash as she took it from him.

He said, "Until tonight," then turned to look across the lake at the blue sky. He did not want to watch her leave.

It was late in the afternoon when Tamano brought his canoe ashore near the village. As he climbed from the craft, he was greeted by enthusiastic young junior warriors who knew and admired him. Admittedly Tamano spent an unusual amount of time among the English, but his prowess in *bagattaway* and his skills as a hunter had won him renown among his people.

From the canoe Tamano lifted a bundle of mink pelts he had carried from Valenya. He also slung a heavy pack over his shoulder, and young men were eager to take the small keg of powder and pigs of lead from the canoe for him. There were steel knives and mirrors, bolts of cloth and bags of English manufactured beads, and there was even a keg of rum—against Tamano's principles, but he knew well that bargaining with these Chippewa for the life of a friend could be done only once. If he failed, McEwan would die when the war parties came back from Michilimackinac.

Tamano strode through the excited village, acknowledging the many greetings of friends and cousins who crowded around to look on the precious goods carried by the youths walking behind him.

As he passed the lodge of Wesah-na, Tamano saw out of the corner of his eye the entrance flap being pushed back. He glanced at McEwan, who stepped out and stopped, shocked, disbelieving what he was seeing. Tamano paused before the young Scotsman and looked him up and down. McEwan was dressed in tattered rags, like the meanest Indian who ever stayed eternally drunk.

Tamano nodded and said slowly, "If they give you to me, brother, be ready."

Then Tamano walked to the council lodge to meet the village elders; he entered the low lodge door, and the flap closed behind him. McEwan had not the least idea what to expect. He went back into his shelter and finished gathering the odds and ends—a knife, a bit of tow, a worn-out blanket—that he planned to take in the escape that evening. In this gathering dusk he would slip away to hide them near the canoes, and there he would retrieve them when Mary met him after dark. He came out of the lodge, straightened up, and was about to head off when a voice called to him.

"Sergeant!"

Dusten. The Frenchman shuffled up, cackling to himself and shaking his head.

"Mon ami, it seems you may get out of this yet. The chiefs desire your presence in the council lodge. If you are fortunate, *mon ami,* you will spend the night under the stars instead of under your sweetheart's blankets." He laughed and beckoned McEwan to follow him to the lodge where Tamano had earlier entered.

Startled, confused, McEwan let his bundle of goods slide

to the ground in the shadow of the shelter. He hurried behind the Frenchman and bowed to enter the lodge of bent saplings, hide covering, and birch bark. Inside, the air was dull with smoke. A small fire burned in the center of a ring of cross-legged Indians, all halfnaked, chests shining with grease. Their eyes were disdainful, and McEwan sought to avoid them. Dusten slipped into the shadows to listen and to cackle.

Then McEwan saw Tamano, tall and noble, sitting at the right hand of the man McEwan knew was the head village elder. The chief looked blankly at the fire as McEwan entered the circle. Then the young sergeant saw the grim face of the warrior who had captured him on the night that now seemed so long ago but was less than four weeks past.

The head chief motioned for McEwan to sit outside the circle, and the Scotsman did so. As he sat down, he noticed a pile of goods clustered at the other side of the circle of warriors. The chief was grunting guttural words to Tamano, who, unmoving, listened closely. At length the chief fell silent. The men were like statues for more than half an hour. McEwan knew it was nearly dark by now, and he wondered whether Mary was at their meeting place. And if he was late, would she wait?

McEwan noticed that the brave who had caught him was staring with hateful, savage eyes. McEwan met and held their gaze and felt anger growing within himself. He would not look away. He was ready to take on this fighter if he must. At last, after a prolonged exchange of unspoken anger between McEwan and the warrior chief, Tamano spoke.

His speech was slow and long. McEwan began to grow more restless as he thought of Mary. From outside, McEwan heard the laughs of children and the soft voices of passing squaws. Now and again, as Tamano spoke, the fire spat sparks over the blackened stone ring that contained it. More than an hour went by. McEwan felt himself begin to sweat. Mary must be there now. She must be waiting, wondering, worrying with every passing moment. He began to grow stiff, uneasy. His scalp prickled. His heart beat harder. She must not be found there at night!

Finally Tamano ended his speech, and after another long wait the warrior chief who had captured McEwan got roughly to his feet, grabbed up the powder keg, bars of lead, bundle of pelts, and walked quickly from the lodge. Left in the pile were the small keg of potent high wine and the bag filled with knives, mirrors, and trinkets. Also the bolt of cloth lay at one side.

Another wait. Then the chief spoke to Tamano, who grunted, rose, and motioned McEwan to come. Tamano picked up the bolt of cloth and led the way out of the lodge.

McEwan, his heart thundering, did not look back as he followed Tamano through the darkened village, past groups of silent squaws and curious children who stared at them. The time for meeting Mary was long past.

The two men stopped at the lodge of Wesah-na, who was standing with hands at her sides, opening and closing her fingers. She gazed at Tamano, who held out the bolt of fabric and spoke to her. Wesah-na's eyes lit brightly as she took the cheap, English cloth in her hands. She turned it over once, twice, felt it, then laughed aloud. Without the slightest look at McEwan, the squaw went into her lodge hugging the cloth and let the flap down behind her.

Tamano touched McEwan's shoulder and said, "You are free now, brother. But we must go quickly. For in one day, you will be fair game for any brave once again."

Tamano was on his way, and McEwan, snatching up the bundle he had left by the lodge, hurried to catch up to him. They were walking near the rendezvous place, and McEwan searched the dark for Mary.

"Tamano," McEwan said urgently and noticed that several young warriors were following like puppies. "Tamano, I was to escape tonight with an English woman. She's waiting for me there!"

Tamano looked around, his dark face stunned. He shook his head slowly. "No, my brother, that cannot be. These young men follow us. If we do not depart together now, we shall never depart alive."

Tamano stepped away faster, and McEwan came up behind him.

"Then walk near those trees there, just for a moment," McEwan said hurriedly and looked around to see whether Dusten was near. He was not.

They walked by the spruce trees where McEwan was to meet Mary. There he fell to his knees, as though he had dropped something. He looked into the shadows at his left. The braves following went on with Tamano, who began to laugh and joke with them. McEwan saw the glint of fair hair in the trees. He had time to say, "Tomorrow I shall come for you here! Tomorrow at sundown, be here, my Mary! Be here! Sundown!"

There was no sound from the girl. McEwan stood up and walked away to Tamano's canoe and the promise of freedom.

As they paddled away into the depths of the night, they heard the sound of gunfire and saw the flashes of scores of muskets from up the shore. Voices whooped and yelled in the Chippewa camp as well as from the source of the shooting. Tamano, who sat in the rear of the canoe, stopped paddling.

"War party that struck Michilimackinac come back," he said.

They floated, watching, as firebrands were carried from the village down to the shore. The shooting went on from what appeared to be dozens of canoes coming closer to the village. In a few moments the shadows of canoes being driven ashore could be seen, and leaping, yipping warriors clambered out and joined the crowd on land. From his canoe McEwan saw several figures stumble and lurch ahead, prodded and struck by Indians all around them.

"Prisoners," Tamano said. "This war party probably has André Breton among them. He killed Donoway's woman, my squaw's sister."

McEwan jerked around and looked at Tamano, who was vaguely illuminated by the fires on shore.

"Donoway awaits us," the Indian said. "We bring you safe to Detroit after we kill Breton, and maybe kill the Delaware chief, Sin-gat, too."

"Delaware?" McEwan thought of Mary's story. She was promised to a Delaware chief. McEwan thought a moment, then said, "I promised to free an English woman, Tamano. I believe she will be given to this Sin-gat. I'll join you to fight them. I'm coming back here tomorrow to fetch her. Will you take me back?"

Tamano paddled the canoe away from the scene in the village and up along the shore to reach Sutherland at their camp. "We do what we can, brother. I save your life, and it cost much. But I do what I can to help you with this white squaw. I think the Delaware and Breton not stay long when they hear Donoway nearby. They not sleep so good at night with Donoway near. Maybe they gone tomorrow. Tonight we sleep, then come back for your woman."

chapter **13**

RETURN TO DETROIT

After the dismay over the reinforcement convoy's being cut off, Fort Detroit's weary inhabitants and garrison settled down once more into the anxiety of a prolonged siege. The ship *Michigan* had been sent off several days ago to tell Fort Niagara of Detroit's plight and to return with supplies, but it would not be back for many long weeks, and there was little optimism among the English and provincials bottled up in the fort.

The news that came in a letter from the captive Captain Campbell did little to alleviate the fears and boredom of the besieged. Campbell's letter said peace had formally been signed between France and England some months ago, and the northwest territory as well as Canada had been ceded to England.

Campbell had sent the letter to Gladwin via a French trader who had no sympathy with the Indian uprising. The captain had learned of the treaty-signing during a conversation with one of the Englishmen made prisoner in the convoy. The prisoner was soon after taken away and roasted to death.

Now it was certain there would never be a French army to join Pontiac's rebellion. That word would pass quickly through the French *habitants,* but it offered little hope of lifting the siege. For one, those French who had aided Pontiac and urged the assault on the English fort would forfeit their lives if news of the peace treaty was conceded by them as being true. For another thing, those French who opposed the rising—and there were many hundreds who did—knew they were virtually unprotected if the Indians chose to take revenge on them before breaking off the war. So the French could not acknowledge the rumor that passed through the English, through the French, and then through the restless Indians. But many *habitants* continued making nightly food shipments to Detroit, risking their lives by secretly rafting provisions to the *Huron*, anchored near the fort's water gate.

Still, food was extremely short. Supplies were drastically rationed. Meager fare was better than none, though, so the hundreds of souls penned inside Fort Detroit did not complain in public. But there were many in the fort who would have gladly risked their lives in open combat against the Indians rather than continue to sit caught in the fort, hungry, without initiative.

All Ella could do for diversion was to play her spinet. But it was a God-sent diversion. Each afternoon before tea—or what passed for tea but was really a concoction of bitter Indian herbs with some suggestion of mint mixed in—Ella went to the council house to play. There were others who looked forward to those interludes, and they joined her, dozens of them sometimes, to listen quietly, intently soaking up the music as though it was the last they would ever hear. In the warmth of late spring afternoons, soldiers, traders, shopkeepers, and their families gathered in the council house to listen to Ella's music. At first she had been shy, but when she realized how much it meant to the others to listen to her chiming spinet, she forgot her self-consciousness and played for them. And she knew her playing had never before been so satisfying, so inspired.

But at other times Ella worried about Jeremy. The boy's face was gaunt for lack of food. He and many other children took little interest anymore in playing together. They were listless and talked morbidly of death and of Indians. It twisted Ella's heart to see him so, and it wrenched her deeply to listen to him talk of misery that a child should never know so soon.

Both her brother and Major Duvall were unbowed by the siege. Their strength seemed unebbing, no matter what the adversity. Even when cholera was rumored among the traders, Duvall and Gladwin maintained calm until it was discovered that the illness was not cholera at all and the population was not in danger. The two majors were everywhere at once, cheering spirits, seeing to the fort's defenses, finding work for soldiers to do so they would not think so much about their plight. Duvall was a frequent dinner guest with Gladwin and Ella, and he assumed the position of Gladwin's confidant now that Captain Campbell was Pontiac's prisoner. Ella saw Duvall as a courageous and capable officer, handsome and polite, kind enough to Jeremy, though he lacked a true camaraderie with the boy.

On the night of June 6, Ella and Duvall were sitting in rockers on the porch of Gladwin's house. Jeremy was asleep upstairs, and Gladwin was at his desk inside seeing to paperwork by candlelight. The occasional sound of Indian gunfire drifted to them from outside the fort, but otherwise Detroit was peaceful, asleep, and the night was lovely with stars.

Ella knitted. It seemed she was always knitting these days—knitting, or spinning in the company of Lettie Morely so she would have more yarn to do more knitting.

Duvall cleared his throat and got her attention. From the shadows he said, "You know, Mistress Bently, despite the horrors we've all seen, and despite the uncertainty of this tragic affair, there has been one aspect of it all that I consider to be most fortunate for myself."

He was leaning forward. The starlight lifted off his boots and gleamed faintly on his brass buttons.

"And what might that be, Major? I confess I have found nothing at all to recommend the present state of things to my good favor. Except to say that I have knitted more socks and caps in the past month than I expect my Jeremy will ever wear."

"Well, my dear lady, I had so hoped you might consider it your good fortune that you and I have met and been given the opportunity of knowing one another better. For my part, I am deeply grateful for that."

Silence. Ella had been rocking slowly. Now she was still. Inside the house Gladwin's chair scraped the floor beneath his writing desk.

"I am honored, Major, that you look upon our acquaintance with such—such—"

"Ardor, mistress." He said it with more intensity than she really liked.

"Well," she replied and started rocking unrhythmically. "I'm not sure I would have dared use that word, Major."

"Indeed, Mistress Bently," he said with a voice that seemed to be under control only with difficulty. "Ardor is very definitely the appropriate word to use in describing my feelings toward you." He leaned far forward in his chair, and Ella worried that it might skid and drop him flat on the floor at her feet. He was speaking in a hoarse whisper. "Who can tell what might come? I cannot wait longer to express my feelings, the very depth of my soul to you, mistress—if you permit me to do so."

Ella felt a chill. Was it the wind? All of a sudden she felt closed in, confined as though the siege had at last cornered her with its unending relentlessness. She sensed the looming walls of the fort, the dark night, the insistent voice of this gentleman speaking so kindly to her, all closing in.

"Major," she said with an appeal that cut him off in mid-sentence, "Major, at this time, under these circumstances, I am really not in a position to respond to your most flattering expressions of friendship, which I appreciate, I assure you. These are not times, as you said, when one is given to clear thinking."

Her knitting held no interest now; she knew she had missed a loop somewhere, but she could not concentrate to go back for it. But the needles clicked on as she tried to find steadiness in her rocking. She cast an uncertain glance at Duvall, who was leaning even farther forward in his chair. Ella was sure now the chair would slip. She begged it would not.

"If you will forgive me, Major Duvall," she said and began to rise.

But he reached quickly to touch her arm and she remained seated. "Mistress Bently, it is you who should forgive if I have spoken inappropriately—"

"No, no, no, Major," she insisted and thought to meet his hand on her arm but held back. "I only hope I have done nothing to give you the impression that I am frivolous or flirtatious—"

"Not at all, not at all, mistress! I consider you a mature and lovely woman, one who has been in my thoughts constantly ever since we first met at Fort Niagara so very long ago. The sight of you each morning makes my heart leap—" she thought the chair would slip out from under him at any minute "—whose lovely face makes it possible to endure the most aching collapse of spirit, the most agonizing plummeting of fortunes—" she was sure he was going to fall; the chair balanced on a razor's edge "—and I assure you, dear lady, I would risk the very brink of the abyss for your—"

"Major!" She stood up rapidly and eased him back in his seat, back from the brink, and then, relieved, she looked kindly at his shining eyes and said, "My dear Major Duvall, you must understand that my wits are not about me at the moment. Please do not consider this a rebuff, but forgive me if I am not more receptive to your kind words. Surely you understand and will forgive if I wish you a pleasant evening. Major, please come for dinner with us tomorrow night, won't you?"

He stood and bowed to kiss her hand. She smiled weakly

and went into the house. As she reached the stairs to her room, Henry Gladwin stepped into the dim hall, and they bumped into each other. He stood back. They exchanged glances and bid one another good night; then Ella hurried upstairs to tuck in Jeremy.

When she was in bed, with Jeremy sound asleep in a cot nearby, Ella stared up at the darkness. In the distance, shooting could still be heard, but she was used to it now, and it was not the shooting that kept her awake and restless.

Duvall was a good man. It was obvious how he felt about her. Her thoughts drifted back to those years between 1755 and 1758, when her husband John was an invalid after being wounded at Braddock's defeat. Henry had been wounded in the same massacre, but not severely—not like John, who had been abed for three years, devoured by the urge to work their little farm, tortured by his inability to feed Ella and the baby. Ella had earned a little by giving music and reading lessons to the few gentry in the neighborhood, but she had done no more than keep the wolf from the door.

The strain had finished John. Brave John. Brought up in New England, he was nothing like Duvall or Henry. He was a provincial—a proud and headstrong one, and she loved him all the more for that stubborn courage and simple honesty. She had met him on a visit he had made to England, and she had decided she would like to make her life in the colonies with this man. She had never regretted this decision. She loved it here, and even after John died, she wanted to be here, for this had been his home. Only after futilely attempting to make ends meet, trying to raise a growing boy by herself, had she finally contemplated returning to England.

No, John was not Alex Duvall. Those few years with him were the happiest and the saddest of her life. She could not separate the joy from the sorrow, the poignancy from the laughter, and she would have been glad to spend her life with that man, even though he could not walk. He could have given her other babies had he wanted to, but he did not want to, and there were no more after Jeremy. Now Jeremy showed the same bright vigor of his father. Although the dismaying lines of war and death already showed on the boy's innocent face, the strength of John Bently shone through. She was glad for that. He was a good boy. He would be, like his father, a very good man.

Ella drifted to sleep. Jeremy rustled and muttered in a dream.

She awoke again. Ardor, Alex had said. A nice word, but John would have said he was mad about her, impossibly, irresistibly in love with her!

Ardor. No, that would never have described her love with John. But no doubt it was just the right word for how Alex Duvall felt about her.

She turned to face the rough wall and tugged the blanket over her shoulder. Perhaps a few years in America would soften Duvall's formality, loosen him up and make him more spontaneous. A spontaneous man felt more than ardor. As Ella slipped back into sleep, she saw a familiar face, but it was not looking at her. The face was looking at a silver pendant. The pendant gleamed and was beautiful. So was the face. But the face did not see her. It saw only the silver pendant.

It had been dark for more than an hour. McEwan, sitting in the canoe with Sutherland and Tamano in the dark shelter of bushes hanging over the edge of the lake, hoped Mary was hiding near the inlet, waiting for him. When the twilight deepened to night, Sutherland steered the canoe into the little cove among the bulrushes.

He felt a kinship with McEwan's fiery determination just then, but it was not yet time for Sutherland to strike. First, McEwan must find Mary Hamilton, who would know if Breton was in the village, as Tamano had suspected. It was likely that Mary knew just where, and then Sutherland would move. Then he would go after Breton, no matter what the risk. If all went well rescuing the girl, Sutherland would go into the village that very night.

McEwan stepped out clumsily and splashed waist-deep in the still water. The others waited in the canoe while McEwan crept with as little noise as a Scots soldier could make along the line of spruce trees.

He stopped in the shadows and listened. No sound. He whispered Mary's name and listened again. Nothing but the wind rattling the branches above him.

"Mary!" he said, a little louder than he should have.

In the canoe Tamano and Sutherland glanced disapprovingly at one another. Sutherland remembered his own early years in the wilderness, when he was as inexperienced at stealth as McEwan now was. He thought to go ashore, find the girl himself, and learn about Breton.

"Mary," McEwan called softly.

No answer. Perhaps she was late. McEwan crouched in the depths of the thicket where they had made love the morning before. He searched the darkness. He prayed she was merely late, nothing else. Nothing else, please, dear God!

The wind gusted and hurried the long grass that grew around the slope of the inlet. Fifteen minutes passed. There was danger for the other two with him. He could not wait much longer. She should have been here by now. The mad desire to slip into the village took hold of McEwan. He moved through the grass up the slope and lay, unmoving, staring across the open ground at the village. It was lit by fading fires here and there. He looked closer at a larger fire in the center of the encampment. What seemed to be stark white cloths hung limply on poles around the fire.

Were they white cloths or rags? Fresh deerskins, maybe? Glowing white, tinged with red in the firelight, there were half a dozen strange objects dangling from those several poles. Then McEwan's stomach turned. He knew these rags were the bodies of English and Scottish men.

Hung, crucified, dead, and destroyed, they were the remains of prisoners taken at Michilimackinac. McEwan buried his face in his hands, fought fury and tears, and found himself hypnotized, gaping at the sight of dead men—men he might have known as friends.

There were no braves in sight. Only a squaw or two walked about the slumbering camp. The men were probably lying in a stupor of drunkenness and sated bloodlust, having spent themselves torturing the last drop of pain and blood and life from their delirious victims. Trembling, McEwan lay in the long grass, tasting sweat and tears.

A twig cracked behind him.

He held his breath. Someone was there. He slid down the slope toward the darkness of the trees. There was a deeper shadow there—a shadow of someone watching him.

"Mary?" He got to his knees and peered at the figure. "Mary, is that you?" No answer. Who was it?

His rage at the atrocity he had just seen swept the fear and caution from him. He would face whoever was in those shadows, and face him to the death if need be.

He crawled toward the shadow, and it moved, quickly crashing through the bushes, trying to escape. Without thought, McEwan was on the figure, dragging it down by the throat.

This was an enemy, and with every angry ounce of strength, McEwan throttled the man to the edge of death.

"Sergeant—Sergeant—" the victim rasped.

It was Dusten! The Frenchman wheezed and begged for mercy, but McEwan's dirk was out, and its point nicked the *voyageur*'s throat. McEwan's knee crushed down Dusten's head so the Frenchman's face pressed against the ground. The man babbled half in English and French. McEwan snatched his hair and wrenched his head back, exposing the jugular.

"Make a sound and you die!" McEwan whispered.

Dusten was afraid, but he was no coward. "Maybe you kill me anyway," he snarled, and his eyes searched for McEwan in the darkness. He grunted as McEwan jerked his neck back farther and pressed the knife cold and deadly just below his ear.

"Maybe I shall, Frenchman! I owe you death! But I need to know something, and if you tell me true, I'll let you live until the next time we meet, and then you'll die. But if you won't tell me now, or if you lie, I'll come for you and kill you in your sleep. You'll never sleep again, *métis!*"

Dusten's eyes were aflame with hatred and fear. McEwan released the man's head, but held the dirk close to his throat.

In a hoarse voice, Dusten said, "Well, *mon ami*, ask."

"Mary Hamilton! Is she here?"

Dusten held McEwan's eyes with his own, which were no longer afraid of death. "She is gone, taken by the Delaware called Sin-gat."

"Where?"

"I don't know—"

"Where?" McEwan drew blood from the Frenchman's temple. One flick and the jugular was opened and Dusten was as good as dead.

But Dusten had found his *métis* pride. "You gave me your word, Scotsman. Take away that blade, and I'll tell what I can. I'll trust your word, and you can trust mine. But if you want me to talk, take away your blade. Otherwise you can kill me."

Shaking with rage, McEwan reluctantly took the dirk from Dusten's temple.

"Where?"

Men were moving in the Chippewa camp. It sounded as though the braves were still drunk. Screeching and wailing went up among them. From where McEwan had caught Dusten on the slope down to the river, he could not see the camp, nor could he be seen from it.

Just as Dusten was about to answer, a pleading cry of agony burst from the village. McEwan felt the blood drain from his head, and he went slightly dizzy. At least one prisoner still lived. The Indians had found him and were starting all over again. The laughter of cruel delight rippled in the air. The victim whimpered without words, pleaded without sense, then moaned long and miserably and began to cough and cough.

"Where, by God?" McEwan's dirk shook so badly that Dusten stretched his head away from it and began to talk quickly.

"Away to Delaware country in Pennsylvania, near Fort Pitt. They left before dawn—in a hurry."

"By way of Detroit?"

The groaning soldier hanging like a suffering animal coughed harder, as though his very soul were vomiting with an ever-wracking, heaving expulsion.

"Detroit," Dusten said and eyed the knife that had come dangerously close. "Then along Lake Erie and south to the Delaware country."

"And Breton?"

"He's with them. A dozen of them, in two canoes."

There was the coughing sound again from the village, and the drunken Indians were laughing and mimicking the dying, helpless man.

"That's all I know. I swear! I swear." Dusten's face showed terror. "Let me live. You gave your word!"

McEwan sat up, straddling Dusten's chest. The coughing scoured his mind. He felt as though his strength was lost forever.

"My word! Yes, I gave my word. What do you know of such things, Dusten?"

McEwan got to his feet, ordered the *métis* to remove his moccasins and leggins, and bound him on his side, hand and foot, with the long leather thongs that held the footwear together. Then he gagged Dusten with the dirty red sash the Frenchman wore around his waist, and left him.

McEwan reached his friends, pushed off the canoe, and told them what he knew. Without further words, they drove the canoe fast and hard out into the river. They would find Breton, Sin-gat, and Mary Hamilton.

The glowing fire of the Chippewa camp, which was now alive

with reeling, whooping warriors, grew smaller in the distance, but over the sounds of drunken braves McEwan still heard the dying soldier coughing. They hurried down the shore of Lake Huron, and even when the light of the encampment's fires had vanished into blackness and there was just the lapping of water and paddle, McEwan was sure that awful coughing could still be heard. It echoed out to him, helpless and deathly, coughing and coughing, haunting his courage, and even purging thoughts of lovely Mary Hamilton, who had promised him an eternity ago that she would live until at last he came for her.

But they did not catch up with their quarry. Night after night of weary paddling brought no success, no discovery of their prey. They dared not travel in the daylight now, for fear of meeting hostiles as well as for worry that, if their pursuit were detected, they would be ambushed by those they were after.

A week passed, and then another. At night they crept close to campfires and searched from the darkness for familiar faces but found none. They asked questions of those they met whom they knew and could trust. Ahead of them, always ahead of them they were told, if they were told anything at all. Breton and his followers were moving fast, as if they knew they were hunted.

On the night of June 29, the canoe knifed past the anchored, silent *Huron* near Detroit's water gate, and Sutherland and McEwan cautiously made their way up to the sally port in the river wall. Tamano took the canoe across the river to find his woman, Lela, and to learn what he could from the Indians there. Sutherland and McEwan would provision themselves in the fort, and McEwan would request permission to go south with his friends, bringing dispatches to Pitt—if an excuse to go were needed. Sutherland would use what influence he had with Gladwin to take McEwan with him if they had to go south after Breton and Sin-gat. But if he were not given formal permission, McEwan swore he would desert.

Sutherland tapped a coded knock against the sally port, and startled soldiers opened the door and let him in. A young sentry stepped back and greeted Sutherland warmly and asked if he had good news, adding, "Who's this 'ere smelly savage you got with you this time?"

"Hold your tongue, Georgie!" McEwan said and swept back the old blanket that covered his shoulders. "You smell worse than I do, and worse than a lot of Indians I know."

The surprised private, mouth slack, mumbled McEwan's name and watched the two men walk quickly away into the compound.

It was past eleven, but Sutherland and McEwan hammered on Gladwin's door. They wanted news of the uprising as much as they sought to tell Gladwin of the fall of Fort Michilimackinac and the hostility of the northern Chippewa.

"Perhaps we should have gone for the duty officer instead, Owen," McEwan muttered and suddenly felt very much a fool as he looked down at his garb of filthy rags. The door was pulled open, and the sleepy face of Ella Bently poked out at them.

"Forgive the intrusion, Mistress Bently, but is—"

Ella gasped, interrupting Sutherland. Her hand went to the neck of her long cotton nightgown.

"Owen—I mean—Mr. Sutherland!" Ella shook herself awake. "Yes, Henry . . . you want Henry. Well, he's not here. He's at the officers' mess; he's with the staff. They've been meeting for—for . . . What time is it now?"

"Late, mistress," Sutherland said, and he marked that she was a fine and pretty woman even in the simplest of garments, such as this shapeless nightgown. "Go back to bed and forgive our disturbance. We'll find him ourselves. Good night."

He was walking away with McEwan's shabby, ragged hulk ambling beside him, and Ella, trying to clear her head, said, "Owen—I mean . . . Owen!" He turned to her. "Is that really you, Owen?"

"Aye, mistress."

"I thought I was dreaming."

"Good night. I'll see you tomorrow."

They were gone. Ella felt a wind drift in from the river. She shivered and closed the door. She stifled a yawn and groped upstairs to her bedroom. It really was him, wasn't it? She wasn't dreaming. Or was she?

Sutherland and McEwan walked into the dark officers' mess, and there they found a mingling of men and flickering candles in the low, stuffy room. There were a score of ensigns, lieutenants, captains, and a few traders of note jammed together, stuck sitting at tables or standing against the walls. As Sutherland and McEwan entered with the escort of a sentry, the officers became silent.

At the far side of the dim room a parchment map of the fort and its immediate environs was nailed to the rude wall planking.

At one side of the map sat Duvall and on the other side stood Major Gladwin, who brightened and gestured for Sutherland to come forward. Embarrassed by his castaway garb, McEwan lingered in the background.

"I'm glad you're back, Owen," Gladwin said. "Have you any news? Our news is all bad. Who's that with you?"

Sutherland surveyed the faces of the officers watching him. Then he nodded to McEwan, who stood up straight and let his blanket fall away, revealing the old, greasy Indian shirt. Those who knew him gasped.

"I'll let your Sergeant McEwan tell you in detail of what he's seen, but first I'll say that Michilimackinac has fallen."

A groan went through the officers, and a few heads shook sadly.

"The garrison? Lost?" Gladwin asked, and his voice nearly trembled. Sutherland nodded. "Good dear Lord." Gladwin's largest dependency fort was gone.

In the next few minutes the major told Sutherland that the situation at Detroit was nearly hopeless. Every dependency fort had fallen, according to reports of French spies and escaped soldiers. Sandusky on the southern shore of Lake Erie was destroyed. Forts Presque Isle, Le Boeuf, and Venango—the "Fort Pitt Communication," forming a chain of garrisons from Pitt northward to the south shore of Lake Erie—were burned. Fort Edward Augustus on Green Bay of Lake Michigan was abandoned under pressure from the Indians there, and its soldiers were said to be in the hands of friendly Indians who were protecting them against hostiles.

To the southwest, within two hundred miles of the central fort of Detroit, the dependency garrisons of Forts Miami, St. Joseph, and Ouatanon were lost, with most of their defenders massacred. These garrisons numbered between a dozen men and a few traders under an ensign, to as many as thirty-five at Michilimackinac under the command of a captain.

From Gladwin, Sutherland learned the uprising had kindled the entire territory. To the east powerful Fort Pitt was under attack by hundreds of Indians, and those few couriers who got past the Indian marauders said Forts Ligonier and Bedford farther east in the settled mountain country west of the Cumberland Gap were also in danger of falling. Fort Lyttleton with its three or four defenders in that region had already been abandoned.

The settlements in the vicinity of Fort Pitt, where whites had filtered in from over the Appalachian mountains, were stricken with panic. Farms and outlying homes and mills were burned down. Hundreds of people—men, women, and children—had been killed by war parties, and many more were prisoners. Thousands of settlers were fleeing in panic from even the rumor of Indians. Many had stood to fight, been cut off, and were massacred.

Then, as though this tale had exhausted him, Gladwin slowly told the tale of the relief convoy that was lost downriver. Sutherland listened quietly, without emotion, until Gladwin's story spent itself with the last words, ". . . and here at Detroit there are more than fifteen hundred hostiles surrounding us. And we have little to eat. Pontiac has offered terms of surrender and has promised we can leave in safety if we lay down our arms. But that I do not believe, not after I have seen how treachery has been the downfall of many garrisons at the hands of Pontiac's followers. Owen, we are facing the greatest uprising of Indians in the history of American colonization. And we are losing the war."

There was a long silence. The officers looked about the room dejectedly, shuffling their feet, clearing their throats.

Gladwin spoke again. "We are in our second month of siege, Owen, and we have not yet received provisions. If not for our brave French friends who have brought us food, Pontiac would have starved us out weeks ago. And if he decides to attack us and sacrifice heavily, there is no way we can stand against him. I realize you are not an officer, and I realize you have certain interests among the Indians, but we would welcome any suggestions you might have for us—any thoughts on how we can get food, for that is our one necessity that is most lacking."

Sutherland looked at Gladwin's dark eyes. After a pause he said, "I'll leave tomorrow with a few provincials and we'll see what we can do about bringing in some fresh meat. We'll go at nightfall, by canoe, and we'll head north, where there are few hostiles. We'll come back in a week. But I can do no more than that. Perhaps we can shoot and salt enough game to last until help comes from Niagara. But, Major, you know I have my own task to complete—though, for the moment, I seem to have been eluded. Tamano is gathering information for me, and he'll be back at the fort in a week. I shall have some food by then, if we get through. But at that time, I must be away on my own mission, which you—"

"Your own mission!" It was Duvall whose voice sounded

like a hungry snarl. "That's just like you, Sutherland. You abandon your own people to attend to your own selfish business!"

"Enough!" Gladwin smashed his fist against a table that rattled and nearly toppled with the fury of his blow. "I'll have no bickering!" He cast a hot glance at Duvall, who stuck up his nose and faced away.

Sutherland looked at Gladwin and said, "Major, I want no part in your war councils. This fight is your government's to finish. I have my own fight to finish. But I'll do what I can to help, short of taking up weapons for you." He looked squarely at Duvall. "I have my own duty to do. It was the duty of your administrators to keep the peace, and they bungled that! They won't spill my blood making this war!"

He swung angrily toward the door, but Duvall jumped up and pointed a shaking finger at his back.

"Treason! Treason, I say! Again you speak like a traitor, Sutherland! Treason! Have you not yet learned the lesson of disobeying His Majesty's Government?"

Sutherland spun in fury, but McEwan and several other officers stepped in the way. Sutherland's hand was on the hilt of the claymore at his side. Duvall's fist rested on his own sword.

But Gladwin's sword was already out, and he swung it down between the two men.

"Stop! Now! Or I'll have both of you in irons! Major Duvall, you are an officer, and you'll behave like one, or you'll have me to contend with! Owen, I suggest you depart. I gratefully accept your offer of hunting for us. Draw supplies from the traders, and tell them to charge it to the army's account. Gentlemen, I declare this meeting finished for now, but I expect you all here tomorrow, one hour after morning muster. Dismissed."

McEwan and another young officer shouldered the maddened Sutherland out into the cool night. There he willed away his black mood and returned with McEwan to the noncommissioned officers' barracks. It was too late at night to go to the Morelys', so he would stay in the barracks tonight, and then, while Tamano spent a week searching for news about Breton and Mary Hamilton, Sutherland would risk his neck on a hunting trip that might end with him becoming the prey.

As he unbuckled his sword in the slumbering barracks, Sutherland wondered why he had agreed to hunt for the fort. Instead he ought to be preparing himself for the chase after

Breton, which could resume at any moment. He lay down on the hard cot, slid under the blanket, and tried not to think about Alex Duvall. He must concentrate on the problems immediately facing him. Duvall had once been a problem, but that was in the past. Yet as much as he hoped he would never be forced to confront that man again, it seemed sure that Duvall would one day stand in his path. And no one could stand between him and André Breton. No one, and survive.

For Sir Jeffrey Amherst, sleep was hard in coming these days. As he sat at his writing desk, a candle flickering nearby, he hated to admit that William Johnson had been right. But even if he had agreed to Johnson's insistence that presents be given the Indians, this conflict between whites and Indians would have had to come sooner or later. Their ways of life were too different, and the Indians held far too much rich land to expect that the two civilizations would not ultimately clash.

Well, that clash had come, and it had proved to be of broader scope than Amherst had thought possible. Certainly he had never expected the Indians capable of capturing British forts and besieging Detroit and Pitt. These matters would not look good at all to the king, not at all. There would be many questions to answer when he returned to England.

Amherst dipped his quill in the inkwell and gritted his teeth. This was a moment for bold action. He had already ordered every available soldier to assemble for relief of Detroit and Pitt, though he had only limited resources to work with now that the great armies of the last war were dissolved or sent overseas. But there were a few understrength regiments preparing for the campaign.

And Amherst had another idea—a diabolical one, even he knew. But he hated the Indians so, that he was willing to go to any lengths to wipe them out. He addressed the letter to Colonel Henry Bouquet, the officer commanding the force now being mustered to relieve Fort Pitt. In the heart of the letter he wrote: *I wish there were not an Indian Settlement within a thousand miles of our Country, for they are only fit to live with the Inhabitants of the woods (i.e. wild beasts), being more allied to the Brute than the human creation.*

The letter ended with the following thought: *Could it not be contrived to send the Small Pox among those disaffected tribes of Indians? We must on this occasion use every strategem in our power to reduce them.*

As Amherst sealed the letter with a drop of wax stamped with his official mark, there was no thought in his mind of just how the smallpox infection, once among the hostile Indians, would be kept from spreading to peaceful tribes—such as Johnson's Iroquois. But General Sir Jefferey Amherst really did not care.

chapter **14**

THE PRISONER

"Yes, if anyone can get in and out of this coop to get some huntin' done, it be thee, Owen lad," said Garth Morely with a nod into his pewter mug of rum. He clinked the mug against Owen Sutherland's, and they toasted good hunting in the north country. Sutherland stood on the other side of the counter in Morely's trading house. It was midmorning, and Sutherland had come for provisions and powder to supply the expedition.

"But take care of thyself, Owen. Me and my missus would be sorry ter see thy untimely end, and if them red varmints captivates thee and they knows thee be a-helpin' us, then thy days be done, lad." He poured each of them another stiff four ounces. "Aye, we'd be almost as disappointed as that nice Mistress Bently ter see thee deaded."

Sutherland paused before he drank. He looked with curiosity at the grizzled trader, whose eyes were alight with humor. But Sutherland ignored the strange comment about Ella Bently and drank the burning rum. Morely went on.

"Yes, yes, Owen, that lass—a good-lookin' woman she be, too—gets to visitin' with my Lettie and they get to gabblin' about this and that, and thee be one of the mistress's favoritest subjects, yes."

Sutherland had too much on his mind to pay more than a little attention to Morely's silly suggestions that Gladwin's sister was interested in him. He hadn't given her much thought, although she was certainly an attractive and capable woman. Morely's clever, twinkling eyes searched Sutherland over the rim of the trader's mug. Sutherland drained the rum and felt it rush to his head.

"That's good Jamaican, Garth," he said. "But I fear your talk is a bit fuddled with it this early in the day. Now, fix me up with some game bags, powder—"

Suddenly there was a general shouting outside in the street. A cannon on the cavalier boomed and another replied from out on the river.

"The *Michigan!*" Morely exploded. "It's back!" He and Sutherland hustled out the door and joined the crowd of people hurrying toward the wall nearest the river. "It'll have supplies for us, lad!" Morely shouted as they ran up the ladder of the parapet. "Thee won't be needin' ter go on that trip now, Owen. We'll be fixed good until reinforcements come enough ter stop this uprisin' once and for all!"

Soldiers, traders, women, and children crowded onto the ramparts, hanging over the stockade's pointed top and waving jackets, handkerchiefs, hats and shirts at the *Michigan*, which was gliding with a good wind behind it up to the fort. Then the sails were furled as the ship came about and anchored a few score yards from the walls of Detroit. Sutherland saw bullet holes scattered all along its hull. Its sail canvas was shredded and pocked by gunshots, and on deck several wounded men were quickly lifted over the side and lowered in hammocks to longboats and bateaux that came out from the fort. At least fifty soldiers were on the *Michigan*, and they waved to the cheering, laughing inhabitants of the besieged outpost.

The crowd on the ramparts shouted at the newcomers, and someone led three cheers in unison.

"Isn't it wonderful? Isn't it just wonderful?" a woman laughed near Sutherland. He looked at her and saw it was Ella Bently. She was hugging a scarlet-coated officer. He thought it was Gladwin, but when they pulled apart and the man swung Ella around, Sutherland saw it was Alex Duvall. He drew his eyes away, but just before they left her, Ella noticed him staring, and she smiled warmly in a way that unveiled to Sutherland how remarkably lovely a woman she really was. He looked back at her, and she was still watching him. Duvall was searching the ship, counting the number of reinforcements, though Ella's forearms still rested in his hands. Sutherland smiled with a self-consciousness that surprised him—a self-consciousness he thought was lost with distant youth. He nodded to Ella and sheepishly lifted his cap.

"Certainly is fine, Mistress Bently. Certainly is."

She said nothing. Sutherland turned away and followed Morely back down to the ground.

"No, Owen, that huntin' trip won't be necessary, not now that we have all these fresh provisions, eh?"

Sutherland walked beside the swarthy trader. "No, but I've a different kind of hunting to do."

Morley glanced up at him as he walked. Then he put an arm on Sutherland's shoulder and tugged him. "Aye, lad, do that huntin'. But don't be away from this place too long, or that Major Duvall will have done his own huntin', and that there Mistress Bently will be faced with the sorry prospect of spendin' her life with a bug-tit English officer, polish and spit an' all."

Sutherland laughed as they walked into the trading shop. He picked up his gear, slung much of it over his shoulder, and said, "Her business is none of mine, Garth. Sometimes you say unfathomable things, trader." As he went out the door, Sutherland said, "Sometimes I think you've been too long among these English, laddie."

After he returned to the non commissioned officers' barracks to get the rest of his gear, a message came from Gladwin that Sutherland was invited to dinner at the major's house that evening. The note was brought by young Jeremy, who was eager and excited to see Sutherland once more. With the boy, Sutherland forgot the stress and restlessness that plagued him when he was not on Breton's trail, and he decided to accept the dinner invitation and wait until morning to leave the fort. He was pleased to be with Jeremy as they stroll leisurely through the fort, past the happy bustle of a frontier garrison reprovisioning after a long period of near-starvation. Hogsheads of salt pork and fish were rolled by the dozen through the streets. Soldiers joined the traders in meeting the laden bateaux that came ashore after emptying the *Michigan* of its ample provisions from Fort Niagara.

Detroit was so busy that Sutherland and Jeremy ascended to an open blockhouse for some solitude. The blockhouse looked broadly over the river to the northeast, and they sat on benches there, talking for the most part about Indians, because Jeremy hungered for knowledge about them.

"Sometimes Menabozho, who was so strong and wise, was outwitted even by children," Sutherland said as he stuck his feet up against the stockade and leaned back on the bench. Jeremy straddled the bench and listened to another tale about

Menabozho, the great Algonquin manitou who fought with the gods and sometimes appeared in the guise of a white hare spirit.

"That doesn't seem right, Mr. Sutherland," Jeremy said and looked down at his scuffed buckled shoes. "How can a child outsmart a god? That seems sacri—sacrilegious, I think is what Reverend Lee would say."

"Well," Sutherland said, smiling and stretching out his long legs, "nobody outsmarted Menabozho for long. And this story is about how the great manitou always got the best of anyone who tried to best him:

"There was a young Ottawa boy who thought he was very clever. And he was. He bet Menabozho he could do something the great manitou couldn't. Now all Indians love to gamble, lad, and if they're gambling, they'll sometimes gamble until they lose everything—even their wives, and there are some who have lost a finger or two. Those are not the best gamblers, of course. But Menabozho is the best of the best, and he knew no child could outdo him. So when the boy asked to have any wish granted if he won the bet, Menabozho laughed and agreed."

Jeremy's eyes were wide.

"Well, without even trying, the boy sat right down, took off his moccasin, and stuck his big toe in his mouth. 'Let's see you do that, Menabozho!' he said. So the manitou sat down on the ground, took off his moccasin, and brought his foot up—almost—to his mouth—but not quite all the way. He pulled and tugged and pushed that toe at his mouth until his face was red all over and sweat was running from everywhere. But still he couldn't get that toe in his mouth. Because the boy was young and his muscles were so loose he could easily put his toe in his mouth, but the old, strong, hard Menabozho, was too stiff to do it." Sutherland slapped his thigh. "So he lost the bet."

Jeremy's shoe was off, his sock limp on the bench, and he shoved his big toe into his mouth with a gleeful, triumphant giggle.

"The boy got his wish, and he asked for a very, very long life. Well, Menabozho gave it to him: He turned him into a tall white cedar tree that was rooted to the spot, although it lived for many, many years."

"Oh, no!" Jeremy groaned. "If I beat the manitou in a bet, I wouldn't give him a chance to trick me like that."

Sutherland laughed. "Don't be so sure, lad. Nobody is as

clever as a manitou, and that story tells you never ever try to outdo him."

Jeremy spat after he stuck his toe again into his mouth. Then the boy looked up with mischief on his face.

"I'm going to try this one! I'm going to make a bet with Major Duvall!"

"Duvall?"

"Yes! I bet he can't put his big toe in his mouth!"

"Hah! No, not without a boot on it! But what will you bet, lad? What do you want from him?"

Jeremy was already climbing down the ladder of the block-house. "If I win," he said and poked his head up above the floor, "he'll have to agree not to court my ma any more. That way, she'll have time for you!"

Sutherland nearly fell backwards off the bench. He caught himself in time and banged forward, flatfooted, on the wooden flooring. His mouth was open so wide that he might have fit in his own big toe, moccasin, leggins, and all.

At dinner that night, Sutherland resolved to avoid controversy with Alex Duvall, who was at the table with Reverend Lee and Ella. But there was little chance for unpleasantness with Duvall, for the major gave over all his attention to Ella, sitting next to him. In the candlelit dining room the conversation was light and avoided the subject of the uprising. Sutherland was glad to see Henry Gladwin looking rested. The commander's garrison had been strengthened by troops from the *Michigan,* and dispatches told that another relief convoy was on the way from Niagara. It struck Sutherland that the table seemed somehow less complete without the jovial Captain Campbell, still a prisoner of the Indians.

By the time the dessert of cream and peaches was finished, Sutherland was uneasy. It seemed to him that he had tried too hard avoiding subjects that were close to the surface rather than freely speaking with Gladwin and Reverend Lee. Also annoying to Sutherland was the steady, low-voiced banter of Alex Duvall joking and mooning at Ella. Sutherland was surprised that she appeared to be enjoying the major's inane display of empty-headed laughter and compliments. He had expected much more than that from a woman like Ella Bently. It took all his concentration to pay attention to Gladwin and the reverend.

Lee was recalling more peaceful times at Detroit, when his

only problem was keeping drunken Indians out of choir practice. Now the Indians were gone from the fort, as well as the Frenchwomen who lived outside, and Lee was left with his nondescript chorus of English singers. He grumbled to Gladwin, "I'd buy a hogshead of beer myself to keep those old Indians happy if it meant this trouble was done with and my Frenchwomen came back to sing for me again."

Despite the great responsibilities he was faced with, Gladwin chuckled, but Sutherland was silent. Ella thought Owen unusually morose this evening. Presumably he was still deep in mourning for his woman, and no doubt his dark thoughts were of taking revenge on André Breton. Pity that Sutherland was so preoccupied, she thought as Duvall said something and laughed. Pity, for tonight—now that the *Michigan* had relieved them at last of the awful hunger that had haunted every moment of the past two months—she wanted so much to be happy, if only for this one meal. Duvall was trying to cheer her, and that was nice of him, but Owen Sutherland's glowering face and his constant absorption in thought dulled the glow of what she had hoped would be a pleasant dinner. Determined to enjoy herself, Ella gave Alex Duvall as much attention as she could muster. At least he was in a good frame of mind.

Soon after the dinner Sutherland began to follow Lee out the door, but Gladwin caught him by the arm and protested that this was the first time in months that they could spend the evening together. Why was Sutherland hurrying off before even the cordials were served?

"Stay, stay, Owen," Gladwin said and bustled Sutherland into a comfortable chair in the parlor, where a chessboard and ivory pieces were set up. "How about a game, Owen?" Gladwin was like an eager father who finally has found the time to play with his son who is unused to the attention. "Let's have a few fills and a game or two, lad," Gladwin said and brought out two long-stem clay Dutch pipes. "Tonight this trouble doesn't exist. Be a good fellow, now!"

Sutherland smiled as Gladwin plumped down in the chair across the chessboard. It was good to see the tension lifted from his friend's shoulders. Then he looked over at Ella, who was sitting with Major Duvall on the divan near the window. She was dressed in a soft blue brocade gown that revealed her lovely neck and arms. She had worn that gown before, he recalled, but he had not really noticed then how well it suited her. In his proud scarlet uniform, white pants and vest and glittering gold adornments, Duvall looked a handsome partner for Ella Bently.

"I think, Henry," Sutherland said and nodded in the direction of the couple on the divan, "that we'll be rather dull company for them if we lock ourselves up in chess and pipes."

Ella heard and was about to speak, but Duvall said grandly, "Not at all, gentlemen! Not at all. Mistress Bently and I were discussing the pleasures of a turn about the parade ground. I commend you both to your sport and your tobacco."

Duvall stood and offered his arm to Ella, who rose with him and seemed to avoid looking at Sutherland. When the door closed behind them, Sutherland was trying to contemplate the chess pieces: He heard Ella laugh as they went down the steps of the front porch.

A scheming look of eagerness came into Gladwin's eyes as he sucked and puffed his pipe to a hot glow. "Now then, Owen! Just like old times, eh? How I've longed for a good game of chess with you these last few weeks. I tried Duvall once or twice. He's solid enough, but not very exciting. No imagination, and he hates to lose more than I do. Too predictable . . . Are you listening, I say?"

Sutherland sighed and gave his attention to Gladwin, who went on about Sutherland's crafty mind, which he asserted was a sly combination of Indian and Scot. Sutherland filled and lit his own pipe. The laughter of Ella and Duvall was gone now. He thought of Mayla briefly, but that was too much pain to consider at this moment.

"Let's get on with it," Gladwin was saying to an unhearing Sutherland. "Which do you want, white or black? I say, white or black? Owen, are you listening?"

"What?" Sutherland noticed his pipe had not caught very well. "Oh, yes, of course I heard you," he said and lit a piece of straw at the candle. "Now, what shall we do, Henry? Do you want white or black?"

In the next hour Gladwin outplayed, outclassed, and outwitted Sutherland at every turn in a game that was slow and uninspired. At last Sutherland conceded defeat and leaned back in his chair to drink a glass of brandy.

"Well, Owen, I daresay that was the worst I've ever seen you play. Tonight we were supposed to get everything off our minds, remember? Well, you've certainly got a lot more on your mind than playing chess. Why, you could have taken advantage of several good opportunities, but you—"

In the background they heard a flurry of musketry.

"That's the detachment I sent out at sunset to fire some French houses where Indian sharpshooters were hiding lately. Must have met some resistance." Gladwin's mind floated away to listen for the shots, but there was no more gunfire. "Stopped shooting. Must be all right. I've given orders to be called if anything is amiss. No," he sat back and put down his cold pipe, "we can't get away from this war even for an hour or two, can we?" He looked weary again, as though the dinner and the chess game had been an illusion.

"They've been gone a long time," Sutherland said and picked up a chess piece.

"Long time? Yes, perhaps. They went out at dusk, but they had a lot of work to take what's worth saving from those houses and give it back to the French—"

"No, not the soldiers. I mean your sister and Duvall."

Gladwin looked closely at Sutherland then. But the Scotsman merely shook out his pipe, tapping the dottle into his palm, not meeting his friend's probing eyes.

"Do you think she needs a chaperon, Owen?"

Sutherland forced a grunt of laughter and stretched his arms sleepily. "I think you ought to ask her consent for a chaperon, don't you, Henry? These are modern days, and she is grown up."

Gladwin chuckled. "Shall I ask her if you'll do?"

Sutherland shook his head and stood up. "I'm spoken for already. There's a *métis* who already has me as his shadow."

"Afterwards?"

Sutherland was too sleepy to continue this idle talk. He turned away to retrieve his hat from a peg near the door.

"Pity," Gladwin said. "You'd be a good chaperon, and I daresay Ella would very much like having you close by."

Sutherland let his hands drop to his sides. He stared at Gladwin, whose cool eyes were unperturbed and steady. This was all very puzzling, Sutherland thought: Again someone was mentioning that Ella Bently was somehow interested in him.

"Henry, I don't know what you're driving at." He tried to yawn casually, but it would not come and left him with his mouth half open. "But it appears your sister has a very able and eager escort already, and both of them are old enough to do without a chaperon, especially one who likes Duvall as much as I do. Good Lord, what am I talking about? You begin in jest, and now you have me talking seriously about this—nonsense. Good night."

As Gladwin rose to walk Sutherland to the door, there was a shout outside and someone in boots jumped heavily onto the porch and banged the door, calling Gladwin's name. The major opened the door to let in a young corporal whose face was hot and sweaty from a run through the fort.

"Major, we've taken a prisoner, sir. The party you sent out ran into some skulking Indians and Frenchmen and drove them off. They caught that translator you said you wanted so bad. Found him hiding in a house. That fellow Breton!"

Sutherland burst out the door, leaped from the porch, and charged up the Rue Saint Jacques toward the western gate. Behind him, stumbling and buckling on his sword belt, raced Henry Gladwin, shouting for Sutherland to stop. But Sutherland turned onto the Rue Sainte Anne with Gladwin far behind. The major shouted for soldiers to stop Sutherland, and a few stepped into his path, but they were immediately bowled over. In Sutherland's enraged mind there was no thought, no reason. He craved only to clutch André Breton's throat.

Ahead, at the open gate, the group of soldiers with fixed bayonets turned when Gladwin shouted to them. The careening Sutherland saw a darker figure in the midst of the soldiers, and he concentrated on getting at it. He did not notice an officer command the soliders to cross muskets and shield the prisoner. People poked heads from windows to see the running Sutherland and the stumbling Gladwin, scabbard trailing, rush past.

Sutherland shouldered into the mass of soldiers, but though several of them were shoved away, they resisted his rush. He hung over the linked muskets and surged forward at Breton, teeth bared, his heart aflame with hatred.

The officer in charge shouted at Sutherland, grappling at his shoulders and threatening arrest. But Sutherland swung his arms free and tossed the officer head over heels onto his back. André Breton stood impassively. Hatless, dressed in torn flannels and buckskin, arms at his sides, fists clenched, he kept his eyes fixed somewhere in the distance.

Gladwin clattered up just as the fallen officer stood and drew his sword.

"Hold!" Gladwin shouted and leaped into the group of soldiers wrestling with Sutherland. Gladwin stood squarely between Sutherland and Breton, who were less than fifteen feet apart. The major drew his own sword.

"If you want to try and get him, Owen, I'll order my men to let you go! But you'll have to do it over me!"

Gladwin stood at full height now, chest heaving. Dressed only in a white shirt and breeches with silk knee-stockings, the major's body gleamed fiery red in the light of torches carried by the soldiers.

With the agony of revenge burning inside him, Sutherland grunted and swore, but he seemed not to see or hear Gladwin. He was held about the waist and shoulders by four soldiers, who had all they could do to keep him from bursting free.

"Sutherland!" Gladwin shouted again. "Hear me now! I am the law here! This man is my prisoner. He shall be court-martialed by me in accordance with the regulations of this post. Stand now, Owen, or you face me. Will you stand?"

Sutherland at last comprehended Gladwin's words. He rasped for breath, took his eyes for the moment from Breton, and saw Gladwin's sword naked in front of him. Then he looked again at Breton, who was drawn and weary, as though the flight from Sutherland had taken much of his strength. Gladwin said, "Get hold of yourself, Owen. Steady yourself now, before—"

"Henry," Sutherland gasped. "All right, I'll not kill him now. I want no quarrel with you. But—" He moved forward, and the soldiers, who had relaxed their grip, wrenched him to a stop once more. "Just let me look for something on this dog's head, Henry. I swear to you I'll not draw his blood. Let me assure myself of something."

Gladwin glanced at the soldiers holding Sutherland.

"Your word, Owen. If you fail me, I'll have you in irons."

Gladwin paused a moment, then nodded to the four men and they reluctantly released Sutherland, who set his eyes on Breton, then stepped forward. Breton cast a wary look out of the corner of his eye. He was tense as Sutherland came to him and reached slowly with one hand at the side of Breton's head.

"Stand easy, snake," Sutherland said quietly. "If you don't stand easy, I may forget my oath and break your neck." Breton flinched as Sutherland touched his long, greasy hair. But the Frenchman did not pull away, nor did he look at Sutherland.

His heart flurrying, Sutherland slowly pushed away the hair covering Breton's left ear. There! Just before Breton yanked his head away and stepped back against the palisade wall, Sutherland saw what he had expected to see: a still-unhealed scar that raked the *voyageur*'s head from temple to ear. Even part of the ear had been shot away by Lela's bullet on that night when Breton had . . .

Awful trembling overtook Sutherland, and blackness came into his eyes. All he could see was the face of Breton staring back at him. Sutherland felt his fists shake, and they came up as of their own will and reached for the Frenchman. But men caught Sutherland by the arms, and Gladwin thrust himself into the narrow space between him and the cornered Breton.

Gladwin growled, "Take the prisoner to the guardhouse tonight." The major's face filled Sutherland's numbed vision. Gladwin's face, nothing more. Then Sutherland was adrift in despair.

Breton was gone, and the soldiers dispersed. A little crowd of French residents and traders had gathered and now stood murmuring nearby. Slowly, with every breath short, Owen Sutherland returned to the present. Gladwin was gone, too.

For some time after the crowd moved off, he stood helplessly. He thought of nothing at all, not even of Mayla. His eyes were blank. Then a gentle hand touched his arm.

Before him was a face profound and sad and consoling, as though it understood the depth of his sorrow, transformed it into compassion, and returned it as comfort. It was Ella Bently.

Sutherland sighed. Despair shivered once within him. Her hand touched his sweaty face.

Then he stirred. She took her hand from his cheek, fitted her arm in his, and moved him away, guiding him back to life, walking with him down the Rue Sainte Anne, where windows were shuttered against the night, and the street was deserted.

But among the deeper shadows near the gate a tall man stood, his hands limp at his sides. He looked helpless, forlorn. It was Alex Duvall . . .

Back in the commander's house Sutherland was composed as he sat with Ella and Gladwin at the table. There was little said as they drank tea. The silence was broken only by the clink of china. Sutherland squeezed the hot wax of a candle.

Gladwin said, "We'll have a proper trial of André Breton— on charges of treason, inciting the Indians—and then later, if you wish, you can press charges against him for—for—"

Sutherland said nothing. He drank sullenly.

"He'll hang, Owen," Gladwin said. "You'll have to be satisfied with that."

Silence.

Ella put her cup in its saucer and said, "That's surely better than having his blood on your hands, isn't it?"

Sutherland looked at her, and his eyes were cold. "That, mistress, I'll tell you when I know he's dead."

Ella felt revulsion at the idea of Breton swinging from a gallows; revulsion at the thought of Sutherland in the act of taking Breton's life. She understood Sutherland's motives, but the thought of him killing Breton revolted her.

"Mistress?"

She hesitantly looked up at Sutherland, and she was surprised that his face had softened somewhat.

"Thank you," he said.

Her lips moved weakly. She nodded and forced the teacup to come up.

"I'm grateful for what you did for me tonight," he said.

She intended to reply nonchalantly with a hearty disclaimer, but her throat refused to release the words, and she felt somewhat stupid. Her eyes were down on the teacup, then she raised them to confront his, and it was unexpectedly easy to look at him. They saw each other in that moment, a moment that lasted an eternity. Then Henry Gladwin yawned and said, "I think I'll away to bed." He rose.

Sutherland scratched an ear and pulled his nose. "Aye, Henry. I'll be going. Thank you, too, my friend, for not throwing me into the guardhouse earlier, though I imagine you would have if Breton wasn't already in there."

Sutherland stood. Gladwin grunted and said, "Sister, will you see Owen to the door? Thanks. I'm fair puckled, as a tired Scot says. Good night. Good night." Gladwin yawned broadly and stamped up the stairs, leaving Sutherland and Ella alone. She sat a moment longer, staring at him as he took his hat from the peg near the door and turned to face her. She got up and came to him.

"I'll be at the Morelys' until the trial," he said. "If I can ever be of service, mistress." He bowed slightly, and she held her hand to him. He took it and kissed it, but it seemed to her as if his thoughts were somewhere else at that moment. She stood within the doorframe as he walked across the parade ground. She wished he would have stayed longer.

"Sleep well, Owen," she whispered. Then she closed the door and went upstairs, thinking of him.

• • •

Alex Duvall reeled slightly. The rum had found him at last. He walked from his private cabin and went to the officers' mess a short distance away. There were men inside, drinking the rum just come out from Niagara. Light filtered from the windows, and a buzz of conversation and intermittent laughter burst out as he pulled open the front door.

He shoved inside and bumped against tables. Young officers cursed at first, then froze when they saw it was the major. They avoided his surly stare as he moved to the back of the room, sat down heavily, and thumped the tabletop.

"Rum here, orderly!" The room went quiet. Duvall looked around at faces blurred by smoke and shadows of candlelight.

"Well, what're you all leering at?" Duvall blared as a flagon of rum was placed carefully on his table. "Get on with your celebration! That's what we're doing, isn't it? Celebrating our resurrection, thanks to the arrival of the *Michigan*? Celebrate! Drink, you officers of His Royal Majesty's singularly squalid bastion of English power in this godforsaken wilderness! Drink, you heroes! And remember that the honor of your regiments is at stake! So drink like officers, like English officers, and be damned!"

The faces turned toward Duvall in the gloom were a mixture of anxiety and hardbitten cynicism. The young officers were tense, unsure of whether to stay or leave. The older men, veterans all of the French wars, drank slowly, and their eyes lazily withdrew from Duvall, who guzzled his rum and clanged the flagon down. His eyes ranged around the silent room, but they were too fogged to see a calm face staring at him from the far corner. It was the face of one who had no honor as an English officer to uphold. It was the face of Duncan McEwan, who had been breveted temporary ensign by Gladwin, and was in the officers' mess for the first time.

Two men emptied their mugs, stood, and departed. Duvall looked up from his flagon, which was being refilled by an orderly, and he saw the door close.

"Hey! Where are they going?" he lifted the flagon, splashing rum about as he waved it at the door. "Can't they drink like English officers? Pah! Probably Scotchmen! Never could be sociable that kind! Scotchmen! Pah!" He belched. Words slid thickly from his lips. "We don't need Scotchmen! We need English officers, then we'd go out and whip these damned heathens, damned slimy heathens! English! That's what we need!" Duvall went on mumbling.

McEwan's anger rose, kindled by a goodly amount of rum within him. A young officer seated with him spoke quietly, trying to distract him from Duvall, joking with him. But McEwan heard nothing. He stared at Duvall, who was talking again.

"Scotch officers! Pah! Pah! Pah! Can't drink! Can't fight! Can't do anything worth a tinker's damn! Damn 'em! I know! I commanded Scotch officers! Not worth a tinker's bloody damn! Better have no officers than Scotch officers! Let them go! Let the bastards go! Let all the Scotchmen go! And we'll fight like Englishmen! We'll drink like Englishmen, and we'll copulate like Englishmen! Hah, hah, hah, hah! Yes, we'll show these ladies how an Englishman can love them, and let the Scotch lie with their sheep and filthy Indians!"

McEwan was on his feet. The next moment he was borne backwards by half a dozen hands that heaved him down into his seat. He fought to stand. Men whispered warnings at him. He swore and strained against them.

A captain distracted Duvall, agreeing and nodding as he hovered over the drunken major, and waving his hand behind his back. The men restraining the sputtering McEwan lifted the young ensign off the floor and carried him to the door. McEwan growled and writhed, but he was dragged away and thrust out into the cool night, where two officers hurried him back to his barracks.

"You'll do yourself no good killing that swine," one said while he prodded McEwan away. "He's not worth it, man. Not worth it!"

Inside, Duvall looked up as the door slammed shut and the remaining officers took their seats again. He was too dazed to understand what went on.

"More Scotchmen leaving, I see!" He guffawed into his mug. "That's what you can expect from Scotch officers. They run. They don't stick by you when it counts. Orderly, rum all around, and put it on my bill! Drink up, lads!"

The officers relaxed now. They joked quietly about what would have happened had McEwan reached Duvall. They drank up the free rum, gave Duvall backhanded compliments, and generally ignored his rambling tirade. But when Duvall snarled the name of Owen Sutherland, all heads turned and the room became silent once more.

Duvall was slouched in his chair, his head lolling. But he struggled to gulp more rum and forced his eyes to penetrate as best they could the dimness about him, searching out faces to address.

"Yes, Owen Sutherland. Now there's a fine example of a Scotchman, a Scotch officer, for you! Take warning, men. I know you all think he's a great man! But I warn you now, don't trust him with your lives!" Duvall's face flared dully, and he pointed his finger at the others. "It's only for your own good that I warn you against that Scotchman! I know he's Gladwin's favorite—"

The captain interrupted cheerfully and tried to change the subject. But Duvall would not be put off. He had come for a purpose, and he was not so benumbed by drink that he would not say what he intended to say.

"You don't want to hear what I have to tell you, but when I'm done you'll never again trust your scalps or your women in his hands. And if you don't believe me, you can search the records of the Ministry of War, and there you'll find the truth about that bloody bastard! Orderly! Drinks all around! Now soldiers, I'll give you a lesson that you'll be eternally grateful for. It's a lesson about Scotchmen, a lesson I learned, and in learning, watched the defeat of an entire army . . ."

Everyone was hushed as Duvall told the story of the battle in Europe, the same story he had told Sir Robert weeks ago. Now and again an officer snickered and winked in jest, hinting at disbelief to a comrade. But somehow the story rang true, and Duvall's swearing that its proof was in military records also generated uncertainty. After all, it was a fair enough explanation of how a man like Owen Sutherland came to this desolate wilderness, a solitary Scotsman among French, Indians, and half-breeds.

Of course Duvall was drunk and no doubt exaggerated the tale, but the story about Sutherland would make for a fascinating tidbit to tell wives and sweethearts—provided, of course, the women swore themselves to secrecy. Secrecy was essential, for a scandal could cause bitter hatred between friends and enemies of the rumor's subject. And in a besieged outpost, harmony was essential to survival. They might relate this story about Sutherland, but they would assure whomever they told that it was only speculation and nothing more. Everyone knew and respected Owen Sutherland, and he deserved that respect.

Just the same, it was an interesting story, even if it were no more than partly true.

chapter 15

PURSUIT

Bells clanging madly shocked Sutherland awake in the back room of Morely's warehouse. He thought they were being attacked. It was the middle of the night. He hurriedly dragged on his hunting shirt and leggins. In a moment he was in the street standing next to Garth Morely. Soldiers were scrambling into tunics and running back and forth, some carrying lanterns and others muskets. Somewhere a drum rattled out muster.

"What's happened?" Sutherland asked as he grabbed a young private by the shirtfront.

"Murder's done!" the boy clamored. "The sentry's throat's cut and that Frenchy spy's got clean away!"

Sutherland wrenched the private against him and gaped in speechless disbelief at the bewildered youth. The soldier pushed away and stumbled off, glancing back once to be sure Sutherland was not chasing him. But Owen Sutherland was too devastated to move.

Within an hour Sutherland and McEwan were supplied, armed, and prepared to leave. A canoe had been loaded with provisions for three weeks, powder, rum, trade goods, and tools. Sutherland had not spoken a word when Gladwin summoned him and offered whatever he could spare to apprehend Breton. Three guards had been killed by an accomplice, who had apparently slipped over the ramparts near the water gate, surprised the sentry there, and made the soldier his first victim. A corporal sleeping in the duty quarters was next, tomahawked in his bunk, and the keys to Breton's guardhouse were stolen. The sentry at the door of Breton's jail suffered the same fate, and all three had been brazenly scalped.

The entire fort was awake, though it was well before dawn. Light flickered at windows. Soldiers came and went, patrolling within a hundred yards of the fort. But Breton was gone.

It was decided that Sutherland and McEwan would cross the river to find Tamano at their prearranged meeting place; and after Tamano gathered information of Breton's route, the three men—with McEwan disguised as a trader in linsey and buckskin—would go after the *métis*.

At the sally port near the river gate Sutherland and McEwan slung packs over their shoulders and bade good-bye to Gladwin and some officers on hand in the predawn darkness. Duvall was not there, and the excuse was that he was sick in his cabin.

Sutherland turned to follow McEwan out into the night, when his eye caught movement on the other side of the yard. He looked closer and saw Ella Bently watching him, her fingers woven and held at her lips. He paused then, and she found herself moving automatically toward him. Gladwin stepped away. Ella stood before Sutherland, looking up at his face. He took her hand from her lips and kissed it politely. Another moment passed. She hardly breathed until he hiked up his knapsack and began to go.

"Owen . . . Owen," she said, and he looked back over his shoulder. "I had hoped that—that you might have been able to stay with us." Then she wondered what she was doing here at this time of anguish for Sutherland. She felt so selfish. She wanted to turn and run away, and she might have if Sutherland had not said:

"One day, perhaps I shall."

Then he was gone, and the sentry was barring the door. Gladwin snapped out orders, then came to Ella's side, put an arm over her shoulders, and they walked back to the house, neither of them speaking.

Tamano discovered what they needed to know: Sin-gat had slipped into the fort and freed Breton. Now they were on their way south, as suspected, heading for Delaware country near Fort Pitt. With them were a dozen Delaware warriors and a young Englishwoman with blond hair.

Pursuit would be difficult and dangerous. Many of Pontiac's Ottawa braves were moving south as well, on their way to harass outlying English settlements. Fort Detroit was too strong to attack directly, but it could be starved into submission as long as supply convoys could not come through and reinforce it. But there were no scalps and little booty to be had around Detroit, so young warriors set off for the settlements to raid and pillage. To avoid war parties, the three travelers spent nights on the water and hid during the day.

At the end of their second week of traveling they landed within the sheltering spit of sand that formed the bay of Presque Isle. There had been a fort here, but Sutherland already knew it had fallen, as had the other two forts between Presque Isle and Fort Pitt. Even though Sutherland was no stranger to death, and even though he was prepared to see the remains of the fort that had been burned down, what they did find there was appalling. It was dusk when they arrived, and in the failing light they saw the blackened, scavenger-ravaged bones of soldiers who had been slain. Though they wanted to waste no time tarrying, they dug hasty, shallow graves and buried the bones.

They concealed the canoe along with much of their gear in a shelter of brambles and scrub trees. They would need it on the return journey, but the next few days must pass on foot. They would move by daylight now because the forest paths were difficult to follow at night, and there was less likelihood of meeting trouble in the woods than on the busy lakes and rivers where there were always canoes.

They slept that night near Presque Isle, ate a cold breakfast of pemmican and dried peaches, then hurried away from the ghostly place without looking back.

A few miles south of Presque Isle, on a stream called French Creek, the second ruin of the three forts known as the Fort Pitt Communication was their objective. They trampled through low-lying country in weather that was hot and wearyingly humid. Mosquitoes were everywhere, plaguing them, biting necks and faces in spite of the smelly bear grease they had smeared on before they began each morning's march. Blackflies clustered like spots of fire on necks and arms, but the hunters pressed on down the narrow trail without pause. McEwan was amazed by the tirelessness of Tamano. He had heard stories of Indians known for their astonishing ability to trek endless hard miles. Now he was seeing the truth of it as Tamano led on. And Sutherland seemed utterly determined to keep up with his friend's grueling pace. McEwan gamely followed. He was as stubborn as the others, and he refused to slow the hunters down, but he was always in pain.

After a half day of marching, they reached what was left of Fort Le Boeuf. Here the scene was much like Presque Isle—charred stockade and blockhouse with its roof caved in—but there were no signs of dead English. The soldiers had either

escaped or been taken prisoner. They pushed on, stopping a
few miles from the ruin to drink from a stream and to snatch
handfuls of parched corn and pemmican.

They planned to split up once they reached Pitt. Sutherland
would move east to Carlisle and learn what he could from the
settlers there—possibly the party with Breton and Sin-gat
would raid settlements to the east, and Sutherland might hear
about them in his travels. McEwan would stay with the commander of Fort Pitt, waiting and listening for everything he
might hear from refugees or from patrols of soldiers who could
tell him something. Tamano would head west into the Delaware
country. There he would have the best chance of learning about
Sin-gat and Mary, and even perhaps about Breton. They would
meet periodically at Fort Pitt to bring their news together.
Henry Gladwin had given Sutherland three letters—one for
each of the members in his party—that explained they were
on king's business and should be given every assistance from
British subjects. All of them, including Tamano, could come
and go as they pleased at British outposts.

They were close to Fort Venango, the third post, trudging
along the trail, when a foul odor assailed them, and from up
ahead came a ferocious buzzing.

Moving carefully, for they knew the stink of death, they
came upon the naked, white, and bloated body of a man. The
buzzing was a cloud of flies. No doubt this was an express
messenger caught by the Indians. He had died less then an hour
from the fort, though it was unlikely that he would have found
safety there either.

Using hatchets and knives, they scratched out a grave and
pushed the body into it with sticks. Most of the flies were
crushed when the earth flopped over them, shoved in with
scoops of elm bark wielded by the three sickened men.

But when they reached Venango, this dead soldier was only
a shadow of the horror found at that burned and blackened ruin.
Naked corpses lay everywhere, and the stench was so dreadful
that they brought the tails of their hunting shirts to their faces
and coughed, gagging. Sixteen men had been killed and left
to rot in the summer sun.

Sutherland and Tamano, standing back at the edge of the
trees, agreed they had no time to bury so many. They must
move on. But when they looked for McEwan, he was nowhere
in sight.

Before they could call out, they heard a low moan from

within the fort's parade ground. The two hurried past the litter of dead and entered the stockade. When they saw McEwan, they stopped short twenty yards away. The ensign was on his knees, his eyes transfixed on a headless corpse that dangled by its wrist tied to the top of a stake. The man had been tortured cruelly before he died. All the fingers were gone. The toes had been hacked to pieces by Indians forcing him to dance around the pole. A great circle of skin was flayed from his back, and his genitals were cut away.

Sutherland moved to McEwan's side; they lifted him to his feet. Then Sutherland saw that McEwan was not staring at the body but at the head, which was impaled on a stake a few yards away. The eyelids and ears had been cut off, but the face was recognizable as that of the fort's commander, Lieutenant Francis Gordon.

McEwan was speaking in a whisper: "Francis was a friend— a friend. No one deserved this—no one should die like this . . ." Sobbing, McEwan put his face against Sutherland's chest. Tamano cut the body down. Even the awful stink of the place was unimportant now. What was important was that they get on to Fort Pitt quickly. But when Sutherland told McEwan they had not time to bury these men, the ensign looked wildly at him and swore he would stay until the job was done. Stumbling off to a place outside the fort, he began to hack away with his Indian axe. Without a word, the others joined him, took off their shirts in the roasting sun, and dropped to their knees, chopping, digging at the soil in silence.

For all his anguish and near madness, McEwan thought to scour the storage shed to find shovels. He went to the small, charred hut and discovered that it had not been completely destroyed. He knocked away the wooden latch that held the door closed. A yelp burst from within, and he sprang back. Tamano and Sutherland ran to his side. Cautiously, hatchets ready, they moved toward the shed. McEwan pulled the door open and looked into the darkness. The yelp came again.

"Sounds like a child," Sutherland said.

Then McEwan was on his knees, patting the ground and speaking in gentle tones.

From out of the little shed came a whining, whimpering sound. Tamano and Sutherland knelt next to McEwan as toward them limped a soot-fouled little puppy no more than a few weeks old. The pup had been brown and white once, with an ear of each color. Its hair was singed, but if it lived, it might be that coloring again. Whining, the puppy came into McEwan's hands, and he lifted it close to his chest. One leg gave it pain, and he was careful to let it dangle loosely. He murmured to the little creature, which tried weakly to lick his face, its eyes huge and afraid. Soon Sutherland had it cuddling close to him, too.

In the shed a young bitch lay dead with six pups, all killed by the heat of fire and by asphyxiation. Only this little she-pup had lived—the sole survivor of Fort Venango.

They spent the rest of that hot day in clouds of mosquitoes and flies, digging the mass grave. They worked without talking; their hands were raw, for they had found nothing with which to dig. Chopping, pulling, scooping out earth, slapping mosquitoes, and sweating foully, they finished the job late in the afternoon. The bodies were so badly decomposed that they could not be touched. They were pushed with sticks onto a blanket, dragged to the graves, and slid down into it, one by tedious one. Handkerchiefs covered the faces of the three gravediggers. They ate nothing during the hours of work, but they consumed much of the rum they had brought along.

When the last earth was stamped down on the grave, McEwan bowed his head, and Sutherland and Tamano did the same. McEwan spoke the Lord's Prayer. Near their knapsacks and food the injured pup whimpered.

Soon they were back on the trail, using the last of the light to put distance between them and the horror at Venango. The pup nestled in McEwan's shirt, sticking its furry head out between buttons, calmly watching the world pass.

That night they camped in a deep hollow near the Allegheny River. In a stream that rushed fast and cold into the greater Allegheny they washed themselves of the filth that had covered them since they left Presque Isle. They swam until their heads and lungs were clear of the evil stink that clung to them. Then they washed their clothes, banging them on rocks and setting them where the morning sun would dry them out. Dressed in clean clothes that night, and secure enough to make a campfire, which was well sheltered from view down in the hollow, the three men gathered their strength.

It felt good to rest by a warm fire now. They would wait until late morning, when their other clothes were dry, before they would leave. The company of little Toby, as McEwan named the puppy, cheered them a bit. It did them good to feed the happy creature, to play with it tugging on a handkerchief, and to feel it snuggle close to them in turn as they slept around the fire. Even its sore leg seemed better already.

They went to sleep hoping for an uneventful journey to Pitt. There was still a long way before them, through country that was beset by roving bands of marauders, but now that they were clean and dry at last, they hoped the worst of the march was behind them.

But that night the rains came. Day after day it rained steadily. Everything about them was wet. When at last they got to Pitt, they were vagrant and spent, clothes in tatters, food gone, and they had slept little for nearly ten days since the rain began. Carefully they slipped close to the besieged fort and were let in by a startled sentry. McEwan brought dispatches from Gladwin to Major Simeon Ecuyer, the Swiss mercenary officer in command of Pitt.

To their disappointment no one in embattled Fort Pitt knew anything about Sin-gat or Breton.

Pitt, with a number of cannon, was a much more powerful fort than Detroit, but it was in even greater peril from attack. The Indians had attempted but failed to assault the place. It was strong, for Ecuyer had constructed a stout defensive works all about the fort. It was Ecuyer who gave to Sutherland news that was stunning:

Colonel Henry Bouquet—also a Swiss mercenary, and a highly respected soldier—was gathering a relief army two hundred miles east of Fort Pitt at the frontier town of Carlisle, Pennsylvania. That news in itself was not enough to shake Owen Sutherland, but it was Ecuyer's casual mention that the bulk of the force being mustered at Carlisle was composed of Scots Highlanders of the Black Watch—Sutherland's old regiment!

The Black Watch had come to New York on rest and recuperation from service in the Caribbean. But even though many were ill with fever contracted in the tropics, the Indian outbreak found the Highlanders as the only intact regiment of regulars immediately available to relieve Fort Pitt. They were hurriedly shipped out to Philadelphia and came up to Carlisle after a long and arduous march, with many of their weakest infantrymen carried on wagons and oxcarts. They were planning to press on west to Fort Pitt soon. Sutherland left Ecuyer's office in a daze. The thought of his old regiment, the one from which he had resigned eighteen years ago, was numbing news. He could hardly believe it possible that fate would twist his life so. Even though most of the men he had served with years ago would be dead and gone if not retired, the regiment was the same. He wondered if old soldiers still with the regiment would remember him. After all, he had been just another ensign courier, a dispatch rider. But there had been some sharp fights, and he had been at the shoulder of the best in the regiment. Perhaps there would be a face that would recall the past, a face that would remember Sutherland's court-martial.

Sutherland decided he would slip through to Carlisle to question the refugees there about Breton—and to see the Black Watch one last time. He was familiar with that country from trading journeys made in the past. McEwen offered to carry dispatches for Ecuyer to Colonel Bouquet at Carlisle. He would go with Sutherland, still searching for Mary Hamilton. Tamano had already left for Delaware villages to learn what he could.

When they set out at dark a few nights after reaching Pitt, Sutherland wondered whether his old regiment could get through the mountains safely. Or would the regiment meet the same end that poorly led Scottish, English, and provincial men had met in the rugged country east of Pitt back in 1755? Then French and Indians ambushed General Braddock in the depths of the forest and killed hundreds. Braddock's loss was the bloodiest defeat ever of British arms in North America. For a moment Sutherland thought about Ella Bently. It was on Braddock's Road that her husband had met the bullet that eventually took his life. Because of that defeat, because of the death of John Bently, Ella had come to Fort Detroit. He wondered why he was thinking about that now. What did it have to do with him?

As he and McEwan set off quickly into the black forest beyond Fort Pitt and headed at a trot toward the east, he let the thoughts of Ella Bently slip away, and before him he held the hateful eyes of André Breton. That is what he must think about, and only that!

Under his shirt the silver pendant bounced against his chest as he ran. There were moments when he wished he did not wear it, for in those moments the memory of Mayla came to him, and that was too much to bear.

At his side McEwan jogged and thought of Mary Hamilton. Her fair face, her golden hair drifted in and out of his lonely mind. Duncan McEwan had never before been lonely. He had always been independent and easygoing; but these days he never expected to listen to a song again, let alone sing one.

Then something tickled him under his hunting shirt. Toby, warm and soft, snuggled comfortably against him. McEwan smiled. The wee mite was stronger already. Before long he would have to arrange for a special bag to carry Toby until she was big enough to run alongside him. He thought then of seeing Toby in Mary's arms, watching the puppy lick her laughing face. He wondered whether Mary Hamilton had ever had a dog.

Ella was scrubbing Jeremy's clothes in a wooden tub when Lettie Morely, breathless from running, burst through the kitchen door.

"Oh, Lord, Lord!" Lettie gasped, fanning her face and slumping into a chair.

"Lettie, what is it?" Ella shook soap from her hands, grabbed a towel, and came to the distraught woman. "You look like you've seen a ghost!"

Indeed the panting woman's face was white.

"If I look pale, it's not for fear; it's for anger! I come right over soon as I heard them filthy lies! Lies, they be! Thee mustn't pay 'em no mind, Ella. Don't believe 'em. Anyone with half a mind won't! No!" Lettie leaned elbows on knees, put her head down, and caught her breath.

"Lies? What lies, Lettie?"

Lettie looked up, her face showing surprise and dismay. "Oh—oh, my—you mean thee ain't heard the lies about Owen?"

Ella knelt at her friend's side. "What? About Owen?"

"Oh, my, my," Lettie muttered and fumbled with her hands. "I thought thee heard, and now it be me has to tell thee. Oh, my, my." Then she hardened and focused on Ella. "Well, all right. Better me than some busybody gossip. There, sit down now and listen to what I'm about to tell thee. But don't believe a bit of it, except what I tell thee to, of course."

Ella gathered the towel in her lap and sat staring at Lettie, who composed herself, then related the rumor of Sutherland's dishonor started by Duvall. It had grown in the telling, and it ground deep into Ella's heart. She learned that the story had swept the fort completely, and that hurt even more. Not that she had any obligation to Owen Sutherland, or he to her, but the vileness of the rumor stung her. Of course she did not believe it. Nor did she learn that it was Alex Duvall who had begun it, for by the time the story had reached Lettie Morely, its origins were blurred. Foremost in Ella's mind was sorrow for Owen Sutherland. After all he had been through, after all he had lost, this insult was a cruel trick of destiny.

"These things always blow over," Lettie finished and clucked her tongue as she rose to leave. "When Owen comes back, he'll put an end to it, be sure of that! He has friends here, friends who won't sit back and let him suffer without givin' him a chance. We'll get to the bottom of this dirty rumor then, though I fear poor Owen will be hurt by it for as long as he lives out here, no matter how untrue the story is."

Then Lettie was gone and Ella returned to her scrubbing board, but there was little ambition left now. She leaned over the tub of water that had turned cold, and she thought of Owen Sutherland, whose past she knew nothing about. But then why should she? What business was it of hers? She shrugged her laziness away. She had no right to intrude on his life, to speculate on him, to daydream about him. It galled her to admit that she speculated and indeed dreamed about him. It galled her so because, after all, what was she to him? She battered a sloppy wet shirt against the washboard, thudding in her anger, in her growing frustration. Enough childishness! In a few months, back to England, and then begin again, anew, with all thoughts of Owen Sutherland purged from her mind—and from her heart.

chapter **16**

CARLISLE

The wild country between Fort Pitt and the frontier settlement of Carlisle was ravaged. Everywhere Sutherland and McEwan went, they saw the sad ruins of farms. Often they found dead families, every one of them, even babies, scalped. There were scenes of terrible pain and misery frozen in time—frozen at the moment of merciful death. Sutherland cut down more than one destroyed corpse crucified and burned by Indians. They circled many farms where the smoke still rose from the charred walls. They could bear to witness no more horror.

Most of their journey was made at night, but in unfamiliar places they traveled by day. They slunk on the edge of forests and hurried across untended fields day after weary day. They avoided besieged Fort Ligonier, which was halfway between Pitt and Carlisle, because scalping parties skulked around the place. On the way they joined a motley crowd of settlers fleeing with whatever they could carry for the dubious refuge of Carlisle, with its worn and weakened soldiers of the Black Watch quartered in a sprawling encampment surrounded by many hundreds of frightened, starving civilians. As Sutherland and McEwan reached the outskirts of the town, they were appalled by conditions there. Refugees in rags slept in barns if they were lucky; in makeshift lean-tos if they had men around; and often out in the open if they had come without husbands or sons to care for them.

Gaunt faces peered from a squalor of shelters. Hungry children stood pale, without hope, watching with big, empty eyes, without even the strength to beg for food. In the two months the frontier had been aflame, the whites had suffered as much from lack of food and shelter as they had from the tomahawk. These were poor people, who had been struggling with every ounce of strength to chisel subsistence from the land.

In the few years settlers had been in the valleys west of the Alleghenies, homesteads had been won only by great sacrifice, courage, and endless toil. For many of the families who fled to Carlisle, everything they had scraped and eked from the land was gone forever. Death had come among them all of a sudden, taking parents and children. Survivors knew their only hope was in the hands of this small force of battle-hardened but tired Scots soldiers and their commander, Henry Bouquet, a brave officer known for courage, insight, and indomitable determination in a fight.

But when Sutherland passed through the rain-soaked, hungry horde of people and came to the field of tents where the regiment was camped, he wondered how these men could stop the uprising. He had expected excitement and the thrill of memory to rise within him at the first sight of a Black Watch soldier. But there was no thrill at all when he encountered weary Highlanders dragging an oxcart filled with unripe corn. There was no draft animal, for as Sutherland would learn later, there were few oxen on the frontier to be bought, borrowed, or begged by the soldiers. Settlers found their draft animals too precious to sell to the army, or they had lost them to Indians weeks before.

The soldiers wore brown breeches, scarlet coats faced with blue and gold, and bonnets that were round tams with red-and-white-checked bands about them. Legs were protected by knee-high boots. They wore no kilts, for they were awkward in the thickets and brambles of the wilderness.

Sutherland stood to one side to watch the soldiers pushing and pulling the laden cart. He had heard these men were recovering from tropical fever, but he had not imagined them to look so utterly devoid of physical enthusiasm and vigor. Yet they pressed on with determination, and now and again a joke was made to prod a faltering comrade. Sutherland listened to the familiar sound of his countrymen's voices, and he knew that although they were worn out, they were tough and would fight well when the moment came.

And it would come. Even if the soldiers did not go out after the Indians, they would be surrounded in defenseless Carlisle and either be starved to death or overwhelmed. These men, Sutherland realized with profound comprehension, were all that stood between the destruction of thousands of white settlers on the frontier as far east as Philadelphia and north to Montreal and Quebec. The defeat of this force meant that hundreds of miles of countryside would be pillaged. But once the might of the British Empire was ranged in earnest against the loosely confederated Indian nations, utter doom would befall the Indians, and tribe after tribe would be wiped from the face of the earth. Sutherland hoped the uprising would end before that came to pass.

The Union Jack fluttered high above the encampment, and somewhere a piper skirled. Then Sutherland's heart lifted to remember his years with the 42nd. He paused to stare at the men walking through the camp. How young they seemed! They were indifferent to him, for he and McEwan were dressed like provincials. Except for the claymore hanging at his side, there was nothing to tell these boys dressed like Highland soldiers that the tall, dark man looking at them was once an officer in their regiment. He knew how far those days had drifted away from him, and in a rush he felt a twinge of sentiment.

There were a hundred tents spread out in the morning sunshine. McEwan went ahead to find Colonel Bouquet's tent, which had a marquee, and Sutherland looked around. He saw a few companies of Royal Americans in their red and buff; there were also elements of other regiments here, filled out in some cases with men who had been disbanded but agreed for a fee to fight again until the uprising was quelled.

In Europe this would be an insignificant force, a small detachment, the kind that would be sent on a scouting mission or designated to protect a battery of artillery. But here, in a wilderness empire, where the king's domain was held by fewer than four thousand soldiers scattered across all of British North America, this army was the strongest force anywhere in the field. It had taken all Amherst's ingenuity and organizational skills to scrape this expedition together, and at that moment there was no way to replace it if it met disaster.

Should Bouquet's army fail to get through and Fort Pitt fall, the wilds north of the Ohio River would be virtually impenetrable to the English for years to come. The flush of victory would further unite the tribes, and the entire British frontier, from Montreal to the Gulf of Mexico, would be hurled back by marauding war parties. Before the debt-ridden British government could form an army large enough to subdue the Indians, the death and destruction would grow to immense proportions. If Bouquet failed to get through, the restless Cherokee and Creek in the south would rise; the Abnaki and eastern Algonquin would attack settlements in the northeast again; and most to be feared, the mighty Iroquois Six-Nation alliance in the New York and Pennsylvania frontier regions would likely shake off the influence of Sir William Johnson and join the uprising.

More than one British governor feared for the welfare of his great city, including New York and Philadelphia. With the defeat of the French, the Indian coalitions hostile to the English had tottered, but now Pontiac had forged them into a power to be reckoned with once again. How that power might grow, and where it would be victorious were thoughts that ran through Owen Sutherland's troubled mind. The answers were all too ominous. But if the uprising could be dealt a severe setback by Bouquet relieving Pitt, then there was hope that peace could be established—a peace that offered security to white and red alike.

But as Sutherland surveyed this hastily gathered army, he found himself slowly shaking his head. He had grave doubts. They were all professionals, but they faced a difficult task— marching nearly two hundred miles through an inhospitable wilderness. The Highlanders were not experienced Indian fighters, and as he waited outside Bouquet's tent for McEwan, gloomy foreboding came over Sutherland. These soldiers had little hope of getting out of the forest alive. That meant the fate of these civilian fugitives was as good as sealed. There was nowhere else to fly, for every road for miles around was infested with scalping parties.

The flap of the colonel's tent was pushed back, and McEwan looked out. He beckoned to Sutherland, who went inside.

In the dimness the stocky Colonel Bouquet stood over a table of planks on sawhorses, reading McEwan's dispatches. Bouquet was in his mid-forties, with a paunch. He looked up at Sutherland, and the Scotsman saw tired but intelligent cool blue eyes. In a voice thick with a Swiss accent, Bouquet said, "I understand you were this ensign's guide from Fort Pitt. Well, I'm in need of guides for the journey back. I've got a pack of fighters here who'll get lost if they go off to relieve themselves behind a bush. I need somone who knows the Indians, someone who can take us to Pitt over Ligonier, Shippensburg, and Bedford. What is your fee?"

Sutherland stood erect, his head just slightly backwards. "I have no fee, Colonel."

"No fee? Come now, man—"

"No fee, Colonel, because I won't be your guide, sir. I was a soldier once, but now I have other business to complete, business which trudging through the woods with a pack of blundering regulars won't permit. So, sir, although I am honored by your offer, I must refuse."

Within McEwan's hunting shirt little Toby stirred and jumped, and the ensign, embarrassed, struggled to keep the puppy still in the presence of the colonel. But the officer seemed not to notice. He was staring with eyes of steel at Sutherland.

"By the sound of your voice, sir, you're a Scotsman yourself. And by your bearing, I see you've had some military training." Bouquet glanced at Sutherland's claymore. Silently, the officer moved around the desk to look closer at the sword. Then, after a moment, he said, "That's an officer's sword of this regiment, sir. How did you come by it?"

Sutherland felt the man's eyes penetrate him, but he was not inclined to tell the whole story to Bouquet. Not now.

"Aye, sir, it's what you see. I was once an ensign in the Watch. But that time is over, and I don't care ever to return to it."

Bouquet was annoyed. He moved past McEwan, hardly realizing that Toby was whining and lurching to escape the ensign's shirt. McEwan's face was set, his teeth clenched, his eyes avoiding Bouquet, who was back behind his desk, leaning over toward Sutherland.

"Surely you realize, sir, that I'll never get out of Carlisle if I have to count on Highlanders as my vanguard. They'll wind up taking me in circles at best. And these Pennsylvanians who are begging me to save them are giving me a dastardly time just trying to supply and equip my men. They won't sell us a thing without charging treble, and they won't lift a finger to provide scouts. You, sir, know better than anyone what will happen to these five hundred men if I don't have good scouts."

Bouquet paused to let his words sink in, but Sutherland knew very well what would happen to this army. Toby squirmed, and McEwan grimaced slightly, apparently scratched by the miserable puppy.

Bouquet went on. "These are your countrymen, sir. And this is your regiment—"

"Colonel," Sutherland said, surprised at overcoming years of discipline by interrupting an officer. "I came here on personal business and as an escort to my friend, Ensign McEwan." Sutherland did not look at McEwan, for, by now, Toby's nose was snorting out of a space between two buttons. "I'll be on my way as soon as I acquire some information from the settlers here—information which I need to complete that personal business. I'm sorry, sir, but I shall not enter the military service and fight against the Indians, many of whom have been my friends."

Sutherland had intended to say more, but he stopped there, for he had made his point. Outside the piper played a familiar tune.

Bouquet harrumphed and clasped and unclasped his hands behind his back, rocking on toes and heels. The pipes skirled.

"Very well, very well," he said. "I won't press you for your personal affairs. But let me just ask you one question." Bouquet pointed to a yellowed map spread over the top of the table, and Sutherland moved closer to look down at it. "I intend to take the old road of General Braddock, and—"

"No, no, sir!" Sutherland said quickly and ran his finger along a trail running north of Braddock's Road, where so much British and provincial blood had once been spilled. "Don't take Braddock's Road, for it's one long trap from end to end. Take this path north of Braddock's. It's broad, and though rugged, there are fewer good places for ambush. This northern route is hilly and a bit harder, but it's safer. There are some dangerous spots, but good scouts could smell out ambush and give you time to—"

Bouquet was looking deeply at Sutherland, and the Scotsman caught himself.

"Yes," Bouquet said after a moment. "We'll need good scouts."

The tent was quiet. Toby had managed to stick her furry head out of McEwan's shirt and was examining everyone with curious eyes; but the ensign was watching Sutherland, the pup forgotten.

Sutherland said, "That's your best route, sir. If I hear of anyone interested in scouting for you, I'll send him along."

Sutherland stepped back smartly and just barely stopped himself from saluting. He bowed slightly, turned on his heel, and went out of the tent to the relief of wind and sunshine.

He breathed in and heard the pipes sound a stirring melody that flew through his heart and soul. His blood surged, bringing a red flush to his neck. With difficulty he shook the emotion away and walked along the avenue between tents that bellied and swelled in the fresh breeze.

"Owen!"

McEwan came running up. Little Toby scampered alongside, stopping and snuffling into things that were none of her business. Now she had her head under a log and was flagging her short tail in excitement.

"Listen, Owen, I'm going back with these lads to Fort Pitt. I can't do much, but I probably will remember a bit of how we came. Bouquet wants to leave tomorrow, so you'll likely still be here when we go. If you hear anything at all of Mary . . ."

"Aye, lad." Sutherland put a hand on McEwan's shoulder. "I'll be out at Pitt in a month or so if I learn nothing sooner. I'll meet you then, and we'll find Tamano. Then we'll go after her, eh?"

Sutherland tried to smile, but he wondered whether McEwan would get through. McEwan nodded and pulled at his shirt front, looked down at it, and shook his head.

"I should have let that pup out when she started jumping," he said. "But I didn't think Bouquet would like it if she pissed on his boots."

Sutherland saw McEwan's shirt was dark-stained about its middle, and he laughed broadly along with the youth, who stripped off the wet shirt and shook it.

"Conduct unbecoming an officer and a gentleman!" Sutherland laughed.

McEwan grinned. "Above and beyond the call of duty, if you ask me, man."

"Aye, Dunkie, you should have let her go. Bouquet's boots could have used a wash."

The two friends walked away, with Toby prancing behind them. Sutherland tried not to think that this might be the last time he would ever see Duncan McEwan alive, but the effort was not easy.

Ella played the tinkling spinet in the council house, but unlike most other days, there was no one in the building with her. She had chosen to play alone early that afternoon instead of just before the dinner hour when she usually played for friends. The sun hung in shafts from the windows and warmed the floor, but the spinet was in shadow this day, and so was Ella.

Why she felt so melancholy she did not know. But she had hoped the spinet would give her some solace. She played softly, and the music haunting the chamber was beautiful and sad. She played for an hour, then at last when her dismal mood had lifted somewhat, she closed the spinet's lid and slowly got to her feet. She walked to the window and gazed lazily out at the parade ground where people hurried here and there. What there was to hurry about in this trapped little world she did not know. Her life was listless nowadays. There was no thought of to-morrow, for every day seemed the same: a struggle with un-happiness. Ella felt too miserable to put up a brave front for anyone, not even for Jeremy, who was off playing with the Morely boys.

She closed her eyes and languished in the soft sunshine pouring over her face and shoulders. She could almost sleep like this.

A shout came from the parade ground. She looked out to see soldiers running off to the left toward the water gate. Sen-tries pulled the gate open, and Henry appeared in haste. Her heart lifted suddenly, and she strained to see whether rein-forcements or supplies had come. She ran to the door and looked down the street at the crowd near the gate. Several men were coming through, and they were carrying something. She eagerly moved toward the crowd, which was a short distance away.

But before Ella reached the gate, Garth Morely stepped out of the milling group and came to her, turning her away.

"What is it, Mr. Morely? What's going on?"

"Stay back, ma'am," he said sadly. "Stay back. It's not right thee see this . . ."

But it was too late. She saw what the men were carrying. Her eyes opened in horror. "Good—goodness—goodness—" Morely pursed his lips and drew her back, putting an arm over her shoulders. Ella's hand was at her open mouth, and she could barely breathe. Her legs began to give way, but Morely bore her up as they walked toward Gladwin's quarters.

Before they reached the house, Lettie appeared and flut-tered, "What's this, now? Be thee sick, Ella? What be it, Garth? Be she ill? Be it the flux?"

Garth Morely shook his head and screwed up his face to quiet his wife. Trembling, Ella pulled away from the trader and Lettie, mumbled an apology, and clambered up the steps into the house, where she disappeared without closing the door.

Lettie turned to her husband, whose eyes were cast down at his dusty boots. He said:

"She just saw them bring in Captain Campbell, lass."

Lettie gasped. "Campbell? Be he . . . ? Be the cap—"

Garth Morely nodded and walked arm in arm with his wife

back to their home. It was enough that Lettie knew their friend was dead. He could not tell her that the captain had been tortured terribly, and his head was not with the body when it was recovered from the river just now. It was a pity, Morely thought, that he had not stopped Ella Bently in time.

Sutherland was walking through the Scottish and English camp with McEwan, followed more or less by nosy Toby, when someone nearby roared a fierce whoop.

From out of a group of soldiers a short, immensely broad sergeant major sprang at Sutherland, who shrieked the same cry in return and lunged at the man coming for him. They grappled, strong arms about one another, closely matched, each straining against the other. The little sergeant's long arms squeezed Sutherland, and he tried to raise the big frontiersman off his feet. Sutherland did the same. The standoff went on long enough to gather a crowd of curious soldiers who shouted encouragement to the red-faced sergeant. McEwan cried for Sutherland and eyed the crowd, making sure no one stepped in to help the sergeant. But the sergeant seemed to need no help.

With a mighty heave he yanked Sutherland off his feet, took several madly quick steps, and threw his victim over an embankment, down into a muddy stream, drenching him head to foot.

The sergeant clapped his knees, leaned back, and roared with laughter. McEwan moved quickly for the man, about to take him on, but before he got to him, the old soldier was down the bank and standing over a vanquished Sutherland, who sat up to his chest in dirty water. To McEwan's surprise Sutherland was laughing, too.

"You never could throw me!" the sergeant major hurled at Sutherland, who lay back in the stream and laughed:

"Not into water!" Sutherland wiped mud away. "Not if it wasn't fermented first."

The soldier laughed and stuck a fist down to pull Sutherland to his feet. Sutherland grasped the hand and began to rise. Then throwing all his weight at the sergeant's gut, he curled an arm behind the other's knees and flipped him high into the air, splashing him head and shoulders down into the stream.

The soldiers at the top of the bank hooted and shouted, laughing and cheering at their noncom. Sutherland yanked his opponent to his feet as the drenched man chuckled to himself. They strode up the little incline, and the sergeant threw his arm over Sutherland.

"Brains against brawn, eh, Munro?" Sutherland jabbed an elbow in the other's ribs.

"Indian trickery, that's what, Sutherland." Munro grunted and wiped dirt from his eyes. "Worse than the damned French, I'd say. Well, what can you expect from a bloody provincial?"

They stepped back and sized each other up. Munro nodded. "Well, you're a bit older and a bit uglier, and you don't look like a Scotsman anymore, though I'll wager you still know how to use that hanger there." Munro looked at the claymore, calling it by the name commonly given an officer's sword—a hanger.

Sutherland took off his shirt. "Aye, the sword still works, though I'm more rusty than it, I suppose." He looked at McEwan standing nearby. "Ensign Duncan McEwan, you're in the presence of Sergeant—that is, Sergeant Major Ian Munro, formerly of Dundee, lately of His Majesty's Black Watch and the more sordid taverns of New York and Philadelphia; a man I once fought alongside, and a man who swore years ago he'd resign from the army and start a cooperin' business at home."

Munro shook hands with McEwan. "Of Dundee, aye, Ensign, but I've seen nothing of New York or Philadelphia taverns, good or bad, and even less of the women. We were no sooner stationed in this wilderness of a country—a place called Staten Island or some such name—than we're told we've to come out to save you bumpkins from a pack of dirty redskins!"

The soldiers near him grumbled assent. Munro turned to them.

"Look here, you lads, and see a man who once knew somethin' about soldierin'. This is Owen Sutherland, formerly of the 42nd—even was an officer . . ." The soldiers showed deference at that last remark. They stared at Sutherland, who was grinning and wringing out his wet shirt. "Ask Sutherland about the tradition of this regiment, and you pups'll learn what kind of men you're followin' so miserably! He was a soldier with me when you lumps were sucklin' yer mither's teats." He looked at Owen and pursed his lips, then spoke loud enough for his mirthful men to hear. "Laddies just oot o' the cradle, as you can see, Owen. I've to change their nappies afore we go into a fight. Aye!"

The men caterwauled and rasped Munro, who shooed them away and led Sutherland and McEwan to his campfire. Munro was a red-haired, weathered fellow of forty. His hands were gnarled and thick and scarred. He had a broad girth befitting his age and rank as sergeant major; and his bowed legs and long arms were stringy and quick.

Sutherland and Munro changed clothes, and McEwan found some pemmican and porridge for Toby, who hungrily devoured the food before snuggling into McEwan's side as the young ensign lay by the fire, where a kettle of water was on to boil. Munro's men came to the fire, and rum was cut with hot water and melted butter for flip. Before long the two old friends had eaten dinner, smoked strong Dutch tobacco, and had told enough lies to delight the other twice over. McEwan lay quietly and enjoyed the rough exchanges between Sutherland and Munro.

The fire burned low, and the camp grew quiet as night came on. More rum was brought out for the occasion, and they all drank too much. Sutherland and Munro had much to tell— Munro of his fighting in the Caribbean, and Sutherland of his new life in North America. McEwan realized that these two had been the closest of friends years ago, for Sutherland told everything, including the story of Mayla and of his hunt for Breton.

When most of the men were asleep around the fire, Munro lay quietly on his blanket, absently puffing on the Dutch pipe he had brought from New York. Sutherland, filled with rum and weariness, listened to the piper in the distance, who played a pibroch, sad and rippling with loneliness—loneliness that only a soldier in a far land could comprehend. Loneliness that every man in that camp—Scot or English or provincial—felt intensely. No man in that little army had any illusions about what they faced on the coming march to Fort Pitt. No man expected anything more from his life right now than the loyalty and complete trust of his fellow soldiers.

Strangely, Sutherland sensed the heart of this army was beating in time with his. He knew in this peaceful moment that all these men could hope for was a brave comrade at each shoulder when the trouble began. That thought was a familiar one to Sutherland, for it had been with him every day of his life eighteen years ago. And it was the same with these soldiers now, soldiers who had been boys in those days.

"When's the last time you heard the pipes at sundown, lad?" Munro asked Sutherland, who was looking off at the warm reds and grays of the horizon.

Sutherland tried a wry smile. "Dinna be sentimental, you auld man."

Munro got to his knees and searched about a knapsack until he took out a flask and held it for Sutherland and McEwan to see. Both men gaped. It was Scots whiskey, all right, something they hadn't seen or tasted for far too long.

"I'd saved it for Fort Pitt." Munro grinned and popped the cork quietly so the sleeping soldiers could not hear. "But maybe it's as well drunk now. Go on, Owen, do us the honor and give us a toast, lad."

Sutherland took the flask and looked at his two friends. "To your journey. May you get there with all your hair." He pondered the flask, then drank, hissed and shook his head as he passed it on to McEwan. "Aye, Munro, that's the real thing."

When Munro took the flask, he drank and then said, "You mean *our* journey, don't you, Owen?"

Sutherland felt self-conscious just then. "No, Ian. Your journey. I've got my own affairs here—"

"You mean you're not a scout? Isn't that why you're here now? I thought you'd signed on to coddle us along and keep these crofters from gettin' lost in the trees."

Sutherland shook his head. "No, Munro. My days as a soldier are over." He moved into his blanket and lay down. "I told you before, I'm finished with the army after what they did to me. I owe them nothing, and I'm not about to fight against Indians when I know they've been done as I was done by these lousy pea-brained English generals. No, Munro, it's not my fight."

Sutherland yawned. Munro went under his own blanket and tucked the flask away. McEwan fondled sleeping Toby and stared into the dying fire, his own thoughts far away, of Mary Hamilton, wherever she was.

"Aye, aye. Well." Munro looked up at the sky and cleared his throat. "I can't say I blame you, Owen. This is no march to be goin' on. Half these lads are still weak with the fever they caught in the West Indies. We're carryin' forty sick men in wagons when we go off. No wonder you don't want any part of this; no, not with a hopeless little army like we've got."

Munro squinted one gleaming eye over at Sutherland, saw he was still awake, then went on.

"Aye, this is no way to fight a war." He yawned deeply and glanced at Sutherland. "None of us look forward to this campaign, not without scouts."

His words hung in the air. The piper had stopped playing. It was dark, and the fire was low.

Sutherland suddenly sat up and stared at Munro, who casually closed his eyes and pretended he was not waiting for his friend to speak.

Sutherland swore and threw himself down on the ground, turning his back. After a long silence, Munro said, "Good night, lads."

McEwan was already asleep. For a while Sutherland said nothing. Then he jerked himself to a sitting position and looked hard at Munro, who opened one eye.

"Go to sleep, laddie," Munro said.

"Now listen, Ian," Sutherland grumbled, "it's up to Bouquet to get some bloody scouts. That's his job! Don't expect me to do anyone else's dirty work. No more!"

Munro took his opportunity and leaned on an elbow. "Aye, Owen, you're right. Bouquet's job. But gettin' this miserable army together was his job, too, and supplyin' them and lodgin' them and plannin' for the campaign was his job, and little help he got from Pennsylvania—they're all Quakers in the government, and they love Indians, especially ones that are Christianized, no matter how fresh their scalps are. They've given us nothin'.

"Aye, it's Bouquet's job, but the man is cut off at every turn. These people here won't sell him a thing, not food, not oxen, not horses. They won't part with what they've saved, and we can't march without supplies. And not a bloody one will serve as a scout. Not one! There might be some willin' scouts up the line, but God knows if we'll ever get up there to use them. Aye, these folks are beggin' us to save 'em from the redskins, but they won't lift a finger to help us, and Bouquet is in between. Aye, laddie, it's his job to find us scouts, and he's tried, but he can't get 'em. And we're told that we've got to set off, scouts or no scouts—"

"You can't do that! Not without scouts!" Sutherland was furious. McEwan was awake now, listening, and even Toby lay with her head cocked, wondering and amused. "Suicide, that's what it is! Suicide! You don't know the first bloody thing about fighting Indians. You'll be out there with Braddock—would have been there for sure if I hadn't told Bouquet not to take Braddock's old road, that death trap—"

"*You* told him?" Munro asked, seeming surprised.

"Aye, I told him it's an easy place to get massacred."

"Well, well," Munro muttered and lay back. When he spoke, he put on the accent of an English officer. "That was uncommonly decent of you, old boy. For old times' sake, no doubt."

Sutherland glowered at the sarcasm and looked out into the darkness beyond the firelight. Sullen, he said nothing, but then Munro looked up.

"Ach, Owen," Munro said quietly. "Sorry. I didn't mean that to sound so hard."

Sutherland poked a stick into the fire and it flared up. The silver pendant lay outside his shirt. It glinted red in the light of the blaze. So did Munro's eyes.

"I know, Ian," Sutherland said.

"Ach, we'll get some scouts, never fear. You go about your business, and I'll meet you in Fort Pitt when you come out, eh? You know, I might like this country, and you might be able to convince me to stay. My time's up in a few months, and if things are as good as you say they are here, I could make a go of it with my pension and what I've put away."

Sutherland softened. "You'd do well here, Munro." He looked at McEwan, who was watching Munro. "Young McEwan here has the same idea. Once this trouble is over, you two could join up with me in the trade. Aye, you'd be welcome, lads. We could form a company proper and do it right."

Sutherland touched the pendant and felt a rising sadness within as he thought of Mayla. He pushed into his blankets and ached from deep inside. He knew then that the chances of Munro and McEwan ever reaching Fort Pitt without good scouts were virtually nil. This army was marching to certain death, and if it did, the frontier would be a battlefield for a generation to come—a battlefield that would easily surpass the years of war against the French with its misery and desolation. Sure as tomorrow's sunrise, Bouquet's army had no hope.

Owen Sutherland brooded until exhaustion bore him away into fitful sleep.

Long before dawn Ella was restlessly awake. It was a morning toward the end of July. Her thoughts drifted from the rumor of Sutherland's dishonor to the welfare of Jeremy, who slept across the little room. She was startled alert. Someone was banging at the door below. She heard Henry's voice as he clumped downstairs. The firing of many muskets chattered and clattered, muffled by distance. She sat up and dressed as fast as she could.

The *Michigan,* recently sent out again for more supplies, had not been gone long enough to be back from Niagara by now, but it sounded as though the Indians were firing on something coming up the river. She looked out at the false dawn and heard the shooting more distinctly. It came from downstream somewhere and was very heavy. She ran out the door and hurried into the courtyard, where hundreds of people were milling and calling to one another. The water gate was open, and armed soldiers were hurrying out toward the river.

The firing subsided, and a cheer went up from a mob on the ramparts. People pressed out the water gate, and Ella came up behind the crowd. Another shout and shrieks of joy filled the fort. Soon the mass around the gate drew back as an aisle was made, and Ella's heart jumped to see a marching column of soldiers led by a young captain, slender and immaculately dressed, and by a huge, burly man dressed in green. More reinforcements! They had come at last!

Ella stood hypnotized as column after column of soldiers marched into the fort and assembled on the parade ground. The garrison and residents laughed and cheered. Within a half hour two hundred and eighty men stood at attention, rank on rank before the people of the fort. Some soldiers were wounded, for the Indians had seen them in the misty early hours and opened a withering fire from the riverbank. But the force had come through safely, led by young Captain James Dalyell and veteran Indian fighter Major Robert Rogers—the man in green—founder and leader of the famous Rogers' Rangers. Without the cunning Rogers, this group would have met the same fate as the first convoy of whaleboats from Niagara, which was ambushed and captured two months ago. Now they were here!

Relief swept through the fort, for there were nearly twice as many men as had been in the entire garrison for the three months of siege. Someone in the crowd broke into a hymn, and the thanksgiving was taken up by hundreds of voices. Women wept, and men laughed. Captain Dalyell nodded to his men, and they, too, broke into song. More than seven hundred voices lifted over Fort Detroit, which no longer was a dreary frontier post.

"A ball, a ball!" shouted Alex Duvall when he joined Ella

and a sleepy-eyed Jeremy in his night clothes, the boy marveling at the sight he saw. "We must have a ball to celebrate!" Duvall laughed.

The officers, their women, and the trader families gave out with a cheer in answer to Duvall's shout. He bowed to Ella as they shared the joy, thrilling at the prospect of an end to the siege.

"Mistress Bently," Duvall said, "would you do me the honor of permitting me to escort you to our victory ball tonight?"

"Why, thank you, Major," she smiled and curtsied a little. "Of course, sir. My pleasure."

He grinned and kissed her hand.

"Until tonight, dear lady. Your servant."

A ball! Oh, how wonderful that sounded! Now the siege was over at last, and soon she could see this beautiful countryside in safety before she departed for England. Ella took her son's hand and led him back to the house. Dawn was on them, bright and already warm. At the top of the stairs she looked out over the river at the sunrise. She sighed and smiled. What a beautiful land this was! More beautiful than she had ever imagined any place could be. She was grateful to have lived out here, if only briefly. It was almost a shame to leave.

chapter **17**

CELEBRATION

Sutherland could not sleep. He lay awake in his blanket until the fire burned out. Before dawn he rose and paced through the slumbering camp, where the only movement was a sentry strolling here and there. Above were stars, and around him were smoldering fires, lost, forgotten spots of heat sprinkled about in the darkness.

The question that tormented Sutherland never stayed on the surface of his mind, for he did not let it. No rationalization one way or the other arose within him. Visions of dead soldiers in the woods were driven from his mind again and again. No thoughts of destruction and misery were permitted to linger in Sutherland's bleak contemplation. In fact it might be said that he had no clear thought in his mind at all. But he walked away and returned and went away again until he knew there was no escape in that.

Then he sat and built up the fire again. It flickered and burned and crackled into a blaze that lit the sleeping men and tents all about. Its heat rushed against him, scalding his face. Unyielding, he stared into the fire, but it gave him no solace.

So he paced again, this time out into the fringes of the camp, where nervous sentries challenged him, where the morning breeze found him and sent him, chilled, back to his campfire once more.

But Sutherland could not keep out his thoughts for all the night. Like the coming of dawn the inevitable truth of what was upon him took form within his heart, took life and color and domination. Like the light that crept upon the wakening camp, reality broke over Owen Sutherland as he sat with his head on knees, weary and hammered into obedience.

At last he realized the others had been awake for some time.

Though none had spoken to him, Sutherland knew that they had seen him and left him in his solitary world. A breakfast of cold scones and warmed porridge sat near the fire. There was tea left over in a kettle, and a cup stood ready for use. But none of the men were about, although the rest of the camp was gathering in preparation for the long march, which would begin soon.

Sutherland picked at the scones and drank tea. He refused to think, but the night had done its work already. He need not think at all now, for decision had gone beyond logic, and duty had risen above emotions. As the piper broke out and lifted his tune above the rustle of voices and clank of metal, Owen Sutherland put aside his meal and walked toward the tent of Colonel Bouquet, even though no crystallized thought had hardened in his mind.

When the commander's orderly withdrew and left Sutherland standing in dim light within the tent, Colonel Bouquet said nothing. He looked at Sutherland, waiting for him to speak. Sutherland cleared his throat and said:

"I'll guide you as far as Fort Pitt, Colonel."

Bouquet hesitated an instant, his eyes on Sutherland's. Then he came around his makeshift table and shook Sutherland's hand, saying, "Our lives are in your hands, sir."

"You must understand this," Sutherland said. "I am serving only as a scout, not as a soldier. Unless I must save my own life, I'll not fight for you. I have no quarrel with the Indians, and I'm taking you through for their sakes as well as for your own. I want this war stopped before more blood is shed. If your command is destroyed, the war will go on until the Indians are utterly wiped out. I know Amherst is just the man who'd like to do that."

Bouquet nodded, his brow furrowed, and he looked at Sutherland with a mixture of confusion and resignation. He knew Sutherland was good and could get them through safely. He would accept him on these terms.

"Very well. It's your scalp." He went back behind the desk and took out parchment and quill. "You surely know we might be attacked. In that case you may have no choice but to defend yourself—that is, unless you know every Indian in these woods personally. Even then they won't take it kindly if you're with us."

Before he began to write, Bouquet looked at Sutherland to confirm again the Scotsman's determination. Then he scribbled quickly, splashed fine sand on the ink, and shook the letter off.

"This will identify you to our officers and quartermaster as our scout. You're entitled to tenpence a day and the normal ration of rum and powder. Fetch what you need immediately, for I'm mustering the men to march after the midday meal." Bouquet handed Sutherland the letter. "Come back in an hour, and my officers and you will discuss the line of march. Thank you, Mr. Sutherland. I commend your motives in this affair, and I sincerely hope your goals will be achieved."

As Sutherland turned to leave, he said, "If they're not achieved, sir, it'll mean this army's bones will be left in the Pennsylvania woods."

Sutherland found Munro and McEwan, who laughed and clapped him on the shoulders when he told them the news. He did not laugh with them, but something stirred within him— something forgotten. He found himself pausing to watch the color bearers flutter the Union Jack from its sheathing. Regimental standards caught the wind and shook out wrinkles. Drummers quickened, and the piper rang out a march so lively and gay that when Sutherland was walking toward Bouquet's tent for the morning council, he felt a swing to his step that made him grin despite himself.

It was intended to be a casual meeting of acquaintances, but the small gathering of officers at Gladwin's house very quickly stiffened into brittle coolness. Ella was about to bring out a pot of tea from the kitchen when she sensed the voices abruptly stop talking. When she brought the steaming pot into the sitting room, the atmosphere was clumsy and dark. Gladwin, Duvall, Rogers, and Dalyell sat self-consciously, none talking. Ella felt tense as she poured each one a cup of tea.

"I daresay my presence among you has called up such politeness that you've all lost your tongues," she said and tried to smile. She cast a glance at Gladwin, whose reply was to tighten his lips. Duvall said something to assure her to the contrary, then fell silent. She left the room with a curtsy and the soldiers mumbled their thanks. In the kitchen Ella listened.

It took some time, after teacups clinked and chairs scraped, before Henry Gladwin said, "I must remind Captain Dalyell that I am responsible for this post, and your soldiers have been placed under my command."

She knew by now that Captain James Dalyell was a favored staff member in General Amherst's headquarters. Gladwin had already told her that the young officer was given charge of the reinforcement because Amherst wished to bless him with an opportunity for military glory. Even though all the officers in the room outranked Dalyell—in experience as well as in grade—the captain was determined to get his way.

"Sir, my orders from General Amherst," Dalyell said haughtily, "were to lead my force to Detroit and to take whatever action was appropriate to quickly and decisively put an end once and for all to this annoying Indian trouble. Be assured, sir, that I have the highest regard for your rights as post commander, but understand that I shall use my own good judgment about what must be done to confront the renegades and nip this uprising in the bud! With that in mind, sir, it is my opinion that we must strike immediately before Pontiac escapes—"

"Escapes?" Gladwin's incredulous voice rang out. "You think Pontiac, with more than a thousand warriors at his call, and perhaps twice that if he has a fight to make, intends to withdraw because a few more soldiers have arrived here?"

"Major Gladwin..." Dalyell began slowly, as a man who is exasperated by the lack of comprehension in those he considers his inferiors. "My good sir, if bold action had been taken two months ago, there would have been no siege, for Pontiac would never have been supported by simple savages who had been shown the power of British arms. But that opportunity has been lost, and now we are faced with another opportunity, which I, for one, am determined not to allow to slip away. Sir, we have the force to meet Pontiac in the field and chastise him as his black Indian heart deserves. If he is such a wise chief, as has been said among those who have sympathy with the savages, then he must sue for peace now that he knows my force has arrived. In fact I have had reports that he has struck camp already and may even, at this very moment, be skulking off with his tribe before we can get our hands on him. And if that blackguard should escape us, Major Gladwin, you shall be held responsible!"

Exhausted by months of relentless strain and by the deaths of many close friends, Gladwin sighed; he had lost his enthusiasm for argument. He spoke, and in the kitchen Ella listened with every fiber.

"Captain Dalyell, if an attack is warranted—after careful study of the situation—then I would be the first to support it. But we cannot attack unless the situation is advantageous. We are vastly inferior in numbers to Pontiac's force, and we cannot afford a heavy loss of life by hasty action. I am of the opinion that we should wait."

"Wait!" Dalyell burst out. Ella heard him rise and stamp up and down the living room as he spoke. "Major, there has been enough waiting by the garrison of this fort already. If you are commanding me not to attack the Indians, then I have no choice but to take my force and lead them to another post where they can be of some offensive use! Am I, sir, to believe that you are ordering me not to attack?"

Ella wished she could see what was happening, for not a sound came from the room.

Then Gladwin spoke, and Ella thought his voice sounded weary, spent, without vigor.

"No, Captain. I am not directly ordering you not to attack. However, it is my judgment that such a plan is perilous if not clearly thought out —and yours is not, sir! As it is, I shall not order my garrison to go, but if they volunteer to join you they have my permission."

Ella heard heels click, as if Dalyell had turned to leave. The door opened, then Dalyell's voice came:

"All of us know what General Amherst demands be done on this enterprise. He wishes this disturbance quelled—and quelled decisively. *I*, for one, am not afraid to undertake that mission! Good day, sirs!"

The door closed sharply. For several moments none of the three majors left in the room spoke. Then Major Rogers, who had accepted the original surrender of Detroit from the French three years ago, said, "I agree with you, Major Gladwin." His voice was deep. "I think we should plan this out better. But I and my Rangers'll go along with Dalyell to see what we can do about keeping that brash young man from getting his soldiers killed."

Ella heard Duvall bid good day without commenting, and he and Rogers left the room. She came out of the kitchen, teapot absently in her hand. Henry was still deep in thought.

He looked up at her when she poured tea into his cup, then he looked away and sighed. Even the ball scheduled for that night seemed to have lost its luster for Ella. After all her brother had done to command the post during the weeks of siege, he deserved better than this from men like Dalyell. She did not speak, and with something caught in her throat she turned to leave. Then Henry said softly:

"Sister." She faced him. He seemed so tired and so very

wizened just then. "Sister, Captain James Dalyell is a very ambitious man."

Sutherland did not immediately move ahead of the column of soldiers filing by fours out of unhappy Carlisle, for he wanted to watch them leave. It had been years since he had seen soldiers marching off to a campaign. In the past he had been moved by pride and admiration. Now he was moved by anxiety; by fear and doubt filled with dread.

No shouts of encouragement rose from the dismal crowd huddled in Carlisle. The faces of the people lining the roads out of the village reflected the tattered spirits of the soldiers. At the column's head the pipes skirled with courage, but there was no insolent swing of the arm, no lift to the step, and no laughter among the men.

Sutherland moved slowly alongside the column to where McEwan and Munro were marching in line. When they reached the edge of the forest, McEwan would join Sutherland in the vanguard scouting out the way. For now, both McEwan and Sutherland walked alone with their thoughts. Save for the comfort he got from Toby, McEwan's heart was dark with anxiety for Mary Hamilton. For Sutherland there was nothing to give him cheer—nothing but the skirl of that gallant piper, who played his heart out and compelled the men to keep their heads high, even if strength had long ago been drained by tropical fever.

The people watching the soldiers go stood silently until the last of the column—a dozen carts filled with sick men unable to walk—vanished in the woods. Not one of the watching refugees truly expected any of those men to come out of the forest again.

It was sunset when Ella and Duvall strolled down the Rue Sainte Anne on their way to the council house, where the sounds of music heralded the ball. She was dressed in her blue gown, pretty arms and throat exposed. A floating minuet drifted above the fort from the council house, where Reverend Lee's chamber group, with reinforcements, formed a makeshift orchestra. The music sounded light and cheerful, as it ought to in a frontier post that anticipates the lifting of a long siege. In the distance the laughter and conversation of people crowding about the entrance of the brightly lit council house drifted toward them.

Despite the unhappy officers' meeting that afternoon, Ella was determined to enjoy herself. She wished only to think of this evening, fresh and clear, with music that lit the very stars. But she could not resist one question of Duvall.

"Major," she said as they walked, "do you agree with my brother that Captain Dalyell's plan is rash?"

Duvall stopped and put his hand on Ella's, which was in the crook of his arm. He looked intently at her, then leaned back and laughed. "Such a question! And at a time like this, when the disturbance is almost over!" He laughed again, and she saw his face was almost too handsome. His eyes were watery; when they looked at her, she felt as if they were consuming her, and it was an uncomfortable sensation.

"My dearest," Duvall said with a light laugh, "why should you worry your lovely self about such things? Those are men's thoughts, a soldier's thoughts. Let us men do such worrying, my dear lady. For such as you I would be grateful to fight against whatever danger, if only I could take the great weight that this irksome siege has lain upon your gentle shoulders."

Duvall threw back his powdered head and laughed again. "Ella, Ella. Here you've been eager for a ball all these months, and all you can talk about—"

"Major," she said with a voice that cut him. She withdraw her hand from his arm and faced him. "Major, you have not answered my question."

He sighed and shook his head. "My dearest Ella, I respect and admire your brother, you know that. But in this affair I agree wholeheartedly with Captain Dalyell. We have waited long enough—far too long!"

She felt cold, and she found herself rubbing her arms. He took her by the shoulders, gazed down into her face, and said, in a whisper, "Ella, I, too, shall join this attacking force. I tell you this in greatest secrecy: We are departing tomorrow night for the assault. Even today we have seen that Pontiac's camp across the river has indeed been struck. They have burned what they could not carry and gone to a new camp on this side of the river, about four miles above the fort. But we'll truly be fortunate if we find an Indian within a hundred miles of Fort Detroit tomorrow night."

He drew her closer, but she coughed and pulled away, then went on walking. He came to her side and said, "My dearest Ella, I hope you'll not hold it against me that I disagree with your brother. After all—"

"Major," she said, trying to be friendly. "For your sake, and for the sake of the soldiers you take with you, I pray to heaven that you are right and that Henry is wrong." She willed her heart to still its racing, breathed deeply to calm herself, and then smiled. "And now, Major, if you please, I am most eager to join our celebration."

They walked into the council house, where scores of candles were set on candelabra about the room. There were more than a hundred guests at the happy affair, and everyone—everyone but Henry Gladwin and, at moments, Ella—was inebriated by the prospect of dancing their way into liberation. At someone's shout the floor was cleared of talkative officers and civilians, many with wives and grown daughters. Major Gladwin and Ella did the honors of the first dance. As they swung into the music, the brother and sister forgot the peril beyond the walls of the fort. Gladwin grinned at Ella as they glided gracefully around the floor to polite applause.

"I daresay we've all needed this, sister," he said, and his eyes twinkled. "You as much as any of us."

She had nothing to say just then. There was only the swirling dance and the music. In a moment the planking of the floor creaked and thumped with the steps of two hundred dancing feet, and Fort Detroit was happy again.

Gladwin swung Ella lightly, and he looked closely at her before saying, "It would be nice if Owen were here now."

She smiled and released a little laugh of resignation.

"I doubt," she said, "that Owen Sutherland remembers how to dance like this." She continued to dance and put Owen Sutherland out of her mind.

The ball was sheer delight. Ella had a different partner for every dance, and she cared nothing about the envious eyes of many younger women who begrudged her being the center of attraction—particularly for the lavish attention Alex Duvall paid her when he was not indulging at the punch bowl. Ella hardly noticed the women staring at her from behind fans, and she was enjoying herself so much that she did not realize how her unaffected loveliness had made her the focus of male interest. Nor did she care. The music and the dancing and the laughter were a cure for melancholy, and they brought relief and contentment, if only for the moment.

Perhaps she had a bit too much punch. Perhaps the gaiety was so infectious that it sparkled like champagne inside her. Whatever the reason for her pleasure Ella Bently enjoyed the ball that evening as she had not enjoyed anything for far too many years.

When the evening drew on and the musicians grew weary, the singing began. Voices lifted in cheerful song, and Lettie Morely, who had made many trips to the punch bowl, said with a giggle that their voices resounded enough to levitate the council house and float it bouncing out over the Detroit River. Garth spent the last third of the evening slumbering in a chair pushed against a far corner.

Singing was a perfect crown on a perfect evening. Ella laughed to hear the soldiers just arrived from the East sing a song with a bright melody that had come not long ago from the more populated places. It was called "The Lass with the Delicate Air."

> Young Molly who lived at the foot of the hill,
> Whose fame every virgin with envy doth fill,
> Of beauty is bless'd with so ample a share,
> Men call her the lass with the delicate air,
>   With the delicate air,
>
> One evening last May as I traversed the grove,
> In thoughtless retirement, not dreaming of love,
> I chanced to espy the gay nymph I declare,
> And really, she had a most delicate air,
>   A most delicate air,

Near the end of the evening a soldier who had been on the whaleboat with Ella on the journey from Fort Niagara began to sing; his voice was so fine that the others hushed to listen. The song was "Drink to Me Only with Thine Eyes," and it brought a sadness to Ella, for she remembered the evening around the campfire when Duncan McEwan sang it and she first met Owen Sutherland. Before long the whole party was in voice with him, humming and harmonizing the gentle melody.

There was quiet at the end of the song, and all listened for something appropriate to be said. Then, after some time of satisfied silence, Alex Duvall struck up "God Save the King." The evening's joy melted off comfortably, and the revelers drifted home, pleased and spent at last.

The giddiness had left Ella as she and Duvall walked back in the early morning hours toward Gladwin's house. He held her arm, but he seemed heavy against her. Perhaps too much punch had found its way into Duvall's glass. He hummed "Lass with the Delicate Air" as they walked.

He chuckled, then looked at Ella. "What a wonderful evening, dearest!"

"It was, indeed, Major Duvall," she said, and they strolled in step down Rue Sainte Anne.

"Alex," he said. "Please: Alex. Nothing, nothing at all could have made it more wonderful."

But something could have made the evening better, thought Ella, although she had tried not to think of it. Perhaps she, too, had imbibed too liberally of punch, for she now found her thoughts reckless, careless, uncommonly bold. In her mind was Owen Sutherland. For most of the evening, she had not thought about him, and she considered that good. But when the soldier had sung McEwan's song, Sutherland came to mind and had stayed there. Admittedly she had done little to remove Sutherland from her mind, and at this moment it felt warm to contemplate his face. She saw him feverish and frenzied in the bed at Gladwin's, and she was bathing him with cold towels. She saw him climb over the gunwale into the stranded whaleboat, and he was grinning, handsome, and wet. She giggled to herself to remember.

". . . and you know, dearest, our mission tomorrow night is fraught with danger . . ." Duvall was speaking.

Ella saw Owen and Jeremy laughing and polishing fishing rods. Their eyes were easy, and their companionship exhilarated her.

". . . please don't be concerned for my safety, my dearest. Merely knowing that you await my safe return is enough, for nothing shall prevent me from coming back to . . ."

They were standing near the water gate, which was kept open for those at the ball to stroll and gaze out at the peaceful river. Duvall was still speaking, but Ella heard little. She wondered where Sutherland was now.

". . . will you, dearest Ella, please tell me you will?"

"What? Oh, forgive me, Major, I must have been dreaming away. What was that? I beg your pardon."

"A token, Ella," he said with a rush of breath.

"A token? What for?"

"Something, my dearest, that I might carry into battle to give me comfort. Something of yours. Anything—a scarf, a lock of hair . . ."

"I—I," she had no words. "A lock of hair, Major?"

"Alex."

"Alex. Why, what shall you do with a lock of my hair, Major?"

He leaned toward her, and his face was near hers. "A token by which I can remember you when we march to battle. A token I shall keep close to my heart. Forever."

Things were a bit foggy then, but Ella suppressed a silly giggle. She looked up at Duvall's watery eyes and with difficulty restrained laughter. Not that he was so ridiculous. No, he was quite charming in his own way. But something—whatever it was she did not know—something was really very funny, very silly, and she wanted so much to laugh. Just an innocent little laugh that wouldn't harm anyone; a laugh that Major Duvall should not think was meant to insult him.

". . . I'll treasure it always, my dearest . . ."

Just as she'd dreamed her lover ought to woo her. Here it was, actually happening, on a starry night, in a passionate wilderness, while a mighty river surged past in the darkness. Even an English major, and a handsome one, too, to play the part.

". . . and there, while we tramp toward the unknown . . ."

Then if it were such a dream come true, why was it so funny? Why was she sure she would giggle? She tried to turn away, but he pushed his face forward to find her impudent eyes again. Oh, he must not be insulted if she could no longer keep in this awfully silly giggle!

"Will you, dearest Ella? A handkerchief? A lock of your hair?"

She simply must think of something sober. Something to keep her from laughing—something serious—and she did: She thought of the rumor about Owen's dishonor, and it soaked the hilarity from her. Even the tipsy warmth of the rum punch drained away, and all that confronted her was Duvall's puppy face, pleading for her hair.

"Major—" She tried to be serious now.

"My dearest?"

"Major—"

"Dearest?"

"Major, please, I wish to ask you something—something that is very, very difficult—"

"Ask, dearest. Ask, and if it is in my power, it shall be yours."

"Major, have you heard—have you heard about this terrible rumor? The rumor about Mr. Sutherland?"

Duvall staggered back a step. In the faint light of nearby lanterns she saw his lips were turned downward in a scowl. She studied his face, and she felt cold. In a moment he composed himself. His voice sounded thick with rum, and it was gruff.

"Rumor? What rumor about Sutherland? Rumors are untruths, as far as I am concerned. What untruths do you refer to?"

"Why, Major, you must have heard it, for everyone in Detroit has been talking about it. The vile rumor about Mr. Sutherland resigning in dishonor from his regiment. Do you know about it? Is it—is it—"

"True?" His voice was of stone. She said nothing, for she was having difficulty catching her breath. How could she have brought up such a subject on so wonderful an evening? No, she must change the conversation. But before she could speak, Duvall said, "Yes, I know the story. I know it very well."

"You have heard it then? Oh, Major, forgive me. Let's not discuss such a thing tonight. I'm sorry I brought it up, for such vile lies are not worth—"

"Lies? What makes you think they are lies?"

It was as though they had become trees, stiff and awkward.

"Why, of course—I mean—how could they not be?"

Duvall slowly shook his head. He looked smugly down at Ella and put his hands on her arms.

"I know, dearest, how much you and your brother admire this fellow, and I am sorry to be the one to confirm the facts, but the story of the man's disgrace is not a lie."

She felt weaker than she ever knew possible. "Not?"

He wore his most sympathetic face. "Not a lie, my dear. Ella, you should know the truth. He was indeed court-martialed. I know, for, you see, I was his commanding officer at the time."

"You!" She did not know whether to gasp or to faint. She stared at Duvall. "You were . . . then, were you the one who—who started this—this story?"

Duvall let his hands drop from her arms, and he stepped back into shadows. He looked down at the ground before he spoke.

"Ella, it appears it was my unintentional indiscretion which revealed the background of Owen Sutherland to the people here and thus to you." He looked up at her, his eyes questioning. "But you must understand, it was all an innocent moment of—of—well, just let me say that I had a rather private discussion with Sir Robert Davers just before he went off on his unfortunate expedition, and I fear that Sir Robert might have let slip some of what I told him in confidence."

He went on speaking, but Ella heard nothing. It was true after all. Owen had been dishonored after all. After all she had refused to believe—after all the dismal unhappiness she felt at the injustice of it.

But it was unjust! A man's past should be forgotten if he has paid for his sins. Sutherland did not deserve to be humiliated out here. But it was true. It was true after all. How very, very . . .

"Now, now, Ella," Duvall said softly. "I know this is a dreadful shock to you. But let's not think—"

She pulled away from him and felt herself tremble uncontrollably. He reached for her, but she drew away again, muttering broken apologies, and she spun away, head down, heart frozen, running toward her house.

Duvall called once, twice, but she was gone in the darkness, and he stamped his foot in anger.

He turned to walk away, but something white caught his eye. Lying on the ground was a silk handkerchief Ella had apparently dropped. He picked it up and brought it to his lips. The scent was hers. He pushed the handkerchief into his tunic. She would forget Sutherland now that she knew what kind of rogue he really was. She would get over this disillusionment, and when she did, she would see clearly how Duvall felt for her. That would all come soon enough. She would eventually swoon for him. They always did.

chapter **18**

BLOODY CREEK

Bouquet's soldiers made eight hard miles before settling down to camp a few hours prior to sundown that first day. The trail over which they plodded on the way to their initial goal of besieged Fort Ligonier was overgrown and rocky. All that day they had trudged up and down hills that tormented their carts. Oxen were hot and thirsty, and the scores of pack-horses and mules were hard put to bear enough stores for this army as well as for the trapped garrisons.

They had pushed on over hill after hill, and at every crest they saw before them a surrounding sea of green, unbroken forest. The road ran like a scar through this wilderness, and behind every tree an Indian might lurk.

Sutherland was constantly busy moving up and down the long scarlet snake of soldiers, keeping them from straying or falling back to drink water. He warned them about the danger to stragglers, and he made it clear their lives were forfeit if they were caught by scalping parties. It took the better part of that first day to accustom the Highlanders to the risk they faced if they left the column even briefly. This was not Europe, he told them, and eventually they understood.

The provincials and the Royal Americans were used to Indian fighting and to traveling in the wilderness, and they kept up a close but loose formation. Less than a third of the five hundred men in the force, they kept a screen of skirmishers thrown out before the column to prevent ambush. The Scots who made up the bulk of the army were trained in massed volleys and fierce charges. None had faced the elusive Indian, who killed when he could not be killed himself and who vanished after shooting from cover. Even though the Watch had served brilliantly in the French and Indian War three years ago, that was ancient history to these new enlistees.

Sutherland knew the Scottish temperament, and he feared that a few days of Indian ambushes would drive the Highlanders to counterattack recklessly, putting them at the mercy of larger groups of Indians who would hide deeper in the forest and wait until a body of men was lured into a trap.

At the head of the column Sutherland marched alongside McEwan, who commanded the vanguard of a mixed group of Highlanders, provincials, and Royal Americans. McEwan had chosen to wear his linen shirt and buckskins for this march instead of his uniform. When not being carried, little Toby ran alongside, scampering back and forth among the soldiers, making three miles for each mile the army walked. And each of those miles was tedious. The men were sweating, grumbling, insect-bitten as they hobbled into their welcome camp that night and waited for the dawn, when the march would begin again, and begin with them all a day wearier—a day closer to their elusive and deadly enemies.

The rattle of gunmetal from soldiers assembling drifted up to Ella's open bedroom window. Voices were hushed, but the tramp of boots and the squeak of leather was like a restless sea out on the dark parade ground. It was well past two-thirty when she got up and hurried into her housecoat. She looked out the window into the yellow light of a dozen smoking torches.

The fort's east gate creaked open. Quiet commands crept up to her, and she heard the slow shuffling of feet. In the gloom, torchlight glinted off brass and bayonets, but it was difficult to discern individual men. Somewhere down there were Alex Duvall, Captain Dalyell, and Major Rogers. Ella felt a rush of relief that Henry was not among those who were marching out on the assault. She pulled on a cloak and went outside.

Standing at the corner of the parade ground and Rue Sainte Anne, Henry and several of his officers were watching the last of nearly two hundred and fifty officers and men file out into the darkness. The east gate was closed and barred. They would march along the Detroit River, past lines of French cabins, toward Pontiac's new camp, which was on the far side of Parent's Creek. The force had to cross a small bridge where the creek entered the river. The plan was to approach Pontiac's camp after an hour's march, form up in battle lines, then charge just before dawn. Even though the attackers were outnumbered four or five to one, the elements of surprise and discipline were expected—according to young Captain Dalyell—to carry the day against disorganized, primitive Indian fighters. Even though Pontiac was reputed to have learned enough from the French to grasp the manner of European fighting, Dalyell was confident in his own leadership. Apparently Dalyell did not know that the great French general, the gallant Marquis de Montcalm, had valued Pontiac as an ally, awarding the chief with one of his own pure white officer's uniforms as a token of respect. Although that fact escaped Dalyell, it crossed Gladwin's mind as he walked through the quiet fort toward his sister.

It was nearly three o'clock. The shooting would start in an hour. Gladwin walked up the steps to his house and went inside, followed by Ella. He lit a candle from a taper kindled in the embers of the fire, sat down heavily in a chair, and leaned his head into his hands, elbows on the table.

In the kitchen Ella rattled cups and saucers down from a cabinet. She was nervous. She ladled water into the iron kettle and hung it over the fire. As she glanced over at her brother, whose head still rested in his hands, he looked up.

"Henry," she began, sitting down in an easy chair near the fire, "shouldn't I be excited that the siege is about to be broken?" Fear curdled within her.

He half smiled. "Perhaps my own anxiety has troubled you unnecessarily, Ella. I'm sorry about that. Yes, you and I and all of us should be excited that Captain Dalyell's mission will liberate us." He looked away, staring down at the top of the table. Then he said softly, "But I don't like it, not at all. I wish we had planned this business more carefully."

Ella poured brandy, and he sipped it thoughtfully. They said nothing more until the kettle boiled and tea was brewed. As Ella placed the pot on the table, Gladwin quickly looked up, listening. "What was that?"

Ella heard nothing.

"Listen!" he whispered.

There. In the distance. Like the crackle of corn popping. Faintly, just a few crackles, then came a rushing burst of popping.

Gladwin jumped up, and his chair fell backwards.

"Too soon! Too soon!" said Gladwin, his face ashen in the dim light. "They can't have reached the village yet! Not yet."

Gladwin burst out of the house, and Ella ran to the door. The sound of gunfire was louder now. Gladwin called his officers together, and soldiers were gathering on the parade ground, everyone talking in low voices. From what Ella could make out, they feared Dalyell had been ambushed, for the soldiers had not marched long enough to reach the Indian camp. Ella pulled her cloak tighter.

The steady rush of shooting stayed at a constant pitch for more than an hour. Dawn filtered into the sky. A light fog hovered above the river. The shooting went on, and the worried people at Detroit huddled in little groups, talking, speculating, praying.

Then a sentry on the parapet above the water gate gave a shout. One of the two bateaux that had followed the line of march along the shore was coming back out of the fog. People ran to the water gate, and Ella barged along with the nervous crowd that funneled through. They were shocked by what they saw.

The Bateau was laden with wounded and dying soldiers, more than a dozen of them, bloody and moaning in pain.

Men clambered aboard the bateau and lifted the wounded clear. Major Gladwin appeared, and Ella heard the young ensign in command of the craft speak to him in a voice filled with dismay.

"Ambushed 'em at that little bridge over Parent's Creek," he said. "Them Indians was ready for us, Major. Waitin' they was, all hidden in the bushes and the Frenchy houses. Cut these 'ere lads down in a wink. The boys are fightin' stoutly, but if they don't get back to the fort quick, they'll all be goners."

A woman near Ella swooned away, and a man caught her as she fell. Ella's horror froze her. Liberation—freedom—was not certain after all!

In the faint dawn the ensign's face showed black from powder; his white eyes were vacant. The men from the fort who had come down to fetch the wounded were struck dumb. Gladwin shook with anger. Then in a flash of determination he began to order soldiers into action clearing out the bateau. He found replacements for the wounded who had been in the boat's crew, and then sent it back on its way. On the craft was a swivel gun. Loaded with grapeshot and canister, it would be a valuable support for the soldiers when they needed their retreat covered, and Gladwin ordered the boat commander to rake the enemy positions for as long as he could.

A few moments later the second bateau arrived with a gory load of dead and wounded soldiers, who were carried back up the slope. The only officer in sight was the young ensign in command of this craft. He was the one who played violin in Lee's group. He shouted:

"Look lively, lads! We're going right back upriver for more wounded! Shove off! Hey, you there! Give us a hand! Push us off! Hop to it! Look lively! Yes, you!"

Ella looked about her and saw there was now no one on shore but her. The ensign was calling to her, not realizing she was a woman, for the dimness and her cloak made her no more than a shadow.

"Come on, you!" the ensign barked and waved to her. "Cast off that line there, fellow! Cast off so we can get going!"

Ella moved to the stake to which the bateau's line was tied and tugged hard at the rope to free it. As she worked, she heard a soldier in the boat say, "Ensign, we need a few more lads in this boat. We need someone to tend the wounded when we get them, else they'll be dead afore we get back!"

The young officer growled and swore. "There isn't anyone else! We got to go, and we got to go now! We don't have time to wait for more to come down from the fort. Come on! Hey, push off there, fellow!"

Ella splashed into the water and heaved with all her strength at the bateau. Her mind whirled. She heard the pop of musketry in a steady rush, crackling fiercely in the distance. Men were dying upriver. More would die in this bateau if they were not immediately bandaged. The bateau drifted away, and the rowers clattered oars into locks as the ensign shouted commands. Without thinking, Ella scrambled over the side of the boat, clumsily trying to get in while the craft dipped and lurched. A soldier grunted assent and roughly dragged her, bumping and bruising, aboard at the bow. The boat set off against the current, keeping to the riverbank. At first no one spoke.

"Good to have yer with us, lad!" the soldier who had pulled Ella aboard said at last. "Keep yer head down when we get up there, and—hey!"

"Row there, soldier!" the ensign shouted from the tiller. "You—"

"Sir!" the soldier bellowed, staring all the while at Ella, whose cloak had fallen from her head, revealing a tumble of hair in the half-light. "This 'ere ain't no lad! It be a—a—"

"Damn it!" the ensign roared. "Row man, or we'll wallow like a goddamned tub—"

"—a goddamned la—I mean, a—" The soldier was astonished. "It's a lady, sir!"

"What?" The ensign scrambled forward and stopped close to Ella. "Why . . . Mistress Bently—"

"I'm here now, Ensign. And I'm staying!"

"Mistress Bently! Mistress Bently, I can't—"

"I stay!" She reached under her cloak to rip her nightgown free and began methodically to tear it into strips. "I stay. We'll need bandages, and this will do!"

The ensign was still wide-eyed. The enlisted men chuckled in admiration of Ella's spunk.

"Mistress, if Major Gladwin knows—"

She silenced him with a cold stare. Then she looked upstream, where the sparkle of gunfire in the dawning was like a host of fireflies. All the while, the soldiers were rowing. The shooting was louder now, not more than a few hundred yards away. "Heave, lads!" called the soldier who had dragged Ella into the boat. "Pull away! We're nearly there! Ho! Say what, Ensign?"

The officer cleared his throat and said, "Very well. Very well, mistress, but you stay in the bateau! Those are my orders!"

She nodded and continued tearing up her gown. The officer returned to the tiller, and Ella took a bucket, tied a line to it, and dropped it over the side. With great effort she managed to haul it in, half full with river water, which would be needed for the wounded.

Daylight was rising from the mist, gray and cool. The shooting was a loud burst from time to time: That was the regulars firing concentrated volleys. Ella's ears rang with the explosion. All the while, a steady clatter of disorganized firing filled the space between volleys: the firing of the Indians. Now as the bateau drifted into brush along the riverbank, Ella could see the outlines of soldiers standing in ranks on the road near the water. In the silhouetted groves of trees, farmhouses, and fence-rows, flashes of hundreds of muskets illuminated the mist as, all around, the Indians kept up steady firing.

The bateau clumped against the shore, and men rushed into the water to pull it under the shelter of overhanging trees. Others appeared, carrying wounded over their shoulders, in their arms, limping from wounds themselves. The crew in the boat jumped out to help load the injured.

Ella was immediately surrounded by groaning soldiers gasping for air, begging for water. Some lay silent. Some seemed already dead. Ella stared about at so much misery. So much more than she could hope to—

Something whisked past her ear, like a large bee, buzzing, then gone. She realized the air was full of whispering, zinging, whiplike sounds. There were other sounds: Indians whooping in the near distance; muskets firing; ramrods clinking into muzzles; men shouting, swearing, weeping. The boat rocked as a burly corporal was pushed over the side and fell limply on the flooring. Ella jumped up, feeling another bee zip nearby. Someone screamed. She dragged the soldier onto his back, and he looked up at her, eyes glazed, face grimy with gunpowder and sweat.

The wounded man rasped, "Water." Ella fumbled for the bucket, dipped a strip of cloth into it, and splashed his face. He licked his lips, and his head lolled a few times. Silently he thanked her. She splashed him again and pulled open his shirt, which was torn and bloody. She ripped away the uniform, drenched the wound in his side, and wrapped bandaging around him as best she could, but it was not enough. She tied the strip tightly, laid the corporal's head back, then hurried to the next man, and the next, and another. All the while, bullets flew around her. The sky brightened, and the mist rose.

The din of battle did not matter now. She was too busy. She tied tourniquets on bloody limbs, then came back to tighten or to loosen them. She gave water until the bucket was empty, dipped it over the side, and gave again. Soon the bandages were all gone, and she tore tunics, men's shirts, anything, into strips to help slow bleeding.

The boat filled up with soldiers, and a few grappled with the oars. Someone shouted "Push off!" Ella looked up. It was full daylight now. The boat drifted backwards, then the rowers stroked the bateau into the stream and downriver. Ella drenched parched lips and faces, wiped away blood and sweat. There was not enough time and, it seemed, no danger, though bullets thudded against the wood of the boat. No time. No danger. Just dying men, bloody wounds, powder-burned faces, and whizzing bees.

Only four soldiers out of the six who had earlier rowed the boat up to the fighting were still there. There was no sign of the ensign. She turned to the fellow who had first pulled her aboard and asked about the officer. His face smeared with blood and dirt, his eyes bright with anger, he said, "Lad's gone!" and went back to rowing. The wounded corporal groaned, and Ella scrambled to him, though there was little she could do. She rubbed his face with a wet cloth. He groaned again and went stiff with pain. He moaned and tried to sit up. She pushed him back, but he was too strong. His eyes opened wide, though he saw nothing. She pushed against him. He began to shiver, his teeth to chatter. He shook as though he would break into pieces. Ella saw Owen Sutherland in a flash. She pressed the soldier down and drove the cloth into his mouth. He bit hard and shuddered briefly, then his trembling stopped. He breathed one great gulp of air and released it completely. Ella gazed at him, transfixed, sure she was watching him die.

But he breathed again deeply, more relaxed. And then again. Ella breathed with him. She spoke to him, and he slowed down, taking more natural breaths. She hovered over him. He closed his eyes. She touched his brow, and he seemed asleep. A moment later he looked up at her, and something passed of mutual gratitude. He was still alive. Ella took the cloth from his mouth and held her hand on his forehead; soon he lay calmly resting.

The boat grounded with a jerk. They were back at Detroit. The shooting was away in the background again, and dozens of people were all around, lifting wounded from the bateau, crowding into the craft as replacements for the return journey. Ella closed her eyes and held the bloody rag against her face.

"Ella!"

Henry was knee-deep in water, reaching over the side of the boat for her. He stared for a moment, his eyes emotionless, then said, "Come. You've done enough." He lifted her over the gunwale and carried her ashore.

"I'm all right, Henry," she said, finding her strength as he set her on the ground. "I'm all right."

"I'm taking you to Mrs. Morely," he said. "Stay with her until all this—"

"Really, I'm fine, Henry, just—just a little—" She shook her head to clear it. "There's too much to do, Henry!"

Before Gladwin could reply, someone shouted to him. He turned and nodded acknowledgment, then ordered a soldier to accompany Ella to Lettie Morely's. A few minutes later Lettie had changed Ella into clean clothes and served her hot tea and bread. After a brief rest she and Lettie hurried to join other women, who were assisting the regimental surgeon in a make-shift hospital set up in one of the barracks.

Outside the sun shone warm and fresh, but within the hospital the sight was dismaying. Wounded lay in cots all along the walls of the narrow building. Blood ran over the floor, and the chorus of despair that rose from the injured was enough to break anyone's composure. The women moved among the men, who lay in agony or in silence. With the others Ella labored hard, changing bandages, assisting the surgeon, cleaning wounds, bringing hot food and drinks to those who were well enough to take them, and suffering when men—really boys in their teens for the most part—were carried out, dead.

The most wretched lay unconscious, awaiting death. Those whose limbs had been amputated shrieked in uncontrolled suffering. Others lay whimpering, groaning in sorrowful oblivion. More than one nurse ran out weeping after working for hours in the hospital. Ella almost fled as well when she saw a young soldier being carried out by the burial party. It was the corporal who had trembled so fiercely on the bateau—the one she had thought would live.

But Ella kept hold of herself and, together with Lettie Morely, labored with a strength that knew no revulsion, with a devotion borne of compassion. Her arms were spent and her apron was bloody; sweat and dirt and blood streaked her face.

The sun was high when Gladwin came for her. He had been everywhere at once, organizing a rear guard to cover the last few hundred yards of retreat, seeing to defenses, preparing for Indians to pursue the beaten force right into the fort. But no attack came, and that danger passed. Those who could had come back to the fort, but twenty-three were dead. Thirty-seven men were wounded, many badly, and the rest were demoralized and exhausted. One out of four had fallen.

By the time Ella walked back to her house, she had been told bits and pieces of what had happened. Henry was drawn and morbid as he related everything.

The column had begun to cross Parent's Creek when hundreds of Indians burst from ambush, firing furiously, shooting men down in clusters. The Indians drove the soldiers like cattle into a tight defense on the open road, where only the cover of night sheltered them. Indians were everywhere—behind rocks, hidden in houses, in thickets, and shooting from woodpiles. The soldiers stood bravely, although comrades fell all around them. The retreat was nearly cut off, but Major Rogers acted swiftly. Gathering his Rangers, he captured a

strong French house and laid down a steady field of fire that
harassed the Indians and allowed the surviving soldiers to make
a fighting withdrawal, leaving their dead behind. When dawn
was bright enough, Parent's Creek was a dreadful sight. The
water ran bright red with blood, and from that day on the stream
was known as Bloody Creek.

It was late morning when all the men who could be saved
had come back. The overconfident force had been shattered.
British arms had suffered a stunning defeat, and Pontiac's uprising seemed even more invincible. The Indians had drunk
much English blood that morning. The siege of Detroit was far
from lifted—on the contrary. The Indians, who normally were
incapable of sustaining a prolonged siege and had never before
kept one up as long as this investment of Detroit, now had
every reason to believe that the English were doomed to die
to the last man.

And there were those inside the little fort who wondered
whether the Indians might not be right in their assumption. All
that stood between defeat and death were the two supply
ships—*Huron* and *Michigan*. If either of those were captured—
as the Indians had tried often but failed to do so far—then
there was little hope of reprovisioning from Niagara before a
major expedition could be assembled and sent west to relieve
Detroit.

Alex Duvall came back safely, but he avoided Ella. Nor
had she sought him out that morning. Instead she was ordered
by Gladwin to go home and rest, and she was glad to do so.

Soon after she came home, Henry returned. He said nothing
as he slumped into a chair at the table, threw his wig onto a
stool nearby, and folded his hands in front of him. He stayed
that way, unmoving, his eyes down at the table, for nearly half
an hour. Ella was tired and shaken, but she worried more for
her brother than for herself. At last she brought a cup of tea
and sat across from him.

"Henry—" Ella said with a faint voice. "Henry, won't you
drink some tea, dear?"

He sighed deeply and kept his head down. Ella tried to think
of something to say—something to lighten his gloom. But
nothing came. She sipped at her tea, and her hands trembled.
At last she could stand the silence no longer.

"Henry, please speak to me!" She tried to control her voice.
"Don't be silent now, when everything—everything is so—so

terrible!" She restrained a sob. She would not weep now. Not now! Her brother said nothing. "Henry, you must . . . you must at least . . . at least drink your *damned* tea!"

He looked up, his face deeply lined, profoundly tired, sad, and—she hated to admit it—so close to defeat. The strain on Gladwin had been more than a lesser man could have borne.

"Henry, forgive me for pressing you like this, but you worry me. I worry for your health!"

Gladwin nodded. He drank a little tea, then held the cup, cradling it in his hands. He said, "Sister, I fear we're done for now!"

"Henry! Don't dare say that!" She never imagined her brother could speak so. He must not! She could not permit him to say he was beaten. But before she could argue, she was halted by the sorrow in his eyes.

"Too much has been lost," Gladwin whispered. "Our fool-hardiness has cost us too much! Too much in sheer physical effort. Too much in prestige with the other tribes that have not yet joined Pontiac. Too much in blood!"

Ella wanted to get up and rush away. But she could not. Henry's sad eyes held her.

"We've lost far too much today, sister," he said, louder now and deadly calm. He put his cup down. "Pontiac will soon have every brave from Niagara to the Mississippi joining him. When ther hear of this beating he's given us, they'll swarm to him in numbers we've never imagined possible. Only the threat of British guns restrained them from rising, but now he's shown them British guns are not enough. Oh, yes, one day our guns will destroy them all—but that day will come too late for Detroit unless . . . unless there's some great Indian defeat some-where. Someone has to whip them soundly—soon—and then the fear of British guns will be rekindled. But until then, sister, Fort Detroit is in grave . . ."

He did not finish his sentence.

Ella had never seen her brother like this before. She refused to accept what he had said. She got up quickly, clattering her cup from its saucer and spilling what was left of her tea. She stumbled upstairs to her bedroom and fell onto the bed. She was exhausted, but her thundering heart kept her awake. As she lay there, she thought of ambitious men and how their pride so often brings suffering down upon them and upon those who follow them. She thought of young Captain Dalyell. On the road to Bloody Creek, his body lay beside many of his best and bravest. James Dalyell, who was once a very ambitious man.

The letter Frances Gladwin received from her husband this July went as follows:

Fort Detroit
May 14, 1763

My Dearest Frances,

I write this missive (brief it must be, for duty presses) to assure you that I am well, as are my sister Ella and her son, Jeremy. By now you no doubt will have heard of the troubles here in the Northwest, but perhaps by the time this letter reaches you, it will all have passed as these Indian squalls generally do.

Though I wish not to alarm you over my safety, I think it best to tell you the truth of it, for the many rumors and reports England must hear about our situation will undoubtedly be more frightening than the actual fact. At this writing we are safe and secure in a strong fort, and the officers and men are behaving well. There is no fear that Detroit might fall by assault of the Indians, though we would be happier with some prospect of fresh supplies and reinforcement. These are now on the way, and their arrival will spell defeat for the hostiles, who, when they see a strong body of men enter the fort with sufficient provision, will undoubtedly melt away into the wilderness whence they came. Indians have never proven capable of sustaining a siege, and it is not expected they will do so now.

Therefore, no matter what rumors you hear, rest assured that your loving husband is safe and expects to return to you as near as possible to the time originally planned . . .

So went the letter from her husband, all full of encouragement and banter about the future. But Frances Gladwin read it with shaking hands, not because of unfounded rumor but because much had happened in the months since Henry had written this letter. Far too much for his words to cheer her with their optimism.

When she finished the letter, Frances shuddered, trying not to weep, but the tears came anyway. After a moment she sighed deeply and stood up. She must read this letter to her father, who asked every day of word from America. It was a pity that Henry's letter had not arrived before the news had reached them of capture of the Niagara supply convoy. It would have been welcome then. Now, despite the endearment and the tenderness of Henry's thoughts, the letter was painful to read. It hurt to read of her husband's optimism, knowing how crushingly those hopes must have been dashed.

Frances Gladwin knew Henry would not be home this autumn. Yet it would be enough, she prayed, if he came home at all.

At Shippensburg, where war parties hovered, ready to strike at any moment, the struggling column of soldiers made camp. They were five days and twenty miles from Carlisle. Bouquet learned that the tiny fort called Ligonier, several days to the west, was in desperate straits. It could fall with the first determined assault, for Indians harried it day and night.

Fearing the fort's valuable ammunition would fall into Indian hands, Bouquet assembled thirty of his strongest Highlanders. Sutherland roamed about Shippensburg and found several willing frontiersmen who agreed to guide the party on a forced march to relieve Ligonier until the main body came up.

Sutherland had offered to lead these men in their expedition, but Bouquet needed him with the column. It was not necessary for Bouquet to explain why, for it was obvious that the chances of those Highlanders and their scouts getting through safely were very slim. The Swiss officer would not risk losing his best scout.

But McEwan volunteered to go, and when the ensign set out, he asked Sutherland to care for Toby. The pup was still too young for such a mission, because these men would be obliged to move quickly and silently. There might be moments when a squealing Toby would give them away, and they would be lost.

"Keep her close, eh, Owen?" McEwan asked and rubbed the whining puppy's ears. Sutherland slipped the dog into a wide pouch hung over his shoulder, closed the flap, and buckled it. It bounced as Toby struggled to get free.

"There," Sutherland said. "Now she won't come after you.

Be careful, Dunkie. Don't forget you've got to go farther than Ligonier, so don't collect any Indian lead, eh?"

They shook hands, then McEwan was gone, vanished into the depths of the woods along a little-used hunting trail. The Indians would be watching the main road through the mountains that Bouquet's army would use, so it was possible that Mc-Ewan's party would be undetected on the shortcut until they came close to Ligonier. From there they might have to fight their way into the fort.

Scenes of hunger and despair at Shippensburg were even more oppressive than at Carlisle. Hundreds of civilians, frightened and hopeless, wept for joy at the arrival of the soldiers. Although they begged Bouquet to stay longer, he fed them what he could spare and pressed on.

Day after day passed, one like the other. Wheels creaked, pack animals plodded, and the only relief was the occasional tune picked up by the army's lone piper.

They came to tiny Fort Lyttleton, abandoned weeks ago. There a garrison of a few men with ammunition and provisions was left to defend the place. The force marched on, hacking their way through thick brush that encroached on the trail. At Fort Bedford the post's haggard commander was delighted to see the soldiers. But they soon left him and again pushed on toward Ligonier. On and on they went, through sweet-scented pine woods on mountain crests, across flat brooks, shallow and dry in narrow valleys that smelled of rotting timber and skunk cabbage. They walked and walked. They moved from dawn to dusk, heading for Ligonier and then on to Fort Pitt. Oxen's tongues lolled in the heat. Men stopped speaking, and on they went.

The journey would take this army two weeks. If Sutherland had been moving alone—as he was when he came with McEwan—he could travel through even this rough country in one third the time. He struggled on, leading the way in doubtful places, directing the oxcarts in the crossing of streams, searching out stragglers and consulting with the few frontiersmen who had joined up at Shippensburg. Though he might have left the guiding to these newcomers, Sutherland had given his word to Bouquet that he would lead on to Pitt, and that word he would keep.

Wherever there had been settlements or cabins, there were now smoldering ruins. Among the ruins were the dead. Parties were organized for burial, and Sutherland made certain he avoided these scenes of desolation. He had seen enough.

It had been a hard march, but Duncan McEwan was amazed, for they had not seen Indians at all. It had been several days of travel through the forest, and the frontiersmen leading these thirty soldiers rushing to Fort Ligonier's relief kept them from trouble. Often they had huddled silently in shelter, waiting until the scouts told them to move. McEwan felt like a blind man. He knew nothing more than the few feet of trees and bushes on every side. He pushed on at the heels of the man in front of him, and behind came another Highlander who knew no more than he.

In single file, moving at a dog trot almost constantly, the detachment hurried in absolute silence on the way to Ligonier. McEwan had lots of time to think, and his thoughts were always of Mary Hamilton. He did not think of finding her, nor did he think of what their future would be. He did not even speculate on what he would say when he found her at last. What Duncan McEwan remembered of Mary Hamilton was the morning when he saw her slipping down to the water to fill her bucket—that first moment when she found him watching her.

That was what he remembered. That, and the brief moments spent in seclusion, when time stopped, on the day they had discovered their love.

On Duncan McEwan ran, like a tethered slave. He ran day and night. He ran until he was beyond weariness, and as he ran, he knew he was running toward Mary Hamilton. Mary, who was waiting for him, who would not die until he came for her. Mary . . .

He nearly collided with the man ahead, who had stopped. The man behind him thudded clumsily up against his back. Orders were whispered to close ranks and prepare for the final rush. The fort was up ahead, someone said. Indians were gathering nearby at that very moment, but the scout believed they could slip through if they were quiet, quick, and lucky.

McEwan checked the powder in his priming pan. The detachment gathered closer together, hiding in thick brush on the edge of a clearing that surrounded the small stockade. McEwan heard occasional firing rattle at a distance and wondered whether the Indians were attacking the fort, for he had seen none at all. Then, just as the lieutenant gave the command for the men to dash across the field, McEwan stumbled on something in his path and fell heavily to his hands and knees. Men rushed past him. He looked back, and there lay the body of an Indian brave, his throat cut, and his scalp taken.

Furious firing erupted on all sides as McEwan scrambled to his feet and rushed headlong into the open. His comrades were well ahead of him now. Gunfire and war whoops were bursting from the woods around them. McEwan expected to feel an Indian bullet at any moment, for lead whirled and whizzed past his ear. Shots came from the fort ramparts, and cheers went up from the stockade. McEwan raced with all his might for an open door in one wall.

Then someone fell before him. He ran past the man, skidded, and lurched back to him. Bullets zipped around them. The man was bleeding and swearing, trying to get to his feet, but his shinbone had been broken by a bullet. On the edge of the woods Indians appeared. McEwan reached down for the soldier and yanked him to his feet.

"Get going!" the man grimaced. "Leave me! Save yourself!"

The soldier's complaint ended in a groan of pain as McEwan dragged him fiercely through the long grass. The others were already in the fort, and men stood at the door, urgent to close it.

McEwan glanced behind and saw Indians after him now. He pulled faster, but the burden was too much. He looked back. They were less than thirty yards away, three of them, tomahawks and knives in their hands, leaping across the grass.

He dropped the soldier and turned. He brought up his musket, aimed quickly, and pulled the trigger. The powder fizzled and smoked, but the gun did not fire. The Indians were on him. He whooped a savage cry and sprang at them, thudding the first warrior to the ground with the butt of his musket. As McEwan swung again, the second Indian dived under the musket and came leaping up, chopping with his tomahawk. The tomahawk deflected off McEwan's musket and bounced to the ground. Up came McEwan's foot, lifting the Indian into the air as it caught him between the legs. Then McEwan was on the brave, his hands at the greasy throat, driving the man down.

The third Indian got McEwan's hair from behind and raised his tomahawk, screeching in wild triumph. A musket banged, and the startled brave jerked forward as though clubbed from behind and fell on his face.

Holding the second warrior, who struggled, legs thrusting

out and in, McEwan squeezed the throat with all his might. The brave's hands scratched McEwan's face, but the soldier held on, tighter, until it ended.

McEwan began to breathe once more. He turned to see the wounded soldier trying to stand. The man was holding his musket, which he had used to shoot the third warrior.

"Come on, then!" the soldier shouted. "If you're goin' to save my life, get me into that bloody fort!"

A group of men ran out of the stockade and opened fire at the forest. Musketry rippled along the top of the ramparts, covering the men outside the fort. Then McEwan was relieved of the man he carried, he was shoved through the door, and it was slammed and bolted behind him. He fell to the ground, breathless, his lungs burning, chest heaving. He was glad, now, that Toby had not come along.

It took more than a week for the army to cut its way through from Shippensburg to Fort Ligonier. There was no Indian opposition, although Sutherland knew they were being closely watched. Early in August, they reached Ligonier, and when they arrived, the Indians who had been besieging the fort melted back into the forest like ghosts.

The reunion between McEwan and Toby was pure rapture for the puppy, and McEwan was no less delighted by his scampering pup, which already was showing signs of independence and growth.

They stayed only two nights at Ligonier, which was little more than a small stockade with a trading post and barracks. The army slept uneasily in the fields around the fort, and in the morning they set off again, leaving behind reinforcements, excess baggage, and the sluggish oxen. The journey was more perilous now, and speed was necessary. At Sutherland's suggestion, most of the provisions were left behind. He said that getting the army through was more important than dragging supplies slowly across hostile wilds. Sutherland said Indian resolve would suffer if the relief force got through safely and quickly. Bouquet took his advice, and the army moved much more rapidly now. The three hundred and fifty pack horses picked their way carefully but efficiently along the stump-crowded alley through the woods.

The country, as Sutherland had warned, became more rugged and steep, but progress was good considering the difficult terrain. The land was hilly, thickly overgrown, and serried by deep ravines where ambush cover was offered to the enemy. Every marching camp was well guarded.

"There's to be only four hours of sleep tonight, lads," Sutherland said as he walked into the bivouac Munro and his company had set up among some large boulders. The men grumbled at that.

"I should be restin' and recuperatin' back on that Staten Island or whatever, not sleepin' on these stones and herdin' this lot," Munro said as he took a kettle of boiling soup from the campfire.

"You're getting too old for soldiering, Munro," Sutherland said and sat on a low boulder, empty cup in hand. "We're only a few days from Pitt, and there you can savor the wonders of wilderness life at its finest. Indian princesses, French trappers, English officers—"

"Ach, away wi' you!" Munro splattered soup into his friend's cup. "What's this about a short night?"

Sutherland drank the scalding brew gingerly, then said, "This ground's too suitable for Indian tricks. Considering our pace, at this time tomorrow we'd be at a place called Turtle Creek. Good for camping, but it's a better place for them to ambush us. We're making a forced march in the morning to reach a closer stream, where the stock can get water, called Bushy Run. Then we stay a few hours, and after it's good and dark, we march all night, slip past Turtle Creek and into better country to stand off an attack. So get some sleep tonight, Munro, you may not get much for a couple of days."

Munro gnashed his teeth and drank in silence.

"Have you ever considered the navy, lad?" Sutherland asked without looking up. "No marching."

Munro grunted. "I get seasick. Don't think I haven't considered it, though. But there's too many bloody pirates and too many bloody officers cooped up with you for months on end."

McEwan came into the light of the campfire, and Toby waddled before him, licking Sutherland and Munro eagerly. Munro pushed a plate of salt pork scraps at the puppy, who hungrily gobbled down the food.

Before they realized it, McEwan had placed a small keg in their midst. Other soldiers materialized, licking their lips. Some already had mugs in hand.

"What's this?" Munro said, picking up the wooden keg. "Looks like army-issue rum, Dunkie."

McEwan grinned and sat down, pulled out his dirk, and

began to dig out the bung. "Aye, Munro, it's the best I could do. But there's not much rum about this country except for army rum. You can drink it or drink nothing."

"I'll try," Munro said and pulled the keg away from McEwan to give him a lesson in freeing the bung.

"Where'd this come from, Dunkie?" Sutherland asked as he shook the dottle from his pipe and pulled out his tobacco pouch.

"Well, Owen, seein' as how you're wantin' me to become a trader, I thought I'd get in some tradin' practice while I could. I got this lot from a good lad in the quartermaster's company. I traded him a couple of ermine pelts I brought down from Detroit."

"Ermine!" said Munro, and the bung came free in the same moment. "You mean you traded ermine pelts for army rum? Go on, laddie, you must be daft! That's no bargain. He'll make a hell of a trader, Owen. Are you sure you want him in our company? Ermine for this? Ach, laddie, you're no trader!"

Mugs were clustered at Munro's knees, and he sloshed rum into them.

"It wasn't the best bargain, I know," McEwan said and picked up his cup. "But it seemed right that we have a dram tonight together. Who knows when we'll get another chance?" Toby was at his feet, curled up, already asleep.

"When we get to Pitt," Munro said and lifted his mug, "we'll make our plans there. I'll get out of this army in a few months, and then I'll show you how a Scotsman's supposed to trade. Ermine for rum! Are you sure you're Scots, Dunkie lad?"

For the past three days Jeremy had eaten little. He was pale and sluggish, and Ella was worried. She understood why he was glum, for the spirit of the entire fort was lower than it had ever been. The defeat of Dalyell, added to the succession of disappointments that had befallen Detroit since the siege began three months ago, had caused the people of the outpost to burrow deeply within themselves. Jeremy seemed to be no exception, his mother noticed, as she bade him good night.

Ella had tried not to press the boy, but at last she could no longer keep from speaking. She was tucking him into bed and leaned over to kiss his forehead, then hesitated and caught her breath, for his eyes were so dark, so blank.

"Tell me, Jeremy, what's wrong?" She sat on the bed.

The boy turned to face the wall. Ella gently rubbed his shoulder.

"Sometimes it's better to talk about things, son. It can't help to brood, you know. Won't you tell me?"

"You wouldn't understand."

His voice was flat, but it was edged with a hint of accusation. Ella felt it cut her.

"Try," she said.

He sobbed and held it in. "No! You wouldn't understand! You wouldn't because you care about—about—"

"Who?" Ella was perplexed and troubled.

"Him! Him! That Sutherland!"

Ella felt the shock of surprise. She pulled her son's shoulder until he faced her. His eyes were red, and tears ran down his cheeks.

"Jeremy, will you kindly explain yourself?"

He buried his face in the pillow, drew up the blankets, and began to sob, jerking and sniffing, though he tried to keep his unhappiness under control. Ella drew back the covers and pulled him up to lean against her shoulder. She was less confused now, but she wondered just what her son felt. She certainly could not express her own emotions, her rational thoughts, or her own unhappiness now. Could this boy put into words what she had only felt? Was he as miserable as she for the same reasons?

"Don't you know, Mama?" he whimpered and pulled back to look at her. "Everyone knows the truth about that Sutherland—"

"Jeremy!"

"Everyone says it! He was a traitor! He was! They all say it, Mama! You must have heard—heard what they say." He was racked by heaving sobs, and Ella felt her own eyes fill up, and her lip tremble. She sniffed and rubbed her face.

She spoke in a whisper, trying to calm him. "Son. You can't think—you mustn't believe every rumor you hear." He just shook his head and looked down at his knees. "Wait until Mr. Sutherland comes back—"

"It's true! The story's been told to everyone, and they say he's a traitor, that he—that he caused men to be killed . . . And he told me he was a soldier, a real soldier, and I—I was proud of him. I wanted you and him to . . ."

He fell forward against her again, and she tried hard not to cry with him.

"Jeremy, Jeremy," she said hopelessly, but hardly a sound came from her lips. She wished the story were untrue, but of that she had little hope, for Duvall had told her the records were in War Ministry files. The past was dead, and one had to start again, regardless of errors. Tears came. What a fool she was to consider herself entitled to these tears! That was the irony, the cruel part: she was weeping for a man who had never even shown interest in her. She was aching for a shadow, a vision. She was pining with her son because an ideal had been dashed. What fools lovestruck women can be! Yes, she knew now, she was in love. The upheaval of the past weeks had brought that truth stark and unashamed to the surface of her thoughts.

Ella was in love with Owen Sutherland even if he had once been disgraced. That did not matter at all, somehow. She still loved him—whatever he was or had been. It was foolish perhaps, and futile, but somehow there was nothing at the moment she could do to change her feelings. And the utterly mad part of it all was that she did not know why she could not change her feelings. But she couldn't. And she wouldn't try.

She tugged the blankets about her son's shoulder. For the boy, she wished there were something she could say. But there was nothing. If only there were some way to comfort Jeremy at least.

chapter 19

BUSHY RUN

The column marched all morning, from well before first light until nearly one o'clock of a blisteringly hot afternoon. Little water had been encountered, and Sutherland was glad they were less than a mile from Bushy Run, where they would stop and camp before making another forced march through the treacherous Turtle Creek country at night. The pack animals were even more thirsty than the soldiers; they seemed to push a little quicker when they sensed water ahead. Dust-choked men were also lifted by the prospect of a drink and a rest at the stream.

The ground was steeper now, rising into wooded ridges above the road. Sharp cuts in the rocks slashed back into the forest. Groves of trees and gatherings of brush kept Sutherland's attention every moment—were they good places to hide, good places from which to shoot?

Ahead of the army was the wave of skirmishers and scouts that protected the main body of soldiers from being surprised by ambush. These men were scattered into the fringes of the woods along the road, walking through the trees as well as along the open way. None walked casually. All were intent on their surroundings, and they did not speak or permit themselves to be distracted from watching the woods ahead of them. The slightest nonchalance might mean quick death.

Sutherland felt uneasy in this country. Restlessness troubled him and had troubled him since before dawn. Not one shot had been fired on the army during all this passage from Shippensburg. It was as though the Indians had withdrawn in the face of the army: withdrawn as though under orders. It was not likely they would have retreated without trying for a stray scalp now and again. But no one had been attacked at all. And the

Indians were too flushed with victory, too contemptuous of
British arms to fly before this small and vulnerable force without offering opposition. Yet the army had not been opposed.
That meant the Indians were undoubtedly gathering for one
decisive massed assault. They were waiting somewhere ahead,
perhaps at Turtle Creek, where the ground favored their fashion
of fighting. Pitt was only a few marches away, so the Indians
must strike soon, before the army joined with the fort's defenders. In Sutherland's bones he sensed the attack coming.

The land was open here; it was a good spot for an ambush.
Moving with the vanguard of skirmishers, Sutherland surveyed
the rocky land that rose on both sides of the road. His men—
most of them in buckskin and hunting shirts, although there
were a few scarlet-coated regulars with him—were spread
across the road. Both ends of the line of skirmishers were well
into the woods. Beside him young McEwan walked in silence.
None of the vanguard had so much as coughed for the past
hour. They even appeared to have slowed down, become more
cautious, more watchful. Behind, at about a hundred yards'
distance, the army marched. The forest was quiet. Not even
a bird twittered. Nothing flew above their heads. Even the air
was heavy, expectant.

"Dunkie," Sutherland said softly, and McEwan turned to
him. "I'm not sure of what's up ahead. Pass the word to go
slow and careful. I'm going back for Bouquet and have him
send a company through the woods on the right flank. We'll
send some skirmishers through on the left at the same time."

McEwan pushed Toby's snuffling head into his leather
satchel and buckled the bag closed. Then he moved to the man
a few yards away on his right and passed on Sutherland's
command to slow down. Sutherland trotted back down the road
toward the plodding column. But before he reached Bouquet,
firing broke out up the trail. He turned to listen. There were
many muskets. Ambush! They were here!

Bouquet, riding a proud, gray charger, met Sutherland halfway. Wheeling his horse, the colonel drew his sword and
shouted to Sutherland, "Is this it, then?"

"I don't know!" Sutherland looked down the road, where
officers were arranging the first companies into attack columns
of six men abreast. "It could be a ruse, or it could be just a
harassing attack. Some forward companies should come quick
up the north side of the road and strike the flank of the Indians!"

Bouquet agreed and yanked his horse back to his men, and

Sutherland ran back up the road toward the advance guard. But before he had run forty yards, the air was so filled with lead that Sutherland was forced to take shelter behind some bushes. The vanguard was already under cover and shooting into the woods, holding their ground, though the Indian gunfire was heavy. In a few moments the cry of charging Scots soldiers broke out behind Sutherland, and he saw seventy men running up the road, bayonets glittering, officers' swords whisking overhead.

But the Indians opened fire on them with a volley that was even more intense than before. It was apparent that hundreds of Indians were hidden all around them. Those first companies suffered heavily, and men fell everywhere. Officers rallied these troops in the open, subjecting them to even more casualties. Heedless of the price, the soldiers formed ranks and, on command, opened a devastating fire into the woods. But the Indian shooting increased even more. The air was filled with acrid, gray gunsmoke.

The battle cry! More light infantry swept past Sutherland, barging fearlessly toward the woods, bayonets pointed, feet flying, and they burst into the edge of the forest.

The Indian gunfire stopped momentarily as the soldiers were swallowed up in the trees. But the shooting broke out more loudly on the left, and the scattered skirmishers there were hard pressed. They began to fall back, running at a crouch while comrades poured lead over their heads. Several fell. Sutherland's rifle was in his hand and loaded, but he did not want to fight. He had come as a guide, not as a soldier. He wanted to shed no Indian blood, but the frustration of helplessness, the feeling of being useless burned within him. He sweated ferociously, and the dryness in his mouth was from more than just lack of water.

McEwan, a dozen men moving with him, ran back to Sutherland's side. He was panting, face stained black from powder smoke.

"There's too many, Owen! We'll never push through this without frontal attack. Those two companies that just came up are lost if they don't come back out of those woods there. They'll be cut off if these redskins come at us from the left, and there's a lot of them over there!"

Indeed the heaviest shooting now came from the left, opposite where the infantry had struck and disappeared in the trees. But soon the shooting at the right grew louder, as though the soldiers there had been met by more Indians. In a few moments men in scarlet appeared backing out of the woods, firing as they made a fighting withdrawal. Some scrambled for safety while others covered them from shelter; then the latter withdrew and the first group fired to relieve the pressure. Gradually, coolly, these two companies—or what was left of them, for they had suffered serious losses by now—shot their way back out of the trees they had just entered.

Indian whooping and scalp yells, musket fire, and the cries of the wounded mingled in a raucous chorus of havoc. All the while, Sutherland crouched, watching, a spectator. He was numbed by his own refusal to fight, but he was in a good spot to be shot down even though he had resolved to stay out of the killing.

The retreating soldiers slowly worked their way back to him, and the surviving skirmishers of the vanguard had clustered nearby, firing furiously at unseen enemies. The shooting filled the forest. It was as though Indians were everywhere, shrieking in wild joy and shooting. They were heard but never seen. Steadily the soldiers withdrew. Sutherland grabbed under the arm of a wounded infantryman, pulled him up and bore him back to the main force. Perhaps at least he could save lives.

Other companies in Bouquet's force came up just then, and they poured a withering fire blindly into the trees. It had little effect. The Indian gunfire was not slowed. Sutherland laid the injured man down in the center of the infantry defenses, which were roughly circular and stretching down the road two hundred yards or so to where the packhorses and their drivers were crowding together in fear.

All around him soldiers fell. Sutherland scrambled to those who were not killed and dragged them back to lie with the other wounded. But he could do no more for them. He had not a drop of water to give. Up the road less than ten minutes away was Bushy Run, with plenty of fresh water. Already the gunsmoke and the hot weather had brought gasps for water from the ranks. From the wounded and dying the cry for water was a plea—a plea that rose to become a moaning begging until the man died or fell unconscious. But there was no water.

Then shooting ran quickly down the tree line on both sides of the army, as though a signal had been given to hundreds of Indians concealed all around to fire simultaneously. The army was completely surrounded, and still not one Indian was to be

seen. Suddenly it all changed. With wild shouting and a heavy
burst of musketry, a horde of Indians sprang from the trees,
charging the packhorses and the handful of soldiers responsible
for defending the pack train. The Indians immediately poured
over the courageous men who stood against them, and then
they were in among the supplies, looting and destroying.
Bouquet on his horse careened past Sutherland, waving his
sword and calling for a general withdrawal to save the column's
supply train.

Efficiently, perfectly trained, and with unwavering discipline, the hard-pressed infantry executed a withdrawal en masse
toward the defenseless train at the rear, where the small guard
there fought to the death with the braves falling on them. The
packhorses would have been lost had not McEwan and Munro
led a heedless assault of volunteers. They threw themselves
across the fifty yards of open land between the main body and
the supply-train guard and fought hand-to-hand with the Indians, standing them off until the organized companies followed up behind the charging Colonel Bouquet. The packhorses
were barely saved, and the soldiers withdrew to form an oval
defensive position, with the animals and wounded all in the
center. Sutherland, who had suffered a half-dozen slight gashes
on his legs and arms from Indian bullets, quickly organized the
building of a ring with sacks of flour in the middle of the
infantry lines.

Within this ring wounded were laid to wait until the surgeon
came to them. Sutherland struggled up and down the defensive
position, dragging wounded to the rear and going back for
others. Lead balls sliced everywhere like a cloud of bees. But
he ignored the fear of death and labored in this loud and dusty
hell to save whom he could. But it seemed there were so many
Indians around them that these wounded being carried back
were doomed anyway.

Despite the hail of bullets the soldiers stood fast, firing only
when ordered to do so, maintaining discipline in circumstances
that a European battlefield would never have thrust upon them.
In Europe the enemy stood in the open, as these soldiers stood.
The battle was decided by sheer force of numbers and by the
bayonet. But now the bayonet was impotent. The Indians struck
at will up and down the ring of defenders, showing themselves
in numbers only briefly before the infantry counterattacked.
But the counterattack inevitably met nothing once it reached
the edge of the woods. Maddeningly, the braves withdrew from

under the bayonet, slipped in force up or down the line and charged another weak spot, harrying and infuriating the soldiers.

Hour after hour the fighting went on, and soldiers lay in scarlet heaps all across the clearing through which the road passed. Sutherland knew the Indians intended to drive fear into the soldiers—as they had Braddock's men years before—forcing them to flight, then butchering them one by one in the country between here and Ligonier. If they broke, they were finished. If they stood, there was hope, but not much.

They stood, but they paid for their strength. After seven long hours of fighting, when nightfall mercifully hid the army in its dark mantle, more than sixty soldiers—one eighth of the army—lay dead or wounded on the field. And the remainder had no water and little enthusiasm or strength left to eat the cold pemmican and corn that was passed among them. They lay in position, waiting for the morning.

Many packhorses had been shot and had fallen still alive in the ground between the soldiers and the forest. These wounded horses shrieked and neighed in agony, but there was nothing to be done. Until they bled to death, the injured horses stirred the gloomy night with their frightened dirge. They whinnied across the dark field, haunting, sad, and hopeless.

All around Sutherland, who sat with his head on knees within the circle of flour bags, wounded men huddled, aching and pleading for life, groaning for water and praying. The forest was silent but for an occasional taunting shout from Indians who spoke English. Now and again an Indian fired aimlessly at the soldiers, and now and again the bullet struck home.

The regimental surgeon moved about the wounded slowly, methodically. He had little in the way of medicine, so he dispensed rum, which only increased thirst, but it eased their aching somewhat. The weary soldiers lay silently in the darkness. Bouquet walked among them, stopping to voice his admiration for their courage, speaking a compliment here, raising hope there, promising that tomorrow they would fight their way out.

But Sutherland, who tried to sleep curled up against a flour sack, was not so sure. He knew that another day's fighting like this would all but finish the soldiers. If they stayed, they would be killed to the last man. If they tried a fighting retreat, there was the ever-present risk that panic might strike as it had among

Braddock's army at a place less than thirty miles away from this battlefield. The army had only one hope—to force the Indians to commit themselves to the open ground, and there meet them on equal terms, where discipline and the bayonet would be felt.

But the Indians knew how to fight. They need not suffer heavy losses. All that was necessary was to shoot from the shelter of the trees, to harass the soldiers with fierce little attacks at weak places until the army either fled or angrily carried out a full-scale assault, breaking up its defense and exposing itself to death.

The night was quiet and hot. Sutherland looked up at a wan crescent moon rising. At his side was the rifle and his claymore. It seemed he would have to use them against the Indian after all.

He would not die without trying to fight his way to freedom.

"Owen, that you?" Munro came out of the darkness and crouched beside him. Sutherland sat up. He felt the searing pain of many slight wounds.

"What is it?"

"The colonel wants to see you. He said to come right away unless you're badly wounded. Then he'll come to you if he must, but he wants to talk to you."

Stiffly, Sutherland rose and walked away with Munro, who was limping gamely.

"You hit, Ian?"

"Not much," Munro said. "No worse than my gout. Damn!"

They walked past the shadowy figures of prone soldiers sleeping on their muskets. Now and again a flash erupted in the dark woods.

Something thudded next to Sutherland. He heard Munro groan, half-turned, and saw the silhouette of his friend crumple to the ground. Sutherland grabbed Munro as he went down and eased him backwards.

"Where?" Sutherland asked breathlessly.

"Ooh," Munro gasped. "That bugger was the real thing. My side, laddie. Ooh."

In the blackness Sutherland vaguely saw Munro's hands move to his side dabbing at blood. Munro was swearing when Sutherland hoisted him roughly and hurried to where the surgeon was working.

"Bugger got me. Got me!" Munro murmured. "Damn!"

Sutherland called to the surgeon, who was kneeling over

someone, laboring in the faint light of a lantern hidden from
the Indians by piles of flour bags. The surgeon shouted back
that he had heard.

Sutherland kneeled at Munro's side. He could just see the
glint of light in the sergeant major's eyes.

"I told you you're too old for soldierin'!" Sutherland said
as he stripped away the tunic covering the wound. "Why, the
greenest recruit could have ducked that one!"

Munro grunted and coughed. Sutherland called again to the
surgeon, who was twenty feet away.

"I hear you, dammit!" the doctor replied hoarsely. "There's
more than one wounded man here!"

"Take your time, Owen," Munro said, and he was short of
breath. "This isn't going to finish me. The bullet passed
through—I think." He groaned a breathless curse and inhaled
rapidly. Impatient now, Sutherland grabbed Munro under the
armpits and dragged him into the light of the surgeon's lantern.
He laid him on the ground behind the surgeon, who did not
look around. The yellow light splashed on the surgeon's back
as if to accentuate the man's stubborn obligation to someone
else. In the haze of the lamp Sutherland saw a keg of rum and
found a mug. In a moment Munro was guzzling the fiery drink.

"Ahh, that's better," the sergeant major sighed. "By morning I'll be back out there. A bit more of this…" He drank
deeply. "Never thought army rum could taste good." Munro
handed the cup to Sutherland, who finished it just as the tired
surgeon turned quickly to peer under Munro's tunic. Sutherland
held the lantern over his friend so the doctor could get a good
view of the wound. With the tunic pushed back Sutherland saw
a ragged tear in Munro's side. The bullet had hit him an inch
or two above his waist and had torn cruelly as it exited near
his back. Silently, the surgeon poked and probed with his dirty
scalpel.

"I hope," Munro said, "you don't want to amputate me from
the lower half down, sawbones."

The surgeon said nothing. He deftly wrapped a bandage
about Munro's waist, pulled it tight, and tore it down the
middle. Then he tied it and reached for the rum Sutherland had
just poured. He drank and spat some on the ground. He needed
the moisture, but had to remain sober.

"You'll be all right in a week or so," the surgeon said. "Just
have your butler answer the door for a while, and don't do
anything strenuous, like fox hunting or attending the opera."

The sallow-faced doctor, whose wide mustaches dripped rum and sweat, looked at Sutherland. "Keep him lying here tonight. The bleeding ought to stop soon. Swab his wounds every hour or so with rum, and don't let him drink it all."

The doctor pushed the keg closer to Sutherland, got up wearily, and began to walk away.

"What about this lad?" Sutherland said, motioning with his head at a soldier lying nearby. "Can I do anything?"

"If you're a Catholic priest, you can give that provincial his last rites. He'll be dead soon, so don't waste rum on him."

Sutherland looked at the man, who lay on his back, eyes fixed on the sky. He crawled to the man's side and looked closely at him. The doctor was wrong. It was too late for last rites.

"Hey, Owen," Munro said with great strain. "The colonel still wants you. Best get over there now. He doesn't ask for someone at a time like this unless he means it. Get going now!"

Sutherland was on his knees, staring at the pallid face of his old friend.

"Get!" Munro said. "Just be back here in time to give me another drink before—before what's in me cools off, eh?"

Sutherland held Munro's head and pushed the cup of rum against his lips. Munro gulped, coughed, and lay back. Slowly Sutherland got up and, after a last look at Munro, who lay in the weak light of the lantern, moved away into the darkness.

But before he had gone ten paces, he heard Munro shout angrily. He spun. In the lantern's glow there were shadows writhing. An Indian was on top of his friend! Sutherland hurled himself with a shout onto the brave's back. The warrior tried to turn, but Sutherland heaved him down, bowling him over, and they rolled, grappling for control of the Indian's tomahawk. Sutherland held the axe hand with both of his own, but the Indian's free hand gripped him powerfully by the hair and jerked his head back. With all his strength Sutherland held onto the Indian's wrist and yanked him around, driving his shoulder up into the man's chest.

The Indian was strong. He grasped Sutherland's shirt front as the Scotsman tried to get on top, and he threw Sutherland bodily away from him. With his grip on the axe hand broken, Sutherland faced the Indian in the darkness, unarmed. Neither man made a sound. The Indian took one feinting step forward, then jumped at Sutherland, bringing his hatchet down quickly. Sutherland sidestepped the blow. He grabbed the Indian from behind, wrapped his arms around the brave's midsection, and rolled onto his own back, flipping the Indian head over heels onto his stomach. Then Sutherland was on top. The brave twisted onto his back. Sutherland held the warrior's wrists, spreading the man's arms wide. Then with a vicious thud Sutherland crashed his forehead into the warrior's face, again and again, until he heard a crunching splinter and felt blood splash. But still the Indian was too strong. Bringing up his legs, he jerked Sutherland up and over, landing him hard on his back. The brave moved quickly and struck with his tomahawk, but Sutherland had already shifted, and the blade bit the ground.

From his leggin Sutherland drew the long-bladed hunting knife that had replaced his broken dirk, and he jumped at the Indian, who, blood streaming from his face, had just swung wildly again. Together they tumbled backwards, and Sutherland thrust up with the knife, driving it into the warrior's heart. He pushed with all his weight, and the knife killed the brave in that instant.

Sutherland got to his knees. In the blackness he could not see the Indian's face. He pulled the knife from the body and dug it into the ground to clean off the blood. He knelt, head throbbing, lungs gasping, and knew the course of his life had torn loose again. Now he was a fighting man, a soldier once more. The blood on his hands attested to that.

Then he thought of Munro.

He jumped to his feet and hurried to the lantern light, where his friend lay. But he stopped when he saw him. The warrior had been swift with his tomahawk. Munro was dead.

In a few moments several soldiers appeared over Sutherland, who was on his knees, head bowed.

"That you, Owen?" It was McEwan.

Sutherland did not lift his head. McEwan saw Munro, fell to his knees, and sighed.

Then one of the men who had come with McEwan to find Sutherland said gently, "The colonel wants you, Sutherland."

Sutherland looked at his dead comrade. Then he nodded slowly. "I'll come." He stood up and said to McEwan: "Somebody better get a guard around these wounded, Dunkie. Munro was killed by an Indian who slipped into camp."

McEwan said nothing for a moment. Then, "Did he get away?"

Sutherland motioned toward the dead Indian. "He's there.

There might be more of them." Sutherland gathered himself and stood erect. He fastened his sword belt, took a drink from Munro's rum, and fetched his rifle from where it lay. "I'll be at Bouquet's," he said, and he knew his restlessness, his uncertainty was gone. "I might have an idea how we can get out of this. If I don't, I hope Bouquet does."

The officers were gathered with Bouquet in the shelter of a grove of fir trees. In the light of two shaded lanterns they huddled on their knees over a piece of parchment spread on the ground before them. When Sutherland was brought to them by a sentry, Bouquet, who wore no hat, said:

"This is a rough estimation of our position." He pointed to the parchment, which showed an outline of the oblong defense and the location of the pack train and wounded. "We intend to counterattack toward Fort Pitt in the morning, Mr. Sutherland, and our plans are to divide our forces—"

"I wouldn't," Sutherland said.

The officers looked up at him. He stepped back from Bouquet's shoulder. "Colonel, your only chance is to force the Indians into a battle in the open."

Bouquet sighed, exasperated. "Good God, man, don't you think I've been trying to do just that? We've been attacking them with the bayonet, but they vanish like ghosts, then appear somewhere else a moment later to nip at us!" Bouquet smashed his fist down on the map. He did not speak but waited for the frontiersman to go on.

"It might be possible we could draw them into a trap, a ruse, that would be sprung when they're in the open," Sutherland said. "They think we're beaten. All they have to do is shoot us up until we break, and then they'll come after us on the road, where we can't defend ourselves, and that'll be the end. But there's a chance we could take advantage of their overconfidence."

Sutherland knelt at the parchment spread between the lanterns. He pointed at the position of the flour-bag defenses where the wounded and the packhorses were sheltered from enemy fire.

"The Indians have been trying hard to get at the pack train, and they must know the wounded are there, too. They've been attacking that area hardest all day, and I suspect they'll continue to do that tomorrow. If they think they can break through there and make off with horses, booty, and scalps of the wounded, they'll go for us there with every man. So far they have been obeying their chiefs, but no chief could hold them back if the braves believe there's an easy scalp and booty to be had."

The officers and Henry Bouquet were silent. In the background an Indian musket popped now and again, and warriors hurled taunting curses at the soldiers. In this little enclave among the pines, men were thinking, absorbed with the strategy that Owen Sutherland began to lay before them. It was a dangerous gamble, but no one had a better plan, and if it worked, it would work magnificently.

As he explained his strategy, Sutherland thought for a moment of the green tatoo the Ottawa had placed on his chest when they adopted him. But right now his loyalty was not to the Indian. It was to this army—an army which faced death when the sun rose.

As Sutherland leaned over the map, Mayla's silver pendant slipped out of his shirt. He put it back in its place and resolved not to touch it again until this fight was finished.

An hour later, just at the first false dawn, Sutherland found McEwan with Munro's company. The youth was lying on the ground, watching the trees that looked darker now that the sky had brightened. Sutherland lay down next to his friend and felt something furry nuzzle against his cheek. It was Toby. From inside a pocket Sutherland took a pull of dried beef, but Toby would not eat it.

"Not hungry, pup?" he whispered.

McEwan sat up and took Toby in his arms. "She's dry as a cork, like the rest of us. Not a drop of water anywhere. If the Indians keep us here another day, we'll go mad with thirst, and that will be that."

Then Sutherland told McEwan his plan to catch the Indians in the open. McEwan offered to stand alongside Sutherland, who would be in the most dangerous place at dawn. Sutherland accepted the offer by saying nothing. After a few moments they got up, Toby was stuffed back into the leather bag, and they began to walk away to where a few score volunteers were mustering. They would form an outer defensive line two hundred yards in front of the pack train and the wounded. As they walked, McEwan said to Sutherland, "I don't know how you managed to kill that Indian last night. He was a big bastard. There he is now."

They were walking past the place where the brave lay.

"Strong one he was," McEwan said, standing over the body. In the light of the false dawn Sutherland looked down at the warrior. Then in surprise he dropped to his knees.

"Dunkie," he exclaimed, "this is Sin-gat!"

The night was hot, and air hung stifling and humid over Fort Detroit. Ella got out of bed again and walked the floor of her room. Jeremy slept fitfully, but at least he slept. Ella could not. Perhaps it was the suffocating heat, perhaps it was worry that troubled her tonight. Whatever it was, she could not remain in that little room. She went downstairs. To her surprise a candle flickered on the table. Henry was up, also, sitting near the hearth.

"Come sit and keep me company," he said to his sister.

She did, and they spoke little for a long time. Then Gladwin said, "Thinking about Owen?"

Ella could not conceal her surprise. She tensed, then relaxed, and nodded. "You've heard the rumor about him?"

Gladwin sighed. "I have, and it's all new to me. But I'm sure Owen can explain it. He's not that kind, despite what the rumor says, to let his friends down. Not Owen."

Gladwin looked closely at Ella, but she was pretending to see the tea leaves at the bottom of his empty cup. Her brother's gaze was too strong for her, and she looked up at him.

"You do believe he's not that kind, don't you?" Gladwin asked.

Ella bit her lip. "I do," she said, and her voice quivered. "I so much want to believe that Owen is not what this rumor says of him. You know—you know I think very highly of Owen. And Jeremy thinks so very highly of him, and I fear the boy has been hurt too deeply by what he has heard about Owen's—Owen's—disgrace. Oh, Henry, I'm at a loss for words! I want so much to be told that all this is a dream! I want to be sure, for Jeremy's sake—for Owen's sake, for he has suffered so much—I want to be sure that this rumor is untrue! But—but Major Duvall said he was the officer who brought charges!"

She shook, and Gladwin stood, came behind her, and put his hands on her shoulders.

"Ella, I for one shall believe nothing until I have first asked Owen Sutherland. I know him too well to do otherwise." Henry's voice was reassuring, and Ella felt anxiety flood from her. "I've never asked Owen why he left the service, and he's never told me. But when I next see him, I'll bring this rumor to his attention, and then, I assure you, we'll learn the truth. We've heard only one side, and that's not good enough for me."

Ella turned and looked up at the kind eyes of her brother. She forced a smile and wiped away her tears. "Henry, I know you're right. And it's not the dishonor that troubles me—if indeed there was dishonor. It's the sorrow I feel to think that such a terrible tale should follow a man like Owen. If he made a mistake, then he has paid the price. But I'm sure that he'll be hurt when he comes back and is told that everyone who knew him here is whispering about his—his dishonor."

"Ella," Gladwin said firmly. "Don't let the scandalmonger trouble you so."

"No," she sighed. "I should be stronger. It's just that I . . ."

Gladwin waited, but Ella could not say the next words, so he said them for her:

"You love him."

Ella did not reply for some time; then she said, "I have no right to love him. I have no right to love a man whose life is falling to pieces. Owen Sutherland needs friendship and loyalty now, not the love of a selfish widow who takes the first opportunity to snatch him up—"

"Ella!" Gladwin came around to face her and brought her to her feet. She looked down and shook her head. "Ella! Let Owen be the judge of your right to love him." She stared at her brother. "Let your love take its own course, its natural course. You can do no less and no more. Now find rest within yourself, and share that rest with him. He'll need it very much when he returns."

"Henry," she said, smiling weakly, "you're a good brother. And I'm grateful for your sympathy. But don't worry about me; I'll find my way. I always have before."

"You have indeed," he said and grinned. "And I can't imagine anyone I'd rather see at Owen Sutherland's side than you, sister."

"Henry." She again shook her head and moved away from him. "I think I should get some sleep, for it's almost morning. Good night. And thank you." She let free a crooked, wistful smile as she stood at the bottom of the stairs. "I'm getting the hint that perhaps you don't want to take me back to England after all."

He chuckled and sat down once more. "Are you so sure," he said, "that you really want to go back?"

"No, I'm not so sure," she said from far away. "But right now I intend to go."

By the time the pale streaks of a red dawn colored the sky, Indian musketry was already picking at the weary, thirsty soldiers. McEwan stood with Sutherland in a thin line of skirmishers thrown out in front at the center of the defense. Toby scratched and whined in the bag at McEwan's side, but he ignored the unhappy puppy. In McEwan's mind was the thought that somewhere out in the forest Mary Hamilton was still a prisoner in Sin-gat's camp.

For Sutherland, who loaded his Pennsylvania rifle and prepared to fight as a soldier for the first time in eighteen years, the knowledge that Sin-gat was here brought home the thought that André Breton might also be in the vicinity. After this fight Sutherland could no longer move freely among the Indians. Those who recognized him—and he anticipated that many would, because there were Ottawa as well as Delaware and Shawnee in the force that surrounded them—would quickly pass the word that he had chosen to fight for the English. If he survived, he would be an enemy of the Indian.

Somehow he was not surprised that it had all come to this. When last he saw Pontiac, he had expected his quest for vengeance against André Breton might make him the Indian's foe in this war. He was resigned to that now. As he stood in the first light of morning, shoulder to shoulder with the men who anticipated taking the brunt of the next Indian attack, Sutherland cleared his mind of unneeded thought. Now, for as long as necessary, he was again a professional soldier. Any other considerations would distract him. Distraction could mean death.

He stared at the edge of the woods, less than a hundred yards away. He was certain the Indians were massing there. This thin line of fighters stretching across the front of the army must look like easy prey to the warriors. There had been no firing from this section of forest, which indicated further to Sutherland that the Indians were intending to spring a surprise attack from there. Sutherland drew his sword and stepped in front of the line of men who stood in a rank less than a hundred yards long. He and McEwan were in the center. For the first time in eighteen years Sutherland was in command of soldiers on a battlefield. He looked up and down the line. Every man had his musket at port arms, ready to raise it, aim, and fire. Daylight was breaking grayish red on them. The plan was to return Indian fire from kneeling positions, then to withdraw slowly and let the Indians come on until the very last minute; then this line of skirmishers would fly for shelter. If they broke too soon, the Indians might suspect a trap and not take the bait. If they broke too late, they would be overwhelmed.

"Ready, men," Sutherland said. "Stand your ground, then withdraw on command. Carry all wounded and pay attention to where you are so you get back to cover."

The men—haggard, tense, with lips dry and cracked— stared straight ahead. Their eyes were ablaze with determination; their gaze held on the tree line.

Then the shooting began. Indian volleys crashed from the trees, and two soldiers crumpled immediately.

"Kneel!" Sutherland shouted. In unison the soldiers knelt on one knee, and the long grass gave some shelter. Only Sutherland and McEwan still stood. Far behind, the white sacks of flour were tinged red in the morning light. These skirmishers, it seemed, were all that stood between the Indians and the pack train. On a straight line to the flour sacks, supplies, wounded, and horses, the ground was flat and open. It was like a funnel that narrowed at the end where the potential booty was sheltered. On either side of the funnel were small trees and a sort of hedgerow that stretched away in both directions, meeting the wide circle of soldiers forming the main defensive line.

The line of Sutherland's skirmishers joined the main defensive ranks at each end at the top of this funnel. Standing in the wide opening of the funnel, the skirmishers were cast precariously over open ground. It appeared that a determined attack could easily overcome Sutherland's men, crack the defense wide open, and expose the riches and trophies of the supply train where the scalps of the wounded were ready for the taking.

Random shooting intensified from the woods opposite Sutherland's little force. At his orders the soldiers returned a few volleys. Several more of his men fell. One of them lay groaning and spitting up blood.

"Steady lads," Sutherland said, and he felt his own tension rise. "Keep shooting back. Pick your targets and fire at will. That's it, keep at them. Make them think we're trying to hold them back. We want them coming after us. That's it. Keep firing."

Worry, fear, and instinctive discipline mingled with hope inside Owen Sutherland on that sunny summer morning. His plan had to work! There would be no second chance if it failed. He refused to consider that he might very well die out here whether his plan succeeded or failed. He concentrated on his duty and on his training of years ago. It had not left him.

Braves began to appear, moving forward, leaping and brandishing muskets on the edge of the trees. Now and again a brave was shot, and he fell, but the Indians kept prancing and jeering, howling and threatening, daring the mediocre marksmen of the soldiers to fire at them. Sutherland called on his men to cease individual firing and to prepare for massed volleys. He called the orders out to them—he would do it by rote, by the manual of arms:

"Handle your chargers!" he called out.

As one man, the slender line of redcoats put their hands to their cartridge boxes hanging at their sides.

"Open them!"

The skirmishers drew out the paper cartridge and bit off one end, taking the bullet in their teeth. In that instant Sutherland gave another command:

"Prime!"

The priming pans were sprinkled with black powder. At Sutherland's next command, "Charge with powder!" the men poured gunpowder down the barrel of the muskets. On and on went the orders, rapidly, smoothly, without second thought, until the musket ball was spat down the barrel and rammed home. Then the command "Present!" was given, and every man aimed. Someone fell and writhed in the grass, but not a soldier flinched.

"Fire!"

Sutherland's excitement rose as the muskets flashed and banged in unison. More Indians became visible as they increased in number and in audacity. They sported their courage, dancing, whooping, and screaming up and down the tree line. They seemed to feel they had the soldiers whipped. He fought down his excitement and proceeded through the manual of arms once more, giving at last the commands: "Present. Fire!"

Indian bullets whisked past, singing, whining around him. His shirt fluttered now and again but not with the breeze. He hardly noticed it, but his clothes were torn by bullets. Still he stepped up and down the line, standing, as a British officer must stand, fearless and heedless of the danger. He directed his men coolly, forcefully, keeping them under control while death darted about their heads.

There was something magnificent about that mad moment, about these silent soldiers, unflinching and stoic even when they were shot. In that realization Sutherland hesitated, recognizing what had lain dormant within him for all these years and knowing how he had come to be the man he was. Much of his character had been acquired at the side of men like these, in times like these, when right and wrong meant nothing, and survival was all that mattered.

Suddenly he sensed it was coming. He spun. The Indians were silent, just for a moment. They crowded, seething, whirling in front of the trees. This was it! They were coming!

A great ululating war cry rose from every Indian throat, and they boiled out of the forest, screaming at Sutherland's skirmish line.

"Handle chargers!"

That feeble spurting volley did nothing to slow the Indians. "Open chargers! Prime! Charge your muskets!" On they came, swirling, howling, headlong, with war lust in their eyes and hatred in their hearts. "Present!" Closer now. "Fire!" The Indians were too close now.

"Retreat!" Sutherland shouted. His men jumped up, dragging their wounded, and ran madly for the scant shelter of the hedgerows and the pack train. The Indians raced after them, shrieking and screaming and glorying in their moment of triumph.

"Skirmishers, halt!" Sutherland shouted, and those not carrying wounded spun and knelt at his command.

"Steady, handle chargers, prime!"

The Indians skidded to a stop, hesitant, bumping into each other, surprised that these soldiers dared stand.

"Present!"

A huge chieftain roared defiance and sprang ahead, and he was followed by the rest.

"Fire!"

Withering this time, with so many targets gathered close together, the volley of Sutherland's unit staggered the foremost warriors. But now the Indian horde was less than forty yards from their enemies, and no soldier could load a Brown Bess in the few seconds it would take a brave to cover that distance. The Indian warriors charged again.

"Retreat!" Sutherland yelled, and this was the last flight—

a race for life over a hundred yards of grass. His rifle slung over his back, Sutherland trailed his running men. In one hand his claymore gleamed. He glanced back to see the first Indians nearly upon him, whooping and yelping, some of them with bloody tomahawks. Others were stooping over the British dead, tearing off scalps and waving them in glee.

Sutherland twisted round to meet a Shawnee warrior, who hurled himself at him and swung his tomahawk down. Sutherland slid by the hatchet blow and slashed out with his sword, catching the Indian on the side of the head, sending him sprawling with a snarling cry of shock and pain.

Before Sutherland could flee, another Shawnee was on him, and he parried the tomahawk blow. He struck back and knew he was lost. A third Indian appeared in the corner of his eye, bearing down for a death blow, coming in too fast for Sutherland to defend himself while engaging the second brave. He leaped aside and thrust at the Indian facing him, dancing desperately away from the third one at his back. He ran his opponent through the throat, then felt someone slump heavily against his legs. He skipped away and looked down to see the third Indian, clutching his smashed skull, kicking his life away without a sound.

McEwan was at Sutherland's side. They nodded once and raced away, with the great mass of Indians nearly upon them. Arrows and bullets whisked thick around their heads as they ran for the flour-bag wall. They fled through the long grass, keeping their heads tucked into their shoulders. In a few moments, they would be over the flour sacks...

"Sir! Help!"

The two of them glanced to their left and saw a half-dozen redcoats clustered under a tree. Some were lying on the ground, obviously wounded. One called "Sir!" again. And in that instant Sutherland and McEwan knew that some soldiers had gone as far as they could with wounded friends. They could not abandon them—it was better to die at a friend's side. They had collected under this tree, for to flee farther with the burden of a wounded man meant they would be caught and killed. "Sir!"

Without second thought Sutherland and McEwan ran to these men and turned silently to face the howling mob descending upon them. Three of the men were standing along with Sutherland and McEwan. Three others, all wounded, were on their sides or their knees, waiting.

The Indian force concentrated on the pack train, surging past this little group of redcoats, but at least twenty braves broke off from the main assault to strike down such likely victims. As they came on, Sutherland felt a vast calmness descend upon him, as though he were watching it all from a distance, as though he were merely a spectator, cold, and without a trace of emotion. He gripped his claymore's hilt.

Standing with muskets aimed, three soldiers and McEwan fired on Sutherland's command. It was as though another voice were giving the orders. Bayonets ready, his group met the surviving attackers head on, roaring as loud as their enemy, striking as wildly and as fiercely as the conquering braves.

Curdling screams. Bayonets and tomahawks. Musket butts and knives. Fists and feet. Sword and strangling fingers. Sutherland's claymore bit and bit, flashing red with blood. He fought his way through the attackers and suddenly found himself alone, with two dead warriors at his feet. He whirled to see the others in a bloody tangle. Sweat poured into his eyes, stinging, blinding. He flicked it away, smearing blood over his face. Two bear-greased bodies flew at him. One wrenched the claymore from Sutherland's hand as he lunged by, yelping and clutching at the sword, which was stuck in his stomach.

Sutherland was bowled over by the other Indian, and they went down, both weaponless, into the grass, tumbling over and over, punching, yanking, seeking a hold, a death grip, on the other. Sutherland could catch nothing of the naked warrior's greasy body. The Indian had him by the hair, wrenching viciously, while Sutherland kept rolling with him, scrambling to get control.

They fought silently, but Sutherland's immense strength told at last. The scratching, biting brave flipped head over heels, and Sutherland sprang to his feet. The Indian recovered and leaped again. This time Sutherland caught him with both hands, crushing his throat, the Scotsman's body bending at the waist from the force of the brave's rush. Sutherland took the brunt and went with it, lifting the man higher off the ground and hurling him to the ground like a heavy log. Then in a flash Sutherland was upon him, smashing his head against a stone.

Bleeding, clothing torn to shreds, Sutherland was up, and he jerked the claymore from the body of the other Indian, who hissed and screamed as it came out. With a yowling Highland war cry, he charged the braves surrounding the others, and with his sword slashing and striking down startled Indians, he drove back six or seven of them at once. Without a moment to recover, the Indians reeled under the blows, and two fled. Two others crumpled with their heads slashed, and the rest sought an opening in this madman's defenses. Sutherland's skill and berserk strength were awesome.

Suddenly over the tumult, the roar of massed musketry stopped Sutherland. Every fighter hesitated and turned for an instant to look into the narrow funnel of trees, where smoke drifted from the left side. Soldiers were hidden there. No more than a heartbeat passed, but Sutherland knew what that volley meant. His plan had worked! The great mass of Indians was stunned, stopped in their tracks at the very brink of victory. They were now crowded at the face of the flour-sack wall.

"Down!" Sutherland shrieked to the men with him, and they dived to the ground. The Indians confronting Sutherland were surprised as they saw him leap into the grass. But their surprise was short-lived. A terrible second volley erupted from more soldiers hidden in the ditches and hedgerows on the other side of the funnel. The Indians near Sutherland gasped and yelled as they fell, gaping wounds spurting blood.

Great swaths of destruction cut through the astonished Indian attackers, and they fell by the score. Warriors crumpled everywhere, and those still standing shrilled with terror and fury. In the next second, two hundred Scottish bayonets glittered and darted from the hedgerows, and the wild Highland battle cry burst like a thunderous storm wind as the soldiers swept across the grass, driving back the Indians, who fled for their lives. Their leading chiefs were dying, bayonetted without mercy where they lay.

Sutherland stood, his chest heaving in breathless agony, rasping for air. At his side were McEwan and two others, both wounded. The escaping Indians dashed past in anger and shock.

"Owen!" McEwan screamed.

Sutherland jumped around. Facing him was a young Delaware brave, six feet away. Sutherland's claymore came up quickly. But the warrior, just a teenager, was unarmed. In his eyes was disbelief. But that look changed as the youth saw the sword tip before him. He was in that moment ready to die.

Sutherland fought for breath. His aching chest heaved as though he had not breathed since the fight began. A soldier moved up, his bayonet pointing at the warrior, who was unflinching. The Indian lifted his chin, and his eyes were cold.

The charging soldiers were almost up to them now. The

Indians who could run were disappearing in the trees. The soldiers were taking no prisoners.

Sutherland's sword dropped. "Run!" he croaked in Delaware.

The youth jerked as though to fly, but the soldier threatened with his bayonet. All in the briefest of spaces the Indian glanced at Sutherland and at the death in the soldier's eyes.

"Go!" Sutherland rasped and jerked his head so the soldier would understand his meaning.

In an instant the brave was off, springing like a deer through the grass, bounding with magnificent speed toward the trees where his brothers had already gone. Behind lumbered the soldiers, gear clinking, voices howling, as they rumbled in pursuit of the fleeing enemy.

At Sutherland's side the soldier muttered with exasperation and let his musket butt clump to the ground. McEwan came to his friend's shoulder, and the two of them stood watching the soldiers pursue their scattered quarry, thundering past, killing and taking vengeance for the comrades they had lost.

"It worked," McEwan said under his breath.

Sutherland stared at the trees and said nothing.

The attack was broken. The Highlanders wailed and shouted in the distance, sparing no one in their path, fighting or wounded. Up and down the circle of defenders, a general bayonet attack—as had been planned if Sutherland's ruse succeeded—took shape. The exhausted army found the last of its strength and charged into the trees after the battered enemy. But by the time the soldiers burst into the woods, word of the staggering slaughter near the pack train, and of the heavy losses of leaders and chiefs, had passed among the Indians, and they melted away.

The Indians had been certain of a great, resounding victory. Now they had been repulsed, cut down, and demoralized by the ambush. Within an hour of the savage Scottish counterattack, the firing died away. The Indians had fled.

Soldiers were laughing and cheering up and down the line. Sutherland's daring plan had worked. Once drawn into the open, and sure of victory, the braves had been easy targets for the massed volleys. When met by the fearless bayonet charge, they were beaten soundly.

Nearby McEwan sat, spent and bloody, and Sutherland, his claymore still in hand, leaned against the great tree where he had made his last defense. Exhaustion and revulsion twisted within Sutherland, and he pressed his cheek into the tree bark. He did not think at all. He only felt the rough bark, felt it hard against his face, felt it scrape and touch his cheek. No thought at all.

Then a shout from McEwan jarred him.

"Owen! Bouquet's here."

A beaming Colonel Bouquet rode jubilantly toward Sutherland, jumped down, and shook his hand eagerly.

Bouquet laughed and pumped Sutherland's hand. "It worked, my boy! It worked!" He clapped Sutherland about the shoulders and heartily said, "By Jove, sir, your plan was brilliant! Brilliant! Hah! They're gone at every front! They've been dealt a blow they won't forget! Hah! Magnificent, Mr. Sutherland! Magnificent! You'll be mentioned in dispatches, sir. I'll personally recommend you to General Amherst!"

Sutherland stared without emotion into Bouquet's delighted eyes. Sutherland felt no joy; simply, he was glad it was over. Bouquet was still talking.

". . . delighted to have you on my staff—as an officer! Yes, Mr. Sutherland, you'd do well in times like these! What do you say, sir? Will you come with me on my staff? You'll—"

Bouquet's bubbling voice was suddenly stilled by a horrible shriek of pain. The colonel, Sutherland, and McEwan turned to see a soldier driving his bayonet into the breast of a young brave lying nearby. The youth lurched up from the waist as the blade went in, and he vomited a gush of blood and fell back.

Sutherland screamed and plunged at the soldier, knocking him away. He threw himself against the brave, lifting the Indian's head and cradling it frantically. It was Molo, Mayla's brother.

Sutherland muttered incoherently, muttered and rocked, calling Molo's name. Then he wept in anguish, crumbling in awful heartache. He held the tense body against his chest, rocking and muttering, weeping and sighing in angry misery, until Molo went limp and died.

For more than an hour Sutherland sat with the body. Molo was dead. And so was Mayla, and so was so much that Owen Sutherland had once loved.

And what lived?

What lived was an offer to become a soldier—an offer that promised a life of killing. Was that really all that lived now? What else could he lose?

Long before Sutherland and McEwan carried Molo into the trees to bury him, Colonel Bouquet departed, his offer to Sutherland unanswered. But Henry Bouquet knew he could never make that offer again. The reply needed no words, for words could never tell the destruction that had been wrought in Owen Sutherland's life.

The dead were buried in long rows of graves beside the trail. The three hundred and fifty survivors who could stand paid homage to their fallen friends, walking past the graves in columns of four. Sutherland stood alone back among the trees. There was still much more to do. He wished it was over. His soul was taken up in the dark silence, brooding over this dismal victory. The forest should have rung with the bittersweet lament of the regimental pipes. But it did not, for the piper, too, had been killed, and all that endured was silence and sorrow.

chapter **20**

SOLDIER

The army reached Bushy Run by afternoon. Men collapsed along the stream's banks, drinking deeply, as many had never expected to drink again.

Frequent Indian sniping went on all day, and the camp the soldiers made there was dangerous. Men walking were shot down, and an occasional sally by small groups of braves reminded the soldiers that the country was still controlled by Indians. But no major attack came. The Indians had lost too badly to renew the battle in earnest.

In that unhappy camp the tally was made: eight officers killed and one hundred and fifteen rank and file killed or wounded. Fully a quarter of the force were casualties. Indian losses were also heavy, although many of their fallen had been borne away before the last fight. In the Scottish counterattack a number of important chiefs had been killed, and Sutherland knew the Indian leadership must be shaken and losing confidence.

Sutherland was sure that the heavy losses the Indians had suffered would inhibit their taste for war. An Indian wanted quick, easy victories. He wanted plunder, scalps, glory, not massed battles and great heroic loss. He did not equate self-sacrifice in battle with gallantry as did the British troops. That was a fool's glory to him. The loss of even one brave took much joy from victory, and prolonged mourning was necessary in a dead man's village before the joy of triumph might be permitted to be expressed by those who lived.

With such terrible losses at Bushy Run the Indian expectation of certain victory over the British had been dashed. Fear and doubt would spread quickly through the tribes. Their leaders had promised easy triumph—and it had been easy until now—but that illusion was gone. Even though the warriors knew the English might was formidable, they had been counting on surprise and rapid victories one after the other to force the British to sue for peace. A few such Indian triumphs, Pontiac and others had promised, would set the stage for an expected French invasion, and the country would be cleared of the hated British forever.

But now, to the dismay of the Indians, the British had snatched a great victory from the warriors at the very moment of success. Despite awesome losses, the soldiers had stood up to the Indians; they had refused to flee in the face of withering fire—Pontiac had predicted they would flee. And they had counterattacked with such savagery that the braves were driven like chaff before the wind.

In scores of villages the death wail was going up; women were blackening their faces with ashes and tearing clothes. Wounded sons were bleeding to death in their mothers' arms, and brave chiefs were sitting silently in council with the specter of doom in their hearts.

Immediate victory had been essential to the greater plan that had raised up the tribes as one people, for the first time ever, in such power and unity. But an unexpected defeat had come instead, and the invading army was still intact, still moving relentlessly toward Fort Pitt, which now would not fall.

Sutherland knew what was taking place in wilderness clearings for miles around. He knew word of the battle was on its way to Pontiac, and that the great chief would be in danger of losing face. Too many young men had fallen. Now, the Indians were thinking, a long war of desolation would begin. The English could not be beaten by the Indian alone. Where was the Frenchman?

It occurred to Sutherland that many tribes would fight on for some time. But the Delaware and Shawnee around Pitt had paid a bitter price in return for the terror and destruction they had spread along the frontier. He hoped those two major tribes would ask for peace. If they did so, that was the beginning of the end of the uprising. Then only Pontiac and his immediate followers in the northwest around Detroit would remain at war, along with a few Seneca who had broken with their brothers in the powerful Iroquois League, which had chosen peace.

When they reached the stream, whimpering, panting little Toby leaped out of McEwan's bag and scampered for a pool of water where soldiers were thirstily scooping up drinks. Tail wagging, the puppy waded through the water, lapping and splashing. McEwan dropped to his knees and gratefully dipped his face into the cool, soothing water, and he groaned with relief. He looked at Toby, who was watching him, as though she was amazed to be here drinking at last. For a moment man and dog gazed at each other, both dripping wet, both completely spent.

"Toby, lass," McEwan said with a grin.

He ducked his head again and let his shirt soak up water. While his head was still underwater, McEwan felt Toby leap on the back of his neck, frolicking and yelping in play. He laughed as he grasped for her, shoving her down and splashing her completely. Toby yelped again and bounded onto dry land, eyeing McEwan and standing like a scrawny water rat, her hair matted down. McEwan slapped water at her, and she skittered away a few feet, looked at him with disdain, and shook herself dry from head to tail.

Shortly, McEwan and Toby were lying in the warm sunshine. He fed her jerked beef, and she ate hungrily. Then he looked up to see Owen Sutherland.

Neither man spoke as the frontiersman sat down. After a while, with Toby half-asleep between them, McEwan said: "What are your plans, Owen?"

"I'll find Tamano and then get after Breton again. My promise to guide Bouquet will be fulfilled when we get to Pitt. You can come if you want."

"I shall," McEwan said and lay down next to his musket. "Mary is here somewhere. I'm told Bouquet thinks the Indians have had enough. As part of the peace, they'll have to bring in their white hostages. It just might be—it just might be possible that Mary will come in . . ."

After a two days' march from Bushy Run, the column came to a halt, just one day from Pitt. Sutherland, in the vanguard with McEwan, encountered a large party of Indians on the trail. They made signs they wanted to parley, and Sutherland passed the word back to Bouquet.

The column fell out along the road in rough defensive formations. Bouquet, two junior officers, and Owen Sutherland smoked the pipe of peace with these braves, who were Shawnee and Delaware head men from nearby villages. The chiefs swore to Bouquet that they had nothing to do with the fighting, al-

though some of their young men had been influenced by bad
Indians. These villages, Bouquet was told, wished only peace
with the English.

"I shall send your appeals for peace to the Great English
Father across the seas," Bouquet told the somber Indians seated
in a circle with him. "I cannot make peace terms, but if you
bring your white captives—no matter how long ago they were
taken, whether in this war or in an earlier war—the Great
Father will smile on you. He will recognize that you are sincere,
and he will treat you as his lost children, who have returned
to him. You must bring these hostages to Fort Pitt within a
month. No matter how old or how young they are, no matter
if they have been with the Indians for many years, and no
matter if they wish to stay with the Indians, you must bring
them to me at Fort Pitt. Do that, and I shall tell the Great
English Father that you are to be trusted and should be treated
kindly.

"Fail in what I command, and the Great English Father will
send armies with mighty thunder guns to destroy you utterly,
and you shall never again walk this land."

Bouquet's words were not lost on these Indians. They went
away after agreeing to bring in prisoners before the next moon.

Afterwards the army continued its march. Hostiles still
lurked on the edge of the woods, shooting into the soldiers,
causing several casualties. But the men were ordered not to
strike back in force, for the object was to reach Fort Pitt and
unite with the soldiers in that garrison. The force could not
spare the time needed to charge into the woods against a few
snipers. The shooting was frustrating, and it occurred with
regularity.

"Pitt is only a few hours' march," Sutherland said to
McEwan as they walked slowly along the road—now narrower
and darker. "I'll tell Bouquet we ought to go on through the
night. We'll be there before dawn."

McEwan nodded and walked ahead, carrying Toby in his
bag. Sutherland turned away. From the woods off to the left
an Indian musket banged. Sutherland ducked and dived behind
a log. He searched the woods for movement. There was none.

He looked ahead. The vanguard had all fallen to the ground.
It was quiet as the soldiers probed the shadowy forest for signs
of the sniper. The only sound was Toby whining in the woods.
Sutherland saw something vague less than fifty yards away.
He slowly brought his rifle to bear. The wind shook the

leaves. The late afternoon sun slanted through the trees. Movement again. A feather flickering. He aimed. Bang! The smoke of his rifle clouded Sutherland's vision until it cleared in the breeze. One of the frontiersmen in the forward guard shouted: "Got the slimy bastard! Got 'im!"

Slowly men rose and advanced, muskets ready, eyes intent for trouble. Sutherland knelt and rammed home another charge. He sprinkled powder from his horn into the priming pan, then got to his feet. Toby was still whining.

Sutherland looked for McEwan. He called his name. Toby whined. She must want out of McEwan's pack. Sutherland thought the pup was used to gunfire by now. He pushed through the grass to where he heard Toby. There was still no sign of McEwan. Something froze in Sutherland's chest. Toby whined louder.

"Dunkie?"

Sutherland moved more quickly to the dog. McEwan lay facedown in the grass. Toby licking him, whinning, and whimpering. Sutherland threw aside his rifle and scrambled to McEwan, rolling him on his back, patting his face. He spoke McEwan's name. No response. Toby licked and whimpered at her master's eyes, but McEwan seemed not to be breathing.

"Dunkie, Dunkie?" Sutherland was dazed. He saw no blood. He opened McEwan's tunic and unbuttoned the shirt. He could see no wound. Nothing! "Dunkie?" Toby whined, and Sutherland pushed her away when she climbed on McEwan's unmoving chest.

"Dunkie? Dunkie?"

Then Sutherland saw the bullet hole. Just a small bluish bruise, right in the center of McEwan's chest. He had been shot through the heart. No blood, because the heart had stopped. Simple and clean. Without even feeling what hit him, Duncan McEwan died. Toby whined.

Duncan McEwan, ensign in His Majesty's Royal Americans, 60th Regiment, was buried in the soldiers' graveyard at Fort Pitt the next day. Owen Sutherland had laid McEwan over the saddle of a packhorse and led the animal himself. He spoke to no one, before or after the brief service at his countryman's grave.

That night, solitary in a corner of the noncoms' barracks, Sutherland sat by candlelight and wrote.

He wrote it once, without revision, and without a title.

Soldier, spawn of misery,
Child of anger, hatred, fear.
Soldier, borne by duty,
Standing bravely, proud,
Against all Soldiers,
Spawn of misery.
Laying down their lives in quest
Of Immortality
And dying with their comrades;
Killing for the hope of peace
That never, ever comes to be
For Soldiers, spawn of misery.

Sutherland did not read the poem, but folded the parchment and pushed it into his knapsack. On his bed Toby slept. The pup was growing fast. Soon she would be big enough to fend for herself. But McEwan would have liked him to take the dog. He reached over and fondled the pup's floppy ear. Toby lifted a leg for Sutherland to rub her tummy. She was a good pup. Might make a hunting dog one day. All right, he would take her along when he went back to Detroit. Tamano had been here in Pitt a few days earlier and left word for Sutherland that he would be back soon. He would wait until Tamano came back, and then they would be on their way once more.

He climbed into bed and put Toby on the floor. She jumped up again. He put her down. Twice more he took her off the bed and scolded her, for it was time for her to learn her place. Then, with the pup looking up at him, questioning, Sutherland lay back and fell into an exhausted, dreamless sleep that, for the first time in three months, gave him physical rest.

Toby jumped up on the bed again, curled into a bundle, and fell asleep.

Far away in the northwest a Wyandot runner scrambled along the hunting trail and burst into open ground near the Ottawa encampment of Chief Pontiac. The man's face streamed with sweat. His eyes were glazed, and every muscle ached, for he had run all day without stopping, bringing news from the southeast—news of defeat, of the setback in the uprising in Shawnee and Delaware country.

The Ottawa were busy with preparations for the evening meal, and shouts went up on every side as the messenger raced through the village, pursued by dogs and young boys. Chief

Pontiac, seated in front of his lodge, looked up as the Wyandot stumbled up to his cooking fire, where the chief's wife turned from her pots and listened to what the man had to say. Others gathered around, until a crowd pressed close to the lodge.

Breathless and anxious, the runner gasped out the story of Bouquet's victory, telling of heavy Indian losses and of the deaths of important chiefs. Pontiac listened impassively, although those who knew him well noticed a muscle twitching in one cheek. The brave said the siege of Fort Pitt was broken, and Shawnee and Delaware villages were being abandoned as the people fled deeper into the forest in fear of the British retaliation that was expected before too long.

When the messenger was finished with his shocking tale, Pontiac rose and walked silently into his wigwam. Outside the Wyandot stood, chest heaving for breath. Pontiac's people began to move away, women wringing their beads or buckskin gowns, the men downcast. Sadness shivered through the village as word of the defeat passed from mouth to mouth. The British had won a victory—one they could never win, according to Pontiac. The war would go on now, through the terrible winter months and into the following spring when massed armies and thunder guns would come into Indian country.

The village on the Detroit River was quiet, as were so many other villages that evening. Here and there a woman sent up the death chant for a man known to have died at Bushy Run. Molo's father, Ogala, sat stone-hard in silence, pondering the loss of yet another of his children. Happiness had fled from the Indian heart just when triumph and the prospects of victory had shone brightest. Now there was little hope for victory. Now there was great uncertainty and doubt.

Among the lesser chiefs who had allied with Pontiac, there was disillusionment and anger. His medicine was proving less strong than they had believed. What conquests the Indian had earned were achieved by other leaders, not Pontiac, for powerful Fort Detroit still stood, stronger than ever. It was a witness to British strength and resolve. And it was testimony of Pontiac's vulnerability. There were many Indians in that moment who wondered whether they should have followed Chief Pontiac in this dangerous gamble at all.

A few days later Tamano returned to Fort Pitt. When the Indian first came to Sutherland's quarters, they said little. Together they walked from the fort and found a quiet place in a grove

of trees in the field outside Pitt. There, with Toby sniffing
around them, they sat and smoked in silence. They faced north,
across the broad Allegheny River, one of the two rivers that
joined at Fort Pitt to become the Ohio. Behind them, forming
the peninsula between the Allegheny and itself, the Monongahela flowed from the south; and the Ohio flowed out to the
west.

After they had sat for an hour in silence, Tamano said, "I
have heard about the battle. The Shawnee and Delaware are
defeated. Already villages are emptying here, and many tribes
are fleeing deeper into the forests for safety. Among the Delaware there is fear and great sadness, for they have lost many
sons and some powerful war chiefs."

Tamano did not look at Sutherland, but the Scotsman knew
his friend was waiting for a reply. They sat cross-legged in the
shadow of birch and poplars. The wind rattled the leaves, and
the sound blended with the steady gushing of the rivers. After
some time Sutherland spoke.

"You have heard the truth, my brother. It was a great victory
for the British. I was there. And, my brother, I must tell you
that I fought alongside the soldiers."

Sutherland looked at Tamano, who returned his gaze but
said nothing.

"I wished not to fight, but if those soldiers were destroyed,
the war would not end until all the Indians were wiped out."
He kept his eyes on Tamano, who was impassively staring at
him. "I am sorry this war has come, Tamano, but I did not
bring it upon our peoples. Yet I must do what I can to stop it,
and if to do that I must join the soldiers, then I *shall* do that,
because the Indian can never win this war. He can only hope
for a just peace."

Toby came and lay between them. She put her head on her
paws and looked up at Sutherland with sad eyes.

"My brother," Tamano said and then paused before he went
on. "There is much sorrow among our peoples now; you and
I are sad for both of them." He paused again. "If this war goes
on for many moons, we shall be outcasts, you and I. We shall
be outcasts unless we choose a side. I see now that you have
chosen." Sutherland looked up, waiting for Tamano's next
words—for his judgment. "It is my belief, my brother, that
you have fought beside the soldier because of what is good in
your heart, and that you must obey. Even if it is a white heart."

Sutherland understood that Tamano was well aware of his

every word, that his words were carefully chosen, as only an Indian can choose them, after sincere thought. Tamano had no illusions that Sutherland's adoption into the Ottawa had purged him completely of his British soul.

"Yes, Donoway, your heart is white, and it will always be white. Yet your heart is good, and that is why you are my brother; for me that is enough. If your people had been destroyed instead of mine, I would be sad for them, but not as sad as I am that the Indian has lost so much and will lose so much more when this war is finished. I know, Donoway, the Indian cannot stand against the English guns, and yet I still have not made my own choice whether to take up the tomahawk in a last fight or to depart as we had planned for the northern country."

Tamano sat erect, proud. But his dark eyes were profoundly unhappy.

"Donoway, I understand your decision, and, my brother, I am grateful to the manitous that you still live."

Some time passed, and Sutherland drew his knees up to his chin. He said, "I wish only good for my Indian brothers, Tamano. But I am merely one man. What can I do? What I have done has cost me dearly in loved ones. You know about Molo?"

Tamano nodded and looked blankly into the distance. As much as Sutherland, Tamano had been Molo's mentor. He had been Molo's teacher in the ways of the brave, and Molo had been Tamano's best and most beloved pupil.

They were silent until Sutherland said, "McEwan was killed."

Tamano closed his eyes.

Sutherland felt anger now. Sorrow was transformed into determination. Breton was in his mind again.

Tamano said, "My heart is heavy, Donoway. I had hoped to share with you good news—news that the Delaware Sin-gat is dead—but now those words taste bitter and cold. They hold no satisfaction now. This day has brought too much sorrow, and it is enough, my brother. Let us rest tonight. We should soon depart for Detroit, for there André Breton has fled with a party of Delawares who seek revenge for the loss of their chief—"

"Then let them seek their revenge from me, Tamano," Sutherland said. "I slew Sin-gat, and every village must learn that. Then they shall be forced to come to me, and with good fortune Breton will come with them."

All that afternoon they sat in meditation until the sun began to sink. Then slowly, with Toby bounding ahead of them, they walked back to Fort Pitt. Sutherland was glad that Tamano would stand by him until they found Breton, but he wondered what his brother would do then. Perhaps the Chippewa would go north with Lela, and maybe Sutherland would go with them—go north as once he had promised Mayla. No doubt the English would come there, too, one day. But perhaps by then Owen Sutherland would be a forgotten man, and Donoway, the son of the Ottawa, would have made a new life. One that would last.

The arrival of the army had broken the siege of Fort Pitt. Hostile Indians were not seen for miles around, although signs of large encampments were found abandoned in the woods surrounding the fort.

The day after Bouquet's army arrived, a force of four hundred soldiers went on a forced march back to Fort Ligonier to fetch the supplies, ammunition, and ox carts left there before the fight at Bushy Run. At Pitt, Sutherland and Tamano learned that Bouquet was planning to march into the heart of Shawnee country in a few days. He would demand capitulation, and if he was bold enough, he might get it. That would leave Pontiac and the northern tribes of Ottawa, Chippewa, Sac, and Fox alone in the uprising, supported only by miscellaneous war parties harrying Fort Niagara. Bouquet's success had intimidated at least half the tribes that had supported Pontiac.

On August 15, the afternoon of Sutherland's departure, a great stir arose in the fort when hundreds of Indians, women and children among them, appeared before Pitt's gate. Among the Indians were white hostages.

Drums rattled muster, and soldiers hurried into files. The gates of the fort opened, and out marched Colonel Bouquet and Major Ecuyer, commander of Pitt, to meet with the chiefs. Soldiers in scarlet formed ranks behind the officers, who stopped a hundred yards away from a score of brightly feathered, stoic chiefs. Among these Indians were the village elders who had met with Bouquet on the trail and promised to return all white captives.

In the middle of the clearing outside the fort a ceremonial fire was lit. The principals on both sides sat in a circle together, with their young men fully armed in a half circle behind each group of leaders. Sutherland and Tamano stood with more than two hundred white traders and settlers, who crowded off to one side to watch the parley. Many within this mob of whites had lost friends and family to the Indians. They prayed fervently that their own would appear from among the host of Indians seated behind the chiefs.

Obeying Indian etiquette, Bouquet and Ecuyer parleyed with the chiefs for more than an hour before anything was mentioned about returning hostages. It was late afternoon when an agreement was reached. Then many seated among the Indian horde stood and moved forward out of the crowd. Slowly, singly, and in little knots, figures who resembled Indians moved past the council fire and herded into a nervous group of thirty or so, stopping a few yards from the white civilians.

Then the tense silence broke. A woman among the fort's people shrieked and ran toward the hostages. A man among the prisoners shouted and, arms wide, hurled himself at her, lifting her from the ground. Others among the civilians ran to the former hostages, some finding who they were looking for, others not. Of the dazed and disbelieving prisoners, only a dozen met friends or relations that afternoon. The rest, suffering still from their degrading experience as Indian prisoners, were taken away by Good Samaritans to be cared for until—as best they could—they reconstructed a new life.

To one side a drama was played out that was typical of many reunions on the frontier in those days. A woman was on her knees before a girl about seven years old. The child's face was impassive. She did not respond, even when the mother pulled the child against her breast, grasped her face, and spoke kindly: "Helen, it's Mama! Helen? Helen, you're safe now. Helen, don't you know me? Helen!"

But the girl's eyes remained empty. She stared without feeling at the distraught woman who was touching her face and kissing her fervently. The child gave no sign of recognition. Frantic, the mother broke down and wept.

Sutherland moved to the woman's shoulder and touched it. The little girl looked at him without expression. The woman raised her tear-streaked face to Sutherland, who had seen this kind of shock before.

"It's my child, mister. She don't know me at all. Oh, Lord! It's been only four months since she was took. But she don't know me." The woman ran trembling hands over the girl's face and hair. "Oh, Helen, Helen, darlin'. What did they do to you? Helen!"

Sutherland knelt at the woman's side. "Do you have a song,

a lullabye or something the child might know?"

Hope lit the woman's eyes. She sniffed and wiped her face. She looked at the girl, then in a low and shaky voice began to hum and then to sing a mother's song. The girl moved her head just slightly. The mother found words that she had not sung since the girl was a babe. Her voice rose, pleading as she sang.

The child listened. She watched, curious. Color came into her face. The woman saw it and sang more ardently. The girl's eyes fluttered. The woman sang, clutched her hands in front of her, and repeated the verses she once had sung to this girl when she was her own. And the girl began to breathe more strongly.

"Helen?"

"Ma—Mama?"

They fell into each other's arms, and the woman wept for joy. The little child simply wept.

As Sutherland moved away, he noticed a violent flurry among the Indian women. A strong, young black-haired boy in his early teens was struggling with two braves, who were dragging him toward the liberated hostages. The boy looked like an Indian, he shouted Indian words, and he fought like an Indian. Two soldiers took over from the braves, and the boy was hurried away into the fort. His Christian soul must be saved, no matter where his heart and mind belonged.

Among the Indian women a squaw was helplessly watching as the boy was taken away. Her hands clenched and unclenched. She stood, shoulders heaving, until another woman drew her away to be forgotten along with those Indian families who had made whites their own: had raised them, had married them, had given them children, and now were torn away in return for a promise of peace from Henry Bouquet. For every happy homecoming there was a heartrending separation of captives who were returning to the world of the white man against their wills.

It was dusk when the parley ended, and the Indians had no more hostages in their midst. The white settlers and traders began to move back into the fort when, from among the Indian squaws, babbling arose. Someone else was coming.

Sutherland saw a group of Indian women walking beside a tall, flaxen-haired white girl, who strode with her head erect, as though gliding, across the field toward the fort. Everyone was silent as they watched the woman approach. She wore a

long cotton gown of pale blue that shone in the fading sunlight.
Her face and yellow hair shimmered. The Indians parted as she
walked through them and stopped before Henry Bouquet. The
colonel spoke quietly to the woman, then beckoned for Sutherland.

"I believe this is someone you have been seeking," Bouquet
said to the Scotsman.

The beautiful girl looked at Sutherland with pale eyes that
held his own. He wondered how he could ever tell Mary Hamilton that Duncan was dead. But he must.

"May I have a word with you, ma'am?" Sutherland removed
his hat as he spoke. "In private."

Wordless, she walked with him to a little glade near the
fort's wall. The aspen trees there shivered and rattled. Sutherland turned to face Mary.

"You are the woman Duncan McEwan was seeking," he
said.

Her breath quickened. "Do you know where he is?"

Sutherland looked down at his feet. "I do," he said and
lifted his face to see hers. "He—was a very close friend of
mine . . ."

She brought her fingers to her lips. *"Was* your friend?" she
whispered.

He nodded. "Duncan asked me to find you, and now I have.
Miss Hamilton, all I can do for you shall be done—"

She went weak, and he held her against him.

"I'm afraid," she said, "that I cannot even cry anymore."
He felt her tremble then calm herself. He eased her back and
was about to speak, but she said, "Sir, I carry Duncan's child."

Sutherland left Mary Hamilton at Fort Pitt, arranging that
she receive the pay due McEwan. She promised she would
write to him and let him know if she wanted to go to Detroit,
where friends could give her a home. Sutherland thought of
the Morelys, and he thought of Ella Bently. Ella was leaving
for England before too long, but perhaps she could assist Mary
in this difficult time.

At dawn he set off with Tamano for Detroit. He gave Toby
to Mary, who was grateful, for she already loved the dog.

In his New York headquarters, General Sir Jeffrey Amherst
nodded with satisfaction as he read Colonel Bouquet's report
of the victory at Bushy Run and of the relief of Fort Pitt. Finally
this uprising was being brought under control. There was still

much to do, of course, with a force to be assembled and sent out from Fort Niagara to Detroit. The destroyed posts must be rebuilt, and the Indians had to be severly punished for their transgressions. But all that was at last under way.

Now if the British could arrange for a truce with Pontiac in the northwest, then Amherst's successor could safely reinforce that region and prepare for a campaign in the spring. Bouquet would handle the subjection of the Shawnee, Delaware, and Mingo in Pennsylvania, and another army would put down any flickering rebelliousness in the lakes regions. Amherst would be going home with his job unfinished, but he hungered to get away from America, a place he despised.

He laid Bouquet's dispatches on the desk and drummed his fingers in thought. The uprising was being overwhelmed, but there would still be an inquiry in London. The ministers would demand an explanation as to why supposedly subjected Indians could have surprised and defeated so many outposts garrisoned by regular troops, not to mention the humiliation of the British Army and the disillusionment of the colonial assemblies with the government that had failed to protect the frontiers. Damn! After all he had achieved against the French, to have a pack of drunken heathens taint his reputation, his honor, his— Damn!

Well, at least there was some compensation. The Indians would pay heavily for what they had done. He nodded again to think about the report of Major Simeon Ecuyer, commander at Fort Pitt, who had told Amherst that Indians had been given a number of blankets as gifts during a parley that summer. The blankets had come directly from the fort's hospital, where smallpox raged.

Amherst almost smiled to think of that. Indeed this winter would be a bitter one for the Pennsylvania Indians. And when spring came, it was likely that very few braves would still be alive to carry on the uprising. It wasn't everything that General Amherst could have hoped for, but it was something at least to satisfy his sense of justice.

PART THREE

The Truce

chapter **21**

COLONEL BROCKHURST

The Detroit River was deep red at sunset on September 1, when the *Michigan* sailed upstream on its return from Fort Niagara. The *Huron* had also been sent out sometime after the *Michigan* and was expected to return shortly. Alex Duvall, recuperating from the wound he suffered during Dalyell's defeat at Bloody Creek, was on board the *Huron*. Henry Gladwin still intended to leave for England before winter set in, and Duvall would be taking command of Detroit soon. With that in mind, Duvall wanted to confer with the commander of Niagara about provisioning his fort before Lake Erie froze over.

A cannon boomed from the fort, and a ship's gun returned the salute. People gathered in excitement on the ramparts overlooking the river, for even though the *Michigan* brought only a handful of reinforcements, it always brought news from the East—news that one day might mean an army on its way to lift the siege.

From her porch Ella saw Henry at the gate greeting newcomers. She was startled when she saw an elderly officer—a full colonel—meet her brother. They headed for the house, and she hurried inside to wait. As they entered, she curtsied.

"Well, sister, General Amherst has sent us some inspiration indeed!" Gladwin grinned and introduced Ella to Colonel James Brockhurst, who bowed pleasantly. Gladwin turned to the colonel and said, "And, Colonel, do you have a regiment of grenadiers following you?"

Brockhurst laughed deeply and said, "No, Major, I'm afraid I'll have to do for now—inspiration, as you said. But if I had a regiment under me, it would not be grenadiers; it would be Scottish Highlanders, for I have commanded those men in the field and did so until I joined the general staff in New York Town."

Ella wondered whether she was hearing correctly. "Did you say Highlanders, Colonel?"

He nodded. As they sat down, Ella calmed herself and said, "Which regiment?"

"Why the 42nd, mistress. The Black Watch. I commanded them for many years."

Ella felt shaky.

Brockhurst asked, "And are you familiar with that regiment, mistress? No doubt you are, because you probably have heard news of its success near Fort Pitt recently."

"Success?" Gladwin asked. "You mean we've managed to win a battle, Colonel?"

Brockhurst smiled broadly. His face was weathered but refined. His eyes were gray, like his hair, and he had bushy eyebrows that danced when he spoke.

He said, "I see news travels slowly out here. Haven't you heard that the 42nd and some other regimental units under Colonel Bouquet have smashed the uprising of Shawnee and Delaware near Fort Pitt? Yes, Pitt is now out of danger."

Gladwin laughed and bounded from his chair. "At last! At last, we've something happy to talk about! Magnificent! Inspirational indeed, sir!"

Ella was thinking that the colonel might know Owen. Could she ask?

"Yes," Brockhurst said, "the uprising in the East is almost quelled, and General Amherst has sent me to Fort Detroit on a very important mission—one which I sincerely pray will end this fighting without further bloodshed."

Gladwin and Ella listened intently.

"Forgive me, Major, for not sending advance word of my coming, but I arrived at Niagara only two weeks ago and was obliged to leave immediately because the *Michigan* was ready to depart. In brief, I have come to inform the Indians that the French war is officially over, as you already know. We realize that the Indians are carrying on this abominable affair largely because they believe they'll get help from the French. Well, my aim is to put an end to that misconception once and for all."

Gladwin looked skeptical. "With all due respect, Colonel, the Indians believe what they want to believe. Their leaders would lose face if they had to admit that the French will not defend them."

"I understand that, Major. But I'll soon meet here with a French officer who is well known to the tribes in this region. Already he is on his way from Fort Chartres in the west. As part of our treaty with France, the French have agreed to assist us in calming those Indians who were once under their influence. I and the French officer will act as envoys to this chief called Pontiac, and together we must convince him of the folly of continuing the rebellion. Our mission, coupled with news of the great victory at Bushy Run, is expected to be enough to break the siege you have suffered for so long, Major."

Gladwin said, "By now, Colonel, you must know that my second-in-command, Captain Campbell, was taken prisoner by Pontiac while on such a mission of peace, and the good captain was foully murdered by this same Pontiac you presume will so willingly accept you and this Frenchman."

Brockhurst nodded slowly. "We're well aware of the risks, Major," he said. The colonel was calm and strong, not haughty as were many on the staff at Amherst's headquarters. He was a man who instilled natural confidence, Ella thought, but perhaps his assuredness in this matter was colored by lack of understanding of the hatred borne by the Indians for the British.

"We're hoping," Brockhurst said, "that you will be able to present us with a volunteer who knows the Indians well and who is trusted by them. English, French, it doesn't matter, as long as he has the respect of the Indians. Then I'll trust to my own powers of persuasion and to the influence of this French ambassador who'll be risking his own life along with us."

"I have one such man, Colonel, but he is not here," Gladwin said. "I have no idea when he'll return, for he's down Fort Pitt way. Perhaps you know him, for he was once an officer in your regiment." Ella's heart whirled when Gladwin said, "His name is Owen Sutherland—"

"Sutherland?" Brockhurst boomed. His face was aglow. "You mean Owen Sutherland is out here? Why, yes!" Brockhurst slapped his hand against his thigh. "That explains it! I thought I knew that name! Sutherland! Then it was he at Bushy Run!"

"I beg your pardon, sir?" Gladwin asked.

"Sutherland!" Brockhurst laughed. "A fellow named Sutherland was mentioned in Bouquet's dispatches to General Am-

herst after the Battle of Bushy Run. How remarkable! Owen
Sutherland, according to Bouquet, won the battle with a brilliant tactic. He fought with the army—"

"Fought?" It was Ella now. She was standing. "Are you
saying, sir, that Owen fought against the Indians?"

"Exactly!" Brockhurst slapped his thigh again and laughed.
"Owen, Owen! Well, one can't keep a good man down, eh?
Yes, Owen Sutherland saved the army at Bushy Run. If he's
the fellow you would send with me to visit Pontiac, I'd be
delighted. Couldn't have a better man!"

"So you know him?" Ella asked, and she struggled to cloak
her excitement.

"Yes, yes, I know him, Mistress Bently. Served with me
years ago. Fine, fine officer. Good man, none better—"

"But, Colonel," Ella began slowly. "Colonel, I don't quite
know how to ask you this, but—but I must. You see, I must
have something explained, and you . . ."

"Sister!" Gladwin spoke sharply. "If you don't mind, Ella,
Colonel Brockhurst will be with us for some time yet. You'll
have every opportunity to ask whatever is on your mind. But
at the moment I suggest we make accommodations for him in
our own humble way, and I'll discuss military matters first.
Would you excuse us, sister?"

Ella realized that her brother knew she was about to ask
about Owen's so-called disgrace, but for some reason he wished
her not to mention it. All right, let Henry do what he apparently
wanted to do. She rose and curtsied to Brockhurst, who with
Henry stood and bade her farewell. Ella went outside and was
met by a clean, cool breeze off the river.

It was very strange, all this. Was Duvall telling the truth?
Was he lying? Why did Brockhurst speak so highly of a man
who had allegedly resigned in dishonor from his own regiment?
She walked across the dusky parade ground, lost in thought.
Her mind drifted to Jeremy. Ella hoped Owen would speak
with him, would tell him his side of the story. Surely the
heroism Owen had displayed at the battle near Fort Pitt would
console her son. It would be a good lesson for him: a lesson
that no one is perfect, even those we most admire. Jeremy must
understand that. Surely his unhappiness would be lifted when
Owen returned.

She would meet Owen when he came back and would tell
him about the rumor before he heard it without warning. He
deserved to be told, and painful as it might be, she was de-

termined to be the one who told him first. Then she would ask him to talk to Jeremy, for she was certain Owen could win the boy's confidence again—and perhaps win it more strongly than before.

As for herself, Owen's story was something she longed for. She knew well that she loved him, although she had resolved not to permit that love to show—he had lost so much that she feared it was far too soon for him to be confronted by a woman in love with him. He needed time to find himself again. How much time that might take, she did not know, but she would not push. She would not be a grasping, clutching woman who pursued a man as though he were a prize to be won. She would leave him alone. Yes, she would control her own emotions for Owen's sake.

With that last thought, relief swept Ella as though a dark cloud had been lifted from her heart. She knew now, whether or not Owen ever recognized that she loved him, she would be independent, happy in her own way. Happy with whatever life brought, as she always had been. As for returning to England—she would wait and see what happened.

The council house stood before her. She felt a gladness that she was here, now that she had resolved what to do. Within the council house was the spinet, waiting for her, and it was a joy to anticipate its soaring melodies. She went inside, groped in the dimness for the flint and tinderbox, and lit a candle. She set the candle on the spinet and sat down.

The light flickered on the black and white keyboard. Her hands lay gently on the keys, and she began to play. The music glittered, pure and crystal bright. In the music, her happiness took shape. Slow and tinkling, the melody gave her peace— peace that Ella Bently needed.

Sutherland came walking up from the river's edge, where he had left Tamano. He trudged toward Gladwin's house. The journey from Pitt had been long and dangerous, for many war parties were still on the move, particularly those that had not tasted defeat at Bushy Run. He was weary.

When Ella's music caught him, Sutherland stopped. He set his rifle on its butt and leaned against it, listening as though his heart had been unchained, delivered from despair. He closed his eyes and let the spinet's melody spill through his very being. It was a moment without grief, the first such moment he had felt in much too long.

Sutherland saw the faint glow at the window of the council house. He moved to the door, opened it, and looked inside. Ella, her back to him, was playing the spinet. Quietly he slipped into the room and closed the door without a sound. He sat against the wall and let the music fill him.

Like that—Ella playing and Sutherland listening—they remained for twenty minutes. At last Ella withdrew her hands from the keys and breathed deeply. She leaned over, blew the candle out, and sat in darkness.

But the darkness was not solitary. She sensed another person there. She turned and looked into the shadows, and then Sutherland said, "I'm grateful for that, Ella."

She caught her breath. "Owen!"

"Forgive me," he said and came toward her in the dark. "Forgive me if I was impolite in listening while you were unaware, but I could not disturb the peace you brought me. For that, I am grateful."

She fumbled with the flint, struck a spark into the tinderbox, then lit the candle. The light brought Owen's haggard face into sharp relief. His eyes were dark, though shining. They looked—familiar—yes, they looked like eyes she had seen before, but never before as the eyes of Owen Sutherland. Gone was the confident sparkle in them that had lit her within. Gone was the brash and carefree boldness she had seen that first day in the whaleboat. Yet these eyes were known to her—from where, she could not yet recall. And their change attracted her all the more.

They looked at each other, she sitting at the spinet and he leaning on his elbows near the candle.

Then in a flash that shocked her, she knew whose eyes he wore! The thought was startling, and she had to look away. When she looked back at him, she saw, indeed, he had John Bently's eyes. Those were the eyes of her husband when he came home wounded from the campaign that brought an early end to his life. Those eyes had followed her across a thousand miles—across a lifetime. That hollowness, that empty space born of too much horror, had also found this man, and it found him on a battlefield in the same blood-soaked country in which it had found John.

Ella shivered and turned away again. In that moment all she had resolved to say to Owen, all she was so certain she would ask him, slipped away.

Sutherland saw uncertainty in Ella. The siege had been

unhappy and depressing, and it showed in Ella's face—a fine, profound, and lovely face.

"Are you well, Ella?" His voice was faint, but steady. "You look—you look worn out. But I'll say your playing just now told me you've not been completely overwhelmed by all of this."

She sighed, and he smiled. His face looked warmer then. The darkness lifted a bit. She smiled, too.

"I'm glad you're back safely, Owen," she whispered. Both felt profoundly tired.

"Aye," he said and touched a high note on the spinet, sending it ringing about the room. "It's good to be back."

He stood up and flexed his shoulders. Then he said, "It's been a long time, and much has happened, though my business is still not finished. Yet I find myself almost too exhausted to carry on. And if you'll forgive my complaining, I'll tell you that there are times when I'm almost too dismayed to want to go on. But somehow I shall. I must. I must go on until I—"

"Don't say it!"

He looked at her. "Don't say what?"

"Until either you or Breton dies."

Their eyes were unwavering. Then Sutherland pursed his lips and sighed. "Life is strange isn't it? There's nothing more I'd like to do than to stop this chase. But I cannot. I'll never rest until I avenge..."

He turned and walked away from the candlelight. Ella closed her eyes. All her brave resolution had vanished, all her certainty that she would be above her passions might never once have been there.

"Forgive me," Sutherland said from far away. "You don't deserve to be burdened with my troubles."

"I'm glad to be, Owen. Truly. I'm glad to do whatever I can for you. Don't ask me for forgiveness; just say what's in your heart." Under her breath she said, "One of us must."

"What?" He came back to her and leaned against the spinet once more.

"Nothing. Just...feel free to speak your thoughts to me. I understand that you need that. For I have also known such loss as yours, and I have been grateful of friends at moments...like this."

He sighed again, and the breath sent the candle flickering and dancing. Ella thought his eyes seemed brighter now. He thought she was a fine woman—a good and loyal friend.

"I think, now," he said and almost smiled, "that even without words my heart has been lifted thanks to you, and thanks to your music. Will you play for me again? Now?"

She turned and let her hands hover over the keys. But then she paused. There was something she must say. The thought of the rumor distracted her. She looked up at Sutherland and tried to smile but could not. Her hands fell to her lap.

"Owen," she said and held her eyes on his. "Owen, there is something I must tell you—something you should know that has happened since your departure."

She stood up and said, "Will you walk with me, Owen? This will take fresh air and walking, so will you walk with me?"

He picked up his rifle and went outside with her. They strolled without speaking down to a corner blockhouse, the one where Sutherland had told Jeremy of Menabozho. In silence they ascended the steps. Above, the wind was stronger, and autumn was crisp in the air. They leaned over the parapet and looked down at the dark, rushing river. The *Michigan* creaked and groaned as it rode at anchor a short distance away.

"So much has happened, Ella," Sutherland said, "that you need not think your news will be too much for me to bear. So tell me now, lass, and don't trouble yourself any longer."

She turned to face him. They stood a few feet apart. In the faint light of the stars, she could see his face, strong now, and it was as though they had always known each other.

"Owen, I must tell you that, since you left, a rumor has passed through the fort. It is a rumor about you. It is a story about your past." She was so surprised at how this flowed now that she was determined to tell it. He listened with such sincerity that she could not hold back—she could not temper her words with anything but the truth. In a moment the story was told. She could not see Sutherland very well, for he was looking out over the river. For some time neither spoke.

Down in the fort, a constable shouted out the time and cried all was well. She wished it were; yet she no longer felt the sharp anticipation of what his answer might be. Doubt that had once worried her was gone. She was calm, waiting for Owen to speak. Canvas on the *Michigan*'s mast snapped in the wind.

Sutherland spoke, but he did not face her.

"Thank you, Ella, for telling me this." He was quiet again. "I suppose I should have known that story would one day follow me here. And to tell the truth, I knew it would only be a matter of time before Duvall let it loose. He had to." Sutherland looked at her. "He had to because he loves you too much."

The icy thrill that stabbed Ella brought her hand to her breast. Owen turned away again.

"Yes, Ella, forgive me if I'm too forward or speaking out of turn. But Duvall feared you might..." He turned and stood closer to her. "...that you might somehow care for me, and so this story has been spread by him. Well, I'm not in a position to deny it, for in fact it is true. I was found sleeping, and I did not deliver the dispatches in time to prevent the French victory. Many good men died because of that. But believe me or not—"

"I believe you," she breathed and hardly heard herself.

"Believe what you will, but I am innocent of what I was court-martialed for. I'll tell you, and I'll tell this to Jeremy and to your brother, and to those who'll believe me! I was drugged by French spies that night, and that is the truth. I was drugged while waiting to give the dispatches to Duvall. But there is no way to prove that, so I'll let the matter drop, and those who choose to believe otherwise can do so."

He looked out at the black river. "No doubt," he said quietly, "there will be many who won't believe me."

"Those who care for you will!" Her hand was on his arm. He looked at her. "You must know that, Owen."

"I do," he said. "But this is not the first time this tale has poisoned friends I knew well. This is not the first time it's followed me. When I was a student in Edinburgh it came among my friends, my professors, and it wormed itself into their hearts, even though they wished not to believe it. And the best of them resolved to be friends anyway—even if it were true."

He gave a little laugh of irony. "Even if it were true. But they were never sure of what I told them. And what about you, and what about Jeremy and Henry?" He was staring at her. "Will you respect me in spite of the fact that the story *might* be true? Even though I *might* have been a lazy scoundrel who cared more about a night's sleep than about the lives of—of so many, many friends?" He laughed again, and the laugh was cynical, hard.

"I'll believe whatever you say, Owen."

"You will? Why should you? Oh, yes, like everyone else,

you'll *want* to believe it, and you'll want to so badly that you might gloss over what some call fact. But always you'll have that gnawing little doubt—"

"Don't say that! You're unfair to say that!"

"I am?" He was cold as ice.

"You are! Very unfair!"

He looked out over the water again. "Perhaps. And if I am, then I'm sorry. But it wouldn't be the first time that a friend swore he did not believe this story and then, as time passed and doubt crept in—"

"Owen! You have no right to say that! No right at all!"

"No?"

"None! I've told you what I could to prepare you for what might face you! At least you can give me some consideration in return. This was not easy. You act as though you and you alone have a burden on your shoulders. Well, Owen, you're unfair to think so ill of those who care for you!"

He looked again, and she sensed he had softened. She felt tears in her eyes and was glad it was too dark for him to see them. But her voice quivered and betrayed her feelings. "Don't think Owen, that all of us are so dull that—that we can't—"

"I don't," he said and moved closer to her. His hands were on her arms. She looked up and saw a glint in his eyes. "I don't, Ella. Please forgive me. I thank you for telling me all this. I thank you for being someone I can talk to. There's little more one can ask for than to find someone like you. I thank you."

He drew her closer. Her eyes closed. He kissed her on the cheek. She burned inside. He felt deeply grateful—and something else, something else of which he was not sure. But he was grateful.

"Owen," she said and held his hands. "Will you speak to Jeremy? He's hurt so by all this. He needs to talk to you so very, very much, Owen."

Sutherland nodded. "I need to talk to him, too. He's a good friend, Ella. Like his mother." He moved to kiss her on the cheek again, but without thinking about it she met his lips, lightly, just for an instant, and then she pulled away. But he followed her and found her again. He touched her cheek with his fingertips, uncertain. Then they kissed with love, and she was lost, and he was suddenly at peace, at peace so unexpected, yet so undeniable.

"Owen!" she whispered. "Owen."

He said nothing, but he felt the love. He held Ella tighter, feeling her tremble as though she were afraid. He stood back and took her shoulders in his hands and looked into her eyes. She was seeking him, and he tried to speak, but his lips moved without a sound, forming her name. His eyes were moist, and she felt a flood rising within herself, too. She bit her lip and tasted tears.

Then Owen was smiling. His hand caressed her cheek and throat. She took it and kissed it. He drew a deep breath and sighed.

"Ella," he said then and kissed her forehead. His voice echoed her name over and again inside his heart.

She looked up at him, and he brushed her lips with his. She drew him against her and kissed him. Her trembling was gone. He crushed her nearly breathless, and she wept for joy.

For some time they stood together in silence, save for the wind and the river rushing past. She leaned close to him, and they thought of nothing at all but felt each other and the cool wind and the soothing, rushing river. Like her music, Ella gave Sutherland rest. Like her music she was pure, everything he needed then, and everything he wanted. In that brief eternity he knew that once again he had found the heart of love.

Ella suddenly gasped, "Oh, my!" and pushed back from him.

"Not something else?" he asked.

"Yes! I mean no! I mean, I don't know what it is to you, but I should have told you: Colonel Brockhurst is here! He came today!"

"Brockhurst! Here?" Sutherland was amazed and excited all at once. "We must go and see him! Brockhurst! Well, then, perhaps there's some good news at last! Brockhurst never knew the truth of that night in the Lowlands, but he trusted me enough to believe I was telling the truth. Ask him what happened if you want to know at all. If nothing else, he'll tell you that the army never found me guilty of disobeying orders. He'll tell you that they could have shot me for what they court-martialed me for—if they'd found me guilty. But the evidence was not sufficient, and to avoid scandal, I chose to resign. Let's go to Brockhurst now, and then I won't have to tell you what happened. He'll do it better than I can!"

At that very moment, in Gladwin's sitting room, Colonel Brockhurst was doing precisely that. In response to Gladwin's pointed questions Brockhurst assured the major that Sutherland's guilt was never conclusively proven. Brockhurst had been on the court-martial panel, and he was the only one who voted in Sutherland's favor. Since Duvall was a brave and successful officer, and since he was Sutherland's superior, his damning testimony carried enough weight to tarnish Sutherland's reputation, causing him to resign in anger from the British Army.

"It pains me to hear that this story has followed Owen even here," Brockhurst said and leaned back in the easy chair before the fire crackling in the hearth. "Then and now, I am certain that all the facts did not come up at his court-martial. I never had a finer officer, Major Gladwin. He was my protégé, like a son to me. And whatever others might believe, I am sure his story is true."

Gladwin chewed on the end of his long-stem pipe. He said nothing, but he was glad to hear Brockhurst speak highly of his friend. Henry Gladwin was not the only one at that moment who was relieved and happy to hear that Sutherland's disgrace might be unjust: At the top of the stairs, listening in darkness to the conversation below, Jeremy Bently felt hope surge into his heart. All he prayed for had come true in those last few moments. Now, no matter what anyone else might think, he was sure Owen Sutherland was the man he had always believed him to be.

Ella and Sutherland walked arm in arm back to Gladwin's house. They said nothing, both drifting in their thoughts. Sutherland felt Ella light and easy on his arm. He wondered how this had all happened between them. Then he knew it had grown, as though it had to be. She was walking, head down, deep in her own world. He wondered again how he had not sensed this feeling for her growing. Now he understood it, step by step, from the time she healed him of his wounds to the solace she gave him when he craved killing Breton after the Frenchman was taken prisoner. Just now in the council house, when he listened to her playing, everything that had taken place between them came to life—a life that went far beyond even the notion of romantic love. He could not explain it clearly, but he could not deny it, even though it might seem all too soon—too soon after the loss of Mayla. But it was right. It was right. Even though it might seem . . .

"Too soon," he whispered.

"What did you say, Owen?"

He stopped walking, and they faced each other. They were outside Gladwin's house. He held her hands.

"I said too soon. It all has come so—so unexpectedly, Ella."

She waited for him to go on, but he did not. She said, "If it doesn't seem right, Owen, then say it, and—and I'll not deny it. I'll understand—"

He shook his head and smiled. He touched her chin. "How could it not be right?"

She put her head against his chest, and he pulled her close. After a few moments they stepped back from each other, and Sutherland said quietly, "Let's go in and see Brockhurst, eh? It will be good to see him again."

She straightened her hair. She went ahead of him up the steps and did not take his arm then, for she wished not to compromise him—to commit Owen as her lover before he had the time to think about it. But just as she opened the door, Owen moved to her side and took her arm. She felt joy as they went into the house together.

"Owen!" Brockhurst roared and, laughing, strode to hug Sutherland in his great, long arms. It was as if a father and son had found each other once again. They clapped each other on the back and looked up and down in search of all the years, found them, and were surprised and delighted. The three men crowded to the fireplace, and Ella contentedly went to the kitchen to make tea.

When she came out to them again, teapot in hand, Ella exchanged a glance with Gladwin, who beamed at her, causing her to blush. Sutherland and Brockhurst were already deep in conversation about the past two decades—conversation that recalled Sutherland's years among the Indians as well as his time as a merchant sailor. Colonel Brockhurst told of his promotion from commanding the Highland regiment to joining the staff of General Amherst.

"I've never fought Indians, Owen," Brockhurst said. "And too many others on Amherst's staff know no more than I do about the savages—or even about the provincials. Amherst has fought with them and against them, but he has no love for Indians, and he'd as soon see them wiped off the face of the earth. He wants this country for England alone, and I believe he sees this war as an opportunity to get rid of the Indians once and for all. If he had the forces to do it, he would kill every Indian man, woman, and child he could find. If this war goes on much longer, if the Indians won't listen to reason, then Amherst will get the army he needs, and..."

The only sound was the fire crackling.

Sutherland lit his pipe and puffed. "That's the whole injustice of this war, Colonel. It was Amherst's lack of understanding that brought it all about. We can't suddenly change two centuries of experience the Indians here shared with the French. The Indians are used to being treated with respect, and Amherst refused to do that. They show respect for one another by giving presents on special occasions. Amherst refuses. They're used to white man's muskets, clothing, and tools, but Amherst won't trade them powder or weapons to hunt with, so they can get the furs to trade for tools. They're going to die because of Amherst's policies, whether soldiers kill them or they starve to death."

They were silent again. Gladwin spoke and told of the Indian prophet, the alarms in the past three years that had nearly caused war on several occasions, and at last he showed Brockhurst the bottle of black rain—the portent of doom that had fallen on the fort a year earlier. Brockhurst turned the glistening bottle in his hands and considered it.

Finally he said, "If this war is not stopped, Amherst will destroy the Indians. It's as simple as that." He looked at Sutherland. "Owen, I intend to go to Pontiac in the company of a French officer very soon. Will you come with us?"

Sutherland looked at the fire, then nodded slowly. "I'll go with you, Colonel. If there's anything I can do, I'll do it. But do understand that my influence with Pontiac may be finished. I tried months ago to keep him from this war, but I failed. Now he'll know I fought at Bushy Run, and he may... Well, let me just warn you that I may not be welcome in his camp."

Ella felt fear for him. She stared at Sutherland, who leaned forward and lit a taper in the fire, then puffed his pipe to life once more.

"We'll send word to Pontiac by Tamano," Gladwin said.

Sutherland shook his head. "I'm afraid Tamano is searching for news of André Breton. We can't be sure when he'll return, and we don't know if he'll get back to Detroit before your French officer gets here. I suggest you send the message to Pontiac through a French resident, and then—then we'll just have to take our chances."

Brockhurst drew a deep breath. "Do we have a chance, Owen?"

Sutherland did not answer. Ella wished he had.

A short time later Sutherland got up to leave, and Ella went with him to the door. On the front porch he took her in his arms and kissed her.

"I'm afraid for you, Owen," she said. "I wish you did not have to go."

"I'll come back," he said. "I'll come back, Ella, but you have to know I won't rest until I find Breton."

Emptiness shrouded them in that moment.

"I know," she said. "I've known that for a long time."

"Perhaps that's why this is all too soon between us."

"It's not too soon, Owen. How can it be, in times like these? How can it ever be too soon? My Owen, let's hope that what we have is not too late."

They held each other.

"Until morning," Sutherland said and went off toward Garth Morely's to spend the night.

Ella hurried up the stairs to her bedroom, eager to lie alone and to think about Owen. For the first time in ages she was excited about waking in the morning.

As she slipped into her nightgown, she heard Jeremy stir. She leaned over to kiss him good night, and he awoke.

"Mama," he said and smiled. "Mama, I heard Colonel Brockhurst and Uncle Henry talking tonight. They were talking about Mr. Sutherland, and they said all these things about him were not really true! They said he was a good man, just as I had hoped he was!" Ella sat on the end of his bed. "I'm glad, because I like him so much."

She blew out the candle.

"I'm glad, too, Jeremy, and Mr. Sutherland is glad you don't hate him. He likes you very much, you know."

Jeremy yawned and turned on his side. Sleepily he said, "I know, and I hope when he comes to Fort Detroit he'll come to see me."

Ella felt happy. "Maybe he'll come to see you tomorrow. He's here already."

Jeremy sat up straight. "He's here?"

Ella laughed. "Sleep now, and you'll see him tomorrow."

"He's here!"

Yes, Ella thought as she went to her own bed. It's good that he's here at last. But how long would he be with them? And when he left, would he return? She forced that thought away and let her mind recall the hour on the blockhouse. That was real. Not what might be or what had been. That was real, and that was what must last. From deep within, she prayed it would.

At Garth Morely's, lying on a cot in the darkness, Sutherland reflected on the events that had tumbled him into the arms of Ella Bently. After what had been, Ella's love was more than he had ever hoped for. It had come without warning because he had been too stubbornly blind, too swallowed up in passions of revenge and mourning to see it. He touched the silver pendant on his chest. What did it all mean? What should he do? And most of all, did Ella deserve his obsessive quest for vengeance? What would he become before that quest was finished? What could he give Ella and Jeremy once André Breton's blood was on his hands, as he was determined it would be? And how long would it take before that search was done? Could he promise Ella anything at all right now? What was fair to her? What was fair to the memory of his beloved Mayla?

Sutherland lay awake, and those questions writhed within him. But there were no answers, and that's what was so frustrating. There must be answers, but he could not find them. He could only hope that one day he would find peace—the kind of peace he knew when Ella played her spinet.

He sat up and lit a candle, then took out pen and paper. This is the poem he wrote:

BRIGHT LAND

Freeborn land that knows no duty
What shall be my destiny?
Whence thy fire and savage beauty?
Whence thy promise held for me?

Cast my life abroad, and plunder
All my past of memory;
Purge my heart with marveling wonder,
Blest by Nature's harmony.

Whence thy fire and savage beauty?
Whence thy promise held for me?
Tell me now, my solemn duty
To, bright land, my hopes and thee?

chapter **22**

THE FRENCH EMBASSY

Sutherland breakfasted with the Morelys that morning. During the meal Garth bantered on about his ambitions for forming a trading company after the trouble was over. Owen listened but did not say much.

"Well, Owen," Morely pressed, "do thee or don't thee want to start this company with me?"

Sutherland put down his teacup and brooded before replying. "Garth, the idea is a good one—if the Indians will still do business with me now that I've fought against them. And if Amherst lets this war end without wiping them out—"

"Wiping them out? Hellfire, man, without Injuns to trap fur there'd be no fur trade at all! And without fur trade, this country's useless to the crown! Never fear, there's too many important people getting fat off Injun trade to let Lord Jeffrey snuff it out like that!" He snapped his fingers. "Yes! There's goin' to be Injuns and furs and white traders, and I intend to trade! This country needs the likes of thee, Owen! Surely thee sees that!"

"Garth, you speak as though you know nothing of what's been said about me since I've been gone. This reputation that's followed me—"

"Pah! I don't give a tinker's damn about that, and neither'll anybody what knows thee, lad! Thy word is good enough for me! Tell me thy side of the story if thee wants to, and then let it rest."

"We'll let it rest, perhaps, but others won't. They think me a disgraced scoundrel. Do you think I can live with that?"

Morely was gloomy. He rubbed his beard, then said, "Look here, Owen, what's done is done. Thy past is of no concern to me. Those busybodies who spread gossip can have their muck, but it shouldn't trouble thee, lad!"

"Maybe not," Sutherland said. "But it does."

"Damned stubborn Scotch pride! That's what it be! Thy damned stubborn Scotch pride, Owen! Don't let it blind thee, no! Damned pride!" Morely muttered angrily and spread butter on thick, black bread. But he had no other reply for Sutherland. He knew his friend well enough by now. Sutherland was indeed stubborn, and his anger at this rumor would very likely drive him from Detroit. Morely, too, was angry now, but he had no words with which to hammer reason into Sutherland's head.

Sutherland thought hard. Yes, it was his pride, but he would not remain where he was thought to be fleeing from past guilt. He was not guilty, though he was certainly fleeing the shame of disgrace. Even though he did not deserve the shame that had been forced upon him, there was little he could do to clear away the doubt that had spread among the people of Fort Detroit. Then let them doubt. Let them wonder about him if they chose to, but he would be gone. He would go north and start again. Then he thought of Ella Bently. His life was getting more complex now. What would he do about her? He loved her, of that he was sure. Perhaps that was all the more reason they should keep their feelings in check. She could never share a life in the wilderness. He could not ask her to do that, as much as she might love him.

"What be thy plans, then, lad?" Morely asked, his mouth full of bread.

"Wish I knew, Garth. But I can't think beyond this embassy to Pontiac. Not beyond that and—and—"

Morely waited, but Sutherland did not continue. The old trader knew Sutherland meant to finish his sentence with a promise to get Breton.

Morely poured more tea and grunted, "Damned stubborn Scotch pride! That's what kills too many good men, Owen. Especially good Scotchmen! Pah!"

Sutherland finished breakfast and wandered out into the fort. Morely was right: Sutherland was stubborn and proud. Perhaps his friend was also right in warning that his pride could very well cost him his life one day. But nevertheless he would go on as before. He would continue until he could go no longer, or no longer had to.

Nearby, Jeremy appeared and shouted his name. Sutherland's face lit up as the boy came bounding toward him. He caught the child and spun him around. In that moment Sutherland's troubles melted away.

Ella searched for Jeremy, knowing he would be with Sutherland, for the child had been eager to leave the breakfast table. To tell the truth, Ella had been just as anxious. She knew where to find them.

At the base of the corner blockhouse, Ella paused and listened to Jeremy's laughter up above. She smiled to herself and then went up the steep steps, and when she looked over the edge of the floor, Jeremy and Sutherland turned from their laughing and welcomed her. The boy ran to the edge of the platform and took his mother's hand, pulling her up. Sutherland stood as she came, and watched her as though he had never seen her before. She was even more beautiful than he had realized; his heart skipped.

"Good morning," she said, almost shyly.

He smiled and took her hands. Jeremy was at their side, so Sutherland was hesitant. But Ella was sure of what to do. She kissed him on the lips, and Jeremy giggled.

"What's so funny there?" Sutherland prodded the boy.

Jeremy giggled again.

Ella smiled at her son. "Jeremy, would you mind sharing Mr. Sutherland with me for a little while? I think your uncle could use you this morning. All right?"

Jeremy glanced quickly at Sutherland and then at his mother. Then, smiling, he climbed down and left them alone. Ella moved to the edge of the blockhouse and looked out over the fort. Jeremy scampered off, turning now and again to wave back at her. It made her feel very sentimental.

Sutherland was at her side, and she turned to face him, but her smile vanished when she saw he was serious, his eyes dim.

"What is it, Owen?" she asked and put a hand on his forearm. "You look unhappy again."

He walked to the opposite side of the blockhouse and stared off at the far shore of the river. He said, "Aye, lass, I'm unhappy." He turned to look at her. "And happy and unsure all at once."

Her fingers linked at her waist, and she walked slowly toward him. "I can imagine."

"Ella." He boldly grasped her arms, and his face was tightly drawn. "Ella, I don't know what it is I want to say, or how to say it, or whether there's anything to say at all, but..." He sighed and looked at her, and he struggled with his words. "Ella, I mean I've got to go—you know that, don't you?"

She weakly nodded. She felt as unsure as he then.

"I've got to go until I do what I must, but even then, I'm not sure I belong here anymore." He waited for her to speak, but she did not. She could not. She knew he had to say this. "Ella, after all that's happened here at Detroit—after all that's been said and done, I want no part of this place ever again. All right, call it Scottish pride or whatever, and it no doubt is, but I'm not perfect, no more than anyone else, and pride or anger or whatever it is will not let me stay here. I won't remain at this place with people believing what has been said about me. There are other places, other people, and there's no reason I should not go—"

Searching for elusive words, Sutherland whirled around and stalked to the parapet again, his fists clenched on the tops of the stakes. There was no way he could put his fustration into words. Now Ella was listening intently, probing the truth of what he was saying, forcing him to voice his thoughts, which came out in a way that seemed so petty, so selfish. The words might be petty, but the depth of his indignation was profound.

From behind him Ella said calmly, "You can run away, yes Owen. There's somewhere else you can go. For a time. But don't you think this story will follow you? It's come across the sea after you. It's found you here. It'll follow you again. Be sure of that. You can't always run from it."

Strange, it seemed to her. She was talking with the bravest man she had ever met. She was telling him not to run away. Strange. It made no sense at all. He turned to face her again, his eyes steady; but they were darker—as they had been when he first returned to the fort yesterday evening: like the eyes of her husband had looked for so very long. She wished she could give him comfort, as she had wanted to give John comfort, but could not.

She brought out her thought: "I wish I could help you."

"You can't. I'll have to do whatever has to be done, and I'll have to do it alone."

She came to him and put her arms around his waist. "Not alone," she said as he held her close. "I want to come with you, Owen. Jeremy, too. We want to go with you—"

He shook away and turned his back to her. "You can't! Don't you see—you can't come! No one can!"

"Owen." Gently she brought him around to face her. "I love this country. I love it because you're here. I'll love it wherever you are."

He shrugged. "Ella, Ella, lass, I've got a long road ahead of me before I'll settle down. I won't ask you to waste yourself with me now, not until—"

"You don't have to ask!"

"Ella," he whispered, and his hands drew her face to his. "Ella, you don't know what you're saying, lass. You don't know the northern wilderness. You couldn't live there. You're not meant to. No . . ."

He tried to hold himself back, but he could not, and he kissed her. They stood in silence, their thoughts racing uncontrolled.

Then she sighed and looked at him. "Tell me something, Owen. Tell me, do you—"

"I love you, Ella. That I do."

Hope and sadness, joy and mad frustration leaped within her, and he took her hands in his and kissed them.

"Don't you know," he said, "that because I love you, I cannot ask you to come with me? Don't you know what it means? I'm sworn to . . ." He clenched his teeth and gripped her hands. "I'm sworn to vengeance, Ella." Then he was without emotion. "No. That's not the kind of man for you. That's no way to live."

"Must you?"

But she knew the answer. He nodded. "I must."

"Then, when you can, come back to me. I'll wait for you—"

His hands fell to his sides. "Don't you see what you're asking for? You deserve more than that! You deserve a man who's free to love you! I'm not!"

"Will you ever be?"

He hesitated then. "I don't know. If I can be, I shall. Perhaps then—"

"Owen. Will you pursue Breton until you die? Have you sworn yourself to that? If you have, then you may already be dead. Then he's killed you, too! And if he's killed you, then something in me will die, too! But if you're not already dead, then—then there's hope, Owen. And hope—that's enough for me. But tell me, are you sworn to follow him forever?"

He put his arms on the parapet and let his chin sink down

onto them. His eyes shone with sadness. Ella knew she could ask no more. All she could do was to give—to give him what she could. But would he take it?

After some time he said without looking at her, "Ella, my life is not my own just now. Soon I'll be going with Colonel Brockhurst to Pontiac, and that may be trouble enough." He turned toward her. She faced him with a strength that moved him. "I don't know what my future might bring, but I do know I want it to hurt no one else." He caressed her soft cheek. "Especially not you, lass. You've been hurt enough."

"Owen, let me be the judge of what my life shall be."

He knew so clearly then how he was living out of time, dogged by the past and chained to the future, and his every moment was devoid of liberty. In that dreadful, dismal revelation Sutherland held fast to Ella, kept her against him until the true vision of his wretched existence filtered away, vanishing but not disappearing completely, for it drifted in the shadows of his soul like a specter.

It would return to him. It would come back to infect his mind. But in this brief time with Ella the awful side of truth was banished. In her arms the world stopped, if only for a fading instant.

"I love you, Owen." Ella said, her head against his chest. "I know you must go, but unless you tell me now you do not love me, I'll wait for you. I'll wait until you come back."

"I love you," he said. Then, as if another voice were speaking, he heard himself say, "I'll come back for you."

He was glad it was said, and wondered why he had not said it sooner. He would come back for her. Somehow, no matter what he must face, he would come back for her. And she knew he would.

In the days that followed, Ella and Sutherland grew even closer together. They spent their time with Jeremy or alone on aimless strolls through the fort. It was still too dangerous to leave the fort during the day, and from time to time concealed parties of Indians would shoot at sentries. But there was little chance of full-scale attack now. With the survivors of Captain Dalyell's reinforcements added to the garrison, there were nearly four hundred soldiers to defend the place. The fort was unusually crowded, and there was always some activity to break the boredom. Officers played croquet on the bumpy ground between the church and the munitions magazine building. Soldiers preened for the attention of the young French girls who lived in the fort, and competitions of all sorts were held, from shooting to fencing or horse races down narrow streets with ponies hitched to the small French-made sulkies.

Yet boredom settled heavily on nearly everyone at Fort Detroit—everyone but Ella and Owen and Jeremy. Their favorite place was the commandant's garden near the eastern wall. It was colorful there in the fall, with gentle reds and rusty yellow in profusion. Ella tended flowers there, and Sutherland enjoyed watching her moving about the garden, reflecting the beauty there and the colors of autumn. For the three of them it was as if grief had fled, and there were no war. For them, these days before Sutherland's mission to Pontiac were precious, aglow with happiness and contentment.

In the evenings Sutherland, Brockhurst, and Gladwin sat before the fire, smoked, and played chess. Brockhurst was a marvelous gentleman, kindly and witty. Ella could well see how he and Sutherland had become such close comrades, though their ages and ranks were far apart. Even Gladwin set aside the turmoil of his daily duties. He relegated the managing of the fort to subordinates. These were his last weeks in America, and he was not without regret that he would leave behind a life so wholly different from the life he would resume as an English country gentleman. He was eager to return to Frances, who patiently awaited him at their estate in Derbyshire. He had not spoken of it with Ella yet, but he presumed she and Jeremy would not be coming back with him. Well, time would tell. For the moment he was thoroughly enjoying the companionship of Sutherland and Brockhurst. Not since those happy days when the charming Sir Robert Davers had stayed with him had Henry been so cheerful. Those days seemed all so very, very long ago, as though it were another life and had happened to another person.

Gladwin had every expectation that Colonel Bouquet's victory near Fort Pitt would help convince Pontiac to give up this war. Though Gladwin feared for the safety of the emissaries, the presence of the French officer—who would arrive any day now—was strong assurance that the Indians would not only honor the flag of truce these men would bear but might even believe what the Frenchman would tell them about peace being signed between France and England.

For Sutherland the few days spent at Detroit waiting for the French officer to arrive proved to him that, indeed, there were many in the fort whose manner toward him had become uneasy, unsure. More than once he heard men talking when they did not know he was nearby, and often they spoke about the rumor concerning Sutherland's dishonor. It angered him and saddened him to see eyes averted, to receive cool greetings from people who once had been friendly. It troubled him, but he braced himself against it, and he was grateful when friends like the Morelys and Reverend Lee were no different than they had ever been with him. But even after Duvall returned to the fort he seldom saw the major—thanks to Lee.

Reverend Lee had been watching the romance between Sutherland and Ella with interest, because in the four months he had been minister for the English at Detroit, he had performed not one marriage. On more than one occasion he hinted to Sutherland that he was getting out of practice, but Sutherland joked aside Lee's light hearted comments. All the same Lee knew Sutherland would like nothing more than to bring Ella to the altar. But that he could not yet do, not until the mission to Pontiac was completed and André Breton caught.

Lee thought them a handsome couple. When Jeremy was with them, the reverend ruefully clucked his tongue and said they already looked like a happy family. He never voiced his own inner fear that they might never realize that future. Rather, he chortled to all who would listen that Ella and Owen and Jeremy deserved each other, and prayed that it might be the will of the Lord that their bliss would endure.

And Lee had done his part to help it along:

The schooner *Huron* had come back from Fort Niagara soon after the return of Sutherland. It was a dangerous trip, for Indian canoes had found the craft becalmed at the mouth of the river two nights before. Under cover of a mist the canoes slipped up to the ship, and the braves scrambled over the side. There were only twelve men on board, including Major Duvall, but they fought ferociously against the attackers. Yet for all their courage, there was no hope. The captain and another crewman were killed, and every sailor was cut, but they wielded pikes and cutlasses without thought of surrender.

The ship was crawling with Indians, and the whites were surrounded on the deck, then the first mate screamed an order for a seaman to blow up the powder magazine rather than permit the Indians to capture it. "Blow it up!" he bellowed. "If we're going, by God, we'll take these devils with us!"

Just as the sailor was about to obey the order, Indians who understood English shouted warnings and leaped from the ship.

In a twinkling, all the attackers were screeching and jumping into the water. To their amazement the survivors stood unopposed on the vessel. Quickly they manned the ship's cannon and opened fire on the retreating canoes until there was nothing left to shoot at.

Spent, painfully cut on his arms from that fight, Major Duvall was glad to return to Detroit. His wounds would soon heal, particularly if he asked the lovely Mistress Bently to tend him. As he lowered himself down the ship's rope ladder to the gig waiting below, Duvall held on with his teeth to a small package he had carried all the way from Fort Niagara. In the wrapping was a Swiss clock, intricate in design and very expensive. He had purchased it from an officer returning to England who had no room to pack all his belongings. The clock would make a perfect gift for Ella.

Duvall went directly to Gladwin's house and there greeted Colonel Brockhurst, who had once been his superior officer. Duvall knew the colonel did not believe in Sutherland's guilt, but he still held the older officer in high regard. Duvall had been told at Niagara that Brockhurst was on his way to Detroit. In that first half hour of conversation, Duvall learned of the Colonel's plans to carry the flag of truce to Pontiac. His offer to join the embassy was accepted.

Gladwin warned Duvall of the dangers, but the Major was not swayed, for no matter what else he was, Alex Duvall was a brave man. Furthermore, if Owen Sutherland was to go along with Brockhurst, it would not do for Duvall to remain at home sitting on his hands.

After his interview with Brockhurst, Duvall set out to find Ella, who, he was told, was in the flower garden. On his way, with the Swiss clock under one aching arm, Duvall encountered Reverend Lee, who cheerfully welcomed him back and asked for news of the East. Duvall impatiently muttered what little came to mind and began to walk on, for he was within sight of the garden, and he thought he could make out Ella in a light brown dress. But he found Lee again at his side, still talking.

Now Duvall was sure Ella was really there. He quickened his pace, but Lee caught Duvall's attention when he said, "They certainly make a lovely couple, don't they?"

Duvall stopped short. "What's that you say, Reverend?"

"I said it's wonderful to see Mistress Bently and Owen together," and he pointed to Sutherland's tall figure leaning against the palisade. Duvall had not noticed him, because the

Scotsman was in the shadows. Lee went on: "And everyone is saying what a lovely couple they make. Don't you agree, Major? They'll no doubt marry when Sutherland comes back from this embassy to Pontiac. That'll be capital, capital, indeed! My first wedding!" Lee became rapturous and babbled on about that anticipated wedding, his bespectacled eyes uplifted to the blue sky, his hands folded before him.

"Wedding, did you say?" Duvall's cuts were even more painful now. His arms felt stiff. The Swiss clock was unbearably heavy, though it was no larger than his fist.

"Won't it be wonderful, indeed?" Lee prattled. "And of course, as future commander of Detroit, Major, we'll expect you to sit in a place of honor in the front row! That'll be so very, very exciting for all of us!"

But Lee's last words were spoken to Duvall's back, for the tall major was stamping across the parade ground toward the open water gate. The package was clutched in one hand, and he swung it roughly, as though it were hateful. As he watched Duvall stamp off, Lee tapped his fingertips together and rocked on his heels. He smiled, and his eyes gleamed. Not even his most formidable sermon had been so decisively successful in swaying an audience. Duvall disappeared through the gate, and Reverend Lee felt just the slightest twinge of Christian remorse at his own scheming. But he looked briefly at Ella and Owen cutting flowers, and his heart danced. He hummed as he walked away and thought it would be appropriate if he asked Ella Bently to supply his makeshift little church—which was still temporarily arranged in a spare barracks—with flowers every Sunday until the frost came. In a way, he thought, he had quite earned them.

At the river's edge a fuming Major Duvall kicked hard at a stone, sending it skittering and splashing into the water. Someone shouted that he should be inside the fort during daylight, for the Indians often took pot shots at men working near the ships. He ignored the warning and swore resoundingly, seething and boiling with fury. He paced up and down the beach, kicking and muttering until it was of no further use. Then, as though his arms were not sore, Duvall leaned back and hurled the Swiss clock far out into the river. It plopped and vanished from sight. He stood, eyes aflame, breath rising and rushing in anger. He had lost after all! He had lost her! And he had lost her to that damned Sutherland!

It galled him. Alex Duvall did not lose easily. And when it came to women he wanted, he had never yet lost at all.

That same day the post and dispatches that came in on the *Huron* were distributed, and Sutherland was surprised to receive a letter from Mary Hamilton. It had been sent, not from Fort Pitt, where he had left her, but from Fort Niagara. Up in the blockhouse he read the letter in the presence of Ella, who listened as Mary told of her journey to Niagara and of her plans to go to Montreal, where family friends could help her pass the winter and prepare to give birth.

"She's a strong girl," Ella said softly, sadly, remembering Duncan McEwan and feeling she was about to weep. She sighed and looked over the wall at the river as Sutherland, seated on a bench, began to read again.

"Toby is well and growing fast," he read. *"She's a comfort to me, Mr. Sutherland, and again I thank you for your kindness in leaving her with me. I know how much you—"* the next two words were scribbled out, but Sutherland knew they were and Duncan—*love Toby as well as I do, so I must assure you that she is in good hands, as I shall be on arrival at Montreal. The military have been most kind in aiding me, and I have received some pay due Duncan, which will bring me through the next few months.*

"Although I do not know whether we will ever see one another again, sir, it is my fondest hope that we shall meet once more in happier circumstances, and in a world where men are kind to one another. But that I doubt will ever come to be in our lifetime. Perhaps in the time of our children.

"Forgive me, Mr. Sutherland for burdening you with my melancholy. Be confident that I and Toby, and Duncan's child who lives within me, will make a new life for ourselves. Once again, my deepest thanks for all you have done. I shall write you once more from Montreal. Your devoted friend, Mary."

They were silent for some time after Sutherland finished reading. Then Ella turned to him and said, "She's strong indeed. I'd like to meet her someday."

Sutherland folded the letter and put it in his coat pocket. "Yes," he nodded. "I'd like to see her once more, and Toby, too, and . . . the baby."

"Duncan's baby." Ella looked closely at Sutherland, who did not look up. "It is . . . his child, is it not?"

Sutherland sighed. "If Mary Hamilton says it's Duncan's child, then I'll believe her. I only pray, for the child's sake, that everyone else believes her, too,"

Two days later Monsieur Pierre de Quinot arrived at Detroit after an arduous journey from the French Fort Chartres on the Mississippi River, five hundred miles to the southwest. He was in his late thirties, a major in the French Army, and an impeccably dressed and mannered gentleman. From the first, de Quinot struck the British officers as a trustworthy and gallant man. He gave them hope, for he had known Chief Pontiac years ago and had fought alongside the warrior against the English. He told them also that he had served in Europe twenty years earlier, in the War of the Austrian Succession.

Sutherland was intrigued by this short, slender officer, who looked familiar to him, although they had never met when Sutherland was the only British trader living in the French-held territory around Fort Detroit. They brushed off this seeming familiarity when de Quinot said he had been often to Fort Detroit when it was French; Owen Sutherland might have seen him then and now recalled a face, but nothing more. De Quinot did not remember meeting Sutherland, but when Major Duvall was introduced to the Frenchman, who was fluent in English, de Quinot stood back and thoughtfully observed the officer.

"Have we met before, Major Duvall?" he asked. "Have you been in this country before? With the British forces accepting surrender of our forts, perhaps?"

Duvall shook his head and laughed. "No, no, monsieur, we've not met before, I assure you. I've only been in this wilderness for four months—and I've hardly set foot outside this godforsaken fort because of all the trouble your redskinned former allies have caused us! No, monsieur, I'd remember you if ever I'd met you before."

Just the same, de Quinot was not put off in his curiosity. But he turned to the business at hand, and a meeting was held in Gladwin's house to plan the embassy. The request for the parley with Pontiac had been delivered by a French resident of Detroit, and the chief had agreed to receive them. De Quinot was warned about the murder of Captain Campbell, and though his face flushed slightly at the doleful story of Campbell's betrayal while going to Pontiac under a flag of truce, the Frenchman was resolute.

"There has been enough bloodshed in this beautiful country," he said softly while sitting at Gladwin's table the day before they were to depart on the mission. "If there is any way I can help put an end to the killing, I shall. The sooner the Indians accept peace terms, the safer will life be for the French who live in this country. They are in great peril also, for at any moment the Indians might grow angry that the French have not risen up with them against your fort, and then my people would be massacred. I have many friends among the *habitants* and *métis* here, and their welfare is in my heart.

"Gentlemen," he said to the others, who included Gladwin, Brockhurst, Duvall, and Sutherland, "my orders are to help bring peace to this country now that a truce has been signed between our kings. Pray to God, we never again shall fight."

They all toasted with brandies, but in their souls these men knew that peace between France and England was only temporary. Peace between those mighty foes had always been merely lulls while a new generation of young men grew up learning stories of their forefathers' valor and with the hatred of the other nation branded in their blood. The liquor was not easy in going down even though every man in the room wished it were.

This dinner at Gladwin's house—with the men who would go to Pontiac joining Gladwin and Ella—was more sober than anyone had intended it to be. Every sally at good humor seemed to fall flat. Cheer and joviality were short-lived and needed constant stoking. By the end of the evening all were eager to get to bed. The tension of anticipation, of uncertainty, gripped them, and each was anxious to get under way.

Only Ella and Sutherland wished to prolong the evening. Duvall, who was dull and morose for most of the meal, and who said few words to anyone, departed early. Ella and Sutherland went for a walk in the crisp air of mid-September. Winter was not far off, and the cold sky and sparkling stars in the deep of night recalled past winters, when the lakes froze and lonely Detroit was isolated from the world.

As they walked, Sutherland reminded Ella of those coming long and suffocating months inside the fort.

"Nothing could have better prepared me for winter here than this past dreadful siege, Owen," she said and tugged her beaver-pelt wrap closer about her shoulders. He drew her to him. Without further words they walked toward the council house.

Inside, Owen pulled Ella roughly against him, and she felt his fiery passion. She kissed him desperately. All that had been kept within surged, released in that instant. All the worries, hopes, and dread burst in that lingering kiss. Ella's mind whirled with love and fear; and he kissed her again and again and again. Tears poured free, and she laughed and wept all at the same time. He ran his fingers through her hair and kissed her face, her forehead, her hands.

"My darling, Owen," she murmured. "My dearest darling, Owen." She wanted to say so much more but could not.

Her heart was pounding with longing. He wanted her then, completely, without thought, only with love.

Ella yielded and held him closer than she ever dreamed she could. For an eternity they touched souls and were one. They were beyond happiness, beyond joy.

Sutherland lit the candle standing on the spinet and closed the tinderbox. Ella sat down at the spinet, and he went to his place against the wall, where he usually sat to listen as she played.

The music rang in minor chords, sad and wandering. Her hands were hesitant, clumsy, and indecisive at first. He came to her and sat at her side. She looked at him and smiled, but tears appeared again. He kissed her, then shared with her his thoughts of the past few days. "My Ella, listen to me. I'm coming back to you. Trust that, darling." He put his fingers against her face and held them there. "And when I come back, we'll make a home here, near Detroit."

She stammered, but he pressed his fingers against her lovely lips, and she kissed his hand.

"I know," he said, "I'll never be happy without you, and I know you can be happy here. We'll never want, and you'll have a life that'll be right for you."

"Owen, I—I'll do whatever you—"

"I'll do what's good for you, Ella." He slowly shook his head and smiled at her. "I see now that Detroit is where I belong. I see that. It might never be perfect, but with you and Jeremy, it'll be nearly so."

He kissed her, and she trembled with fear and joy. Now she just needed the strength to wait for him.

"I know you'll come back to me."

He gave a little smile, and his eyes shone in the glint of the candle. He looked happy at last. She kissed him softly and prayed with all her might that Owen would return safely. Safely, please, Lord, and with those same happy eyes that caressed her now. She had made this prayer before for a man she once loved, but her wish had not been granted. Now with every essence of her being she prayed that Owen be restored to her, complete, and loving her as he loved her now. Was that so very much to ask?

After Sutherland returned to the Morelys', he sleepily sat on his cot, a board across his lap. On the board was another sheet of paper. At his feet lay a dozen crumpled pieces, all scribbled in Sutherland's steady hand. Concentrating, he read again— for the fifth time—the words he had written so haltingly, so inadequately.

Yes, that said it as best he could. Perhaps in the morning it would be hopeless as so many poems were when exposed to the day. But for now this expressed his heart. He dipped the quill into the pot of ink on the floor, and at the top of the paper he wrote, "Ella."

chapter 23

TO PONTIAC

The morning, fresh and bright, could not have been more beautiful. The air was cool, with the smell of autumn and smoke in the breeze; a strong wind gusted down the straits, but it was not powerful enough to hazard the canoe being readied to take the four men up to Pontiac's camp. Hauled up on shore below the fort, the canoe was laden with presents for Pontiac and his chiefs. There were beads, English knives, axes, bolts of cloth, and several soldier's hats bundled in the bottom of the craft.

Sutherland carried a pistol stuck in his belt, as did Duvall. All the officers wore swords, and Sutherland's claymore hung from his waist. They looked a proud and capable party as they stood at the edge of the river and bade farewell to those who had come to see them off. More than a hundred residents of the fort stood uneasily in the background, hopeful that these men would not fail. All had been sickened by the long siege and wanted peace before the coming of winter.

Gladwin shook hands all around, then Ella came to Sutherland, who kissed her cheek and held her close for a moment. Duvall, standing nearby, looked away. He realized they were unaware of his presence. As he stood with Gladwin, Brockhurst, and de Quinot, mechanically exchanging with the men final words of farewell and encouragement, he thought that *he* should be the one whom Ella was embracing. He was the better man, and he would prove it.

As Ella and Sutherland parted, he reached inside his hunting shirt and drew out an envelope.

"When, I'm gone, open it." An impulse brought Sutherland's hand to the silver pendant, which had slipped out of his shirt and hung free. For an instant he thought he might put it around Ella's neck, but she reached for it, her eyes on his, and placed it back beneath his shirt.

"For good luck," she smiled.

He saw the tears brimming in her eyes as she moved away to stand alongside her brother. The canoe was pushed into the water, the men climbed in, and a soldier gave it a last shove away from the bank. Sutherland, who sat at the stern of the craft, waved once, took up a paddle, and thrust it deep into the water. The others followed his stroke, and soon the canoe was shooting out into the current.

Ella lingered with Gladwin after the others had gone back to the fort. She looked at the envelope in her hand. Henry put an arm about her shoulders, and they walked back up to the gate. Before she entered, she turned once and saw the vanishing speck of the canoe.

She asked Henry to tell her son she would come soon, then went alone to the blockhouse where she and Owen had discovered their love. There she sat on the rough-hewn bench and opened the envelope, breaking the red sealing wax with nervous fingers. There were two sheets of paper within. The first was a letter from Owen addressed to her. She was on the verge of weeping as she read it, for it said she would inherit all that he owned should misfortune befall him on the mission. She did not want to read such a depressing letter, but she forced herself to finish it, and she read again and again Owen's closing, "With all my love, dearest Ella."

She did not know what to think and preferred not to think anything just then. She tucked the letter into the envelope and unfolded the second paper. As she read, her heart filled with joy.

ELLA

> My time of searching passes on,
> Like wind through winter grass,
> And all my soul finds comfort here,
> Takes heed of love at last.

The wind blew dry leaves that rustled along the river wall and dusted the blockhouse. Cold, forgotten ashes of another season. But Ella did not feel the cold. Inside she was aflame with happiness.

He would come back! He would!

All along the bank of the Detroit River, crowds of Indians gathered to watch the passing canoe. They had not seen an English party moving in peace on the water since those leaves that now were dull reds and withered yellows had been green buds. The men in the canoe sat stoically, not heeding the thousands who watched them. More than once Sutherland wondered if André Breton was among them. More than once he suggested they paddle farther away from shore to prevent a hostile Indian from shooting at them.

Brockhurst had never seen so many Indians before. Duvall was glum and wordless, and the Frenchman, de Quinot, seemed lost in reveries that recalled days when this land was under the French crown. The only occasion on which de Quinot spoke was to ask Duvall once more whether they had been previously acquainted. Duvall had replied without much interest that they had not, as far as he could tell.

At last they arrived before the great village of Chief Pontiac, which had been moved back again to its original site on the other side of the river. There were hundreds of wigwams made of skins and bent saplings and shaped like rude upside-down bowls. At least a thousand people lived in this village alone, though hundreds more had come to witness the parley between their chiefs and their enemies. The presence of a French officer startled many Indians. As they stood back, gaping at the men disembarking from the canoe, the Indians muttered with surprise to see de Quinot in his gleaming white uniform accented with gold and black. Of all the members of the little party the Frenchman was most impressive in dress. The scarlet English tunics on Brockhurst and Duvall were no match for the splendor of the Frenchman; and if Sutherland had not been so well known among the Ottawa, Chippewa, and Huron who saw him come, his frontier hunting shirt would have obscured him despite his height and stately bearing.

Without the slightest sign of fear the four men strode through the Indian village, ignoring dark and hateful looks on every side. It took discipline to walk so unflinchingly, and more than once Sutherland—who went first—had to kick away a snapping dog that sensed the hostility all around. Sutherland's thoughts raced. He felt at home in this encampment, where many former friends and family still dwelt. Here were Mayla's people, and here he had taught Molo much and learned from him as well. Here he had lived from time to time as one of the tribesmen. Here he had once been welcome as a family welcomes its beloved son.

But now Sutherland felt only anger in these faces. He was an outsider now. After all those happy years Owen Sutherland—Donoway, once—had again become a white man, an enemy. Not just any enemy, but one who stood with men who symbolized the doom of the Indian nations. As much as it troubled him. Sutherland thought he would never again be an honored son of the Ottawa. Yet no matter what had come to pass, he must strive with all his power to bring peace to this unhappy country. Today, standing before the judgment of the greatest chiefs for hundreds of miles, Donoway would speak as one who loved the Indians, even if they loved him no more.

Ahead, through an alley of Indians and squat huts, was a great crowd of warriors and chiefs around the council fire. These would hear the words of the English and the French who claimed to own this sacred land the Indian knew belonged to the spirits and could never be owned by a man. The village was utterly silent as the four whites approached, walking through the alley into the broad circle of silent humanity. The smell of smoke was in the air, and meat cooking, simmering on small fires, wafted its fragrance throughout the village. The odor of curing hides and bodies smeared with sweet bear grease was overpowering to Brockhurst. This experience was utterly new to him. They came into the center of several hundred warriors, sitting cross-legged, bedecked with feathers and bright blankets, painted vermillion, and blackened in the face with soot.

Pontiac was there, massive and imposing, glowering and grim. His shoulders were covered by a shaggy buffalo robe, but his chest was bare and adorned in ceremonial swirls and streaks of red and blue. The small bone crescent dangled from his nose. Sutherland stood before Pontiac, and the others came behind. The Scotsman laid his bundle of presents at the great chief's feet. Saying nothing, Pontiac motioned with a hand for the whites to sit on his left. Still no one spoke.

Stone pipes were lit by the score and handed to all the seated men. A half hour passed before the tobacco was smoked, and everyone in turn had puffed. Sutherland looked straight ahead, above the heads of the Indians, most of whom were watching him closely. He had told Brockhurst and Duvall what to expect during the ceremonies, and de Quinot needed no advice. They waited patiently for Pontiac to formally welcome them.

At last, when the ground began to feel hard and their bones were stiffened from sitting, the whites saw Pontiac rise and stride into the center of the council. He stood at the roaring fire, oblivious of the smoke that buffeted around him when the wind changed, and raised an arm laden with silver jewelry above his head.

"Welcome, white brothers, to the council of the Ottawa, Huron, and Chippewa in this village," Pontiac began in a booming voice that carried far above the crowd of braves listening. Sutherland was surprised that the chief called the English by the courteous term "brother." He wondered what that meant, for he had expected the Indian to express only scorn and hatred for the English. Now, even at this early stage in the parley, Sutherland had hope for success, but he did not yet know why.

"It has been too long since the son of the Great French Father has sat in council with the Indian, and it has been too long since the sons of the English Great Father have come to us with words of peace." Sutherland was astonished at Pontiac's kind words. What was he up to? What did he want? Was this another deception?

"And welcome to Donoway, who once was a son of the Ottawa, but who has now returned to the arms of the English. We welcome Donoway, even though he has fought against us and even though we promised him death if he did so. We welcome him because he brings with him delegates who seek peace with the Indian."

The fire crackled and sparked furiously, and the smoke rushed among the audience. But for barking dogs, the village was silent. After a lengthy and unexpectedly generous welcome, Pontiac sat down, and Sutherland, who had translated, waited the appropriate ten minutes of polite contemplation of the chief's words before rising to speak. He looked about at the mighty force of warriors, resplendent in warlike finery. For a fleeting moment he saw what they might become: fighters, lying by the hundreds, feathers flickering in the wind, destroyed by English cannon. Then he spoke and gave the proper lengthy introduction:

"My brothers, we are grateful that you have greeted us in peace. For there indeed has been too much war between the white man and the Indian. We have come with a promise of goodwill and love from the English Great Father whose children you are, and from the French Great Father, whose children you once were. Before you we have laid these gifts, and after we return to the fort, we shall send back many more gifts for all of you, so that your hearts and ears may be open to our words of friendship, and you shall understand them."

Sutherland spoke for ten minutes before coming to the point of his oration. Then he said, "For those who have been the loved ones of Donoway, I say this—Donoway loves his Indian brothers and sisters still. It is because he wants peace that he has fought to stop this war. It is because Donoway desires his Indian people to live in happiness and prosperity that he has come among you and brought these other white men who shall witness to you that the great war between the English and the French has come to an end at last."

The warriors and chiefs stirred and grumbled at these words of Anglo-French peace. Seated nearby, neither Brockhurst nor Duvall understood Sutherland, who spoke in Ottawa, but they felt hostility rise from the braves all around them. Duvall looked around the circle at the faces, and he saw they were angry and sullen. Then he looked up at Sutherland, who continued to speak in a firm and brave voice, and he suddenly wondered who indeed was the better man. Here was the man he condemned and despised, resolutely standing in front of hostile Indians, attempting to bring peace to all the peoples of this harsh land. What had he, Duvall, done? Nothing, nothing at all. Maybe Duvall had lost after all.

The Indians continued to listen to Sutherland, who was now mentioning the Paris peace treaty, and they began to mutter to each other. Then the Indian whispering rose to a level like waves breaking on a shore, and Pontiac raised his hand and held it aloft until the crowd quieted. Then Sutherland introduced Monsieur de Quinot as the son of the Great French Father, "who has come to bear witness to the love that now exists between the English and the French."

Proudly, nobly, and with a deep baritone that resounded about the council grounds, de Quinot addressed the gathering. He drew out a scroll of parchment he had kept in a satchel at his side, unrolled it, and read a translation of the French proclamation that was authorized by King Louis himself.

"Open your ears, my children, that my words may penetrate even to the bottom of your hearts. It has pleased the Master of Life to inspire the great King of the French and Him of the

English to make peace between them, sorry to see the blood of men spilled for so long. It is for this reason that they have ordered all their chiefs and warriors to lay down their arms, and we acquaint you of this news to ask you to bury the tomahawk, doing it, I hope, with joy in seeing the French and the English smoking with the same pipe and eating with the same spoon . . ."

The Indians listened; they understood, and their hearts were heavy, for they had been abandoned. As de Quinot spoke, all hope of a French army coming to support the uprising faded and vanished. There would be no alliance with the French. There was only the poorly armed Indian to stand against English thunder guns. Every warrior present who had seen the white armies in battle during the French and Indian war respected their power. Even though the English soldier had been viewed with disdain at the outbreak of the hostilities, the outcome at Bushy Run and the failure to capture Forts Pitt and Detroit had proven that they were not cowards. No Indian in that encampment deluded himself into believing that they had yet seen the full might of English firepower.

But they had hoped a French army would arrive before that power was brought to bear. The uprising had begun successfully, and the Indians had done much to clear the way for the once-anticipated French. Now, as de Quinot read the proclamation calling for the Indians to stop fighting, warriors and chiefs knew there was little hope of victory. All they could do was fight to the death. Yet many were willing to do just that, for they were courageous men who knew that to lose this war meant the beginning of an end to their way of life.

De Quinot went on: "I, the great King of the French, depend on you, that you do not make me lie, and that your young men will not take up the tomahawk. Leave off, then, my dear children, from spilling the blood of your brothers, the English. Our hearts are now one. You cannot at present strike the one without having the other for your enemy also . . ."

And so it went. The Indians were cast down into the abyss of solitude. All they had done melted into futility with every word de Quinot spoke. Their father was now the English king. Their destiny now lay in the hands of a people who refused to give them gifts out of respect, who withheld precious gunpowder and ammunition, and who scorned them as lower beings.

When de Quinot sat down, the Indians were silent. Sutherland felt the excruciating weight of dismay settle on the masses around him. He glanced at Pontiac, but the chief was impassive, sitting erect, head up, proud, and unperturbed. Just then it occurred to Sutherland that the crafty old warrior might have known all along this news of French abandonment was coming. That might have been the reason for Pontiac's gracious welcome to the embassy. Perhaps the chief fully expected what he had just heard and had resolved to make the best of the situation. Winter was coming on, and the majority of Indians must travel southward to winter quarters, where the game migrated, and where there was provision for bad weather.

Sutherland realized that the Indians could never keep up the siege of Detroit throughout the bitter winter months. They could never sustain themselves in the crowded country around Detroit. As much as anyone else they needed a respite from the war. They needed to depart—at least until springtime.

Now doubt began to form in Sutherland's mind. It was possible that—despite the loss of French support—Pontiac sought merely to move to winter quarters in safety, without fear of English attack, and then he would resume the war in the spring. That was likely. But whatever Pontiac's motives for receiving this delegation of peace, Sutherland was grateful that the Indians now knew the bitter truth about the misplaced hope for French intervention.

After an appropriate wait Sutherland stood and introduced Brockhurst, who rose before the crowd and spoke with dignity and in as imposing a voice as had the Frenchman. Sutherland stood at Brockhurst's side and translated for the Indians. The colonel said the English regretted that the war had broken out through misunderstanding. He promised to present the Indians' complaints before the king, and he said the English wished their Indian children to live in peace and happiness until the very end of time.

But as Sutherland and Brockhurst sat down, it felt as though the colonel's words had fallen on skeptical ears—ears that had already closed to them.

After some time Pontiac and his chiefs arose and departed from the council fire. The other warriors also stood and crowded away. Several young braves came to the whites and led them to a small lodge, telling them to remain within the bark-and-skin-covered shelter until morning, when Pontiac would give his reply to the English offer of peace. Remain, they were told, and do not wander through the village—for their own safety.

Ella was in the parlor reading Shakespeare's sonnets when she heard a soft tread on the porch, followed by the clump of a soldier's boots. She answered the knock at the door and was startled to see Tamano with the young corporal of the guard, who removed his hat and asked for Gladwin. Ella said the major was meeting with his officers, and the soldier spoke to Tamano, asking the tall, dark Chippewa to follow him. But Tamano said to Ella, "Where Donoway?"

"He's gone to Pontiac's camp with an offer of peace for the Indians," she said. "He left this morning with other officers."

Tamano's face hardened.

"Tamano," she said quickly, "have you news for Owen? Is there trouble?"

The Chippewa straightened up and said, "Breton come. He go to Pontiac soon. Want Donoway. Plenty trouble, sure. Plenty big trouble."

As Tamano began to follow the corporal, Ella fought back the fear that gripped her and called to him, "Tamano! Can you do something? Can you help him?"

The Indian stood still and stared at her. Then he said, "Tamano go. Maybe too late."

Ella felt faint. Tamano and the soldier walked away in search of Gladwin.

Ella returned to her parlor, but she had lost what little calm contemplation she had earlier called up. The book of sonnets lay closed in her lap. She gazed unseeing out the window. Indeed, waiting for Owen to return would be a lonely vigil. She closed her eyes, wishing for peace. How very much she wished for peace, but it would not come.

It was dim in the Indian lodge, and the air was rancid with smoke, sweat, and old leather. The four men lay on blankets around a small fire. Firelight flitted on their faces, and all but de Quinot smoked pipes. They had been silent for some time, pondering Sutherland's suspicion that the Indians might want only a temporary peace until the winter was past. They knew there was no choice other than to accept even a sham peace treaty if it were offered. At least Detroit could be reinforced by a stronger army, and plans could be laid out to strengthen

the frontier garrisons and display force that might dissuade the
Indians from rising the following spring.

De Quinot sighed and yawned and removed his white coat
and breeches before sliding under an Indian blanket. Sutherland
pulled the woolen blanket up over his shoulders and tried to
sleep. He had seen no sign of André Breton, and there were
no Delaware warriors present at the village, as far as he could
tell. He wished he had his rifle with him, but he had known
in advance that he would not be permitted to carry a rifle into
the village. He was glad that he and Duvall at least kept their
pistols by their sides. They were not much, he knew, but better
than nothing at all. Well, Pontiac's answer would come in the
morning, and they would go soon after; Fort Detroit was only
a short distance away.

Sutherland heard Duvall and de Quinot talking quietly. The
conversation was about the war in Europe twenty years ago.
Then suddenly de Quinot slapped his forehead and sat up.

"*Sacre bleu!* Of course! Of course, *mon ami!* Now I remember everything! Duvall! Yes, yes, that was the name! It
stayed with me all these years because it was a French name!
Of course, *mon ami,* we have indeed met!" The Frenchman
was staring at Duvall across the flickering fire. Duvall was
sitting with his head cocked, listening. Brockhurst was next
to him, and Sutherland could see all of them in the semidarkness
as in a reddish haze.

"The Lowlands!" De Quinot said eagerly. "You were in the
Flemish Lowlands, no?"

Duvall said nothing, but nodded vaguely, almost suspiciously. Sutherland was listening more closely now.

De Quinot chuckled softly and said, "Do you not remember
me, monsieur? I was only nineteen at the time, and you were
a young captain, were you not? Yes, that was a stiff fight, a
stiff fight, indeed, *mon ami.* I remember it well."

So, thought Sutherland, after his country had been defeated
in North America, this Frenchman had found something he
could boast about. Each of the men de Quinot addressed at that
moment had suffered at that battle in Europe. But certainly the
Frenchman did not realize the painful memories he was calling
up. On Duvall's face anguish was already showing, and his
eyes were shaded, avoiding the French officer's eager gaze.

"Do you not recall me, the one named Antoine?" De Quinot
thrust his face forward so Duvall could look more closely at

it. But Duvall actually seemed to shrink from the face, as though it frightened him. Sutherland was curious, and he listened closely. Brockhurst, paying little attention, puffed absently on his pipe and watched the fire.

"No?" De Quinot asked and leaned back. "Major Duvall, you must remember me, eh? The one who knew so much about the Flemish beauties! Aha! Aha! Yes, I think I see a gleam in your eye that recalls those days, that night: that lovely lady I brought to your quarters!"

Sutherland saw Duvall's eyes were gleaming, but with anxiety, not fond recollection. De Quinot was laughing.

"But *oui*, Major Duvall, we have met. One day we must—"

"*Yes!*" Sutherland growled and sat up. He crawled close to de Quinot, who was startled by this outburst. "Yes, you both certainly have met, monsieur, and so have we!"

"Eh?" The Frenchman was unsure of what Sutherland was saying.

"Nonsense! Nonsense!" Duvall grunted and crept back against the side of the lodge. "We've never met, monsieur! I fear you are mista—"

"He's not!" Sutherland was angry. "You know him, Duvall, he was one of your Walloon spies!"

"Monsieur, monsieur," de Quinot muttered nervously. "It is hardly appropriate to be specific in this matter! I do not know where you got your information, but I must decline to discuss this matter further. I had no idea you were in any way aware of what I was saying. I apologize most sincerely to Major Duvall, for I had no intention of . . . of . . ." De Quinot looked distressed as he eyed Duvall, who was huddled in the shadows.

"Of embarrassing Major Duvall?" Sutherland said calmly. "Is that what you were about to say, sir?"

"Why, why, this is none of your affair!" De Quinot was truly sorry he had brought this up. He had meant to hint at it with Duvall and then, later, share recollections of those days in Europe. But now it appeared as if he had indeed put Duvall in an embarrassing situation. The Frenchman tried to elude Sutherland's penetrating stare.

"Monsieur!" Sutherland said. "It is most certainly my affair. Look closely at me—Antoine! Look closely and think about that dispatch officer you met at the inn. Yes, I am he! I am the one you drugged!"

De Quinot was speechless. His mouth hung open. He

glanced at Duvall and back to Sutherland. They were silent. Brockhurst sat, eyes wide, his pipe in his hands. De Quinot peered at Sutherland, then nodded faintly. "Indeed, you are the one."

Before Sutherland could speak, Duvall raged and threw aside his blanket in fury. "Enough! Enough such gabbling about the past! Let it lie! It's dead and gone! There's peace now, don't you both see that? Why talk about—" he met Sutherland's hard eyes "—the—the—past?" He sat back once more and brought his knees up to cover his face.

Sutherland turned again to the flushed de Quinot.

"And, Antoine, I must say you did your work very well—"

"Monsieur, I really do not wish to go into this at the moment. As Major Duvall so aptly said—"

"The past is not dead for me, sir." Sutherland said and knelt before the Frenchman. "Not yet. You see, when you drugged me and stole the dispatches—Hah! Yes, yes, Monsieur de Quinot, you were very good at what you did!" Sutherland was grinning warmly, and the Frenchman, abashed, found himself smiling. "Very good, indeed," Sutherland said and clapped his thigh. "I only wish we had a few like you on our side. Tell me, what did you use in that drink? It worked in a wink. Best night's sleep I've ever had!"

De Quinot laughed good-naturedly. Then he leaned toward Sutherland, put a finger to his lips, and whispered, "That's a secret. Old family recipe. My grandmother used it when grandfather became too passionate. Worked every time. It had to; she already had ten children!" De Quinot burst into roaring laughter, leaned back and laughed and laughed until he realized that he heard only his own laughter. He looked around. Duvall was lying on his side, face buried in his blanket. Brockhurst was pale, and Sutherland was staring at the ground.

"Well," de Quinot said, annoyed. "I thought the English had a sense of humor! No? Well, gentlemen, I'm sorry if my joking was inappropriate. I realize you lost very heavily in that campaign, and I realize full well that the success of our espionage was instrumental in it all. But, dear me, gentlemen, there's no need to be so morose at a time like this. We're at peace. I'm sure you all have a few stories you could use to tease me! Never fear that I'll be so grim about your tales and exploits! My, my, gentlemen, what's all this sobriety? It seems to me your country won the war, after all! Come, come!"

But de Quinot's appeal fell hopelessly, without response
from the others. Glumly, he huffed and went back under his
blanket muttering something about bad manners.

Sutherland's voice cut into the quiet.

"Tell me, monsieur, was Duvall with a woman when you
drugged me? Was he drunk?"

De Quinot sat halfway up and leaned on an elbow. "That,
sir, you'll have to ask him."

"If I must," Sutherland said and drew his dagger from his
leggin, "I'll make you give me that answer."

"Owen!" Brockhurst hissed. "Steady yourself, man! Put that
knife away! That's an order!"

Sutherland was calm. De Quinot was as grim as he. Sutherland said, "I'm not in the army now, Colonel. I'll have the
truth now. I'll have it, or—"

Brockhurst stood up quickly. He towered above them all,
his legs spread apart, and he looked every bit the leader he had
always been.

De Quinot sat up and said, "Monsieur Sutherland, if you
are a gentleman, then you must fully understand that I'll never
answer your question. If you seek satisfaction in the field, then
I request that you wait until we return to Fort Detroit. At that
time we shall settle this matter in an appropriate manner."

Sutherland felt the breath leave him all at once. Above him
Brockhurst stood ready for trouble. This Frenchman was jus-
tified in refusing to submit to Sutherland's threats. In de
Quinot's place, Sutherland would have done the same. Even
Duvall was sitting up now. He stared uncertainly at Sutherland
and de Quinot.

Sutherland relented. He let his knife hand fall. "Forgive me,
monsieur. You are quite right. I have no quarrel with you, and
I wish none. I understand your position, and I respect it. Now,
Duvall." He looked at the major. "Will you tell Colonel Brockhurst the truth or not?"

Silence again. Deadly, heavy silence.

Duvall's lower lip trembled slightly, and Sutherland was
startled to notice that his eyes were filled with fear and helplessness. "I have nothing more to say in this affair, Sutherland.
All right, so you were drugged. So you have a reason to be
forgiven. All right! Colonel Brockhurst has heard that. Isn't
that enough for you? Isn't that enough?" Edges of hysteria
crept into Duvall's voice.

Sutherland slid the knife into his leggin. He looked at Brock-hurst, who sat down again.

Brockhurst spoke. "I've heard all I need to hear, Owen. I promise you now that a full report of what Monsieur de Quinot has revealed here tonight shall be sent back to the War Ministry." Sutherland heard the elderly officer's words as though in a fog, in a dream. "I'll do everything I can to clear your reputation. Under the circumstances, Owen, I daresay that's enough."

Sutherland looked coldly at Duvall, who had curled up again and was lying facing the wall. "Enough. Yes, it'll be enough for now, Colonel. I want no revenge on the likes of him!"

Silence again.

"Let's sleep, gentlemen," Brockhurst said wearily. "We've more listening to do tomorrow. Let's pray that what we hear will mean a new era of understanding between the Indians and our government. Let's sleep now, and permit the past to die."

Sutherland went under his blankets. De Quinot lay on his side staring into the failing fire. Brockhurst was on his back, gazing up at the darkness. Sutherland tried not to recall those days so long ago, when he was young and hopeful. He had been betrayed by Duvall. He ought to hate the man, but strangely he did not. He wanted simply to be rid of him. He already had enough vengeance to take, and there was no need to add Alex Duvall to his adversaries. Duvall released a shaking sob, and then another, and the only sound in the lodge was his quiet sobbing. Suddenly all the anger dissipated from Sutherland's mind. Duvall had troubles of his own—troubles that in their own way were more terrible than any Owen Sutherland ever had to face. Duvall had to live with himself. Sutherland had to live for Ella Bently.

A chill September sun was low in the sky when the embassy sat again within a great mass of Indians. The braves were somber as they smoked the traditional pipes of tobacco to begin the council. Then Pontiac arose and with great dignity gave his reply to the English offer of peace.

"Englishmen, open your ears, that my words may reach your hearts and you shall understand them." His guttural, hoarse voice lifted and swept across the crowd. Sutherland quietly translated for Brockhurst and Duvall.

"Englishmen, you have come to our lands as enemies, but

we offered you the hand and pipe of friendship. Yet you ignored our hand and you broke the pipe. You knew well what the Indian needed to live, but you refused to give it to him, and for two terrible winters the Indian has starved for lack of ammunition with which to hunt. We have been unhappy."

Thus did the great warrior Pontiac elaborate at length on the injustices perpetrated by the English against the Indian. Thus did he tell why his people had taken the warpath, and why they were willing to fight to the death if need be to protect their families and the land from destruction by the whites. He told of insults at the hands of soldiers, of cheating by dishonest traders, of the rape of the land by an increasing tide of English settlers who put plow blades to the heart of the Earth Mother. The Indian—whose divine right it was to live upon this land, and who permitted the whites to dwell upon it out of generosity—had never once been asked permission for the use of their holy country. Instead they were scorned and threatened at every turn.

"Englishmen," Pontiac said in conclusion, "for these and other reasons I have raised the tomahawk against you. We have laid waste your settlements and slain your people. We did not want this war, but you brought it with you, and we accepted your challenge.

"Englishmen, we have believed that the Great French Father had awakened from his sleep and would send his armies to fight with us and drive the English away. But now his son sits before us and says peace has come between you and we must no longer fight, for he cannot help us.

"And so, Englishmen, I see that we can make war no longer, and unless you force us to continue to stand against you until we spill the last drop of our blood, then we shall bury the tomahawk as our French Father asks."

The Indians stirred, but not a word was spoken against Pontiac's decision, which had been reached this morning after the leading chiefs and medicine men had slept and dreamed and found counsel in sacred visions.

"The message which my French Father has sent me to make peace I have accepted. All my young men have buried their tomahawks. I think you will forget the bad things that have taken place in the past. Likewise, I shall forget what you have done to me, so we should think of nothing but good. My people, the Ottawa, and the Chippewa and the Huron are ready to speak with you to discuss the terms of peace. We await your answer."

With profound gravity Colonel Brockhurst and de Quinot rose and accepted Pontiac's pledge. The Indians slowly departed until the council ground was bare and lifeless.

Soon Sutherland and the others were in their canoe, paddling away from the village. Brockhurst turned back to Sutherland and asked: "Do you think he'll honor the peace?"

"At least until the spring, Colonel," Sutherland replied. "He can't afford an army coming after him when he's in winter camp and has nowhere to run. He'll honor it until the ice is out of the lakes, but I don't know about beyond that time."

Sutherland thought about the possibility of war beginning again next year. He hoped it would not. Yet he knew the Indians were not satisfied, and the young braves and war chiefs would be hungry for a fight when warm weather returned.

Lost in speculation and concentrating on guiding the heavy craft through shallows at the edge of the river, Sutherland did not notice two sleek canoes shoot out of a thicket three hundred yards behind.

chapter **24**

THE PENDANT

One canoe held five men, the other six, paddling in unison, driving their craft with all their might, skimming over the water in pursuit of the canoe ahead. In his canoe André Breton sat at the prow, and in his hands was a rifle.

Steadily, silently the pursuers closed the gap between themselves and Sutherland's craft. The four men in the canoe out in front were yet unaware of Breton's presence. Closer, closer the *métis* canoe came. The dogged Delaware braves rammed their paddles deep and thrust the canoe to within less than a hundred yards of their quarry. Breton was ready. He was within good range for a shot now, even though the canoes were leaping and jerking in the water. Ninety yards. In a few more minutes, he would have a fair shot at Sutherland's broad back. He would get a shot off before anyone spotted them.

Eighty yards. The wind was at Breton's back, and the Delaware surged ahead. Sutherland had no idea his canoe was being pursued. His party stroked at their leisure, not talking, pondering the possible peace that Pontiac seemed willing to accept. Then, strangely, Owen Sutherland felt a chill at the back of his neck.

Seventy yards, and Breton rested the stock of the rifle in his palm. He sighted down the long barrel. If it were dry land instead of a bobbing river, Sutherland would be impossible to miss at this range. But Breton must be careful to judge the rise and fall of the craft. Sixty yards.

Then, from the distance behind Breton, a musket cracked. Sutherland jerked around. He saw his enemy and quickly wrenched his craft's prow toward the shore. Breton fired, and lead zinged past Sutherland's ear. That distant warning shot had startled Sutherland into action and, at the same time, had

384

disturbed Breton's aim. Now Sutherland's canoe was racing for the shore a hundred yards away. Behind, the Delaware whooped and charged their crafts forward. Brockhurst stopped paddling, turned, and snatched the pistol from Duvall's belt. He aimed, resting his elbow on Duvall's shoulder. The shot was deafening.

"Got one!" he grunted.

Breton's canoe skidded and nearly capsized as a brave grabbed at his face and fell overboard. The second canoe swerved to avoid a collision. Now Brockhurst had Sutherland's pistol in his hand, aiming coolly at the delayed pursuers.

Another shot. Brockhurst grinned savagely. "Well, I haven't forgotten everything yet!" In Breton's canoe another Indian slumped, shot through the chest. Brockhurst's accuracy gave his comrades just enough of a lead to allow them to run onto the shore ahead of the Delaware, who now were wary of their quarry's marksmanship.

A flurry of firing burst from the Delaware, who had stopped paddling in their fury. Breton swore and shouted at his men to push into shore and not fire their muskets. But several braves ignored him, reloaded, and fired again. The men they were after were clambering ashore. The Delaware whooped when Brockhurst stumbled and went down in the water.

De Quinot thrust an arm under Brockhurst and dragged him to his feet. The colonel was shot in the thigh. Duvall took the officer's other arm and, with de Quinot, helped him ashore. Sutherland held his own pistol, but the one carried by Brockhurst was wet and could not be fired. Sutherland aimed and sent a bullet at the enemy but missed.

Breton was aiming his long rifle again. He fired, and his shot just missed, tearing Sutherland's shirt near his left ribs. Before Breton could reload, the four hunted men crashed away into the underbush and out of sight. Fort Detroit was three miles downstream and across the water.

Brockhurst leaned on Alex Duvall, who helped him along behind Sutherland as they ran through the scrubby trees. They were a mile upriver from Valenya, heading there in the hope of finding weapons and a canoe. Sword in hand, de Quinot brought up the rear, glancing furtively behind him.

Sutherland could not move as fast as he wanted because Brockhurst was stumbling. His wound was clean, but ugly, and he was losing blood. The bullet had cut the leg but fortunately went on through, without breaking the bone. However, the leg would take little weight. When he tried to use it, the leg sent Brockhurst sprawling in agony. Duvall supported his superior and held the useless pistol in his free hand.

They ran and ran, sweating and gasping for air. De Quinot helped Duvall support Brockhurst, but they moved no quicker. Within two hundred yards of Valenya Sutherland called a halt. He did not know whether Breton and the Delaware had gone ahead by canoe to intercept or whether their pursuit was from behind, but he was taking no chances that they come to Valenya in a loud clatter of dry leaves and thumping boots that would alert anyone lying in ambush.

"Complete silence," Sutherland whispered. He looked quickly at Brockhurst, who was pale and thirsty but did not complain. "We'll leave this trail and come in behind the house. There's a small path through the rocks that overlooks the house. If anyone's there, we'll see them first. Come on!"

They trotted down a shady path that turned away from the trail to Sutherland's home. They moved quickly at first, then after a hundred yards slowed when Sutherland raised his hand. They crept along as quietly as they could. Brockhurst grimaced in pain but was silent. With Sutherland in the lead, Duvall at the rear, and de Quinot carrying Brockhurst, they slipped into the shadows of the massive rocks that stood behind the log cabin.

These were the singing stones that gave Valenya its name. They were twenty feet high, rusty black, and stood straight up, seven of them, as though deposited by an ancient giant. Brockhurst leaned against one, his head lolling dizzily. For a moment Sutherland thought Brockhurst might cry out in pain. Around the standing stones were crowds of black birches that offered little cover for a man intent on stealthily approaching the house, which was forty yards away in a clearing. Nearby was a wooden cross in the ground: Mayla's grave. Sutherland felt a twinge, for this was the first time he had come back to Valenya since Mayla died. In that thought all the anger and hatred for Breton rose again. He drew his claymore from its scabbard, held the pistol in his left hand, and moved to the corner of the cluster of stones.

He watched the clearing around the house. There was no sign of movement. At the river's edge, his master canoe lay upside down. That was their only hope: If they could get to the canoe and cross the river suddenly before Breton could cut them off, they would be able to paddle straight for the fort.

Sutherland sensed Breton and his party were lingering under cover in the river's shallows, watching for just such an attempt. If Sutherland waited until darkness, they might get away. But Breton would never wait that long.

The thought that now, when Breton was so close and was even looking for a fight, he had to run from him, consumed Sutherland. Perhaps he could draw off Breton and let the others escape while the *métis* and the Delaware were looking for him. Yes, that might work! If he moved into the open and they came after him, he might even come to grips with Breton. It was dangerous but worth the gamble. He scurried back to where his companions huddled behind the great stones.

"Colonel," he said and knelt at the weakened officer's side. "Sir, I've got an idea. There's a canoe on the beach there. If you three take it, you'll be able to make a dash for the fort at nightfall. I think Breton's out there on the water, watching for us to try that. If I let him see me and pretend I'm running, I think he just might come ashore and follow me first. It's me he wants, not you. Sir, I need you to clear my name, so keep up your strength. You'll be at the fort an hour after you set out!"

Brockhurst's eyes were glazed with pain, but he was conscious. He nodded at Sutherland. "I'm in no position to disagree with you, Owen. Do what you think is right. I'll—I'll see to it—" He was in agony. "I'll see to it that your—your record is cleared once and for all. I promise you that, son. I—promise you that!"

Sutherland did not look at Duvall, who was binding Brockhurst's leg with strips of the colonel's shirt, but if he had he would have seen that the major's eyes had a sad and faraway look. Nearby, de Quinot was staring at Sutherland's house for any sign of movement. He saw something.

"There!" he whispered and pointed at the edge of the woods near the trail they would have used if they had not taken the cut-off path. "I saw an Indian move there, I'm sure!"

Sutherland knelt on one knee and nodded. "All right, I'll let them see me, then I'll lead them off downriver. When they go after me, move closer to the canoe and take your chance if you're sure they're not watching. If you think they haven't all come after me, then wait until night before you go!"

He shook hands with Brockhurst, who sat up and gritted his teeth as he got to his feet. Already he looked stronger. "Good luck, Owen!" he said.

Sutherland, sword and pistol at the ready, slipped through the rattling stand of birches toward the clearing. He, too, saw the Indian half-concealed at the opening to the trail. He moved through the trees, scurrying in a crouch to get a running start before he revealed himself.

Then he gave a fierce war cry and fired his pistol at the brave near the path, who yelped and ducked into the bushes. Sutherland sprang for his escape route, but he took no more than three steps when something crashed down on his head and he went totally black.

Soft, contented chuckling came from the groggy distance; chuckling hollow and soulless. Sutherland saw dim light. He was lying on his back looking up at the sky. It was still full day. Above him, wind-stirred branches leaned down and seemed to be pointing at him. Pointing as though they thought him a fool who had no hope, no hope at all.

Pain drummed through Sutherland's head. He tried to lift it, but his head clumped back onto the ground again. He blinked his eyes. The laughter had stopped. He looked up through a fading blur and saw a shadow above him. It was a man. Someone was laughing once more. Sutherland shook his aching head clear, and saw André Breton laughing scornfully. Sutherland breathed deeply. He kept his eyes partly closed, though he could see and hear enough. His head rang with throbbing agony. He squinted at Breton looming above him.

"Wake up, Sutherland," Breton chuckled in English. "Wake up. I did not hit you so very hard, eh? No, no. I would not kill you so very easy, eh? Not so very quick, *mon ami*. Wake up. I have been waiting for you for nearly an hour. That's better. Now you can see me. Good. My braves are impatient for you to awaken. They want you to join our celebration, eh? Yes, that's it, sit up."

Sutherland struggled to lean on his elbows. He felt blood trickling down his face and into the corner of his mouth. He touched a gash on his forehead.

"Ha, ha!" Breton clapped and stepped back. "Suits you, no? *Oui*, that pretty scratch suits you very well, Sutherland. You'll look very fine when my friends here give you more pretty scratches for your face. Nice, eh?" Breton cackled. "Come, sit up, *mon ami*. As you can see, we have not been without amusement while we waited for you. Look!"

Breton gestured toward the trees at the edge of the clearing. Sutherland gasped when he saw de Quinot's limp body tied between two trees. It was stuck with a dozen arrows. Revulsion and horror rent Sutherland, but he restrained his fury and let it channel into a scheme. He would get Breton, somehow, even if it meant his own death.

Brockhurst! Where was he? Sutherland felt some relief when he saw the man, apparently unconscious, seated against a rock nearby. The colonel was still alive at least, but there was no sign of Duvall.

"*Oui*," Breton said. "You came into my open arms and, well, what else could I do but accept your offer, eh? Your friends? Well, they were a surprise, for I thought they'd gone another way. Pity they did not, for as you can see, my Delaware friends have found them and can have their sport."

Sutherland was fully alert now. Pain was overwhelmed by resolute anger. He saw a glimmer in Brockhurst's eye and realized that the officer, who was untied, was only feigning unconsciousness. Sutherland quickly assessed the situation. There were only two Indians with Breton.

One brave, a young warrior painted in red and black, naked from the waist up and with long hair down his back, stood near the slumped Brockhurst. Across the small clearing the other brave sat on a log near the body of de Quinot and grinned with cruel, fierce glee.

Sutherland looked again at the colonel. Yes! Now he was certain Brockhurst was conscious. But where was Duvall? Run off apparently, or already killed.

Breton laughed again and slipped a wicked hunting knife from his belt. He kicked aside Sutherland's claymore, which was lying useless nearby, and he looked down at Sutherland.

"Now that you have come back to us, *mon ami*, we shall finish our work. I wouldn't want you to miss anything at all." Breton turned and reached down for Brockhurst. The brave sitting on the log leveled his musket at Sutherland in warning. Brockhurst remained limp as Breton yanked him to his feet and began to half-drag him toward the tree where de Quinot's body hung.

Suddenly Brockhurst tore free and booted Breton between the legs. The Frenchman, powerful as he was, groaned and went down on one knee. The Indian with the musket, startled, spun at Brockhurst, who lunged and savagely slammed him to the ground. The second Indian charged Brockhurst, and Sutherland leaped for Breton, bringing him down hard, smashing his face into the earth.

A gunshot rang out, followed by a fierce war whoop. Breton roared and threw Sutherland from him. Like a sack of rags Sutherland tumbled head over heels and thudded onto his back. The air was driven from his lungs, and he felt Breton grappling for him. Dazed, Sutherland scrambled to his feet, but he was helpless. He expected Breton to hurl at him. It was over for him.

Then he heard cursing and shouting. He shook away the fog and spat out blood. In a flash he saw Breton struggling with Brockhurst.

He lurched forward, reeled with nausea, and fought for balance. Breton and the redcoat scrambled like furies in the dust. Sutherland moved, but not before Breton's knife plunged once into the redcoat's chest. And again! Sutherland shouted and tore the *métis* off the soldier, dragging him to the ground. With every wild muscle straining. Sutherland rammed Breton downward. The *métis* broke free. Then Sutherland snatched the knife from his leggin. Breton rushed him, thrusting his own blade cleverly, wickedly, and Sutherland took it deeply in his left shoulder and staggered backwards from the force of the assault. His knees buckled, but as he fell he savagely slashed upwards and stabbed the *métis* beneath the chin. Breton gagged and gurgled horribly. Sutherland kneeling, watched as Breton hesitated, swayed, and with surprise in his face jerked the knife from his throat. Blood gushed over his chest, the blood of a slashed jugular pouring onto the ground. Stupidly, Breton stared at the knives in his hands. Then he looked at Sutherland, whose shoulder wound was bleeding but, unlike Breton's, not mortal.

"Ah," Breton gasped and nodded once. Both men knew he was as good as dead. It would only be a moment now.

But he was not dead yet. His eyes hardened, and in a barely perceptible movement he shifted the knife in his right hand, ready for throwing. They were only ten feet apart, and as Breton's hand flashed, Sutherland had only an instant to turn sideways. The blade grazed his shirt as the knife flew past. They stood facing each other. Breton still had Sutherland's knife. Nearby lay the claymore. If Sutherland could reach it before Breton attacked—

The *métis* laughed and nodded again. He tried to speak, but blood came up, and he spat. His shirtfront was bright red, and his arms were covered with blood. Sutherland, whose head still spun from the blow he had received earlier, knew Breton would spend the last of his strength trying to kill him. Breton switched the knife to his right hand, then he came on. Sutherland dived for his claymore. There was no time to unsheath it. Breton was a step away when Sutherland whirled on his knees and brought up the sword, parrying the Frenchman's blow and knocking the knife out of his hand. Sutherland swung the sheathed sword and struck Breton across the face, driving him back. The sheath slid from the claymore, and in the next moment Sutherland, with naked steel in his hand, faced the unarmed Breton.

Sutherland had him. At last, this was the moment he had longed for, had struggled for through so much agony. He had Breton. This was the moment of savage triumph, the end of Sutherland's quest. He felt the hatred burn and boil as he brought the point of the sword to the dying Frenchman's bloody chest.

Then the face of Mayla came to Sutherland, beautiful and tranquil, a dream vision that made Sutherland tremble with sadness. He shook it away. There was Breton again. Mayla's voice spoke, and the image of Breton blurred. Sutherland did not understand what she was saying. Breton came into focus again. His eyes were defiant. The sword flickered, ready for the final thrust that would spend Sutherland's hatred in the passion of revenge. Breton swayed. He would be dead in a few seconds. All that kept him standing, his eyes burning, was his force of will. He expected that cruel thrust, and he was ready to take it, to take it without showing fear.

Mayla spoke again, and Sutherland understood the words. But they were not her words, they were Ella's: *Will you pursue Breton until you die? Have you sworn yourself to that? If you have, then you may already be dead . . .*

Then voices of Ottawa braves burst in like a storm:

Kill, kill, kill him!

Ella's voice again: *Then he's killed you, too. And if he's killed you, then something in me will die, too!*

Sutherland's hand clenched on the sword hilt.

Kill, kill, kill him!

Breton's eyes raged, unafraid, scornful.

Sutherland felt an explosion within, and he shuddered as he understood how a man could die in so many ways. A man could sacrifice too much in taking revenge.

He breathed deeply to calm himself. The sword thrust would not kill André Breton. That was already done. But it might kill something within Owen Sutherland . . .

The sword point came down. In Breton's eyes, defiance melted and became confusion. He swayed suddenly. He blinked and looked down at his feet, then met Sutherland's impassive eyes again. With a grunt Breton slumped to his knees. Doubt, then anger crossed his face. He wanted that thrust. He wanted to defy death. Then he knew it was over. Resignation came, and his eyes closed. Through gritted teeth, Breton forced a short, gurgling laugh, then fell heavily, face down in the grass.

Still dizzy, Sutherland stared at his enemy. But Breton was unmoving. It was done at last. Breton was dead. Sutherland reeled, then caught himself. His vision fogged, and he shook away nausea. Breton was dead.

The forest was silent. Only the wind and the river could be heard. The river rushed onward, unending. The wind sang through the standing stones, hollow and careless, neither lamenting nor rejoicing. Neutral, like the river.

Mayla appeared in Sutherland's mind, then vanished. He tried to see her, but could not. She, too, was gone, and the wind sighed through the stones, neither lamenting nor rejoicing.

With sudden shock Sutherland remembered Brockhurst, who had saved his life and had taken Breton's stabs. He hurried to where the officer lay twisted in a pool of blood. He turned the man over, then froze. It was not Brockhurst at all! It was Alex Duvall lying there as though deep in slumber.

Sutherland pressed his ear against Duvall's chest. There was no heartbeat. Duvall was dead.

After all, after everything that had happened, Duvall had saved Sutherland. Nothing made sense, and everything made sense to Sutherland then. But somehow none of it mattered at all anymore.

A hand took Sutherland's shoulder, and he jerked around. Looking down at him was Tamano, whose sad, dark eyes held his. Sutherland stood up, swaying, and Tamano gave him support. Then Brockhurst was there, wiping blood from his face, which was streaked with dirt and sweat. No one spoke until Brockhurst said, "Come on, Owen. There's no more we can do here."

Sutherland found his breath and raised his head. His shoulder needed bandaging. They went to the house, where cloth was found for Brockhurst's leg as well. As they prepared to fetch the bodies of their comrades and take them wrapped in blankets back to Fort Detroit, Sutherland said weakly in Ottawa, "There are other Delaware, Tamano. There was another canoe of Delaware with Breton—"

"No, Donoway, they'll not trouble us now," Tamano answered. "I met them on the trail here, and those who live are in flight. They have had enough today."

Sutherland said, "What happened? How did you come? Duvall?"

The Chippewa looked at the carnage about him; Colonel Brockhurst leaned on a stout stick and listened. "I follow you," Tamano said in English, so the colonel could understand, "see Breton canoes waiting. I come but cannot go so fast as Delaware. I fire warning shot from far off. You hear?"

Sutherland nodded and sighed. He remembered that first distant shot that had startled him just as Breton closed in.

"I get here, come up trail from where you leave canoe. Behind me come other Delaware. I catch 'em. They run away. I come to Valenya, but too late. I see this soldier—" he nodded at Brockhurst—"kick Breton. I shoot one Delaware then, come quick and kill Indian fighting with this soldier. But cannot help Donoway in time. This one, this Duvall, come from woods like madman. He try shoot pistol at *métis,* but pistol wet, no shoot. Then he jump *métis,* who has knife; he jump quick, no time to pull own long knife."

Sutherland understood Tamano meant Duvall had not used his sword when he leaped at Breton.

"Why not?" Sutherland asked. "Why didn't he use his long knife?"

"No time," Tamano said somberly. "No time if he want to save Donoway's life. He jump Breton mighty quick, my brother. If he wait, you dead man."

Sutherland looked at Brockhurst, whose face was stony. Tamano moved away to stand over Duvall's body.

"Plenty brave soldier this," he said and knelt to pick up Duvall.

Sutherland came and reached down for Duvall's legs. They bore him off toward the canoe at the river's edge. Sutherland said, "Yes, Tamano, this one was a brave soldier."

While the others prepared in silence to depart, Sutherland wandered slowly to Mayla's grave near the singing stones. The wind whirled and gusted through the great rocks, and a mournful sound rose all about Sutherland as he stood, head bowed, over the grave. He sank to his knees and touched the earth, grown over now, and blown with dry leaves. He closed his eyes and listened to the wind, his heart slowly beating. In the center of the grave a yellow wild flower grew, bright and bobbing in the wind. The wooden cross stood erect and straight, and Sutherland thought again about the granite marker he would place here one day.

The wind dropped once more, and the stones made no sound. He sighed and began to rise. Then he paused. From his neck he removed the silver pendant. He held it in his hand a moment, considering. Perhaps it should have been buried with Mayla. Perhaps . . . But it had not been buried with her. He had it still, as he had the sweet memory of her. He closed his hand on the pendant, then slipped it into his shirt pocket.

After a moment Sutherland stood up and looked out at the river. He thought of Mayla then, saw her running down the beach, brown legs flying, hair streaming behind her. And he smiled to think of her as he must always think of her.

It was a sad and pensive journey across the river back to Fort Detroit. Brockhurst briefly told Sutherland what had happened while he was unconscious. After Sutherland had been stunned, Breton and the three Indians had found them. Duvall had run off, and one of the braves chased him.

"But," said Brockhurst as he shifted his weight in the canoe and grunted, "it seems as though Duvall took care of that one. I had no idea he would come back for us. I thought he'd abandoned us. Then the savages wasted no time butchering poor de Quinot." Brockhurst slowly shook his head before speaking again. "Well, Owen, thanks to Tamano and Duvall, we're alive to tell the story."

Sutherland, seated in the prow of the canoe, looked back at the blanketed forms of Duvall and de Quinot lying in the bottom of the craft. He faced front again. A few hundred yards away, Fort Detroit jutted up from the low, reddish-brown shoreline. It was good to see it again. Here was Ella and the beginning of a new life.

As the canoe reached shore, crowds of soldiers and civilians ran down from the fort. They stopped short, groaning in horror when they saw the covered corpses in the canoe. Women moaned and began to cry. Men swore. Gladwin came down quickly and hurried to Brockhurst, who staggered through the water with two soldiers supporting him.

Gladwin and Brockhurst stood for a moment, looking at each other.

"You've failed then?" Gladwin asked.

Brockhurst took a deep breath. "No, Major, this is the work of André Breton. We've come to terms with Pontiac. We'll have peace now—at least for the winter. Despite what you see here, the siege is broken."

With that the mob whooped and cheered, tossed hats in the air, and swung one another in delighted circles. They capered and clapped each other on their backs. The siege was ended! Peace at last!

Then, as quickly as the joy had swept the crowd, they fell silent when four soldiers with stretchers carried the bodies of Duvall and de Quinot up the slope to the water gate. Civilians and soldiers parted to make way for the stretcher-bearers. Hats were doffed, and heads bowed. Women averted their faces, and men kept their eyes on the ground.

Slowly, painfully, Brockhurst and Sutherland walked up to the fort, Gladwin alongside them, and they entered the gate, where more people had gathered. The onlookers stepped back, whispering about peace. One by one the people of Fort Detroit learned the happy truth. One by one they let fall away their decorum and respect for the dead passing among them. After the two bodies were taken out of sight, the residents and soldiers congratulated one another. They laughed and even sang. Somewhere a fiddler struck up a gay tune, and some boys found old snare drums to beat through the fort. In a few minutes every street was alive with jubilation. Music and singing, laughing and drinking erupted everywhere in an uproar of boisterous inspiration. The siege was ended! The Indians had given up! Truce! Peace again!

As he walked at Brockhurst's side, Gladwin spoke, almost to himself: "Well, well, well. After all, I can write something cheering to Frances . . ."

"What was that, sir?" Brockhurst said.

"Eh? Oh, forgive me, Colonel. I was just thinking out loud . . . Thinking about home," Gladwin said, and he put a hand warmly on the limping Brockhurst's shoulder. Sutherland stopped and watched them walk away toward the infirmary. Henry Gladwin, like the others in Detroit, had good reason to rejoice. When a new commander was chosen to replace the major, he would be free to depart at last.

But Owen Sutherland did not celebrate. Slowly, with every

step reminding him of Alex Duvall's sacrifice, he walked alone through the milling crowd and wandered among the masses dancing and cheering on the parade ground. Yet he was now aimless. He walked with purpose, searching.

Then, as he had hoped, Ella stood before him. She had come in haste from the infirmary, where she had often gone to help care for the sick and wounded quartered there. She stopped short, as did he. The sleeves of her gown were rolled up, and hair straggled in wisps over her flushed cheeks. Their eyes held each other for an instant, saying all that was necessary. Without a word Ella came to his side, and he leaned against her. She pulled back the torn cloth at his wounded shoulder.

"You must see the surgeon, Owen," she said. Though her voice was low, and the crowd swept in gay celebration all around their tranquillity, he heard her. He shook his head and said:

"Not yet, Ella. Come with me, lass." Slowly they turned back the way he had come, through the teeming streets, arm in arm and out the water gate. They did not speak.

As they walked, Ella looked across the mighty river, and it seemed she had never seen it before. The air was sweeter, the breeze fresher; they were free again, and Fort Detroit's rough walls were no longer the boundaries of her life.

They walked down the grassy slope, and the tumult within the fort faded. On a mossy place, dry and crumbled with old leaves, they sat down to gaze across the river. The river rushed past, as it always had, as it always would, no matter who sat on its banks. A moment passed, then Owen turned to her.

"I'll tell you everything another time, lass, soon."

She moved against him. Her arm slipped under his, and she let her head rest on his shoulder. Their own peace would last forever.

His hand lifted her chin, and before her eyes dangled the silver pendant. Her breath caught, and she sat up. He reached to fasten the chain about her neck, but she took his hands and kissed them.

Hardly breathing, she said, "Owen, I can't wear this. I can't. It's a remembrance of someone—someone you loved so. No, Owen, it means too much for me to—"

A voice shouted to them from back up the slope, and they turned to see young Jeremy's head poke up over the fort's ramparts. He was waving. His head disappeared as he set off to join them at the river. Ella turned back to Sutherland, who still held the pendant close to her.

He said, "Once you told me you also had a remembrance of someone you loved."

She recalled that day when she had tended Owen's wounds, and she had said that about her son. Yes, he was a remembrance... Her eyes flitted out to the river and came quickly back to Owen's.

He said, "I'll be glad if you'll share the boy with me. As I'll be glad if you'll share this."

And her heart rushed as he secured the pendant around her neck, then kissed her gently. She touched it, hesitantly at first, and then with heartfelt gratitude. Owen took her hand.

Behind them, Jeremy shouted again and bounded through the rustling grass. They stood up just as the whooping boy reached them and charged into Sutherland's arms.

"Careful! Careful!" Ella scolded kindly. "Mr. Sutherland's hurt, son."

"Owen." Sutherland said looking down at the eager boy. "It's Owen, at least for now, lad."

"Owen," Jeremy said breathlessly, "now we're at peace with the Indians, can I meet some Indian boys and learn all about those things you said I could?"

Sutherland touseled Jeremy's hair. For a fleeting, cloudy moment he thought of Molo. Then he saw the shining face looking up at him.

"That I don't know, laddie; things have changed. Things have changed a lot since I was with the Indians. It might be that I'll never again return to them—"

"You shall!" Ella surprised herself by saying that so emphatically. But somehow she was certain he would go back among the Indians. "Surely," she began in a more controlled voice, "you'll always belong close to them, Owen. It's important you go back to them, back as someone they can trust. It's important—for all of us."

Sutherland said nothing, but his eyes searched hers, and they were glad for what they found. Then, hand in hand, all three walked together up the slope. In that moment Ella wondered whether she could ever be close to the Indians. Perhaps she could. Her fingers lightly touched the silver pendant at her breast. Yes, perhaps one day she would be. Perhaps she already was.

An exciting preview of

CONQUEST

the next great book in the
Northwest Territory series.

*Coming from Berkley in
September 1982.*

Old Mawak beached his canoe near the deserted landing at Fort Detroit, ending a short journey from his lodge at the Ottawa village a few miles upstream. For all his uncounted years, Mawak's gnarled and sinewy body was still strong, and he climbed out of the canoe with the vigor of a young warrior, splashing through the icy water and hauling the craft up on the shore. He moved quickly because he was excited, happy to be back at the English fort after a forced absence of nearly five months.

He turned to face the high stockade on the crown of a slope rising from the river, and he saw the Union Jack fluttering in the September afternoon breeze. For a moment, Mawak wondered if Chief Pontiac was as wise and all-knowing as he claimed to be. After all, anyone who looked up at the strong walls and massive blockhouses of this place should see that no Indians could capture it by storm.

Standing at the water's edge, Mawak felt small and insignificant in the shadow of Fort Detroit, even though he wore his finest eagle-feather headdress and had put his very brightest red shirt on top of four others of less importance. It did not matter that Mawak was a respected elder in his tribe of warlike Ottawa, and it did not matter that once he was first on the warpath and first in hunting buffalo. On the riverfront under the guns of the strongest fortress in the northwest, Mawak was just another redskin whose chief had sued for peace after leading the Indians in an uprising against the British forts of the northwest territory.

When Mawak saw a sentry wandering on the rampart at the top of the palisade, he stopped gaping at the fort and reached down into the canoe for a blue blanket, which he threw with great ceremony over his shoulders. The soldier was standing watching Mawak now, and it was important that the Ottawa make a good impression on him from the start. Mawak drew himself up as best he could, considering his stiffening old bones, and began to stride solemnly up the slope toward the door in the fort's river gate, which was closed. He stopped at the sally port just below the young sentry, who scowled down at him. The pale-faced boy on the ramparts above did not need to hunt, to travel many miles to find the game the Indian needed to feed his family. This boy, who would be helpless man-to-man against a warrior his age in a fair fight, represented a king who supplied his fighters with ammunition, food, warm clothing, and rum.

Rum. Mawak suddenly felt thirstier than he had ever been before. He longed for a good drink of rum, and he thought again of why he had come to Fort Detroit, when most of his people were packing up all they owned and heading southward to the Illinois country, where game would be found during the cold months.

Mawak cried up to the young man peering down from the rampart, "Hey, solder! Me come wedding! Me big Christian! You know Prince o' Wales?"

The soldier was a private in the 60th Regiment. Mawak had never seen him before, although the Ottawa had earlier spent months in Detroit and knew most of the garrison by sight. Apparently the fellow was new, for he showed no recognition, but instead spat over the wall, aiming close at Mawak's feet.

Mawak did not stir. He cried again, "You know Prince o' Wales?"

"Do I know the Prince o' Wales?" the soldier sneered. "Yeah, old man, I know 'im. 'As 'e been askin' for me again? Well tell 'im sorry, but I'm too busy ter come ter 'is birthday ball this year! Tell 'im I'm protectin' 'Is majesty's American bloody empire for 'im. Tell the prince 'Arry Tompkin's too bloody busy keepin' murderin' bloody savages like you from murderin' bloody farmers. Tell 'im that, yer lordship, an' get yer scurvy tail outa 'ere before I call the corporal o' the guard an' clap yer in irons!"

Mawak drew out a white card with writing on it and held it up for the sentry to see. "Soldier," he said in his deepest, most gravelly voice, "Prince o' Wales come to fort for weddin'. Prince come for Owen Sutherland and squaw. Soldier, this Injun—" He thumped his chest once, hard. "This Injun sing in Rev'nd Lee choir, hear? This Injun name Prince o' Wales, hear?"

Now the soldier was surprised and confused. He cast a quick glance over his shoulder, as though looking at something down in the fort. Then he turned back to Mawak, looked him up and down, and shook his head slowly.

"You? Sing in the choir?" he asked, half to himself, and stared at the shabby clothes hanging on Mawak's aged body. Mawak stood in silence, serene and proud. The soldier continued muttering to himself, gave Mawak a dubious glance, and then finally cried down behind him, "Let this ragamuffin in, mate. Check the card 'e be carryin'. Says 'e come for the weddin'. Says 'e sings." He scratched his ear as another soldier opened the sally port and Mawak handed over the white card.

The second soldier took the card and mumbled to himself as he turned it one way and then another. He was poor enough at reading the King's English, but this writing was pure confusion. As he stared at the card, Mawak walked placidly into the fort. The guard grabbed him by the arm and shoved the card at him, saying, "What the hell's this all about? It's Injun writin', if there be such a thing!"

Indeed, the card was covered with designs and pictures, which to Mawak said Owen Sutherland had invited him to come to his wedding that day. With great dignity, Mawak held the card under the private's nose, while from above the first young soldier looked on. The Indian pointed a bony finger at each symbol: "Donoway. Ella squaw. Marry. Mawak's sign. Come today."

The soldier was squinting as Mawak made sense of the pictographs for him. He took the card and began to puzzle through it once again, and Mawak walked ahead, toward the broad Rue Sainte Anne, where a surging, milling throng of every caste and type of human being in the northwest wilderness was represented. Filling the streets of Detroit like a surging flood of color and noise, hundreds of French, English, Scottish, provincials, halfbreeds and even a few Indians, flowed around the log cabins and whitewashed clapboard dwellings of the little community. Mawak grinned to see the marvelous spectacle, and he stood even more erect to know he was in the very best of company.

There were British officers in scarlet coats, trimmed in white and glittering with gold adornments. Wealthy traders, British and French, paraded through the host of revelers, wearing fine fur caps or broad beaver hats adorned with amazingly large cockades of white tinsel ribbon. The merry *voyageurs*, most of them French and Indian halfbreeds called *métis*, strutted in their gaudy finery, spangled with earrings and bracelets, feathers and broad red sashes at the waist. These men, who traveled the rivers of the northwest in their canoes, selling their goods, now looked every bit more gloriously adorned to Mawak than even the women, whether squaws, *métis*, or British.

The French *habitant* women wore explosive blues and yellows, costly gowns worth more than the very homes they lived in. Their hair was curled in masses that cascaded down their backs, and nothing was spared of bright ribbons that tied their hair, their waists, their arms, and even their ankles. Though they were as poor as their broken fingernails were dirty, these proud folk loved a wedding, and they dressed far beyond their means. Thus it was that for the wedding of the widow Ella Bently and trader Owen Sutherland, these important members of Detroit's small community felt confident that their dress did justice to their station as the wives, daughters, and sweethearts of prosperous merchants. The tyranny and burden of the long siege had cut off all chance of profit for the time being, but that same siege had crushed the fort's usual social life and left its people desperate for a reason, such as this wedding, to celebrate.

Mawak waded into the gushing, laughing mob, saw old friends who knew he had not been in Pontiac's war band, and was welcomed among many he had thought not long ago were doomed to die. Somewhere in the fort Sutherland and his woman were being married, but where did not particularly atter to Mawak. He would congratulate them later, but first needed to drink some rum, to wash away the sorrow of the st, to drown the memory of those who had died, and to ease the spirits of his ancestors, who would be glad to have ne of their own drink to their eternal happiness.

Nodding and bowing as he went through the crowd, Mawak followed the fragrance of roasting beef and came out onto the parade ground, where two whole oxen were spitted over fire pits. His mouth watered to look at such food, for it had been too long since any Indians had eaten well. The hostilities had kept the traders from them, and the fighting had exhausted most of their power and lead, so it was difficult to hunt. Mawak had eaten mostly wild rice and cornmeal for the past two months.

Now he gazed longingly at the roasting oxen, closed his eyes to smell the aroma, and knew in the depth of his heart that he no longer loved war. For all the white man's ignorance and rudeness to Indians, whites had much that the Indian craved and needed. Mawak considered himself well on the way to becoming like the whites, because already he was a Christian. Singing in Reverend Lee's choir had made him a Christian, though not as big a Christian as the reverend or the white members of the choir. But he was a bigger Christian than the other Indians who had come to choir meetings back in the days before Pontiac started the war. The others mostly came for the coppers Lee gave them for beer. Not Mawak. He had come and listened when Lee told them about hellfire and the baby Jesus and the angel Satan. Mawak was able to sing the melodies of some of the hymns Lee taught them, and he had an idea about the words, sometimes. No Indian was better at staying awake when Lee spoke about the white man's god. Only once had Mawak slipped a little off his chair when Lee was speaking, but that was not because he was sleepy; it was just that he never could sit well on chairs, French or English.

Mawak heard the bell ringing on the tower of the French Church of Sainte Anne. His eyes opened as the mob pushed hard toward the big council house across the parade ground from the church. Mawak was borne along with the press of people, and Mawak soon found himself near the council house door. He preferred to be at the far end of the parade ground sniffing the roasting oxen, but he had no choice. Then he saw why the mob had come this way.

The door to the massive building of squared logs opened, and out came Sutherland and his new wife, Ella. The people roared and tossed flower petals and pieces of bright ribbon at them. The bride, a pretty, fair-haired woman, was wearing a blue satin gown and a linen cap, and she carried marigolds in a bunch, which she threw in joy to the crowd. Somehow, the bouquet wound up in Mawak's hands, and he was shoved and scratched before it disappeared as magically as it had come.

To Mawak, Owen Sutherland looked strange. In the past war, much had happened to this Scotsman. Today he was wearing fine clothes instead of his usual linsey and buckskins. As Sutherland and Ella walked smiling under an arch of crossed swords and past a rank of soldiers who clattered to attention in their honor, Mawak thought the Ottawa son named Donoway might even be dead now. Donoway had never worn such a handsome dark-blue frock coat, nor a buff waistcoat and breeches. As for the blue tricorn Owen Sutherland waved to the crowd, it would never have belonged to Donoway, the great hunter and fighter, who always wore a broad-brimmed black beaver hat.

Mawak thought too much in the world had changed in these last few months. Then his stomach grumbled as he again smelled the entrancing aroma of the beef, and he edged back out of the crowd that was milling and singing in honor of the newlyweds.

It was Sutherland who went to Pontiac and talked peace with him—even if peace would last no longer than the winter.

The mob parted, and Sutherland and Ella came through, hand in hand. Mawak stood in their path, and they welcomed him warmly, he and Sutherland speaking in Ottawa. The rest of the wedding party came next, with Reverend Lee at its head. The minister was beaming with satisfaction, and he nodded once to Mawak as he passed. The choir was right behind Lee, garbed in long linen gowns of natural color, each member carrying an English hymnbook, even though a few of the dozen members of the choir were French Catholics.

Mawak saw the wedding party moving directly to the banquet tables, where some chairs were set, and he envied them for their fortunate place in the world. He could almost taste the roast meat, and he thought the rum kegs must be leaking out their spirits, for he could feel their heady power already creeping into his blood.

The wedding party arranged itself on either side of the newlyweds, everyone standing in front of the table. On Sutherland's left side was the choir; on the right, next to Ella, was her brother, Major Henry Gladwin, tall and formidable in his scarlet uniform. Gladwin looked happy, but pale and drawn from the strain of commanding the fort during the siege. Next to Gladwin was the big Chippewa brave called Tamano, a close friend of Sutherland's and a fearless fighter well known to Indians all over the northwest.

Then a tousle-haired blond boy of eight appeared at Ella's side, and Sutherland drew him between them. It was clear from the look of the boy that he was glad to have Owen Sutherland for a father, and, judging from Sutherland's expression, the feeling was mutual.

Reverend Lee moved to the fore and raised his hands, one of them holding a hymnal and the other a Bible.

The crowd gradually hushed, whispering and rumbling, then growing still. Lee kept his hands raised for a moment as he began to speak in a ringing voice that carried across the parade ground.

"Ella and Owen Sutherland, dearest of friends to all of us who are gathered here to bestow our best wishes for a full and happy life, blessed by our heavenly Father in the coming new age of peace in our bountiful country . . ."

Lee went on, recounting the service Sutherland gave the army in the recent fighting, and describing Ella as his most gratifying conquest of all. She colored at this; Sutherland smiled a little, and Lee went on longer than he should have in praise of the newlyweds. As the minister spoke, Mawak saw his chance and moved closer and closer to the gowned choir, until he stood just behind them. Now, as far as he was concerned, he was a member of the wedding party and entitled to all its privileges. Reverend Lee ended his speech with, "It gives me boundless joy to offer up this token of our boundless regard for both of you—a gift of song!"

Lee spryly turned to his choir, and its members raised their chins in anticipation, a few clearing throats and licking lips. Sounding his wooden flute, he gave the keynote. Every eye was on him, including Mawak's at the rear of the two rows of singers. Lee pushed the spectacles back on his nose and smiled at the choir. Giving a sharp, then sweeping gesture with the flute, he led them in a Scottish hymn, much to the satisfaction of the Sutherlands, who stood close together, listening to the beautiful harmony.

Not only Owen and Ella were pleased with Lee's choice of hymns, but old Mawak was delighted, too, for it was one he knew thoroughly—in his own way. He rocked back and forth, closing his eyes and sensing the rhythm—unfortunately, he was much better at rhythm than melody. When he chose his moment to join in, he released a dull, grinding baritone, throaty and painfully loud. The choir's bright melody faltered and began to deteriorate, and the singers—except for the happy Mawak—hesitated and looked over their shoulders at him. Lee, frozen in disbelief, stood with his flute high in the air, his face ghastly pale. The crowd began to laugh, but the Prince of Wales sang on and on.

A few months ago, Lee would merely catch Mawak's attention at moments like these, and would politely hand him a few coppers to buy some beer, dismissing him from the choir room, with no one particularly troubled. But on this special day, when hundreds were in the audience, and when the hymn his choir had practiced so diligently and flawlessly for weeks was being destroyed, Reverend Angus Lee forgot his Christian charity.

Trembling with the fury swelling in his breast, Lee stammered, "Y-Y-Y-You, you, Indian!" He was not heard by the sole person still performing, and Lee threw down the flute before advancing on Mawak.

But Ella, her hazel eyes alight with humor, stepped between Lee and the Indian and touched Mawak gently on the arm. Opening his eyes and seeing Ella, Mawak stopped singing and gave a grand and toothless smile, saying, "Donoway woman have much happiness. Many little ones!" He drew from a pouch at his side a thin string of blue and white wampum beads. Handing his gift to Ella, he rumbled, "First Prince o' Wales sing, then big feast! Drink good lady health! First sing, eh?" He looked up at Lee, expecting to see him pleased, but instead found the minister quivering with anger.

Sutherland stepped forward and put a hand on Lee's shoulder, smiling and saying softly, "He's a big man among the Ottawa, even if he can't sing so well, Reverend. You'll get your choir back; just wait a minute."

The Scotsman took the wampum from Ella, holding the string up for all to see, and addressed Mawak: "We thank you for your good wishes, Mawak, the one we call Prince of Wales. Your gift wipes away the bad feelings that have lately come between our peoples, and in return, I offer this token of our respect and affection."

Sutherland handed his new tricorn to Mawak, whose eyes opened wide at such a fine present so worthy of his high position. Proud of the honor done him, the old Indian accepted the hat and jammed it on his head, grinning with delight.

The people watching appreciated this little ceremony, and they applauded with good cheer. Ella leaned forward to whisper something in Mawak's ear, and he beamed even more happily, folding his arms and standing between the newlyweds. Ella said to Lee, who was perplexed and still annoyed, "You may begin now, Reverend."

His lower lip working, Lee hissed, "Not if he's going to spoil it—"

"It's all right," Ella said gently. "Please sing!"

With some effort Lee gathered himself, gave Mawak a withering look that the Indian did not notice, and went back to his choir. Once again he summoned their voices and, after a few otes, eyed Mawak suspiciously. But the man was silent.

Now the beautiful hymn rose in perfect harmony above the solated fort, and Lee's good little choir sang with all their earts. The first time through could not have been more stirring, nd halfway through the second, those who knew the song oined in and those who did not hummed contentedly. Behind he back of smiling Mawak, who stood once more with eyes losed, Ella and Owen joined hands. The song ended and everyone was quiet. Then came a whoop from a Scottish Highlander nd a shout from a French *voyageur*. The entire crowd roared, nd Sutherland drew Ella against him.

"What did you say to keep the old fellow still?" he asked er quickly.

Ella giggled. "That the choir was singing in his honor!"

Sutherland laughed and said, "You'll make a frontier woman et, lass. Maybe even a diplomat to the Indians."

When the sun rose over the northwest territory the next norning it found summer gone. The frosty touch of cold nights ad flushed maples yellow, and here and there on the hillsides vere pools of orange and red. Ghostly mists hovered over akes, and far to the east of Fort Detroit, the Niagara River oiled and hissed through a deep gorge in its hurry to flow over he mighty waterfalls between Lake Erie and Lake Ontario.

On the crest of the river's eastern cliff a flash of brighter ed appeared among the autumn foliage, and like a scarlet snake t wound along the portage road on the edge of the heights. The steady sound of water rushing headlong through the gorge nd swirling into a great whirlpool called the Devil's Hole was ounctuated by the rhythmic tapping of a military snare drum. Through vague mists rising from the steaming river far below, a long column of mounted Redcoats with a drummer on foot nd a crowd of civilian teamsters in their midst was making ts way from the upper landing at Fort Schlosser on Lake Erie oack down to the lower landing at Fort Little Niagara. There vere twenty soldiers, commanded by a mounted sergeant, and hirty muleskinners and bullwhackers weary from hauling military goods to the upper landing all the way from Albany far o the east.

On the right side of the portage road the forest was thick nd dark. It crowded the road close to a sheer cliff that fell lizzyingly down to the swirling, rocky river. Along this narrow lefile these fifty men traveled in a straggling column of twos

and threes, the soldiers on nondescript horses mingled among
the men walking. As morning drew on, the column marched
even more casually because everyone was fascinated by the
sight of the cataract foaming below.

Frequently, teamsters cried out to the sergeant that they
wanted to rest near the cliff and look at the magnificent scenery
all around before going down to the lower landing; but the
gruff leader of the detachment refused, ordering the civilian
to keep moving and shouting at them to close ranks, even
though there was no real danger of Indian attack here. Through
out Pontiac's uprising, the only tribe from this region which
had joined in were the fierce, cruel Senecas, westernmost nation
of the Iroquois League. But the Senecas had struck toward the
south, taking three British posts between Fort Pitt and Lake
Erie. Here, close to powerful Fort Niagara, there had been only
sporadic disturbances and a few random killings of white trad
ers, but no major attack. With the coming of winter it was
apparent that Indian momentum was almost gone.

Word had recently arrived of Pontiac making peace in the
west, and the soldiers of this escort counted themselves unfortunate to have been selected for such a tedious, annoying
task as guarding a transport train. The teamsters shambled along
like so many unruly sheep, and once the sergeant accused them
of being slower-witted than the oxen they drove.

The leader of the teamsters, a big, handsome fellow with
blond hair and massive shoulders, shouted back at the sergeant
in a good-natured way, "We can't be all that ignorant, Sergeant,
or we'd be in the army, wouldn't we?"

The teamsters laughed, and the soldiers returned with hu-
morous barbs of their own. It was a crisp, fresh day, and the
civilians were cheerful. Once they got back to Fort Niagara
later that afternoon, the big blond one, called Peter Defries,
would present his bill to the commander there, and he would
collect their pay. Then they would all get good and drunk
before starting back for Albany, where most of them came
from. They would sit out the winter very comfortably with
their earnings from the work just completed.

Like his men, Defries was in an excellent mood, fairly
prancing along the bumpy portage trail, kicking rocks aside
and over the cliff, and leaping like a child across fallen trees.
It was no wonder Defries was happy, because he was about
to make a small fortune as the brains and leader of the supply
column. At twenty, Defries had used the ties of his Albany-

Dutch family and the confidence of friends to bid for an army contract supplying the western posts, and now he had carried out his end of the bargain. The goods so desperately needed at places like Fort Detroit were now at the landing, waiting for a schooner or sloop from the frontier, and Defries had not a worry in the world. It had been a grueling, difficult trek from Albany through friendly Iroquois country to Fort Schlosser at the upper landing, and in organizing and leading the expedition, Defries had proven himself a prodigy in the military-supply business.

Not only had he raised the capital to buy the goods, ammunition, and foodstuffs at Albany, but he had found the men and stock to ship it four hundred miles through rough terrain— none rougher than this portage road above the Niagara River. For years Defries had labored as a hired teamster or bullwhacker for other men who made the real profits. He had been the best at his trade, well paid and respected even at the age of seventeen. But last spring he heard about the western uprising, and he went after a military contract with all his native genius and determination.

He won it, thanks in part to the influence of the most powerful man in Indian country: Sir William Johnson, Superintendent of Indian Affairs, adopted member of the Mohawk nation of the vast Iroquois League, and a friend of Defries's father.

Yet all Sir William did for the young entrepreneur was to recommend him to military procurement officers. The rest, which was almost impossible considering the shortage of supplies and goods within reach of Fort Schlosser, was Defries's own accomplishment. Even before the contract was formally awarded to him, Peter Defries had prepared a list of precisely the right kind of goods and went from merchant to merchant in Albany, placing orders and requiring that the merchandise be held in instant readiness until he called for it.

Since no one else in Albany—the main supply source for the northwestern posts—was able to find additional goods, thanks to the foresight and gambling instinct of Defries, he was the only man who could provide the army on short notice with what it needed. Sir William was glad to have been able to put in a good word for Defries with the officers; but he had been as proud as an uncle that young Peter had fulfilled his contract with such mastery and efficiency.

Yes, Peter Defries had cause to be happy with himself on this fine autumn day. His future was bright and held the promise of wealth now that his reputation with the military was firmly established.

As the run of comical insults between soldiers and teamsters swept up and down the column, Defries spoke to the young boy walking beside him, tapping cadence on a drum that seemed almost as big as he was.

"If you'll listen to me, lad, you'll get that lobster coat off your back quick as you can and become a free man, like we are!"

"Why?" asked the boy, whose childish face already had hard lines about it, the marks of a soldier's harsh life. "I aim to see the world, and the army's the place to do it. Besides, I got no taste to goad oxen for a livin'."

Defries laughed as the soldiers nearby cheered the boy. Then the big fellow said, "Rather goad the ox than let the ox goad you, son! Right, Sergeant?"

The sergeant turned in his saddle and gave Defries an obscene gesture, but before the man had finished his motion, the forest came alive. The trees exploded in a tremendous roar of fire and smoke, and the happy world of Peter Defries burst apart in war shrieks and blood. A tomahawk blade whisked past his head, and he ducked instinctively, turning to see a terrifyingly painted Seneca warrior swing the tomahawk again, leaping in and screaming for his enemy's death.

Defries roared and shouldered into the warrior's gut, ramming him back, at the same time grabbing for the elusive tomahawk hand. The slippery, bear-greased Seneca threw his free arm around the teamster's neck and tried to drag Defries down, but the Dutchman was too strong for him. With a shout, Defries lifted the Indian into the air, staggered three steps to the edge of the cliff, and wildly hurled the screaming warrior over. He turned to fight again.

But Defries realized his companions were lost. In a flash of sudden comprehension, he saw ten Indians for every white man. The portage road was swarming with redskins dragging soldiers from their horses, killing teamsters writhing beneath crowds of attackers. Defries had that split second to choose—fight and die, or escape over the cliff.

In the next instant, he glanced down at the river and knew he would die that way, too, as several men already had died in desperate attempts to escape. Then he saw trees growing a little way down the slope, and knew they were the only possibility.

Bestsellers from Berkley
The books you've been hearing about—and want to read

___**THE FIRST DEADLY SIN** 05604-X—$3.50
Lawrence Sanders
___**MOMMIE DEAREST** 05242-0—$3.25
Christina Crawford
___**NURSE** 05351-2—$2.95
Peggy Anderson
___**THE HEALERS** 04451-3—$2.75
Gerald Green
___**SMASH** 05165-X—$3.25
Garson Kanin
___**PROMISES** 04843-8—$2.95
Charlotte Vale Allen
___**THE TENTH COMMANDMENT** 05001-7—$3.50
Lawrence Sanders
___**WINNING BY NEGOTIATION** 05094-7—$2.95
Tessa Albert Warschaw
___**THE CONFESSIONS OF PHOEBE TYLER** 05202-8—$2.95
Ruth Warrick with Don Preston
___**VITAMINS & YOU** 05074-2—$2.95
Robert J. Benowicz
___**SHADOWLAND** 05056-4—$3.50
Peter Straub
___**THE DEMONOLOGIST** 05291-5—$2.95
Gerald Brittle

Available at your local bookstore or return this form to:

Berkley Book Mailing Service
P.O. Box 690
Rockville Centre, NY 11570

Please send me the above titles. I am enclosing $_____
(Please add 50¢ per copy to cover postage and handling). Send check or money order—no cash or C.O.D.'s. Allow six weeks for delivery.

NAME_____

ADDRESS_____

CITY_____STATE/ZIP_____ 1 M

More Bestsellers from Berkley
The books you've been hearing about and want to read

__THE AMERICANS Alistair Cooke	04681-8—$2.95
__DUNE Frank Herbert	05471-3—$2.95
__FAT IS A FEMINIST ISSUE Susie Orbach	05544-2—$2.95
__THE LAST CONVERTIBLE Anton Myrer	05349-0—$3.75
__DREAM DANCER Janet Morris	05232-X—$2.75
__CONFEDERATES Thomas Keneally	05057-2—$3.50
__WIZARD John Varley	05478-0—$2.75
__THE MAGIC LABYRINTH Philip Jose Farmer	04854-3—$2.75
__THE SECOND DEADLY SIN Lawrence Sanders	05545-0—$3.50
__THE SUNSET WARRIOR Eric Van Lustbader	04452-1—$2.50
__WAR WITHIN AND WITHOUT: DIARIES AND LETTERS 1939-1944 Anne Morrow Lindbergh	05084-X—$3.50
__CATHERINE THE GREAT Henri Troyat, trans. by Joan Pinkham	05665-1—$3.95

Available at your local bookstore or return this form to:

Berkley Book Mailing Service
P.O. Box 690
Rockville Centre, NY 11570

Please send me the above titles. I am enclosing $_____
(Please add 50¢ per copy to cover postage and handling). Send check or money order—no cash or C.O.D.'s. Allow six weeks for delivery.

NAME_____

ADDRESS_____

CITY_____STATE/ZIP_____
#85M